The Blissmaker

by Royce Richardson
Author · Composer · Artist

First edition published by

Ancient River Publishing Company
P.O. Box 1329
Duvall, Washington 98019
Tel: 425-788-6193
AncientRiver@AncientRiver.com
www.AncientRiver.com

Publisher's Cataloging-in-Publication
(*Provided by Quality Books, Inc.*)

Richardson, Royce.
    The blissmaker : a novel / by Royce Richardson.
    -- 1st ed.
    p. cm.
    LCCN: 00-101214
    ISBN: 0-9677200-1-X

I. Title.

PR3568.I285B65 2000   813.6
                      QBI00-446

Published in the United States of America
Printed in Singapore

My heartfelt gratitude to Shankara, for his love and wisdom, and for always being that sweet voice in the wind.

My thanks to those in the unseen, who assisted with this project on so many levels, especially to Charles Dickens and the poet, Rumi.

My thanks to all of the people who contributed to the creating of this book: To Marisa Lovesong, for her constant encouragement and for insisting that I listen to that voice in the wind. To Alison McIntosh, for her years of dedication and for the many contributions that she gave through her talents as an artist and an editor. To Stan Cummings for all of his support, for laughing when the writing was brilliant and funny, and also for telling me when it was not. To Connie Krontz, for her refined skills as an editor and for helping me write my own words with such clarity, style, and purpose. To Alinda Page, for her faith, and for creating the sanctuary where such a voice as Shankara's could be heard. To my parents Eleanor and Lawrence Richardson, for being a constant sounding board and for always loving, regardless of the path I traveled.

To the following people who were there from the beginning, who sat with Shankara at the original fireside gatherings and who listened to the music and explored the *Journeys* for no other reason than to do it: Laney (Karil) Friesen, Melanie Barlow, Alexandra Hepburn, Marleena Louisa François, Brandon Pole, Dunja Ruljancich, Sasha Stjepanovic, Julie Newcomb, Tanya Clamper, Jay Wilder, Alison McIntosh, Alinda Burke Page, Richard Page, and Ukiah (Ky), the fireside cat.

Thanks for your assistance: Holly Omlin Rubach, Debbie Pezzner, Joe Klice, Molly Murrah, Diane DeFuria, and Chanté.

Dedications

Note to the Reader

For Marisa Lovesong

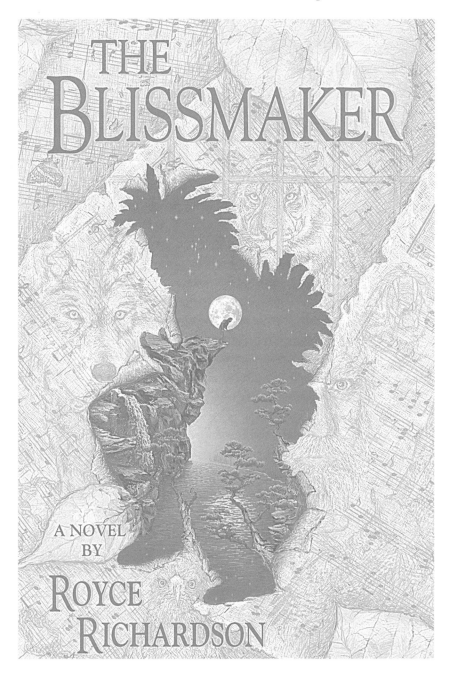

THE
BLISSMAKER

A NOVEL
BY

ROYCE
RICHARDSON

This novel is filled with sheet music presented as illustrations—visual enhancements for the reader. Musicians are invited to play the scores for a deeper understanding of the main character. However, it is not necessary for the reader to have musical knowledge in order to fully experience this book.

Samples of the music can be heard as recorded by author/composer Royce Richardson at www.Blissmaker.com. The actual sheet music can be downloaded from the website. The appendix at the back of this book includes a complete listing of these pieces.

Some readers may choose to experience this story's journeys as they read by playing the narrated music available on the CD included in the deluxe edition of this book.

Blue skies are waitin'
and the sun be a bakin'.
Take me to the edge of the world.

1

Mirror, Mirror

Once again the intrusive mirror caught me taking inventory of the familiar collection of wrinkles so persistently preserved on my face of only thirty-eight years. This confidential accounting revealed lines on my forehead keeping a precise record of every frown and glare—not to mention childlike dimples that had grown into gregarious caverns without my even noticing. Then of course there were the crow's feet around the eyes. Smile lines they are called by those who are so pleasantly possessed; those infamous wrinkles that occasionally cooperate as the photographer coaxes you to smile, only to betray you later changing from plum-age to prune-age in the blink of an eye.

My hair, on the other hand, had fared better through the years. Having not yet abandoned me, it remained reasonably bountiful and relatively unchanged, the encroaching gray still cleverly disguised by my hair's dusty blond color. Unfortunately, the somewhat darker hue of my beard and mustache now quite willingly displayed glimpses of several shades of gray, as did the hair hidden under my shirt. As for the rest of my wares, well, it was probably to my advantage that my short mirror did not reflect back to me the twenty-five pounds that had been added to the one hundred and seventy-five that once sprinted the local college campus.

Today, sixteen years later, I walked that campus with a slightly slower pace. For the past twelve years I had taught a variety of music courses at the local college. Teaching was a means of financial survival; the ideal place for an unsuccessful composer to camouflage himself while impatiently waiting for the uncooperative world to discover him. So far the plan had worked perfectly: my talents were still well-concealed, and no one was the wiser. Even my closest companions were relatively unaware of the large volume of music I had written and rewritten over the years. I suppose I found it to be less debilitating (not to mention less humiliating) to have created only a few undiscovered masterpieces rather than an entire trunkfull. My scheme though had not taken into account the impending dissatisfaction that had been making its daily visitations into my . . . tediously . . . monotonous . . . existence.

I took a leave of absence. The time had come to end the mundane, to perhaps find the remains of a lifelong dream that was currently somewhere over the rainbow. The spontaneity of my sabbatical was not without justification though; even now my middle-aged countenance revealed a glint of hope. One thread of the dream had made its way back through the pages of my life, rendering the wrinkles somehow less tragic, the futile efforts more vindicated. As I stared at my own reflection, my mind was already conceding that the universe was truly in its right order after all. Perhaps the passing years had been kneading the clay for the sculpture about to be made.

Today, I was to finally meet a man who was a model of the dream I had yet to achieve. In the realm of great musical extravaganzas, the name of producer John McDowell was in some way attached to each of them. Be it the theater or the symphony, the opera or the cinema, he was considered the lord of musical accomplishment, the Robin Hood of undiscovered masterpieces.

Eleven years of returned parcels and disregarded phone messages were apparently the fertile ground in which the seed of my opportunity had finally taken hold. A collection of my compositions had been delivered to McDowell by an old friend who had worked with him on a theatrical production in New York. Nine months later the impossible had been achieved. I was to meet with McDowell himself, and I was to bring *all* of my compositions.

For more than a decade I had reverently collected every piece of passion I had ever known. Each emotion was described and revealed through a melodic testament of my existence. My morning walks had become preludes; brief encounters danced as sonatas. My liaisons bloomed into overtures, while nightmares had borne symphonies. The whole of my life was preserved on the faded parchment in my worn leather satchel, a library of notes and staves, measures and stanzas.

The mirror released me, leaving me with the image of a timeless dreamer who had possibly found the courage to begin again.

In my studio, which also doubled as a living room, I found the television still on from the night before. Miraculously, it had changed from broadcasting an evening with the symphony to a Monday morning evangelist. A middle-aged woman, doing a bad Barbie impersonation, was drunk on—*praise God, thank you Jesus. Praise God, praise God.* With a click of the remote, the religious drivel was silenced.

My appointment with McDowell was for 11:00 A.M. This gave me ample time to drive to his office in the heart of the central district. Grabbing my coat and the leather satchel, I paused at the doorway and looked back into my studio. Melodies had been born there and emotions had found immortality. Propped on the brow of the grand piano was a piece of sheet music I'd been reminiscing with the night before, composed years ago for just such a day as this.

Dreamwalker, take my dream to the far side of this life.
And hold my vision in your arms,
it's your promise of the night.
Feel my passion. Feel the wonder of all that I desire.
Dreamwalker, set my dream on fire.

As the door slowly squeezed the images out of my view, the telephone rang, pleading for me to return.

My immediate thought was to deny its persistent request—to allow nothing to distract me from my morning's destination. As I stood outside the door, my hand still on the knob, the thought occurred to me that it might be Mr. McDowell's office. I retraced my steps and lifted the receiver.

"Hello."

A woman answered, her voice surrounded by the indifferent clutter of office sounds. "Hello, is this Mr. Jared Grayson?"

"Yes," I said, "this is Jared Grayson."

"Mr. Grayson, my name is Sarah Neburg. I'm a nurse from the emergency room at St. Anthony's Hospital. I am calling to see if you are related to a Mr. Benjamin Grayson."

Taking a quick mental inventory, I could find no Benjamins—Grayson or otherwise. To my great relief it appeared that this phone call was a mistake. The interruption would not hinder my departure. A sigh escaped as I answered her question.

"No, I'm sorry, I have no relative by the name of Benjamin Gray—" The name caught in my throat. I had a sudden memory from childhood: Uncle Ben. He never went by Benjamin. He was my father's younger brother and, after the sudden death of their parents, we lost all contact with him. It was rumored he had moved far up into the mountains intending never to be found. Throughout the remainder of my father's life, as well as the years that followed, my family believed that Ben was no longer alive. The voice on the phone interrupted my thoughts

"Hello, Mr. Grayson, are you still there?"

"Yes . . . excuse me . . . I'm sorry, what were you saying?"

"Mr. Grayson, are you or are you not a relative of Benjamin Grayson?"

"Forgive my hesitation, but I'm not really sure. I was just now recalling an uncle I used to refer to as Ben. His last name would have also been Grayson. I have not known his whereabouts for over twenty years. Is there a problem? What is this all about?"

"Mr. Grayson, we have a Benjamin Grayson, approximate age

fifty-five. He was brought in about an hour ago with a head injury. Apparently he had a bad fall, somewhere in the mountains north of here. His condition is considered critical. Our emergency room physician is running tests to determine if he will require surgery. If he does, we will need immediate authorization from a family member. So far you are the only person we have found who might be related. We got your number from the local directory. There was no identification on the patient other than a name on an envelope in his shirt pocket. Mr. Grayson, does this sound like your uncle?"

My eyes became fixed on my watch. If I was still going to make the appointment, I would have to leave immediately. My heart was pounding. I wished now that I had never answered the phone.

"Miss, to tell you the truth, I don't know if I'm related to this man or not. Could you describe him?"

"Yes," she said. "He has a full-faced beard that, like his hair, is now mostly white. My guess would be that he is about six-foot-four and that he weighs around 260 pounds. His skin tone is somewhat dark, like he spent a lot of time out-of-doors."

I could find nothing in her description to show that this was someone other than my uncle. However, having not seen him for so many years, it was impossible to know for sure. With both of my parents deceased, I would probably be my uncle's only living relative. Regardless, the question remained, was I actually related to this man?

"Mr. Grayson," she continued, "as long as there's the possibility of locating a living relative, we will not proceed without consent. If there is no one, he will be considered a ward of the state, and the attending physician will be given the authority. I see by your address that you're not far from the hospital. Under the circumstances, the best course of action would be for you to come immediately to the emergency room."

The responsibility of this precise moment was inescapable. I was the only one who could quickly shed some light on this regrettable situation. Try as I might, I could find no other logical solution. She was right, I had to go to the hospital. I had to surrender to the situation at hand.

"Very well," I said, "I'll be there as quickly as I can."

I hung up and slowly placed the satchel full of music onto the bench, knowing full well that along with it I laid down the dream that perhaps had made its last attempt to be realized. The truth of this stranger's identity was as yet unknown, but the consequence of this day, and its effect on my life, was more than evident. My body sank forward and seemed to collapse inside of itself. Questions filled with disappointment and anger stumbled over each other, repeating in my mind. *What kind of an explanation could there be for such circumstances? Why had I been brought at last to the table if there was no banquet to be held? What kind of a God could be so entertained by such futility?* The list was unending and well-rehearsed. All were thoughts I had grappled with before. They were the familiar cornerstones of the last twelve years of my life.

Before leaving the house, I quickly phoned McDowell's office, hoping to explain and beg fervently for some other time to meet with him. The agitated tone of the busy signal clashed with my own quickened heartbeat. Not only was I going to miss my appointment, it would look as if I had not even bothered to cancel. And, I would be unavailable if they called me. Salvaging my golden opportunity—or even a remnant of my shattered credibility—seemed hopeless. I hung up in total defeat, putting the bleating busy signal out of its misery, wishing that someone could do the same for me.

2

The Hospital Maze

It was true that the hospital was but a short distance away. Today though, the journey seemed endless as my thoughts meandered among the emotions that now held them captive. A lifetime of disappointments accompanied me like an unwanted passenger who stared woefully out the window as I maneuvered my jeep along the city streets.

As I passed the red neon EMERGENCY ENTRANCE, I could find no part of me that cared whether or not this man was my uncle. And if he was, it was of no consequence to me whether or not he survived. He was but a stranger who had somehow attached himself to me by the common name of Grayson, a name I saw only as another legacy from my disheveled lineage, the members of which were all but deceased.

I stepped out of the warm jeep into the cold late morning air. Walking toward the sliding doors, I could already feel my face finding its plastic expression of concern, my body still searching for a more formal demeanor. I welcomed the commotion around the admissions desk, hoping that my honorable duty would be brief. With any luck I would ease by with a slight case of mistaken identity. Or better yet, the more definitive conclusion that the man had simply died in the interim. The eyes of the receptionist finally found me as did her generic question of, "Yes . . . may I help you?"

"My name is Jared Grayson. I am here in regard to a Benjamin Grayson. There was a question about my being related and giving some kind of authorization."

"Oh yes, Mr. Grayson, I remember . . . as it turns out, we discovered after our conversation that the patient's wife had already arrived. She made her way in to see her husband without stopping at the front desk and checking with us . . . so it appears that . . . well, I believe we do have someone from the immediate family after all. I hope that your trip to the hospital was not an inconvenience."

Stunned, I stared at the pages on her desk. Perhaps by reading the upside-down lettering, I might decipher some secret message as to why this small oversight had been allowed to create such havoc in my life. If my efforts and personal sacrifice had been for some gallant cause, I could have found a remnant of satisfaction within this fiasco. But to have my noble gesture appear simply as some ironic jest to which only God-the-Novelist was privy was a stretch, even for my sense of humor. The receptionist interrupted my melancholy trance.

"I must say Mr. Grayson, it was rather a surprise to us as well to find one of his relatives and to learn that she was right here at the hospital all along. She apparently found her husband in one of the cubicles in the emergency area. Someone overheard her talking to him behind the curtain—even though he has yet to regain consciousness. It drew the attention of one of the nurses, and that's how we discovered she was here. In fact, I believe she's there with him now. Would you like to go in and see them?"

For several seconds I debated involving myself further. If I suddenly made my entrance into this dramatic scene not knowing anyone in the room, this affair would not only become exceedingly uncomfortable, but I would have discovered yet one more opportunity to be unveiled as a total buffoon. If these were indeed members of some long lost branch of my family tree, then did I really want to rekindle all of those perfectly good reasons why they had generated themselves to be long lost in the first place? Maybe I should leave well enough alone and not disturb what for some twenty years had been kept so perfectly vacant. Finding no resolution to my dilemma, I responded. "Well, I'm not actually sure that I'm even related to any of these people. Did you happen to catch the wife's first name?"

"Clair, I believe it was. Would you like to speak with her?"

Silence followed as I hung on to her words with great hesitation. What for an instant had been clear and concise was once again murky and questionable. Cautiously, I answered.

"Ah . . . yes, I think I would like to have a word with her. . . . Yes, a word with Aunt Clair would be very . . . engaging."

Speaking to my Aunt Clair (as I remember) was always a challenge, but I had the feeling that this encounter with her was going to be rather exceptional. Clair Grayson, my uncle's wife, had died some time ago.

My mind began calculating the odds of there actually being some other Ben and Clair Grayson coexisting on the planet. There could be some perfectly gracious couple who just happened to be called Ben and Clair Grayson, who by mere coincidence lived in the same city as I, but were of no relation. This absurd notion was dismissed as swiftly as it arrived only to be replaced by the childhood images I could recall from my Aunt Clair's funeral. Maybe it wasn't really her in the casket that day, but was some imposter that just—

"Mr. Grayson," said a cheerful voice, breaking through my jumbled thoughts.

"Yes," I said to the nurse who approached, a small Asian woman with large glasses and a gracious smile.

"Well, of course you must be Mr. Grayson, you have such a strong resemblance to . . . is it your father?"

I fervently shook my head *no* and said, "I think he's my uncle."

"Oh . . . well, Mr. Grayson, your uncle has been moved up to intensive care, and his condition is no longer considered critical. As of yet though, he has not regained consciousness, so they are still monitoring him. He's on the fourth floor in room 417. You can go on up and look in on him if you like. Oh, and Mr. Grayson . . . would you remind your aunt that we still need her to fill out the appropriate forms . . . as soon as possible."

As I walked to the elevator, I noticed how inviting the exit sign looked. It glowed with that wonderful green "GO" color, and it hung over the front entrance, which led to the sidewalk—which led to my jeep—which could lead me to anywhere other than here.

The fourth floor spoke with a ghostly orchestration of beeps and tones from machines and monitors that seemed to be in every corner. As I searched the hall for room 417, I suddenly caught the features of a face that, to my own disbelief, I remembered so well. Even from across the hall and through the silence of a window I knew it had to be him. Like a child, I peered through the pane of the glass at a small handful of my history, a memory that I thought was all but forgotten. I was amazed at how well I remembered his face and how well he had aged over the years.

I stepped into the quiet of the room, greeted only by the mechanical bleeps of a sleeping man's heart. He lay idle and frozen underneath the folded pale linen as though possessed by a spell that had yet to be broken. His hair was white, sketched with patches of gray as if his face had been brushed by the sun, his skin still bronze from the exposure. His beard was grayish-white, full and well-groomed; his nose was strong and broad on his face. Even with the frenzy of tubes that now cradled his features, he held onto that noble appearance that was so much the image of how I saw him as a child. I remembered being frightened of his size and his strength: he seemed to tower over most other men. He was a sensitive man though—too sensitive, my father would say—yet so filled with life—a quality I now searched for some remnant of. Like a great sleeping giant cast in stone, he rested perfectly still, unaffected by me or the world around him.

There was no sign of any Aunt Clair, and being alone in the room with him gave me an eerie feeling. It was a discomfort like that I had experienced during numerous encounters at funerals. I stepped closer to look for more signs of life, when a male voice startled me from behind.

"You must be his son . . . I can tell by the resemblance." A man wearing a tweed jacket with a stethoscope around his neck stepped around the back side of the curtain. His thinning blond hair and thick mustache were accentuated by his dark tan, probably the result of a recent tropical retreat. His vibrant eyes and healthy demeanor seemed somehow out of place in this haven for disease and depression. With a strong hand he reached out for mine and spoke, "I am Dr. Stiltson . . . Sam Stiltson. I'm one of the physicians assigned to your father's case."

"Hello, Doctor," I said shaking his hand, "I'm Jared Grayson, but I'm not his son. I'm his nephew and I haven't seen him for some twenty years. They tracked me down because they couldn't find anyone else, that is until they discovered his wife was already here at the hospital. I thought I'd find her here."

With a puzzled look, the doctor replied, "I haven't seen her or been notified about his having a wife. So far you are the only one to come in and see him, at least since he was moved into intensive care. . . . Is his wife here at the hospital?"

His timely question was also one of mine, but the real question was whether our dear Aunt Clair existed anywhere at all. Once again I found myself enmeshed in some muddle that was no-business-of-mine and expected to explain what was no-understanding-of-mine. Surreptitiously, I glanced toward my uncle, perhaps checking to see if he was secretly listening. Or maybe it was because I felt uneasy about speaking in front of him on the information I was about to share.

"Well, Doctor . . . there was a woman in the emergency room who claimed to be his wife, my Aunt Clair. She apparently did not check in at the desk, and no one seems to have any idea where she is now. I myself have not seen her for many years and I have no idea whether she is even a relative of his, or of mine. And quite frankly, Doctor, I don't know that I am the appropriate person to be handling this. I hardly know this man and would really rather not be in this position. My being here was sort of a legal family obligation because they couldn't find anyone else."

"That's all right," he said, "at this point it doesn't really matter. There aren't any decisions to be made on his behalf. Currently he is in a comatose state that is not uncommon with someone who has had a traumatic injury, especially one that involved such a heavy blow to the back of the skull. The damage from the impact was severe, but not necessarily permanent. Our greatest concern right now is that he has several arteries in the damaged areas that are extremely narrow for appropriate blood flow to the brain. This may have been a condition that he had earlier and the accident has just compounded it. At any rate there is a very high probability of his having a blockage or clot in one of these arteries. This could result in an aneurysm or a stroke . . . even death."

"So, Doctor," I said, "is this the reason for the sudden coma?"

"We're not really sure why people go into a comatose state. In his case, it could be a reaction to the trauma as well as his delicate arterial condition. His brain may be shutting down all unnecessary bodily functions in order to minimize pressure to the arteries, which could lessen any chance of a disaster. Some people believe that a coma is an immobilized state in which the body then focuses on an ailment in an attempt to repair the problem. In any case, there is no way of knowing how long the coma will last, or if he will come out of it at all."

"If he does come out of the coma," I asked, "will he be alright? I mean, will he be able to function in a normal way?"

"The brain is a complicated mechanism," he said. "It's impossible to know the extent of the damage. He may already have some mental or physical dysfunction. We will be able to know more after further testing. He might regain consciousness and be perfectly normal. But he will then have to live with the threat of the aneurysm. With even a small amount of mental stress or physical strain, perhaps even for no apparent reason at all, the aneurysm can occur . . . and without any warning."

"In other words, Doctor, if by chance he does return to some kind of normal activity, he will always be a walking time bomb ready to explode at any moment?"

"Yes, that's about it."

"Is there any chance for surgery or some kind of treatment?"

"We can give him some medication to thin the blood, which will help minimize the clotting. As far as surgery, with the existing arterial problems, the risk factor is extremely high, and the odds for any kind of success are not good."

The doctor rambled on about my uncle's condition,

compounding the reasons why I wished I had never gotten involved in the first place. After he finished, he gave me his condolences, which left me feeling that it was unlikely my uncle would survive for very long. I suppose I was relieved. After all he had been through so much, and the quality of his life would be restricted. Maybe it would be best if he just never came out of the coma and simply died in his sleep. Of course, I could not deny my more cunning notion. If he would just go ahead and die, I would not have to take up any responsibility in the situation and could quietly go back to my mundane life.

The doctor and I slowly wandered towards the hall. To my surprise, as Dr. Stiltson passed through the door, he leaned back into the room and said, "Well, goodbye Ben. We will stop in and see you again tomorrow." At that particular moment, a verbal gesture seemed rather odd, since for the last twenty minutes the doctor and I had been carrying on as if Ben weren't even in the room. Not to mention that I now appeared to be the coldhearted bastard who didn't even bother to say goodbye at all. Surprisingly, he added, "There is something about this one, your uncle."

Before leaving I stopped at the nurses station, reluctantly giving them my name and number and what little knowledge I had about their patient. Again I asked about the woman who had claimed to be his wife, but there was no more information. I told them to please notify me if they had any further communication.

As I again passed by the doorway of my uncle's room I heard what I thought was a part of a conversation from inside. "Well, I've got to go now, but you have a mighty fine rest, Mr. Grayson, and we'll be talkin' with you again real soon," were the closing remarks of a woman's voice. Startled by the possibility that Uncle Ben had awakened and was talking to someone, I slipped back into the room. My abrupt entrance nearly caused me to collide with a short Black woman carrying a bucket and a mop, the handle of which did clap me on the side of the head.

"Well, hello there," she said, in an outspoken fashion, unaware that she had just assaulted me with her mop. She then turned toward my comatose uncle and exclaimed, "Ya see there, Mr.

Grayson, now here is someone else whose a comin' to talk with you, and I'll bet that this is your son, too . . . the resemblance and all." As I secretly searched for a fresh gouge on my head, the woman glanced back towards me from her exit out the door and said, "Well, you two have a real nice visit now."

I stood there feeling pressed into the scene as though an audience of ghostly bystanders were now expecting me to strike up some lively conversation with a man that was completely nonresponsive, in a room that, except for my presence, seemed as vacant of life as the city morgue. I felt ridiculous and uncomfortable, having been launched by this crazed cleaning woman into the opening lines of some artificial conversation that I thought was totally pointless. My body throbbed with a silent animosity as my participation in this senseless drama continued to escalate.

For the life of me I could not understand what possessed any of these people to talk with him. He couldn't hear them, and he was unable to respond even if he could. It seemed deranged to me that they would behave as though they could cleverly communicate with him in some emotionally-disturbed language only they could decipher. Furthermore, I had no appreciation whatsoever for their insightful observations of how I so strongly resembled this frozen figure. After all, he was a half a foot taller, sixty pounds heavier, had stark white hair and a beard, a big nose, giant ears, and looked like he'd been dead for at least a week!

Just then, I heard a chuckle from the direction of my uncle's bed. My heart jumped; I gasped for a breath of air. When I first turned to look, I saw nothing. Then with a series of clatters someone pulled open the curtain between my uncle's bed and the bed next to it. A young man in green hospital scrubs appeared holding a tourniquet and a syringe full of blood. Lying in the adjacent bed was a very small man, a midget compared to my uncle, but just as silent and equally comatose. The attendant laughed and tried to reassure me.

"Don't mind Emily, our maintenance woman," he said. "She tends to act . . . just a little touched sometimes. . . . Up here, you know." He tapped the side of his own head affectionately. "She always jabbers on that way with everyone. In fact, tonight she said that your friend here even spoke to her. But, of course, as soon as I walked in the door, well, he immediately stopped talking and went right back into his coma," he said with a self-satisfied laugh. "Well, like I said, Emily's a little touched. She's probably the only one that *he* would ever talk to, and no doubt *she* is probably the only one that could ever hear him. . . ." He chuckled again, "If you know what I mean?"

At this time, I had to admit I wasn't sure what he meant, nor had I any desire to find out. I lamely smiled and left the room, once again maneuvering down the hall towards the elevator, trying to wash my mind of a solitary phrase that kept popping up. *Just a little touched . . . just a little touched.*

3

The Elevator

That evening I drove into the central part of the
city. I longed to regain some part of my everyday
existence that was at least vaguely familiar. A gray, misty rain
seemed to saturate the pavement as I walked along Seventh
Avenue, observing people who were pretending to be unaffected
by the cold and wet. A few buildings down, at the Regency
Theater, a performance was letting out. Three or four limousines
out front signalled to onlookers that it was probably opening night
for some aspiring writer or the miraculous debut for the works of
a newly discovered composer. Perhaps I would pretend that it
was me and slip into the open door of one of the limos. I would
tell the driver to pull away and then masquerade with the success
of another composer's life, no one ever knowing the difference. I
smirked at the thought and then glanced up at the marquee to
read the letters that would come to haunt me yet once again.

THE TIME KEEPER
Produced by **John McDowell**

The name taunted me like a relentless ghost. Not only had I
bungled my private meeting with John McDowell (one of the
greatest producers in the country), but I did it on the same day
his latest production opened. He would have been excited and
inspired—looking for something new to take on. He would have

been happily searching for some raw undiscovered talent he could bring into the spotlight and—*BUMP*.

My body was jostled by an awed and excited crowd of people pouring out of the theater. They quickly filled the sidewalks and overflowed into the wet city streets, some of them peering into the many limos that began to receive their long-awaited passengers. One of those passengers was undoubtedly John McDowell, although I had no idea which one. People said he was very much a pacesetter and ran with the richest and most stylish people in the country. Undoubtedly, he knew only the right people and was invited to all of the wildest and most glamourous parties. He was outrageous and eccentric, and had more than enough money and popularity to get away with it. He was the epitome of my most extravagant dream personified, and he was probably in one of those last limos that had just disappeared into the darkened street.

I spent the majority of the next morning dancing aimlessly with my idle furniture, trying to reorganize the pieces of my life to see if at least two or three of them might still fit together in some logical fashion. So far I had managed to dismiss the notion that I was a complete failure. I had all but decided that my life had simply fallen into the hands of one of God's court jesters, and that before the end of time the scoundrel would be caught, and that all would be put back into good order. I had also managed to avoid contact with the hospital all morning and was fervently pretending that the situation would just handle itself. By mid-afternoon though, I was beginning to realize that not knowing what was happening with my uncle might mean that others (unbeknownst to me) could be plotting to involve me with him even deeper. I finally decided to call and see if there had been any change.

"Hello," I said. "This is Jared Grayson. I'm calling in regard to Benjamin Grayson. . . . He is in room 417."

"Yes, Mr. Grayson. I've been working with your father this morning. There really hasn't been any change since last night.

He is holding his own though, which at this point is a good sign."

"Nurse, has he shown any signs of regaining consciousness?"

"No, but he did have a visitor today. A very nice, young woman who has been talking to him most of the afternoon. We have all been hoping that he might respond to her. In fact, I think that she is still with him now."

"What!" I exclaimed. "Who is she? What is her name?"

"I believe she said that she was his niece or something," she replied. "Would you like to speak with her?"

"Yes, I . . . I mean no," I stuttered. "Just ask her to stay at the hospital, and I will be there in a couple of minutes."

"All right, Mr. Grayson. I'll tell her."

"And nurse," I continued after a short pause, "that man is not my father . . . I'm just his nephew . . . a distant nephew."

I made my way to the hospital as quickly as possible, realizing now that, with all of the strange occurrences, I should have taken the time to speak to the mystery woman on the phone. Once inside I maneuvered through the crowded lobby and catapulted myself through the closing jaws of the empty elevator that was, according to the green light, going up. I pushed the button for the fourth floor and leaned back in the silent isolation that the elevator briefly provided. I pondered the recent visit from the other woman who was claiming to be my Aunt Clair.

If she had known Ben or had been related to him, then why wouldn't she leave her real name and number? Or for that matter, why would she bother to say she was his wife if she had no intention of playing out the role? Is it possible that this was just some strange old lady wandering through the hospital, one who had simply misplaced a few of her own faculties and was chronically grieving over some lost husband that she probably never really cared for at all?

My mind continued its relentless pedaling for the misplaced logic in the situation. Within the confines of my privacy, I spoke to myself out loud. "Besides, who's to say whether any of these people who have been carrying on lengthy conversations with my nonresponsive uncle are even in their right minds. Perhaps what is actually called for in this situation is a little psychiatric intervention with each and every one of the these mysterious visitors." *DING*. The elevator chimed.

My words were interrupted as my private chamber came to a stop. Like the eye of some great dragon, the elevator doors opened to look once again into the world. An onrush of light and sound came flooding through the opening. In the midst of this flurry, a young woman stepped up to catch the moving doors. She had long, straight auburn hair that hung down around her shoulders. Her light peach colored garment draped all around her like an invitation to the wind that might at any moment take her up in a dance. Her attire looked Mediterranean, or perhaps East Indian, but very modern as though she had just come from some gallery opening on the far side of town.

"Are you going down?" she said. Her voice surprised me as did the intensity of her light brown eyes. Without thinking I quickly answered her. "Ah, yes."

She struck me as being very beautiful in a modest way, with a soft milky complexion and very little makeup. Her naturally high cheekbones accentuated the almond shape of her eyes which seemed to smile somehow, even during a mundane ride up the elevator. There was a pleasantness about her, everything simple and balanced. She felt familiar to me, although I would venture to say that this observation was likely just another example of my middle-aged roguery surfacing to be noticed.

She reminded me very much of a young woman that I knew years ago by the name of Katherine . . . "Katherine with a K," she would so often announce. In fact, I had intended to marry her had she not decided one afternoon to depart for Nepal, following some infamous guru, whose name I could never pronounce. I can still remember the last letter I received from her:

"Dear Jared, I have decided to live in Nepal with my true guru and mentor. I believe this to be the path of my ultimate destiny. Being pregnant may also be a part of my destiny since there is a possibility that I may be. Even though you are more than likely the father, I want you to know that I assume full responsibility and that I release you of any parental obligations. I am leaving no forwarding address so that we can both start our new lives without any historical difficulties. Sincerely, Katherine. . ." or something to that effect.

Such were the scenarios of having lived through my unstable youth. I was never to hear from her again. Throughout our relationship she had been adamant about never having children. Whether or not a child had been born, there was no way of knowing. At the time, I had neither the finances nor the passion to pursue finding out if I had become a father. I reluctantly allowed all such speculations to fall from me, as I did in time the memories of my life's dawning romance.

As my mind wandered within the past, I noticed the elevator had begun to fill with the scent of roses. It was a subtle aroma, not that of a perfume, but more natural, almost edible somehow. I glanced up at the elevator numbers to refocus myself. The red light reading 5 had just gone dark. A charge of my own electricity jolted my body back into the awareness that I had just missed my stop. Needless to say, though, the fourth floor had not gone by unnoticed. It was undoubtedly the floor where the attractive young woman had gotten on. In addition, the elevator was obviously not going down as I had told her. It was going up on what appeared to be a ghost run, since no other buttons on the board had been pushed.

I could feel her awareness of the situation as if she too was now wondering who I was and whether I was really trying to get anywhere at all. I decided that if I was to leave this elevator with some semblance of dignity (not to mention the appearance of some sanity), I would simply get out on whichever floor the doors chose to stop at next. I would step out with great assurance as if I were in total control of my situation and knew exactly where I was going and what I was doing. As the light beamed 7, the elevator stopped. I stepped confidently out through the doors onto the tile floor, only to bring myself two steps later to a complete halt.

The elevator had opened to a small area, which was barricaded with waist-high countertops. Glass extended above the counters, completing the enclosure to the ceiling. Behind the glass, off to one side, was a security guard who promptly stood up as I stepped out. A woman dressed in a gray suit sat at the counter and peered through a large hole cut out of the glass. At first, the space had the appearance of a small but rather secure bank lobby, that is except for the large black letters mounted safely behind the glass: PSYCHIATRIC WARD. The security guard's voice echoed through the hole in the glass as he leaned towards the woman and spoke.

"Were they sending someone up to be admitted?"

My shadow turned and leapt for the elevator door, but my body surrendered and sank back onto its heels, knowing full well that it was too late for any such escape. There was a slight giggle from the elevator as its doors closed firmly behind me. I glanced again at the lettering on the wall, hoping I might have read it wrong the first time. To my grave disappointment, this was not the case. As I looked back at the security guard, I noticed that his left eye was now open slightly larger than the other, its accompanying eyebrow had likewise raised for the question.

Caught in this scene, with all of its irony, I could not help but laugh in spite of myself. What began as a chuckle more closely resembled an abrupt outburst, which probably did not help my present situation. I took a deep breath to regain my composure, preparing myself to cope with the truth of my absentmindedness.

I informed the guard that I was not paying attention, and I simply waltzed out onto the wrong floor. Then the guard informed me that the elevator does not stop on this floor unless they are sending someone up to be admitted. He also said that new patients are always accompanied by, and are under the watchful eye of, a security guard, who in my case now appeared to be missing. Although this new information helped explain why the elevator had stopped on a floor that had no button to push on the panel, it did not explain why the elevator had randomly chosen this floor and spewed me out into the world of straitjackets and padded cells. My puzzlement was shared by the security guard, who then cautiously guided me to a small wooden bench alongside the counter. There I was to wait while he made some phone calls to find out if anyone had been sent up to be admitted or if anyone had been reported missing.

As he made his call, I directed my attention to the skeptical features on the face of the woman behind the glass.

"This is all just a simple mistake," I said. "My uncle is down in intensive care on the fourth floor, and I was on my way to see him. I missed that stop, and for some reason the elevator stopped here and I got out in error. In fact, I called the nurse on the fourth floor just a short while ago and arranged to meet with someone. They are waiting for me at the nurses station." After a slight pause, I persisted, "You can call them and verify it." She motioned to the guard who was just finishing his call, and then repeated to him what I had just said. She then stiffly addressed me through the opening in the glass.

"What is your name and the name of the patient you were here to see?" I gave her the names, and she continued. "And what is the room number of that patient?"

I answered. "It's room 417."

She started to write it down, but then slowly turned to the guard and said, "Isn't that the room that you went down to last night? You remember, the Indian guy with the long ponytail who was ranting and raving over that patient, the big white-haired guy in a coma. Wasn't that 417?"

The guard clasped his chin with a squeeze of suspicion and said, "Yeah . . . that was 417—" Before he could complete his sentence, both he and the nurse rotated their faces simultaneously to fix their eyes on me. Behind the blank and bewildered look that I was sure now possessed my own face, my mind shouted into every vacant cavern within to awaken me from this metaphorical nightmare. To no avail—the echoes came back leaving me with the inescapable conclusion that this was no dream, and as this drama unfolded, I was to have the next line. It was a classic case of speechlessness. I was caught in the clutches of some cosmic hospital melodrama with no idea which part I was playing. Striving to portray some innocence, I questioned their last response.

"There was someone in my uncle's room last night?"

The guard shifted his eyes and caught the gaze of the woman as he answered. "Yeah, it was about two in the morning, and he was making some kind of voodoo over the old guy, trying to wake him up. The night nurse called and said he was chanting and waving feathers around—which had them all in a panic. When I dealt with him, he started acting like a wild animal. So, I put him in restraints, and he soon found himself admitted to the Psychiatric Unit." He chuckled sarcastically, revealing a pirate-like grin. "He's here for a 72-hour observation until they find out what's going on with him."

To the guard's uneasiness, I came to my feet and attempted a lively but feeble defense. "I don't know anything about this man, but if you would just call the nurses station, I assure you that they know who I am." At this the woman behind the counter picked up the phone and called the fourth floor. The nurse there apparently verified who I was and that she had been expecting me for some time.

With this the guard ushered me back into the elevator, and I was delivered to my original destination. He escorted me to the nurses station as though I were a child in tow. Then he made a sluggish about-face, in the direction of the elevator. At last the steel doors swallowed the fine constable and transported him back to the psychiatric ward, where he was probably better suited as a patient than a security guard. Turning to the nurse I asked, "Could you tell me where I will find the young woman who came to see my uncle?"

Looking up from her clipboard, she said, "Oh, she couldn't wait for you. Perhaps another time, I think she said." At this, my patience all but gone, and with the nurse walking away, I knew I would have to be more persistent.

"Excuse me," I said, "did she understand that I was on my way to speak with her?"

"I'm sure she did," she replied. "She ran out of here like she was in an awful hurry."

I remembered the woman who had dashed into the elevator, the young lady who had been the catalyst of my seventh floor psychiatric detour. She would have been leaving the hospital about that time. I called to the nurse as she continued to walk away.

"Was she wearing something of a peach-colored dress that draped everywhere?"

"Yes, that's the one," she said, disappearing into one of the rooms.

I had more questions, but allowed the conversation to come to its natural end, having noticed that I was standing by myself— talking to myself—in the middle of the empty hallway. Having so recently made my escape from the comforting arms of the psychiatric ward, I thought it best not to create any more commotion. For now, I would be silent, even though I had not yet asked about my uncle or inquired about the mad late-night crier with whom I had nearly become roommates on the psychiatric floor.

I strolled down the hall and slowly entered my uncle's room. Again I could smell a light scent of roses lingering among an assortment of sterile and therapeutic odors. My uncle, ever so still and silent, appeared unaffected by the commotion from the recent visitations. I moved closer to study his private and peaceful expression. Standing in the dim light of the open doorway, I spoke to him out loud.

"For someone who is so silent, you surely do have a barrage of visitors. And lady visitors at that. The nurse said that—" I caught my own words as they merged into a murmur of laughter. I smiled and shook my head. Perhaps the deranged halls of the psychiatric floor weren't so inappropriate after all. Here I was talking out loud with him as the others had done, making light of a situation tangled with confusion and grave uncertainties. I suppose I should have been more melancholy, but try as I might, I could find no grief inside me.

I looked at the gentle lines around his eyes, curious as to how his skin could appear so soft and alive amid the deeper wrinkles of a face that had always placed itself into the wind. I thought about how full of life he had once been and could not help but wonder just how near that life was to me now. Was there some presence here that I had previously allowed to slip past me undetected? Or had my imagination simply been triggered by the day's circumstances and the collection of strangers who had come to visit him? Had I allowed some possibility to make its way into the annals of my mind? I could not be sure what I was truly feeling, but as I stood over him, I knew the feeling was different than before. For the first time, I very much wanted to be there. I wanted to come in and find him sitting up, making jest with some young lover with whom he had recently had an ecstatic affair. I wanted him to reminisce, telling me of those missing years that had passed and of all those summer days that had been so good to him in his life. My hopefulness frightened me, yet it seemed to have found some place inside me where it was now most welcome.

My eyes followed the many shades of his silvery white beard down below his chin. Around his neck I noticed pieces of red and orange color. As I pulled back a part of his garment I discovered vibrant rose petals scattered about his throat and nestled in the white hair on his chest. Again I could smell the sweet scent I had noticed when entering the room. I called the nurse to show her what I'd found. We discovered that Ben's entire body had been covered with the fragrant petals. Like a bouquet scattered by the wind, a delicate array of orange and red adorned him from head to foot.

The nurse quickly began to remove the petals, trying to restore some order to her domain. A bewildered smile overtook me as I walked into the hall. I could still remember the spirited face (as well as the giggle) of the young woman in the elevator who had witnessed a small sample of my disoriented behavior. I could easily envision her as the artful maiden of the rose petals. Quite possibly she was not only the ghostly reminder of a tarnished memory, my first love Katherine, but she may have also been the painter of this most auspicious portrait of my uncle in his ever-so-floral attire. I had no concept of the purpose behind the scattering of the petals and could not help but wonder just what manner of visitors had been drawn to the bedside of my silent relation. As I took my leave, I glanced back through the doorway to say goodbye.

"Well, Uncle, what do you have to say for yourself now?" I smiled and again shook my head as we both started to laugh— I mean, I started to laugh.

4

Silent Situations

The next morning I was roused by the insistent and repetitive whine of the telephone. I could tell by the shadows in the softly lit room that night had not yet surrendered to the day. Darkness still harbored my mind as it slipped in and out of any conscious awareness. The telephone's relentless ringing was accompanied by the familiar sounds from the awakening streets, sounds that played the prelude of dawn slowly making its way into my comfortable slumber. Then I remembered Ben and the hospital. I grabbed the receiver as the other half clamored helplessly to the floor.

"Hello." My mouth struggled to make the word.

"Hello, is this Mr. Grayson?" The obtrusive clear voice of a woman entered uninvited into my still-sleeping thoughts.

I hesitated as if I had forgotten my own name. Then finally I replied, "Uh, yes, this is Jared Grayson."

"Mr. Grayson, well, this is Emily Hewson from St. Anthony's Hospital." Her speech had an urban Black character about it. Her words were hurried and difficult to understand.

"I apologize bein's I'm callin' you at such a late hour and all, but it's about that uncle a yours."

"Yes," I replied.

"Your uncle, Benjamin Grayson. That is your uncle?"

"Yes, what is it?"

"Well, Mr. Grayson, I thought it was important to let you

know as soon as possible, with you bein' the only living relative of your uncle and all—and even though Dr. Stiltson said he would notify you in the morning about what's happened, I felt that with this situation—that time was of the essence. I felt that you would want the information firsthand. And since I'm fixin' to leave the hospital soon, bein's that I work the night shift and the night shift is nearly through for the night, well, I thought that you would want to hear it from someone who was actually there when it happened, you know someone who actually—"

"What is it! What's happened!" My questions broke through her wandering words in an attempt to rescue the critical information drowning within her explanation. After the bombardment of disjointed rhetoric, the empty space that followed my interruption seemed equally endless. Despite the momentary lull, she resumed her monologue with the same intensity as before.

"Well, Mr. Grayson, although it is true that at this present time your uncle is appearin' to be, or perhaps we should say has returned to bein' his comatose self, and accordin' to all of these talkin' machines, well, they show no indication of—"

"Nurse, what happened with my uncle? Is he alright? What's going on?" My random questions echoed my frustration. This time, with no delay, she continued.

"Well, Mr. Grayson, that's just it. To look at him now, why he's as still as a statue, and sorta elegant like one too. But it was not two hours ago that me and Melissa—Melissa, she be one of the nurses on the night shift. Anyway, me and Melissa, why we had the nicest conversation with your uncle, and we even got ta laughin' too. All of us, even your uncle. And I mean to tell ya, that man, he do be havin' a way with words. He must be some sorta philosopher or somethin'. Why he not only answered some a our questions, but he even turned one of them into a story. That's right, Mr. Grayson, he even told us a story. Why, alls I asked him was, why did he talk to me and not to anyone else? And do you know what he said?" There was a slight pause and the sound of paper rustling. "Just a minute, Mr. Grayson, I had to write it down bein's I didn't understand it at first."

After a moment or two she continued. "He said that he talked to me and not to anyone else because, *I allowed the possibility to be, and because I believed that life was present even in the most silent of situations.* That's it, that's what he said I did. Well, ya know Mr. Grayson, I always talk to all of the patients on my route. It don't matter to me whether they answer me back or not. I still talk to all of them just the same. Even these real quiet ones. The doctors say they're comatose, like nobody's home. Well, they're not foolin' me. Just cause they're not talkin' for a while doesn't mean that they don't got nothin' to say."

I was truly at a loss for words; my tongue had taken refuge and was off somewhere in hiding. I'm not sure which I found more unbelievable, the information I was just given, or the manner in which it was presented. As I listened to her explanation, my mind had created the image of a very stout Black woman strategically squeezed into a very tight, white nurse's uniform. This may or may not have been the reason for the rapidness of her speech. In any case, her creative use of the English language gave me cause to question the reliability of her information, not to mention her status as a nurse.

In an attempt to sort it all out, I ventured to ask, "Nurse . . . what you are telling me is that my uncle not only regained consciousness, but he also went so far as to carry on a conversation—which by and large became the telling of a story— after which, he promptly fell back into a coma?"

"That's right, just like you said it, word for word. Except for the part where you called me the nurse. I'm not no nurse. I'm the maintenance person that works the night shift. You know, the cleaning-type person. Don't you remember? I bumped into you the other night in your uncle's room and quite frankly, Mr. Grayson, this is the second time that your uncle has spoken to me. A course the first time I mention it to the others, well, they didn't much believe me. But this time when he starts to talkin', why I ran to the nurses station to get Melissa. When I told her . . . why, she not only goes in to see for herself, but she grabs one of the doctor's dictation recorders. You know, one of those little machines that they talk into all private-like, like they was tellin' a secret or somethin'. Anyway, she records the whole conversation with your uncle and—"

"What!" I blurted.

"That's, right Mr. Grayson, the whole conversation and the story, too. Ya see, Melissa, she knows I'm no fool, and she believed me when I told her about it the first time. So she thinks to bring in the recorder. You know, just in case that after he's done talkin' he decides to slip away again. She records the whole thing, and now she's got proof that perhaps Ol' Emily here do know what she be talkin' about after all."

An undeniable satisfaction had found its way into the voice of this woman, undoubtedly referred to by her most reliable friends as Ol' Emily. With this, our conversation ended and I hung up the phone. In the silence that followed, I tried to gather my thoughts. Was it possible that someone could move in and out of a coma, being so alive in one moment, and yet so dormant in the next? I thought about what she had said, that he had told a story and appeared to be some kind of philosopher. From what I could remember, my uncle had a very limited vocabulary. He was a man of few words, and he used most of them to talk about fishing. Nothing that I had heard reminded me of the uncle I had once known.

Later that morning, I received yet another phone call from the hospital giving me similar information about my uncle, but in a far less colorful manner. This call included an apology for the early morning ramblings of the maintenance woman, as well as an invitation to come and see one of the hospital's resident psychiatrists. The caller, a Dr. Schultz, had been assigned to my uncle's case. I was to meet with her to review the tape the nurse had recorded. She was hoping I might know something from his past that could shed light on the confusion that was now brewing.

The only clear memories I had of my uncle were the late summer visits with him and my Aunt Clair at their lake cabin.

These encounters, the only actual contact I had with my uncle, were due solely to my father's insistence that I spend at least a few days a year with Ben. I never really understood the importance of this annual event for it was more than obvious that my father's interaction with him was even less frequent than mine. The two of them seldom communicated. Still, my father always spoke highly of Uncle Ben, saying Ben was one of the finest men he would ever know.

Trips to my uncle's lake cabin were designed to be great excursions for a young city boy, adventures into the wilderness (or so I thought). Ben had built a cabin from timber off the land. There was no electricity, and the nearest access road was a quarter-mile hike away. Far from being shortcomings, these circumstances had been well-planned by my uncle, for he loved solitude and to live simply with what nature had provided. Because surviving off the land was a great passion of Ben's, I made it a point to never question the supply of store-bought goods we consistently packed into the cabin every three or four days.

Aunt Clair, on the other hand, was not so fond of this rustic lifestyle. Quite often she would stay in the city, leaving me the sole survivor of some of Ben's most famous fishing tales.

Fishing was Ben's first love, and, although I was fond of fishing with my uncle, I could never really muster up the passion he had for those cold, wet mornings. Nor did I relish the idea of any morning that started with any activity other than eating. Ben always insisted that a man needed to catch his own breakfast. Of course, this did not explain the large helping of sausage and eggs that accompanied his ever so small lake trout. Not to mention those frequent mornings when there was no trout at all.

In keeping with Uncle Ben's lake-side traditions, all fishing expeditions began with the raising of his coffee mug (and whatever the liqueur for the day) and his proposing a toast to the noble trout that would be his breakfast. He would swill down most of the drink and toss the remaining splash over his shoulder into the lake.

"That half is for the trout," he would say, even though it was never anywhere near half, I always thought. "For with such a fish I will share my drink. After all, we are very old friends, the trout and I." Ben respected all the creatures of the lake and believed that each one had a spirit like his own. He said that the fish all knew which one of them was to have the honor of dining with him that morning. I remembered how much I believed those words and how much I loved those early days with him on the lake.

The lake itself was small, more like a large pond, I suspect. However, it provided Ben with a fish now and then and a place for the moon to shimmer on clear summer nights, his sleek wooden canoe sliding through the sky's reflection in the cold, still waters.

The only other distinct memory I had of my uncle was an image of him and his rocking chair molded into one ghostly silhouette. Together in the evening hours, they would sway and haunt the rough-wooded porch that extended like a small pier out over the edge of the lake. Gold and orange embers from his pipe tobacco gave out a glow that generally signaled the end of one of his stories, the substance of which I have no recollection. Ben always said that when it came time for him to leave this Earth walk he wanted to slip away, sitting in that old rocking chair at the end of the dock, surrounded by the water and the pale moonlight.

Arriving at the hospital, I was promptly greeted at the elevator by the resident psychiatrist who had spoken to me on the phone. Dr. Schultz was a tall stately woman, probably in her mid-forties. Her dark brown hair was cropped far shorter than mine and in her navy blue suit (with uneven shoulder pads) she could have easily been mistaken for a man—even from the front. For that matter, from the front she more than likely would have been mistaken for a man had it not been for the bright crimson lip gloss that resided underneath her not-to-be-noticed mustache. She spoke with a firm clear voice and attempted to make an equally firm impression with her handshake, which clenched my unsuspecting paw, her bony fingers digging into my flesh.

"Mr. Grayson, is it?" she began. "My name is Dr. Hedda Schultz. We spoke on the phone this morning."

"Yes, Doctor," I replied, gracefully trying to retrieve my perforated hand.

"I'm glad you could come so soon. There are still a lot of unanswered questions about your uncle. I thought we would begin by having you listen to the recording that the nurse made. I've arranged for you to review this tape in your uncle's room."

"Doctor, has he been conscious at all since that incident?"

"Mr. Grayson, I need you to understand that we're not exactly sure your uncle ever regained consciousness at all. Even though the nurse on duty has a reputation for being reliable, according to our technical people there was no change in the machines that were monitoring him. There is some concern about the validity of this recording, as well as the lengthy conversation between these two women and your uncle."

Sliding back into my familiar state of frustration, I asked, "Doctor, why would they create a recording that was a fake? What would anyone have to gain from that?"

"Well sir, that's why we're still giving these two women the benefit of the doubt. We're also hoping you might be able to recognize if it's your uncle's voice on the tape."

Timidly, I replied, "The last time I heard my uncle's voice I was about nine years old. I hardly think that I will be a very good judge of this."

Unwilling to satisfy me with any response, the doctor allowed a lull to form in our conversation. My initial impression was that she had taken this time to tug aggressively at her suit jacket in order to adjust the inanimate shoulder pads, which up to now had been quite mobile and alive inside her apparel. Having little success, she remained quite crookedly cocked as she then led me down the hall and into my uncle's room.

"Here we are, Mr. Grayson." Abruptly she pulled closed the curtain between the two beds, giving as little cognizance to the comatose man in the other bed as he likewise gave to her. "You can sit right here alongside your uncle and listen to the recording.

With these headphones you will be able to hear the voice more clearly, and no other noises will distract you."

I was sure she had some psychological reason for plopping me down right next to the coma in question. Had I been allowed to arrange myself, I could have easily found several other less conspicuous places to sit while my memory was coercively probed. Although it appeared that my uncle was now lying in an altogether different position than I had seen him the last time, it was obvious that this new posture was the result of being puppeted by the nurses who had left him in a most awkward pose. Before I sat comfortably by his side, I courageously rearranged his appendages by putting his arm back into his shoulder and reattaching his head to his spine, so that he no longer resembled some game hen about to be plucked.

"Mr. Grayson," Dr. Schultz continued, "the recording only lasts about ten minutes. I will leave you alone during that time, then we can discuss it when I return."

Having issued her final commandments, she marched out of the room and intently down the hall. I stayed . . . imprisoned by the situation, bound by the task before me.

5

The Forgotten Garden

As I slowly placed the headphones over my ears, the dissonance of hospital sounds was smothered by a blanket of silence. For a moment I felt stunned. It was as if I had somehow joined my uncle in some other time or dimension, one that I was sure had long since been forgotten. I glanced over at his face, nervously expecting to find him conscious in this silent place. To my great relief he remained quiet and empty, completely unaware of my imagined intrusion. As I closed my eyes to shut out the lifeless expression that enveloped his noble features, the recording began to play.

"... but when you were a child, something else happened. For you not only stepped away from the magic—the spirit of your true being, you also stepped away from your freedom. You lost the passion—the fire and the drive to create from infinite possibilities that were once inherent in you as children. It was then that you unknowingly began to be programmed to be the adult who followed limited rules, who allowed the altered truths to slowly pull you away from the purity of your spirit.

"Now ... you surround yourselves with so many others who are ignorant of this understanding, but who are most willing to enslave you in their world of probabilities. As a result, your own world of possibilities lies abandoned, a forgotten garden longing for you to come and be in it."

As the words entered my head, it was as if my mind became divided. One half was remembering clearly the low gruff voice with its slow gentle words that rang so true as my uncle's. The other half was bewildered by the way the words were arranged. The voice was like a Shakespearean sonnet, so eloquently spoken, and yet the accent or the dialect was impossible to trace. It seemed to be Old English and French, Italian and Greek, but also broken as if from a foreigner who was Tibetan or Chinese. It embodied every accent and was loyal to none. And, while the words were English, the content was from beyond.

"When you were a child, you did not walk about chanting to yourself that anything was possible. This was an understanding that was so innate to you that you did not have to contemplate that which was already in motion. You simply played in your garden of possibilities and were so satisfied with the moments you created. You walked in an unlimited understanding where your footsteps were blessed . . . always.

"And so, my dear woman, when you would ask, why I would speak to you and not to any others? It is because you allowed the possibility to be, and because you believe that life is present even in the most silent of situations. Perhaps I will tell you a story about such possibilities and the child in you. All right?

"There was once a small boy whose papa had taken him and his younger brother to the temple or church. Like most young boys who are confined in such a place, he was restless and fidgety, and not particularly interested in what God, or what anyone there, had to say.

"Daydreaming, his eyes wandered until off in the distance he saw this beautiful figure. At first it was like glitter that seemed to fall in specks of white and gold light. Then it swirled and turned, creating substance and shape. It materialized into an image that was of such sparkle, and color, that it made him laugh and giggle at how it danced about the place. This was not uncommon to him, for he had seen such things before. It was an angel or some sweet spirit that had simply glided through the wall—for walls gave it no boundaries and doors were even less. And this filled the boy with such pleasure that he could not hold on to all that was his bliss. He shouted, 'Look, papa, look, at that bright spirit, there!' and he pointed to an alcove dressed with colored windows.

"His papa, quite disturbed by the boy's outburst, shushed him and said in a harsh whisper, 'That is not a real spirit, it's just a statue of an angel. Now be quiet and pay attention.'

"The boy, quite aware that his papa had not seen the real spirit that frolicked above what was a statue of an angel, persisted. 'No papa, there in white and gold light, the real angel.'

"Hearing this, the littler brother, now drawn to the excitement, joined in with a voice of such innocence and unbridled enthusiasm that his words echoed throughout the temple. 'Where is the spirit . . . where, papa, where?'"

"The littler brother squirmed and turned, looking all about with an anticipation and a desire that could only be quenched by the sight of such a being. Then this little one saw the bright spirit and became silenced solely by his awe of the sweet vision.

"The papa, now aware that his children had drawn the attention of the surrounding people, put a roar into his whisper. 'Be quiet! It's not a real angel. Young boys cannot see such things. Only great beings like saints and wise sages can see bright spirits. It is just your imagination. Now stop your pretending, and pay attention to what is truly here.'

"Well, the young boy continued to watch the bright spirit and began to contemplate what his papa had said. The more he thought about the words, the more he believed what the words had told him. As these words solidified inside the mind of the boy, the image of the bright spirit began to dissipate. Before long the image was gone from his vision, and the boy became convinced that his papa was right. Never again would he see such a spirit, for through the words of the limited thoughts, his mind would begin to close. He would lose the ability to see such things and would now limit his thoughts to the probabilities of what he had been taught. He would leave his world of possibilities, never to return to the garden, to play in the magic of its truth . . . ."

I searched the archives of my memory for a time or a place where I had heard my uncle tell this kind of story or speak so eloquently. I could not. Perhaps it was simply madness as a result of the accident or the pressure on his brain. Yet no explanation seemed to account for his unrecognizable dialect or his unusual use of the language.

Scattered among these conflicting thoughts were glimpses of my own childhood memories—impressions that seemed to have been triggered by the story. They danced in and out of my awareness paying no heed to my rational mind. In an attempt to block them out, I once again concentrated on the recording.

". . . all of you have had moments in your lives when you were told that the bright spirits and the visions that you saw were not a reality in this world. You were taught that it was your mind in its imagination that had created such things. You became programmed into an understanding that gave you reasons to dismiss everything that had once been magic in your lives. You were convinced of this, at a time when you were nigh two or three years old.

"Even now, if you try, you can remember some time or place where all of these things happened. Perhaps it was your home. You can still see yourself there in your play clothes, or perhaps you had lost your garments along the way, and now you are wearing nothing upon you. You are outside of your house under a warm sky, because you so loved to be there.
Out amongst the trees and the flowers
of your garden.

It was your kingdom,
    and it was the world that went on forever.

You used to sneak out to the garden,
into the flowers and tall grasses.
You can still feel this little one inside you now,
with small hands,
and feet that longed to run.

You dance about the wildflowers,
and the puppy or the kitten
is running around your feet
with unconditional love.
Always doing whatever you want to do.

And now a butterfly lands upon your hand,
tickles your palm, and wriggles out to the ends of your fingers.
You are in awe of its beauty.

It flies from your hand,
so you chase after it,
through the garden you run, ever so free.

Then you see in the distance a shimmer of light,
like a tornado of tiny stars being spun by the wind.
Excitedly you watch as the sparkles begin to take form.
You remember the feeling of this one who comes in the white
and blue glitter,
and you are delighted to—

Suddenly you hear a harsh voice calling you from the house.
The voice says, "You must come immediately."
    You do not want to.
You keep watching for the sparkles, the spirit that approaches.

The voice becomes louder than before,
and you recognize whose it is.
    The voice says,
"You have been very bad.
Come here to me now."
Sadly, the sweetness breaks,
and the sparkles slowly fade.

The voice frightens you,
a heart-wrenching emotion
you remember even now.
With trembling anticipation,
you step up to the porch.
The door has been left ajar.
You can feel the anger that waits just inside.
An uneasy silence lingers all around.

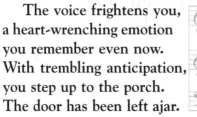

**Slowly, you step up to the opening.
With your small hand you push at the door.
It creaks once . . . then twice.
Suddenly you see—**

"Mr. Grayson . . .
are you all right?
Can you hear me?
Mr. Grayson. . . ."

A muffled voice came flooding into my thoughts, causing them to collapse as though they had been suspended just above me. This same intruder began to paw at me, taking the player out of my hands, dragging the headphones away from my ears, and pulling me from my tranquil shell of words and music into a conscious place of chaos.

"Excuse me, Mr. Grayson . . . I believe you fell asleep . . . Mr. Grayson. . . . It's Dr. Schultz. I'm sorry I was delayed. You must have dozed off after the recording stopped."

I paused for a moment to catch my breath and then firmly said, "No, I was not finished. The recording was still playing when you stopped the machine."

A peculiar expression settled on the good doctor's face accompanied by a welcome display of speechlessness, which was genuinely pleasant in comparison to her usual abrasive manner. However, as her silence stretched to the point of discomfort, I too became concerned.

"Mr. Grayson," she said in a more cautious tone, "when I came in, I asked the nurse if the recording had finished. She said the machine clicked off about ten minutes ago. Because your eyes were closed, she chose not to disturb you. According to my calculation, I also anticipated that the recording would have been over about ten minutes ago. And Mr. Grayson . . . the tape recorder was already off when I took it out of your hands."

I turned toward the nurse on the other side of the room and said nervously, "Well, someone here must be mistaken, because I was still listening to the words when I was interrupted."

The nurse shifted her eyes toward the doctor. With this one silent, blank stare, she was able to telegraph her opinion to the doctor and avoid embarrassing me by saying what she had seen.

Turning again in my direction, the doctor said charitably. "Well, Mr. Grayson, you probably just dozed off in the middle of the tape and were dreaming or something when I disturbed you. That sort of thing happens all the time when people wear headphones. . . . It's perfectly alright."

What was less then perfectly alright, and more than perfectly obvious, was that I was now being addressed as the Village Idiot. Oddly enough though, under the circumstances, I could not be absolutely sure that I had not become the Village Idiot. I reluctantly smiled at the doctor as if in agreement, knowing full well that by doing so I was condemning myself to playing the fool. The nature of my conscious experience of the event made me painfully aware that for about ten minutes some part of reality had gone askew, and my mind had followed in its footsteps. I was also aware that any attempt to address the good doctor with a more psychological approach to my experience would have entitled me to hours of grueling mental mayhem, which at all costs I intended to avoid. So the Village Idiot I decided to be— at least for however long it would take me to find my way out of my hospital-of-horrors and back to my complacent world of Oreo cookies and reruns of *Star Trek*.

"So, Mr. Grayson," the doctor continued, "what is your perception of this recording?"

Unable to find even one analytical bone in my depleted and tired body, I answered her as bluntly as I could. "Dr. Schultz . . . I have no idea what any of this is about. All I can say is yes, that is my uncle's voice on the tape, at least to the best of my recollection. And no, I have no idea what he is talking about. At the age of nine I knew him only as a fishing fanatic, not as a philosopher. I don't believe there is anything I can tell you to make this any clearer."

Accepting my somewhat rude response, she continued. "Father O'Brien, our resident priest, suggested that there may be some other reason for your uncle's strange behavior and for the unusual content of his ramblings. Even though I myself don't really give this concept any credence, he believes that some spirit or demon may be taking control of your uncle's body while he is in this weakened condition. Father O'Brien says that he's seen this kind of thing before and that these demons can be deceiving, speaking quite differently than the person they are possessing. If this is the case, he suggests some sort of an exorcism or something . . . if you believe in all of that. . . . Anyway, he asked to see you. He has an office on the second floor next to the chapel."

The doctor then gathered up the tape player, shook my hand, and disappeared into the hall. The nurse followed closely behind, leaving me alone with the two comatose bedfellows.

In the quiet of the room, I tried to figure out what had just occurred. I stared at my inert uncle wondering who he was and what had truly happened to me during that brief lapse of time. Was this simply my own insanity coming to the surface or was the voice that I had experienced not really my uncle's? Could the priest be right? As unbelievable as it sounded, I actually considered it a possibility. Strangely enough though, I distinctly remembered how disappointed I felt when the recording, about the field and the garden, had abruptly ended. If the voice I heard was a demon, it surely was a pleasant one.

Then there was the music that had graciously filtered its way into my head about half way through the story. It was a sorrowful melody, not actually on the recording, but something I had written many years ago. My brain had started playing it as if in reaction to the words I was hearing.

I could make no sense of this puzzle, the pieces of which lay tangled in my mind. Was there some underlying theme here longing to surface? Or could the design of this puzzle be extracted only by some poetic madman whose mind had been quite properly disengaged, granting only him the privilege of its true understanding? Was my uncle such a madman or had he designed the puzzle, the solution to which he held captive within his silence?

I allowed my eyes to wander about the room, searching for a distraction from my confusion. On a side-table, partly hidden by the curtain, I saw a small vase with three roses that I had not noticed before. I lifted a small card from under the vase and opened it.

This new discovery only heightened my befuddlement. Who is Shankara? My uncle? And Sharee, is she his secret love? Is she the older woman, or perhaps she's the young woman with the rose petals? Given the bizarre occurrences so far, nothing seemed out of the realm of possibilities. Feeling the need to gather evidence, I stashed the small card in my coat pocket. Then, remembering the rose petals that had been scattered on my uncle, I carefully checked to see if he had again been so adorned. I was almost disappointed that he hadn't. I started to laugh at myself when suddenly a male nurse entered the room.

He said hello and went about his business with the patient in the next bed. He pulled open the curtain, revealing the other man, who appeared to be comatose like my uncle, but was about half his size. He was barrel chested with a large head and stout features that seemed to be out of proportion with the rest of his body. He had several days' growth of beard, and both his hair and overall appearance were mangy and ill kept. The nurse spoke to the man in a lighthearted and therapeutic way. As the nurse was the only one in the conversation, I decided to interrupt.

"Excuse me," I said, "is that man also in a coma?"

"Yes," he said cheerfully, looking up from his patient. "He was in an accident and never regained consciousness."

"What's his name?"

"To tell you the truth, nobody really knows. He is a transient, one of the homeless. He came in with no identification, and no one has come to claim him. Just one of your basic John Doe-types, I'm afraid."

"What kind of an accident was it?"

The nurse allowed a chuckle to surface before he began to explain. "Well . . . according to the policeman on the scene at the time, this small, but very theatrical fellow, was perched on the top of a parked car. He was giving instructions to some unfortunate woman who was desperately trying to park her Rolls Royce in the space behind. The woman evidently was not skilled at driving her expensive car, or parking it for that matter. The man standing atop the other car was merciless with the woman and her predicament. The officer said that he carried on like a Shakespearean actor, reacting and playing off of each of her attempts to move the car forward and then back. The police were called to the scene because the man's spontaneous performance had begun to draw a crowd, which of course had this poor woman in a total frenzy."

We both started to laugh as he continued. "Anyway, the officer said he believed that, in her panic, the woman lurched forward and then, desperately trying not to hit the parked car, tried to hit the brake. Unfortunately, she hit the gas instead and slammed violently into the parked car. The impact was so hard that this little guy," he said, pointing to the man in the bed, "went airborne and did a perfect swan dive off the parked car. He landed head first on the hood of the Rolls Royce with a gonk and a major groan.

The momentum carried his body forward, bringing him to rest with his butt staring through the windshield at her and his feet resting comfortably on her roof."

We launched into a fit of laughter. When the nurse regained his composure, he continued. "Well, the woman . . . of course, she faints dead away and this unfortunate fellow here . . . well, he just never came out of it."

"And he's been this way ever since?" I asked, chuckling.

"That's right," he said. "Evidently he couldn't believe it either, and he has yet to recover from the shock."

As my laughter finally gave way to a semblance of poise, I had to admit that the scenario I had just heard about was even more unbelievable than the one I was presently caught in. Before he left the room, I asked, "Where did this accident take place?"

"Down towards the waterfront, near the old square. I guess the merchants say this guy's theatrics are pretty common. He never hurts anything, and he gets the people laughing now and then."

"Well, if people see him around all the time, why doesn't anyone know his name or know where he lives?"

"Like I said, he's probably homeless . . . moves about a lot. When the officer asked the local merchants for the man's name, they all affectionately referred to him as the Village Idiot."

The nurse then promptly walked out into the hall, leaving me alone to look for my jaw, which I assumed had probably landed somewhere between my size-ten feet. I sat on the end of the bed and started to laugh again, unable to believe my own ears. Village Idiot was a name that, up to now and through an entire lifetime, had never been a part of my conscious reality. Today though, I not only heard it in reference to another, I contemplated it as a reference to myself just moments ago. Could it be that I had just witnessed a strange premonition of my own future? Was it my destiny to end up as some spread-eagled hood ornament launched head first from the roof of a parked car?

All two hundred and three pounds of me seemed to shake with delight at the thought. Perhaps losing my mind was going to be a lot more fun than I had ever imagined. There was a certain synchronicity to this mock madness, which teased my sense of humor with its collection of coincidences that were rather obvious once I began to notice them.

I felt giddy about these coincidences, like the child on the recording who had run wild in the garden. I suppose that's also why I found myself scouting the room for even more mischief to entertain me. My mind seemed open to all kinds of prankish possibilities. Then I spied the poor forgotten little man in the next bed, which gave me a wonderfully devilish idea.

Reaching over, I plucked the petals off one of the roses, carefully discarding its plundered stem. I then pulled back the bedding covering the fellow in the other bed and sprinkled the petals all over his body. After all, just because he was poor and nameless, he did not deserve any less treatment at the hospital than anyone else.

Perhaps this stunt was a bit childish for a gruff ol' guy like myself, but why should I be the only one in this situation always in a state of confusion. I think delirium should be shared by everyone who is participating, especially the nurses and why not . . . of course! Dear Dr. Schultz. She would thrive on this sort of bizarre incident. Why, it would occupy her for hours.

I pulled up the sheets and tucked the small man back in with my final words of encouragement. "It did wonders for my uncle," I said. "He came back to life, spoke out loud, and even told a story." I chuckled at my juvenile behavior as I began to imagine this stout little fellow suddenly awakening. In his most theatrical mode, he would stand up in the middle of his bed. Like some crazed elf, he would leap to the floor and scamper out the door in a fit of giggles and cackles. I could just see him jumping up on top of the nurses reception counter, being as waggish and merciless with them as he had been with the woman in the Rolls Royce.

At this point, there was nothing left to do but to make my escape before I was discovered. As I hurried out the door, I whispered goodbye to the both of them and jetted down the hall. I aimed for the elevator and that bright green exit sign that would lead me to the front entrance of the hospital and to the garden—I mean my freedom.

The elevator doors opened slowly as I quickened my step to catch the vacant compartment. Pushing the L button for the lobby, I noticed that the indicator for the tenth floor was lit even though no one else was in the elevator. Attempting to defy the intent of the great sluggish machine, I pushed urgently at the L button trying to change the elevator's mind, for I had no interest in riding all the way to the top, just so I could then ride all the way back down to the bottom.

To my great surprise, the elevator finally stopped at my insistence. I leaned back against the brass railing extremely satisfied with my accomplishment and waited for the steel beast to start down as I had instructed. To my even greater surprise, the elevator instead simply opened its doors as if to rid itself of me without any further adieu. I started to chuckle at the elevator's obstinacy when as the doors stretched wide, I saw the black letters on the wall: PSYCHIATRIC WARD.

My heart jumped as I was engulfed by panic. I slammed my body to the side of the elevator as though to paper myself to the wall, my legs and arms spread wide, my cheek smashed up against the cold panel. I reached frantically for the "close door" button, poking it several times in the hope that it would *please* save me from yet another spontaneous encounter with the Mental Morgue. I waited frozen, second after excruciating second, praying wildly to the doors to assist me in my most well deserved escape.

The doors though, while cleverly disguising themselves as inanimate objects, defiantly left me helpless to be discovered by the first person who might peer into this entrapment. Slowly, a set of light footsteps approached. They were gentle clip-clops, not like that of the security guard, but more like that of a nurse, or perhaps like—

"Mr. Grayson. . . can I help you with something?" said a voice from a navy blue jacket with uneven shoulder pads.

"Dr. Schultz! What are you doing here?" I gasped, quickly leaning back, folding my arms and trying to cross my legs.

She answered in her usually cold and authoritarian tone, "Well, I'm a psychiatrist and this is a psychiatric ward. What are *you* doing here?"

"Well, I guess the elevator must have just stopped here by mistake, but I'm so glad that I ran into you again," I said rambling. "I wanted to ask you earlier if it might be possible for me to see the man who created so much commotion in my uncle's room the other night. You know, the one admitted to this floor for observation. I thought that by chance it might be some old friend of my uncle's or some distant relative I didn't know about."

I had absolutely no idea where this absurd notion came from. Nor, after having said it was I at all sure that I wanted to see this man or get more involved in any part of this scenario. My request, though, had managed to catch the doctor off guard. She proceeded to stumble into the conversation without pursuing her own interrogation of me about my sudden appearance in the world-of-the-bewildered.

Looking mildly puzzled, she said, "Well, under the circumstances I suppose it would be all right for you to take a look at him . . . . Yes, I believe that it might actually be a good idea. I don't know why I didn't think of it myself."

Her words gave me very little confidence. If I was now conjuring up ideas the good doctor wished were hers, then my rational mind could be in a lot of trouble. At this point I knew that I had to proceed with extreme caution, contemplating more deeply my own spontaneous inspirations before just blurting them out. As usual, the doctor then took up the reins in the situation. She led me out of the elevator like a jockey guiding a sauntering horse back to the stable, still wondering aloud why she hadn't come in first on that particular notion. With little resistance I clopped along, receiving an education on this, the seventh floor, a place that had already become far too familiar.

6

Iyokipiya

Early evening, having crept into my long exhausting day, was now apparent on the psychiatric floor. Very few lights were kept on during these hours, giving the long hallways—bare but for a smattering of straight-back chairs lurking at each end—a dark sorrowful atmosphere. As we slowly approached one of the wide steel doors, Dr. Schultz suggested that, at least for now, I should just view the patient through the window to see if I recognized him. Then later, if I wanted to speak with him, she could perhaps arrange a meeting.

Gazing through the framed glass mounted in the door, the doctor commented, "He's pulled his bed away from the wall again. For some odd reason he insists on having the bed directly under that window. See for yourself."

I carefully walked up to the small opening, its checkerboard wire securely reinforcing the double-pane glass. Inside, a gloomy resonance seemed to saturate the space that harbored only a single bed, which resembled an army cot with a mattress thrown on top. Lying with his feet aligned towards the tall barred window was a man probably in his late twenties. The moon, as though standing watch, filled the room with an iridescent light. It streamed through the bars in the window, casting long narrow shadows that appeared to cage both the bed and the man in an illusory prison. He wore only the pants of his hospital clothes leaving his upper torso bare, the dim light sculpting the contours of his smooth chest and arms. His hair, which was black and straight, hung over the edge of the bed. He looked to be Native American or, perhaps, part Latino as evidenced by the black mustache that cradled his broad nose. Balanced on his stomach, looking up towards his chin, was an open pair of oval wire-rimmed glasses. His arms lay out evenly at his sides with both hands draped slightly off the bed, his fingers unfurled as if something had fallen from them.

As I looked more closely at the glasses resting on his body, I noticed two sets of scars grooved into his chest muscles. These parallel markings were identical and were the only markings of any kind on his body, which appeared to be very strong and fit even in the midst of his slumber. Turning towards the doctor, I said, "He looks rather harmless now."

"Yes," she said, "he has been quite cooperative for the last couple of days. When our security guard first tried to restrain him, he went off like a wild animal, clawing and growling. Do you recognize him?"

"No . . . he doesn't look familiar. What's his name?"

"When they first brought him up he referred to himself as Shadow Wolf, but the next morning after he calmed down, he said his name was Michael Talon. He apparently has no criminal record and hasn't been admitted to any of the psych units before."

"Do you have any idea why he was trying to see my uncle?"

"Not really, the guard heard him say something about trying to free the man who was asleep inside the coma."

"And why was he committed?"

"As I said, when they tried to get him to leave your uncle's room, he lashed out at the guard and the nurses like an animal."

"Do you know what caused those scars on his chest?"

"No . . . but as out of control as he gets, it's really hard to say. He may have even stabbed himself at some time or other."

"Then what is his story? I mean, does he say much?"

"He won't talk at all about the incident on that first night, but he did ask to see some kind of competency lawyer who came in to visit him yesterday."

"Really," I said, with some disbelief as I again glanced down at his peaceful figure in the gray light. "And so what happens now?"

"As of tomorrow they move him out to South Providence, the long term care facility. Because there have been other complaints, he will be there for a few more days of observation."

A page for Doctor Schultz interrupted our conversation. "Well, Mr. Grayson, I must be on my way. Thank you for your time. I will walk you back to the elevator so that I can key you down."

"Yes, Doctor, thank you for allowing me to take a look."

Once back at the elevator, the doctor placed a key into the panel and then waited patiently until she had seen me safely off the seventh floor, which was most definitely to my satisfaction as well. By now I was more than anxious to leave these premises, having had ample hospital calamity, at least for one day.

I stepped through the sliding front doors of the main lobby and out into the cool night air, the fresh smell-of-nothing filling every part of me. Totally soothed, I closed my eyes and gave a satisfying sigh. I was finally free at—

"Excuse me, Mr. Grayson . . ." said a female voice from amid the subtle noises of the outside world.

I opened my eyes to find a woman, probably in her late twenties, standing directly in front of me. She was wearing a denim jacket over a blue hospital uniform. Her dark shoulder length hair was straight, and she wore glasses that accentuated the size of her eyes. She seemed a little shy; her mouth crimped slightly to one side as though she were nervous about what she was going to say.

"Yes," I answered.

"Mr. Grayson, I'm Lela Carrow, and I work here at the hospital. I am doing my practical experience on the psych unit, you know, on the seventh floor. I was wondering if I could talk to you for just a few minutes. It's about the man Dr. Schultz took you to see."

Though I was not ten steps from the street, and perhaps fifty steps from the parking lot, I agreed to sit with her on the nearby bench and see what else could possibly be added to this memorable day's impressions. She pulled some wrinkled papers from the side pouch of her purse and began to tell me her story.

"Mr. Grayson, I need you to know that I could get into a lot of trouble for what I am about to share with you, but I believe you should have this information. What I have to say may seem pointless, or maybe even crazy, but still I think you should hear it.

"The man you observed on the psychiatric ward is Michael Talon. He is, or was, a professor at Northwest University. He is well-known for his study of altered states such as dreams and hypnosis. However, others at one of the rival universities strongly disagree with his work and have done everything within their power to discredit him. This type of psychic research with altered states has always been a touchy subject, especially with all of the studies that were done during the LSD experiments back in the Sixties."

"Professor Talon's work does not involve drugs. His approach is really more from the opposite point of view. He believes that the real doorway into our psychic or subconscious states is through combining both science and spirit. He teaches that without some sort of spiritual knowledge, we have no true means of understanding who we are on a psychological level, or any other. He adheres to no particular religion but believes that—"

Abruptly, she stood up and started pacing about ten steps from the bench as several doctors and nurses came out through the sliding doors. A couple of them nodded to her as they passed by.

"Sorry about that," she said returning. "I really have to be careful with this. It could mean my job here and at the university."

She cautiously sat back down on the bench and continued. "Anyway, I had better make this quick. Late into the evening, several hours after Professor Talon had been admitted, I was doing some work in the room across the hall from him. He was, of course, locked in his room, but I saw him motioning through the small window for me to secretly speak to him. I'm sure that he remembered me from one of his classes. So I spoke with him through the glass. He asked me to bring him several sheets of paper and something to write with. When I asked what he wanted them for, he said that he needed to write down everything that had happened to him throughout that night. It was as though he somehow knew that I would do this for him and also keep it confidential. All I could find was this brown butcher paper that we use to line the shelves of the cabinets." She held up several torn pages of tan-colored paper with intense displays of writing on them.

Feeling her deep need to hand me the scraps of paper, I said, "This is all very interesting, but what does this have to do with me?"

"This is an intricate description of a meeting that apparently took place with your uncle up in the mountains. It also tells what happened the night he went into your uncle's hospital room. Mr. Grayson, Professor Talon obviously had a specific reason for being there and for trying to contact him. I believe he was on some sort of a vision quest with a wolf spirit to help him. And even though what is written on these pages may seem like a wild story, I feel it's very important.

"This evening," she continued, "when you were looking at the professor through the glass, you asked about the scars on his chest. Do you remember?"

"Yes," I said. "What are they from?"

"Professor Talon is part Lakota Indian. In the Lakota tradition there is a ceremony done by the young men called the Sun Dance. Its purpose is to renew the spirit of the man and to bring back his power and his union with the Creator. In this ritual the men have their chests pierced with two pieces of bone so that the tips are protruding on either side of the flesh. It is very painful and requires great emotional preparation. They then take twine or a thin piece of hemp, one end of which is tied to the two ends of the bone on both sides of the chest. The other end is tied to a tall pole. Generally several men go through this piercing process at the same time, and all are tied to the same pole. They form a circle facing the pole so they can lean back with their weight putting tension on the twine. This pulls hard on the bone that has been pierced through their chest. They then dance in a circle around the pole and stare directly at the sun. Occasionally they lean back to put pressure on the twine and the pierced flesh."

My entire chest was quietly aching from her graphic description. I longed to reach inside my shirt to massage my own flesh. "Why would they do such a thing?" I asked.

"Through the intense experience, they go into an altered state where it is said that they give up their human forms and become one with spirit or the Creator. Professor Talon has participated in this dance, perhaps many times. He is a warrior of the heart, Mr. Grayson, a man of great courage and unwavering character. He should not be locked up in this place.

"I also believe that Professor James Wilkes, one of his rivals from Stratton University, is the reason they were able to keep him here. Wilkes uses the hospital for practicum work with some of his students. Each year there is a psychology grant given to one of the universities. Professor Talon and James Wilkes have always competed for this, and Michael Talon generally wins. That is also why when Dr. Wilkes saw him, the morning he was admitted, he took the liberty of telling the attending psychologists that he felt Michael Talon was a danger to himself and others. He encouraged them to lock him up for as long as possible.

"I saw Michael Talon when they brought him in, and there was no doubt in my mind that he had been in an altered state. This was a vision quest that had started out in a spiritual place, but ended in tragedy because of the guard's abrasive handling of the situation."

Holding up the pages in her hand, she said, "This will help to explain why he was there. If placed into the wrong hands it could be very incriminating for the professor."

"Why did he give these papers to you?"

"The following morning, they took him out of his room and, after several interviews, they put him into a different room. When I found out, I immediately went back and found the papers stashed under his mattress. While I was reading his description of the experience, something told me to pass it on to you. I have transcribed a copy for myself, which I will return to the professor whenever that is possible. I hope that by giving you this I'm doing the right thing."

"How did you know who I was?"

"I was behind you in the hall when you asked about the professor's scars. I could tell by the way that you phrased your questions that you were not just another intellectual there to analyze him. When I learned that you were related to the man the professor was trying to see, I felt that you should see this."

Carefully she handed me the torn pages, looking intently into my eyes as if we were subliminally exchanging some sort of secret vow.

"There is nothing to be afraid of," she said. "It's really just a story about a wolf that gets caught in a steel trap and how the professor was asked to save it. In the writing, Professor Talon refers to a vision or spirit that he calls Iyokipiya."

"What was that again?"

"Ee-yoh-kee-pee-yah, I think is how it's pronounced. Anyway, according to the admitting report, it was the name the Professor was shouting in your uncle's room that night. I myself am not familiar with this name, but it may come from his native Lakota dialect. In his description of the vision, this spirit instructs the professor to free the wolf from the steel trap—the entrapment of humanity with all of its disharmony and dysfunction. The wolf, like all creatures, still lives as a spirit that holds the knowledge of the original plan of the Creator. Iyokipiya tells the professor that he must become like the wolf so that he can truly understand his union with the Creator. He was to use this knowledge to teach others how to become like the animals, to once again be in harmony with the true laws of nature. He said that *if the children of the planet did not heed this warning, the dance of the human experience would soon be over, and the music of the wind around the world would play no more.* He said that, *to save the dance, the children would once again have to sing the original song,* that is the song of the Earth, of the Creator."

Amid her many words, the phrase *save the dance* seemed to catch in my brain. It circled around and around, longing to not be filed away in the crowded archives of my mind. Somewhere I had known this phrase before. The faintest of memories, it had an existence of its own, and yet it seemed to have no other references attached to it.

"Mr. Grayson," she continued, "I realize that all of this may seem very strange to you. Most people would probably just disregard it, not ever really understanding what it means. Perhaps you will do the same. Or perhaps it will help you to know more about what may be happening with your uncle. . . . Anyway, I must be going now. I'm sorry I don't know more. It's all still a puzzle to me as well. Please don't mention this to anyone."

With this, she said goodbye and ran out into the street, carefully dodging a slowly passing car. Mysteriously she disappeared from the sidewalk, swiftly moving out of the spray of light beaming down from the last street lamp. I looked at the tatters of paper she had given me. The tan pages were crowded with a scribbling of tiny words. In the dim light they resembled hieroglyphics intricately etched on some ancient parchment, its sepia-brown writing still waiting to be deciphered.

I stood there motionless as if someone had pushed a pause button, allowing time to continue on indefinitely without me. I was overwhelmed by all that she had said, not only about this Professor Talon, but about my uncle, and her assumption that he (or some aspect of him) had been at the core of this. Although there was a certain intrigue to this adventure, the seriousness of how these scraps of paper were dropped into my hands made me very uneasy. She had taken a tremendous chance trusting me with them. I was emotionally torn between the unbelievable circumstances that had created this information and the sincerity with which the woman shared it with me.

I was greatly moved by her description of Professor Talon's story, about the wolf and the welfare of the Earth. Once again I was shamefully reminded that, as a people, we have been very poor stewards of this planet. Perhaps these ideas would naturally strum the awareness of anyone who was conscious of these concerns. Nevertheless, her descriptions of it in the story felt almost intimate to me. The words *save the dance* seemed to slosh back and forth in my thoughts, constantly trying to wash ashore a familiar memory or two. I was haunted by their presence and still somewhat apprehensive about reading these pages now staring helplessly back at me.

One thing was certain though, if there was a river of curiosity rising inside of me, its flood waters would have to wait until tomorrow. If I did not rest soon, I would most assuredly drop where I stood. I carefully folded the papers and tucked them into my coat pocket. In doing so, my fingers rediscovered the card with the signature that had been with the roses in my uncle's room. I pulled the card from my pocket and slowly turned it over. Once again I read,

To Shankara, from Sharee.

Shankara, I assumed, referred to my uncle. Yet, the professor in his story had used the name Iyokipiya. These totally different names didn't even seem to be from the same language. This made no sense to me. If there was some logical correlation in all of this, why would the names be so different. There must be some—

All at once I felt my thoughts rudely nudged out of focus by my exhausted mind. I shook my body like a dripping wet dog who had been left out in the rain far too long. I could not think about this any more. I had to rest. I placed the card back into my coat pocket with the scraps of paper, vowing to my collapsing carcass that both would remain there until morning. My mind was well past its saturation point, and before I could take in anything else, my body would require massive amounts of sleep.

Arriving home, I gave credence only to my drooping eyelids, coaxing me to close out the world for the night. As my ragged bones folded into the bed, I was more thankful than ever for the quiet empty nothing I was about to enter.

7

Misplaced Melodies

Dreams (from my perspective) have always been involuntary stumblings in that, if they were not at least inviting (or at best erotic), they were easily dismissed and eventually forgotten. Now however, as I woke in this unknown hour, I knew none of these circumstances would apply, for my slumber had been far from empty. In the dream from which I was returning, my subconscious self had managed to waltz me through several of our history's most bloody confrontations. In the course of a few hours, I had been given a world tour of the chronicles of war. Six or seven scenes of explosive battlefields reeled past me, each with its weaponry, flags, and regalia characterizing the era in which it had taken place. And, strewn amid the military ruins were the remains of all plant and animal life that had innocently fallen in the devastation.

Woven within the gore and mayhem, I witnessed a woman wandering through these war-zones. Step by step she walked, aware of the brutal combat, but somehow immune to its destruction. Stepping through the carnage and debris, she spread handfuls of some sort of herb or leaf, which she broke from a small tied bundle. This tiny wrapped bale, like the fishes and the loaves, appeared to be infinite in its abundance, never changing in its size or shape. The image of this woman's angelic procession dominated every scene. Her devoted action seemed to have some great significance, yet I, in my *limited* understanding had absolutely *no* understanding of its purpose or of the reasoning behind any aspect of this woeful dream.

As I lay in the dark staring at the ceiling, I found but one consolation as to why this nightmare had not been immediately banished from the boundaries of my bed curtains. The woman who walked through the destruction was the same woman I had encountered in the hospital elevator. Perhaps she was also my maiden of the rose petals, and there was some correlation between her spreading of the rose petals on my uncle and her spreading of the leafy substance in the dream. At any rate, in both cases her peaceful expression and the charisma of her presence were striking and unforgettable.

I rolled over in my bed and began a blind man's search for the table lamp. If I could light the familiar space of my ill-kept room, I could rid myself of the dramatic images. With a subtle click, the soft shapes of my surroundings slowly returned, bringing me home to a more recognizable clutter. I welcomed the feeling of security and sat back against the headboard, still baffled by the dream from which there seemed to be no escape.

I was haunted by the image of the woman passing through mass destruction. I had never imagined warfare that could be so devastating as to make the bare ground burn or to fill the sky with black smoke so dense it turned day into night. I thought about the terrain where the battles had taken place— unrecognizable, its ecological balance changed forever. I also thought about the professor's story, about the wolf and the spirit who had foretold that to save the dance, the people of the Earth would have to—

Startled by the alarm of that single thought, the words *save the dance* again became caught in a loop, circling inside my head. I had stumbled on this phrase before, but this time there were the scratchings of a melody line and surrounding music. These were not just words, but lyrics to a song, some lyrical score I had begun to compose years ago. One solid theme with its haunting voice rolled and churned this phrase over in my mind. I could feel all of the notes, but the melody and its remaining lyrics stayed just out of reach. Like a faint whisper, the scattered words called out for me to remember them.

My growing frustration only hampered my memory's search. With a long deep breath, I tried to relax into a space of clarity. Slowly, I surrendered, half-conscious and half in slumber, to the revelation that finally emerged in my mind. The words *save us a dance* gently tumbled into place.

I rocketed from my bed, intrigued and excited. Throughout my life I made a habit of keeping the remains of any uncompleted creation. Beginning with the humble seat of my piano bench, I rifled through every piece of manuscript, every notation that might arise as the reincarnation of this work. It had to be among these forgotten compositions, gallant causes, once washed ashore, unfinished and unfulfilled. Having exhausted all possibilities in the bench, I next tried the filing cabinet. Then it was on to the bookcase, as my studio floor began to fill with the discarded debris of undiscovered masterpieces. Possessed by this melodic excavation, I sprinted up the stairs past the second floor and into the attic, where no compartment was exempt from my search.

As my quest continued, so too did my memory's relentless attempts to piece back together some recognizable rendition of this neglected melody. Patches of the music and lyrics kept starting and stopping, like an old engine trying to catch fire, hoping to once again spin and roar down a deserted highway.

Page after page, I feathered through the titles until at last, preserved on the parchment's faded ocher face, I found the words that had teased both my anticipation and my longing. *Save Us a Dance*, handwritten above the lines and staves, was drawn out word by word, as though it had been penned only the day before.

To my surprise, the enthusiasm of my search was soon swallowed by a decade-of-disappointment as I stared down at the page with its display of notes and words.

It's the hour of all tomorrows.
Shadows cross this land.
The balance has been broken,
and now time slips out.
And the dreams of all tomorrows.
In an hourglass of tears.
Hoping there'll be time enough, for those dreams to appear.

    With time enough to reason.
    Time to understand.
    Time to walk upon the land.

Save us a dance . . . on the crystalline waters.
Save us a flight, on the breath of the wind,
    through a clear blue sky.
Save us a ride . . . through emerald forests.
Pilgrims of Earth . . . . Hear my prayer . . . . Save us a dance.

These were the poetic words of a fiery young man who had an
enormous passion for life and all its creatures. They were thoughts
born out of a truth that had no fear about being written,
completely unaffected by the opinions of others. They were
phrases filled with spirit, immune to the competition for the
almighty dollar. They were the words of my heart, which for the
past decade I had forgotten to write.

I felt myself slide into a great sadness. I reminisced with many
of these unfinished songs, each reminding me of a specific event.
While it was difficult to remember the exact circumstances under
which each of them had been created, I was very much aware
that they had come to me at a time in my youth when passion
was my motive and anything was possible. There was a purity in
these memories, an innocence that even now sifted through this
lamentable history that had been so neatly filed away in one
cardboard pouch.

Long faced, I plodded through the sheets of music. Somewhere along the way, I had stopped writing lyrics to my music. I guess I had come to a place in my life where I no longer believed in words. So often I had seen them used as but a convenient tool for altering the truth, some phrase or sentence cleverly arranged to serve someone's ego. For me, words had become the property of politicians and salespeople who catered quite shamelessly to the rhythm of propaganda and profit.

Was it possible that by abandoning my belief in words, I too had become numb and complacent? Had I lost my own desire to explore and experience this world? Yet somehow, I was sure that through my instrumental compositions, the essence of truth had survived, at least in my private, speechless world.

Now though, here in my hands were reflections of that truth, inscribed with the strongest of words: paper remnants of my passion as well as its shadows, melodically colored both light and dark and all shades in between. At this precise moment, I felt both empowered and frightened. I was not sure whether to treasure these forgotten lyrics for their innocence or to purge them in some ceremonial fire. Perhaps I could rid myself of the attending disappointment once and for all by setting ablaze my studio floor and its carpet of compositions. Or better yet, with a little encouragement, the entire house might catch fire. Then I could become one of the homeless and take on my new identity as the Village Idiot, leaping atop parked cars, delivering extraordinary orations on the more aesthetic properties of *forward* and *reverse*. If madness was to be my deliverance then I welcomed it like an old friend, as long as that friend kept me from living a life that was diluted and mundane.

I wanted to free myself from the stagnation that cocooned me, from the frightened attitudes that were in me and around me. I wanted to know my passion again, to find the words and the lyrics, and to sing again, for no other reason than to do it. I wanted to revive every lyrical piece that I had ever written, bringing them back to life along with my own passions. And most of all, I wanted to dream again.

Anxiously, I looked down at the pages in my hand, at the

many choices from which I could begin my expedition back into the living. Among them was a song I had written after Katherine, my first love, had left me and gone to live in Nepal. Skittishly, I skimmed over the words, girding myself for my return back into the rawness of my emotions.

So if you
Sail You Home
catch me watching for those ocean breezes,
Oh stormy vision . . . of a lonely heart.
Always waiting for that setting sun
to cast a spell on the wind
and sail you home to me.

Though slightly painful, these words were real and resonated with feeling. Difficult or not, they felt alive and whole inside me. Turning the page, I found the letter Katherine had written after her departure for Nepal. It was safely tucked inside the music as if I had known so long ago that I would one day remember to find it here.

Dear Jared,

I have decided to move to Kathmandu, Nepal with Master Ramya Shankara Ananda. My greatest desire is to become a student of this teacher. I know this is difficult for you to understand, but it's something I must do—

Abruptly, I was jarred out of the writing. That name . . . Master Ramya Shankara Ananda was intently familiar. In fact it was strangely similar to the name on the card with the roses. Slowly, a wave of anxiety began to swell inside me as I whispered to myself, "Oh please, let it not be so." At this point, I was somewhat afraid to compare the card and the letter. But in view of all that had been happening, I was even more afraid not to.

Trudging down the stairs, I waded through the rubble of my studio to the closet. Retrieving the card from my coat pocket, I held it next to the letter. For a second I was stunned. The name was the same. Shankara.

Every cell of my body collapsed into the sound of my response, a long and exasperated, "Oh-h . . . No-o . . . ." Feebly I drooped like a leaking inflatable toy until my rump came to rest on the white-papered floor. Perhaps a diluted and mundane life wasn't such a bad concept after all.

I sat there among the disarray of pages with the letter in my hand, wishing now that I had put a bit more volition into my notion of an indoor bonfire. I felt like a two-hundred-pound babbling infant who had been plopped back into his playpen, back into all of the coincidental confusion that, in my fleeting moment of passion, I had temporarily forgotten.

I hadn't minded so much all of the drama with my uncle or the strange adventure that warranted a visit to the (shall we say) committed professor. I was even quite intrigued by the coincidence of the professor's words *save the dance* and the lyrics of my own song "Save Us a Dance." But to have my long-lost comatose uncle receiving flowers from some mysterious young woman who referred to him by the same name as the deranged guru who whisked my fine Katherine off to Nepal over twenty years ago—never to be heard from again—was more than my poor brain could handle.

My mind staggered around in this information hoping to fall over some reasonable explanation. Perhaps the name Shankara was just a title like Reverend or Your Holiness. Or maybe it was just a— *RING RING.*

I scanned the room to regain my bearings and locate the phone buried under the fallout of paper. Four or five rings sounded before I found it behind one of the piano legs. My search had not only revealed to me the whereabouts of my phone, it also informed me that morning was patiently waiting for me to draw open my curtains and welcome in all that cheery sunlight. Whoever was calling at this hour had most certainly not been briefed on my usual morning's agenda of sleep, sleep, sleep. Moreover, calls that arrived before I opened my curtains were always calls with a problem. As I picked up the phone, I closed my eyes and spoke through the haze of my reluctant anticipation.

"Hello?"

"Hello, is this Mr. Grayson?"

I could tell by the background noises that the caller could be nowhere other than the hospital. Mingled in my mind, with my more generic responses, were irrational remarks. *Just say no and hang up, they won't know the difference*, or *sorry, there is no one by that name at this number*. Then, of course, I would actually have to change my number or move to a different city. I might even have to relocate to another state or foreign country where I could change my name and just—

"Hello, is there anyone there? Are you there, Mr. Grayson?"

I put my hand over the receiver and spoke softly like a ghost, "No . . . No . . . No one lives here anymore . . ." Before she could hang up, I unwillingly replied out loud, "Yes, this is Jared Grayson."

"Mr. Grayson, I am calling about your uncle. We seem to have run into some problems with him. Well, not actually with him, I guess it's more about him."

"Yes," I groaned. "What is it?"

"Well, Mr. Grayson, we're not exactly sure how it happened, but all of the outward signs give us the indication that, well . . . your uncle appears to be missing."

While I could have anticipated innumerable words to finish that particular sentence, by no stretch of the imagination was the word *missing* one of them. Words like *improving* or *weakening* would have been appropriate, while other words like *conscious* or *talkative* might have been most agreeable. Even a word like *dead* would have been tolerable. But the word *missing* was totally unacceptable. I wrestled with my anger, like a snake trying to devour the phone's receiver.

Regaining a morsel of my composure, I cynically replied, "Excuse me . . . can you tell me exactly how you misplace someone in a coma?"

"Well, Mr. Grayson, we're not really sure. You see, it isn't just your uncle who is missing. The small man who was in the bed next to him—who was also in a coma—well, he is also missing."

"What! What kind of a hospital are you running? Don't you keep any account of your patients? Especially the ones who can't even move?"

"Well, Mr. Grayson, like I said, we're not exactly sure how it happened since there seems to be no one here at the hospital who witnessed anything unusual. We are currently addressing our suspicion, though, that they may have been stolen."

"Stolen?" I said with a mixture of anger and sarcasm. "Stolen . . ." I repeated the word as my voice then exploded from inside of me. "For Christ sakes! Who in the hell do you think would want them? I mean there's not a tremendous market for comatose bodies these days. Like they were going to put them in a display window or something, for crying out loud. . . ."

"We are very sorry, Mr. Grayson, but we notified the police, and they are presently here doing an investigation. They have requested an interview with you as well . . . that is, now that you have been notified. They asked if you would come to the hospital as soon as possible. Mr. Grayson . . . is that possible?"

Is that possible? I said to myself. Is that possible— If it was possible for a hospital to misplace two full-grown carcasses without anyone noticing, well, then it was now obvious to me that anything was possible. Perhaps the two of them just got up, unplugged themselves, and went for a little stroll.

Then my own internal fury was interrupted by a thought that was as ghastly as it was comical. I saw myself just the day before, dusting that poor helpless man with rose petals, babbling about their rejuvenating properties and of the miraculous affects that he might encounter. This notion, although wonderfully absurd, was also rationally terrifying. I rubbed my forehead like a sleepy child trying to rid myself of this nightmarish thought. Then my mind was bombarded by the memorable words of Emily, the maintenance woman, as she quoted my uncle, *"it was because I allowed the possibility to be and because I believed that life was present even in the most silent of situations . . . .That's it . . . that's what he said I did . . . that's what he said I did . . . that's what he said I did . . . that's what—"*

"Mr. Grayson!" The woman's voice came screeching in like the sound of a welcome scratch rescuing a stuck phonograph needle. "Mr. Grayson . . . is that possible?"

"What?" I blurted.

"For you to come to the hospital . . . is that possible?"

"Yes!" I shouted, "As soon as possib—Yes, I will be there as soon as I can."

8

Raha Muumba

Before beginning yet another frantic expedition to the hospital, I needed to pull over and spend just a minute puppeting through my morning routine. Uncle or no uncle, missing or not, I had to do a check and balance on my cereal-box existence to see if I was indeed alive and well. Examining the memory bank of my phone machine, I discovered that (as usual) it was empty. So was my refrigerator, my butter dish, and my sugar bowl. My garbage can was full, though, along with my dishwasher, which often doubled as a cupboard while it waited to be relieved of its miraculously spotless dishes. Wandering to the front door, I found the offerings on my porch were a bit more abundant than usual, with not two or three, but four daily newspapers. In the living room, my cat Jethro, whom I generally referred to as Mouzzer, was most comfortably contoured to the (absolutely-forbidden-to-be-on) couch, having just returned from one of those long and arduous nights of being a cat. Aside from the extra newspaper or two, everything else seemed quite normal.

I gathered up the papers and threw them into the recycle bin. Then I walked out to the street where a single post with a beam supported three mailboxes for myself and my two neighbors who lived on either side.

In the house to the west of me was a very private sort of fellow who simply went by the name Marshal. He carried a rather stocky frame and wore a full-faced beard with a long draping mustache that nearly concealed all of his teeth when he laughed. The stoutness of his facial features and the shape of his furry smile gave him a grizzly bear appearance, though he was more of a teddy bear in his demeanor. I often saw him out working in his yard wearing a pair of army fatigues, which made me think that he might have spent some time in the service. While he was not unfriendly, he basically kept to himself, limiting our communication to comments about what was growing in each other's back yards, about which, of course, I knew absolutely nothing.

The house to the east was an entirely different story. That is why I now strolled nonchalantly out to the mailbox so as not to draw the attention of my more meddlesome neighbor, Mrs. Nurple. She often took such an opportunity to rendezvous with me for a little neighborly chat. If she had already spotted me today, she would no doubt be out of her house and on her way to the mailbox allowing her screen door to slam shut behind her at precisely right about— (*SLAM*) now.

Naomi Nurple and her husband Fred had been my next door neighbors for the three years that I had owned my house. Actually, I can't say that I remember Naomi's real first name, but with the last name of Nurple, I figured that her first name had to be Naomi or something like it. She was a robust woman with puffy round cheeks, short curly brown hair, bright smiling eyes, and a double chin that was about six times larger than her real one. When she talked, which was always with a rapid tongue, this excess around her jowls became quite active, making it difficult not to stare.

Without fail, she wore a cotton dress printed with the tiniest of pastel flowers. There was usually a white apron tied tightly around her waist, which not only accentuated her watermelon breasts but also framed her bountiful hips into an impressionist painting—the tiny pastel flowers jiggling into a blur while she busily waddled about her front yard.

Mrs. Nurple was an excitable woman who filled the majority of her exciting days living vicariously through the boring lives of her neighbors, whom she intruded upon with uninhibited regularity. In the past three years, I had become quite skillful at avoiding her, which I am sure made me one of her primary targets. Today though,

I had not been so fortunate.

"Jaaared . . . Oh Jared," she yodeled, as she caught up with me at the mailbox.

"Good morning, Mrs. Nurple," I said smiling through my rubber face.

"Now, Jared," she scolded, "don't be so formal. . . . Call me Nadine. After all, we're neighbors, practically family. Speaking of which, is there maybe going to be a new addition to your family . . ? Hmm . . ? Hmm?" she pried, with her eyes open wide and grinning like a Halloween pumpkin.

I chuckled politely. At what? I'm not really sure, since I had no idea what she was talking about. Perhaps she was referring to my uncle, although I was sure I had not told anyone about him. "What do you mean?" I asked, hoping not to give away the fact that I was obviously dumbfounded.

"Don't be silly you cagey old bachelor—that darling girl who has been coming out to your mailbox for the last two days. Why she's just as pretty as she can be. Where *have* you been hiding her?"

Needless to say, I was startled by her announcement that someone had been scavenging through my mailbox. I stood there numb in my puzzlement, searching for an appropriate response. Mrs. Nurple, who was now leaning out over the ends of her toes with her ears fully flared, waited impatiently for my answer. Although I definitely wanted to hear more about this culprit (especially being that it was a darling girl), I didn't want my babbling neighbor to know just how baffled I really was. Nor did I want to give her any more information to chew on than she already had. Taking a chance, I played along with a bluff. Smirking, I said, "Why, whatever darling girl would you be talking about?"

She quickly cupped her hand over her mouth trying to suppress the string of giggles bubbling out of the small oval shape. Scooping up her mail, she said through her laughter, "Oh Jared, you are a crafty one. I know, I know . . . it's none of my business." She pawed her hand towards me as if to say *pshaw* and started back towards her house. Gleefully, she added, "Well, when you get ready to show her off, you bring her right on over, ya hear . . . And I mean that!"

So much for my bluff. She climbed back up her porch steps and through the front door allowing the screen door slam behind her. Now I not only had some darling girl ransacking my mailbox, I was too embarrassed to ask my nosey neighbor for any more details. I pulled three days worth of mail from the box and headed back towards the house. If there was something missing from this arm-load of papers and envelopes, I would never know it. In any event, I couldn't imagine why anyone would want to go through my mailbox. There had been nothing of interest in it for the past decade.

Mrs. Nurple had said she saw a young girl. Perhaps she really meant a young woman. After all, she made such a blatant jest about this darling girl and my middle-aged mischief. She had to have meant a young woman. Of course, I suppose that I should be more concerned that someone may be spying into or robbing my mailbox rather than wondering if that spy or robber might be an appropriate dinner date. I was actually somewhat surprised that I wasn't more disturbed about this incident. I guess in view of the rest of my unfolding drama, it didn't seem that serious. Besides, with my uncle and his four-foot-tall roommate now missing, I had plenty to think about for one morning.

Grabbing my coat, I jumped into my jeep and sped out of my driveway. Mrs. Nurple, who was watching me from her window, pretended not to notice as I drove past. Regardless, I waved obnoxiously and continued on my way.

The scene on the fourth floor of the hospital resembled an amusement park ride. Like a dozen or so talking bumper cars, the doctors, nurses, police detectives, and a priest or two, ran about bouncing questions off each other with no one coming up with any answers. They had no idea what happened to the two men who had apparently vanished in the night. I deduced this from all of the reassuring anecdotes that, one by one, they offered me. Although there were several theories, no one seemed willing to commit to any of them. The situation reminded me of those wonderfully absurd multiple choice questions on the written part of a drivers test.

*(Multiple choice, **A B C D E** or **F**)*

1. What could have happened to the two men who, although both comatose, disappeared from the hospital without a trace?

A. They were victims of a very dangerous prank by a group of medical students who stole them as part of a fraternity initiation.

B. They were taken by some left-wing, anti-establishment group holding them hostage until the hospital lowers its medical fees.

C. They both had miraculous spontaneous awakenings at exactly the same moment, leaving the hospital immediately, without any clothes and without anyone noticing them.

D. One or both of them became possessed by the devil or other assorted evil demons who have stolen their bodies in order to carry out their dastardly deeds.

E. They were both picked up by mistake and taken to either the hospital morgue or to the center for organ donors where they are presently having selected body parts removed.

F. None of the above.

Needless to say my first choice was **F.** None of the above.

After hours of endless interviews, my patience fully exhausted, I asked the officer in charge if I was through for the time being and could go home. Reiterating one last apology, he said that it would be fine. I confirmed my departure with the nurses desk, where I was handed the personal belongings of my now missing uncle. The bundle was made up of a pair of well-worn hiking boots, some heavy black trousers, and a dark green and red flannel shirt. Obviously the hospital had dismissed the thought of finding my uncle, at least anywhere on the grounds. It was as if I had been given the clothes of the deceased, an action quite final and complete. I thought about his condition, of how an artery in his brain could so easily burst. I wondered if I would ever see him conscious and alive again.

Passing by my uncle's old room, I noticed a woman sitting at the end of the bed of his former roommate. Standing next to her was the hospital's resident priest. He appeared to be consoling her as she sat slumped over and sobbing in a very emotional state. I thought of the male nurse who days ago had told me that this nameless man was probably homeless, so I was very curious about who this woman might be. She was dressed far too well to be a fellow transient or some personal acquaintance. Remaining in the hallway, I stepped closer to the door to see if I could find out who she was.

It was difficult to tell, but she looked to be in her mid-thirties. She had an overabundance of bleached-blond hair that at one time must have resembled a well-constructed bird's nest. Now though, with her head lowered into her hands, her hair was matted and coming unraveled. Her eyes were puddled with tears that caused streaks of black and blue color to run like tiny brush strokes down over the heavy makeup on her cheeks. Her face reminded me of circus clowns I had seen who painted on lines of tears as part of their mask to accent the illusion of their sad harlequin faces.

Noticing me near the doorway, the priest whispered something to the woman and began to walk towards me. The woman, unaware that he had left her side, quietly mumbled, "I know that God is punishing me, Father . . . he really is. I was tempted by Satan and now God is punishing me." She again started to sob as the priest joined me in the hall. Gently he guided me by the arm further away from the doorway.

"She's taking this pretty hard," he said sympathetically. Then reaching for my hand in a more formal manner, he continued. "My name is Father O'Brien. I don't think we've been introduced."

"Hello, Father, I'm Jared Grayson."

"Yes, I know," he replied.

"Father, who is she . . . I mean, is she a relative of his?"

"Do you recognize her?" he asked.

"No, not that I know of . . . should I?"

"Not necessarily. She does have quite a recognizable face though. Her name is Jessica Williams. She is a singer and, for lack of a better title, a television evangelist."

Looking back through the doorway, I could see her more clearly as she began to wipe her tears and attempted to mend her appearance. I did recognize her. She was the woman I had verbally slain after clicking on the religious channel a few mornings ago. Needless to say, she looked quite different now, but it was definitely the same woman. "Does she have some personal connection with him," I asked, "that short fellow who is also missing?"

"Yes, I guess you might say so. She's the woman who was driving the car that caused his accident, putting him into a coma."

"This was the woman that slammed into the parked car?" I exclaimed. "The one that was trying to park her Rolls Royce?"

"Yes, and she's still quite distraught. She is feeling responsible not only for the accident, but for his disappearance as well. She sees it as a chain reaction of events in which God is punishing her. For what exactly, I can't really say. I've tried to convince her otherwise, but she is still too emotional to hear much of anything right now."

We both stood there in a kind of mournful silence until the priest spoke again, changing the subject. "Mr. Grayson, I know that you may not put much credence in my explanation of what may be happening to your uncle, but I wish you would consider it."

Then I remembered that he had asked Dr. Schultz to have me contact him, which I never did. From our joint participation in the investigation, he knew that I was aware of his theory that the two men may be experiencing some sort of demonic possession. Knowing full well that he was putting me on the spot, he continued.

"I imagine that without ever having witnessed such an occurrence, the concept of a person being possessed by a dark spirit would be very hard to believe. Perhaps, in the future if you have the opportunity to interact with your uncle, you might see signs of this.

My office is next to the hospital chapel. I can be reached through the service at the front desk at any—"

"Father O'Brien," I interrupted. "I don't really know what to think about all of this. I can't say that I know enough about my uncle to recognize just how he would act. But I will consider what you have said."

Pressing me one last time, he reiterated, "Mr. Grayson, I truly believe that your uncle is in need of an exorcism."

Staring at the floor seemed to be the only response I could find. It was hard to conceive that either of these men were even conscious, let alone ravaging the countryside attacking Christians. Feeling my uneasiness, he finally ended the conversation by saying, "Well, you know how to reach me."

I briefly looked up again and politely said, "Yes . . . thank you."

He patted me on the shoulder and walked off, leaving me stalled there in the middle of the hallway. I waited motionless, like a statue in the center of the town square, as nurses and hospital workers maneuvered around me, going about their duties.

Then, for a second, I thought I heard someone whisper my name.

"Psst . . . Psst . . . Mr. Grayson," said the same voice a second time. Looking all around, I could find no face among the human traffic trying to get my attention. I thought perhaps it was just another hint of my own madness creeping in. Then, with an abrasive and piercing whisper, I unmistakably heard, "Psst . . . Psst . . . Mr. Grayson . . . over here."

I followed these words to the voice of a woman who was hiding in what appeared to be a janitorial closet just off the hallway. Even from where I was standing, some twenty feet away, I knew who it was. With that Cheshire cat smile and those large brown eyes peering out from behind the half-open door, it had to be Emily, the maintenance woman.

"Psst . . . Psst . . . Mr. Grayson . . . in here," she said, motioning incessantly for me to come and hide with her in the closet.

I stopped briefly to truly consider what was happening in that instant. It was as if my life had become some bad drugstore novel complete with the possessed uncle who needed an exorcism and the hyperactive cleaning woman with a secret in the janitor's closet.

My real problem, though, was that this crazed cleaning woman usually knew more about what was going on in this hospital than anyone else. Yet, I had to be out of my mind for even considering climbing into that confining cubicle with her. During our last encounter, she not only compared me to a half-frozen corpse, she assaulted me with a mop handle. Now she was frantically waving for me to leap into that janitorial dungeon filled with menacing mops.

"Psst . . . Psst . . . Mr. Grayson . . ." she whispered impatiently, jerking her head several times to one side without breaking her insistent stare. "Psst . . . in here . . ." she insisted.

I cautiously turned, looking over one shoulder and then the other to see just how incriminating my next insane act was about to be. Then, as it appeared that no one was watching, I took three brisk strides into the closet and shut the door behind me. To my surprise, as the door closed, the light inside the small space went out causing total darkness.

The woman reacted immediately by bumping into me several times saying, "Oh no, Mr. Grayson, you can't be shuttin' the door. It automatically turns out the light." In her attempt to get past me to reopen the door, we collided in the dark. Suddenly, a chain reaction of mop handles, cleaning bottles, and whatever else (I'm not sure), came tumbling down on top of us. Or I guess I should say on top of *me*, for when the light finally came back on, the woman was standing up against the door, and I was bent over in the center of the cubical half buried by the fallout.

By dislodging several brooms and mops, I received two or three fresh cracks on the head. In addition, while stepping lively to dodge the flying mops, I also managed to kick over a small bucket that, to my relief, was only slightly filled with soapy water. Grateful that I was now standing in only a *small* puddle of soap, I attempted to pull myself together as she nervously tried to help.

"Are you all right?" she said, trying not to laugh while showing her deep concern. "I'm so sorry, Mr. Grayson, I should have warned you about closin' that door . . . the light and all."

Attempting to cover my embarrassment, I reassured her. "It's really not a problem," I said, lying with my every breath. Receiving this verification, and with the closet nearly back in order, she continued with her fast and panicked monologue.

"Well, anyway, Mr. Grayson— Can I call ya Jared?"

Before I could answer she quickly rattled on.

"Well Jared, I don't know if you remember me. My name is Emily Hewson. I was the one that called that morning your uncle got ta talking. You know, when me and Melissa made that recording . . . you remember?"

I nodded regretfully, remembering the early morning phone call. Trying to stay focused, I listened to her story, which she delivered like a high speed chase.

"Anyway, I need to tell ya what I saw, and let ya know that it's not my fault that your uncle and that other man are missing. I mean, it wasn't like I just woke um up and told um to leave. I can't help it if your uncle keeps comin' to life and talkin' to me. Besides, he talks ta me every time I see him, so how am I supposed to know that he's supposed to be in a coma? Why, the doctors around here, they don't tell ya nothin'. And anyhow, when your uncle, he starts to talkin' ta me, well, what the hell am I supposed to say? *Don't you be talkin' to me, 'cause you is supposed to be in a coma!* I mean it's not like they told me they was leavin' or anything."

"Wait a minute!" I interrupted. "Slow down, slow down . . . what are you saying . . . that my uncle and that other man just got up and walked out?"

Standing defiantly, she stuck out her chin and said, "That's right, just like you said. But I didn't say a word to make um do it!"

"Wait . . . wait . . . just a second," I said. "First, calm down a little. Then start at the beginning and tell me exactly what you saw."

"Well, Jared, that's just the problem, I saw um both up and walkin' around and I didn't tell nobody. It all looked perfectly natural to me. But if the hospital was to find out that I saw um just before they walked outta here, well, I'd be in a world a trouble. I'd probably lose my job, I would. They'd say . . . 'Oh that ol' Emily Hewson, well, she probably just stood there and watched um both walk bum naked out the door, and didn't do a thing about it.' Now, Jared, that isn't entirely true. Ya see, once they turned the corner at the end of the hall, they weren't even headed for the door, so I went back to my work. After all, it's none a my business what a body do. Like I was expected ta be nosey or somethin'. But I *had* to tell you, Mr. Grayson, 'cause he's your family and all." Stepping closer, she lowered her voice and added, "You won't tell the hospital will ya? I mean it's not like we was breakin' the *law* or anything."

"No," I replied. "It's all right. Your secret's safe with me. But tell me what happened with my uncle, I mean, what did he do? Did he talk or anything?"

"Yep, he did. In fact, the both of um did. Well, it was actually your uncle first. I was in their bathroom cleanin' the potty bowl, when through the crack in the door I heard someone talking. When I opened the door just a little, I could see your uncle in the dim light. He was standin' up, leanin' over that short fella in the other bed. I think he was sorta singing to him a little bit. Then your uncle, he touches the man's forehead with his fingers all funny-like, and kinda brushes his hair back. He says to him 'Mohan . . . *it's time to come back now.*' That's what he called him, Mohan, I remember. Well, that little fella he starts to stir and pretty soon he looks up at that great big white-haired man and says in a his dry, raspy little voice, 'Who *are* you?' Then your uncle, he does the strangest thing. He starts to tell the man his name, but right before he says it, he turns and looks through the crack in the door, directly into my eyes. He says, '*My name is Raha Muumba.*' He said it like he was meanin' to tell it to me and not to no one else. Like that other fella wasn't gonna remember it anyway.

"Well, I mean ta tell ya, it gave me sweet chills when he said it. In fact, I was so beside myself that I had to shut the bathroom door and sit right down on the pot for a minute 'cause I felt so funny. It all seems kinda peculiar to me now. Never heard that name before. I told it to my grandmother later, and she said that it definitely sounded Swahili. She always said that Swahili was her great-grandfather's native language.

"Anyway, when I come out a the bathroom, why they were both

gone. So I stepped out into the hall. Just when I found them, right at that very second, your uncle turns and looks back at me with the most peaceful smile, like he was lettin' me know that everythin' was all right. And that's about it.

"Then off they went down the hall, the big tall one with the little one by the hand, sorta helpin' him along. They was movin' kinda slow the both of um, their furry white bottoms just a waddlin' back and forth—showing through the back of their open hospital gowns. Well, I thought it was just the sweetest thing I ever saw, them takin' a little stroll together. Like two little naked children, they was. Now how could I be findin' anything wrong with that?" Her voice began to swell again in her nervousness. "And after all, they didn't have no shoes on. So how's I supposed to know that they was fixin' ta leave? It's not crime just to be takin' a walk now and then. I mean, it's not a prison, Mr. Grayson, if ya know what I mean?"

I held myself suspended, searching for some kind of response. I was excited that my uncle was conscious and alive. I was also terrified that he might be out of the hospital walking around in some irrational state. He would have no way of knowing about his dangerous condition, the high possibility of a brain aneurysm. I'd have to somehow notify the hospital and the police that the two men were conscious and on the loose. But, I didn't want to get Emily fired. After all, she was a comrade to my fumbling reality and, as crazy as it sounded, the information she had given me felt most like the truth.

Feeling somewhat overwhelmed and extremely claustrophobic, I decided it was time to end this conversation and figure out what I was going to do.

"Well, Emily, thank you for coming forward and . . ."

"Oh no, Jared, that's not all," she expounded. "There's more."

I felt like scolding myself. What was I thinking? Of course there was more.

"Do you remember the morning that you were listening to that recording of your uncle?"

"Yes," I said, "what about it?"

"Well . . . now believe me when I say that I know it's not right to listen in on other people's conversations, but sometimes ya just happen to be in the same vicinity and ya can't help but hear what's bein' said. And, well, if you've overheard the first part of what someone is sayin', well, don't ya think a person ought to keep listenin' to the second half? I mean so that you get the whole story exactly right in case ya need to repeat it later to someone else? Don't you think so, Mr. Grayson?"

I chose not to share my initial response. *Yes well, of course, I believe that we should always hold the highest of integrity when we eavesdrop. That way, when we gossip about it later, we will be sure not to miss any of the details.* Instead I simply replied, "Well, yes, I suppose so."

She continued. "Well, it just so happens that on that same evening, I overheard Dr. Schultz talkin' *real* private about how you sorta went off somewhere in your mind, while you were listenin' to your uncle's story. You know, the one that was on the recording about the garden. Well, to tell ya the truth, Mr. Grayson, it really wasn't much of a secret. I mean the entire fourth floor was talkin' about it after you had that experience. Anyway, what I'm wantin' to tell ya *now* is that you weren't the only one that it happened to.

"Ya see . . . the morning that Melissa and I made that recording of your uncle, well, I sat down and listened to it right then myself, before we ever showed it to anybody. And I mean to tell ya, the exact same thing happened to me. At first I was just sittin' there with my eyes closed, enjoyin' the story. I could just picture myself out in that field, chasin' that little butterfly. As the story went on it got more and more real. In fact, it got so real that I thought it was actually happenin' to me right then and there.

"It was like your uncle took me on a journey back to when I was a little girl. And do ya know who I run into when I was there . . . ? My Grandma Sadie. Now mind you, runnin' into Grandma Sadie— who passed on some twenty years ago—was not such a big thrill for me. I mean, we *hated* that ol' bitch, all of us kids. Why behind her back we always called her the Hag-from-Hell. She used ta beat our butts somethin' fierce. But this time when I was in that field of flowers and started to see all those sparkles a comin', why all that glitter turned into my Grandma Sadie. It was like she was alive and well. Why it was the damnedest thing I ever saw. And this time she was beautiful, and real nice, too. I almost didn't know who it was 'cause she was so different. At least that's what it all looked like in that dark place behind my eyes.

"Well, she come on over to me with a whole bunch a flowers and told me that she wasn't just my imagination—she was real. And she said that all those sweet visions I used to see when I was a little one, what people used to say I was just imaginin', well, she said that all of them were real, too. She also said not to let anybody tell me different. Why, I remember when I used to get walloped somethin' awful if I talked about what I saw in all that sparkly light. And do ya know who used to beat me the worst of all for doin' it? Why, it was my Grandma Sadie. Do you believe it?

"Well, Jared . . . ever since then, I have been walkin' round in a most wonderful feelin'. Like some burden has been lifted from me. That's why I had to tell you, that I know it's all right to take a little walk on the outside now and then, if ya know what I mean."

I shuddered to think that I did know what she meant. I suppose it was true; I may have experienced some of what she had. Perhaps if I hadn't been interrupted by Dr. Schultz, I might have seen even more. Her account also reminded me of Professor Talon's story and of the pages I had forgotten were still in my coat pocket. One thing was certain however, I had to get out of this closet-of-claustrophobia before I lost whatever sanity I had left.

I thanked Emily again for all of her information and maneuvered towards the closet door. She asked if I could please send her word if I heard anything more about my uncle. I assured her that I would.

I backed out of the closet so as to not be recognized. Not that my reputation at the hospital could be any more tarnished. I simply wanted to make my escape without further complications.

I tried to imagine where my uncle and the other man might have gone. As for my uncle, in the years that I had known him there was only one place that he ever wanted to be—in the mountains as far away from people as he could get. The only other place I could think of was his lake cabin. I didn't know if he still had it or if it was even standing. I heard many years ago that the state had run off many of the residents in that area who had built cabins on old homestead sites because the area was zoned as national forest. Whether or not my uncle's cabin had been torn down, I had no way of knowing. He had built it far from any road on a plateau surrounded by a fairly high ridge. It was a difficult hike in, as I well remembered having dragged many a backpack full of groceries up the hill's craggy face.

The police report said he had been found by a hiker not too far from a road in the Echo Ridge Reserve area. They brought him in by one of the forest service's helicopters. I wasn't great with the geography of the local area, and trying to locate him with no clue as to where to start seemed pointless. My only logical choice was to see if I could find his old cabin. Maybe it was still standing; perhaps he would return there. Besides, a few days in the mountains and away from this hospital looked far more than just inviting. It would give me a chance to sort things out, time to read the story that the professor had written.

I had a strong desire to find my uncle, but an even stronger desire to find out how all of the pieces of this puzzle fit together. I was becoming more aware that this was no ordinary situation and that there were obviously no rules and apparently no logical guidelines. In the course of only a few days, my entire reality had taken on the characteristics of a three-ring circus, and it was now emphatically clear that I, beyond any shadow of a doubt, was not a spectator.

9

Edge of the World

My decision to go on a mountain expedition also seemed to usher in an end to the many days of fog and drizzle that had been escorting me back and forth to the hospital. Today the sun was shining, and the morning air was cold and clean. The spring rains had brought out several fresh shades of green that made the old dry pines of the area appear newly dressed for another season. Occasionally, tiny wild flowers crept up the side of the road, while puffs of steam from the patches of wet grasses were slowly finding their way back to the sky. Even my old jeep seemed more than happy to be climbing the winding mountain road that was guiding me into the canyons of my past.

I had not been on this road since I last visited my uncle some thirty years ago. What I might find, I couldn't imagine. It felt good though to once again be surrounded by the shale and granite mountains that allowed only the most insistent evergreens to grow. Because of the rough and rocky terrain, very few people built dwellings in this region. The road, which was now primarily used by the forest service, was poorly maintained, its ruts and boulders becoming larger and more treacherous the higher I climbed. This gravel passage and many of the landmarks were surprisingly familiar, reminding me that I too had been young and adventurous.

Appearing just ahead was a deep blue sign with crisp white letters. The sign looked obtrusively modern against the dark green majestic forest: ECHO RIDGE MOUNTAIN RESERVE. A jolt of excitement raced through my body. Just beyond the cul-de-sac in the road was an old rickety building that looked well-inhabited with a junk yard display of assorted rocks, rusty tools, and antiques. There was also a half-decayed wagon that had probably sat in that very spot for the last quarter of a century. In fact, I believe this building may have been the local supply store my uncle and I used to visit. An old wooden sign hung at an angle crooked with the roof: ECHO MOUNTAIN TRADING POST. Although there was no one in sight, the front door stood wide open like a permanent invitation to come in and wander about.

Parking my jeep, I accepted the open door's invitation. As I stepped over the threshold, I found a bountiful museum of junk, the value of which could only have been fully realized by the most devout of hermits. Numerous streams of sunlight filtered through the fine haze of shimmering dust that had been suspended, flickering in the afternoon air. The breeze of my entrance, though, sent the dust into a flurry, causing much of it to surrender and fall, joining other layers that had settled on the shelves and tarnished articles of this forgotten room.

The only object not yet so dusted was the hermit in question, who appeared to be sleeping in a straight-back chair leaning strategically against a window ledge. The front legs of the chair, about two inches off the ground, waited patiently to return to the roughly planked floor, as did the nervous mug full of coffee cradled loosely in his calloused hand, anticipating his waking and its precarious fate.

His thick coarse hair, beard, and eyebrows were a confused patchwork of color varying in shades from coal black to a silvery-white and seemed to grow unattended in all directions. A large tuft of white hair on his chest protruded through the open buttons of his red long-johns, while his perfectly round belly stretched tight the few buttons that were actually in use. More relaxed were the buttons on the lower part of these crimson drawers, which had stealthily crept out of the widely opened fly of his jeans. His pants, worn for especially high waters, revealed the last of his red suit. A band of red hung down below each pant leg just above his boots, which appeared to be rooted to the floor.

Being careful not to startle him, thereby upsetting his well-balanced pose, I quietly said, "Excuse me." After a second or two I tried again in a louder voice, "Excuse me."

Then with both eyes still closed, through a half-snoring mouth, he mumbled what I thought were the words, "Myrtle . . . now don't be messin' with me again. You know that once is all you get. Now go on."

Obviously, his response was intended for someone other than myself, although I was more than a little curious to know if Myrtle was his wife or his mule. Giving it one last effort I raised my voice slightly and repeated, "Excuse me!"

One eye opened and circled the room as though sent out as a solitary scout to see if there was really any reason to rouse the rest of the body from its comfortable slumber. His one eye eventually found my two, which caused him to start as the chair legs hit the floor and a wave of the cold coffee bathed his lap.

Pretending not to notice the spill, he took a quick sip from the cup and said, "What can I do for ya?"

Trying to hide my smirk, I replied, "I was wondering if you might know of a man by the name of Ben Grayson. He used to live around here years ago and had a small cabin on a pond somewhere on the other side of this ridge." I pointed out the door in the direction I thought it might have been.

"No, never heard that name, but you're probably talking about Lake Cameron. I haven't been up there in a long while. I see a few hikers heading that direction. They say, though, it's pretty hard to get to since the stream flooded and washed out the old foot bridge and part of the trail. Now you gotta climb around the back side of the ridge. It's a good long hike, take ya two or three hours."

"Do you know if there is a small cabin near the lake?"

"Can't say as I remember. It's been a lot a years since I was able to climb up that far."

I followed him as he limped through the door and out into the open parking area. "Just follow the stream up that direction," he pointed off to the left. "When you come to the adjoining creek, look up towards it and you'll see a ravine and two granite peaks.

Climb between those peaks and the lake should be just below on the other side. At least that's what I've been told. Never been that way myself. You think you might be going up there?"

"Well, I think I might head that direction."

"Need any supplies?" he asked, anxiously.

I looked around wondering just what he had that I could possibly need. Perhaps an old wagon wheel or maybe part of a plowshare. Top that off with thirty or forty pounds of his assorted rocks for my backpack and I'd be all set. "No thanks," I said, politely, "but is it alright if I park my jeep here for a while?"

"Suit yourself," he said, hobbling into the old shack and presumably back to his afternoon nap.

I followed the stream as best I could for there was no trail to speak of, and the brush was prickly and dense. The turbulent water having washed its way along the narrow gully revealed a bed of logs and jagged boulders of varying shapes and sizes. I could tell that the stream was still young because the older trees had remained standing in the center of the flowing water, the soil yet to be eroded from their shallow roots.

It was not long before I found the adjoining creek and, as the old-timer had said, up its ravine I could see the two granite peaks. These, unlike myself, were now heavily shaded by a thick blanket of dark clouds. It was obvious that these clouds were headed in my direction, giving me the distinct impression that I was going to be on not only an interesting expedition, but also a wet one. However, the peak's summit wasn't far, and there was a chance I could make it over and down to the lake before any real deluge started.

Although I intended to pick up the pace of my hike, the climb soon became more difficult, with the massive rocks creating a much steeper terrain. My muscles stretched and pulled as I slowly found my way up the ravine's jagged face. Some of my attempts were in vain as sheer rock walls or huge boulders forced me to backtrack and try alternate routes. I could feel my body becoming fatigued as the dark mask of clouds now shaded me and my surroundings in an illusion of nightfall. A chill wind accompanied this shadow, and the smell of an oncoming rainstorm filled my nostrils.

A distant rumble of thunder greeted me as I pulled myself up through the last crevice to the summit. Like centurions, the granite peaks stood on either side of the opening as though guarding the entrance. The view was still hidden by the tops of pine trees and a gray forest of fog. This dense layer of clouds had already claimed the small valley below. It now rose to blow through me, the cold wet breeze misting my face, then continuing down through the ravine I'd just climbed. A quick flash of lightening lit the billowing mist followed by a loud crack and a heartfelt rumble that seemed to vibrate the surrounding rocks. Its roar echoed back into the gray nothing of the terrain before me.

Panic was becoming a reality, as I could now feel my pulse in several parts of my body, my breath becoming more rapid to support this new flow of adrenaline. A few heavy drops announced the rain's arrival as I scampered along the rocky terrain trying to find safe passage down the other side. I squinted hard to see through the dark thick fog. Dread slowly crept down my spine as the rain made small spattering noises all around me. I knew I had to get down off these rocks and under some shelter in the trees below. Soon the boulders would be too slick to climb, and I'd be stuck up here with no cover.

Unable to see what was below, I finally aimed myself in the direction of the treetops I had seen just before they disappeared into the mist. I climbed out onto a smooth rock face, the incline of which seemed less treacherous than the sharp vertical formations on either side. Not trusting the smooth slippery surface of the stone, I used the large horizontal cracks along the rock face like a ladder. With every step the rain seemed to come down harder, the sky becoming even darker. I knew I had to hurry.

Finding the remains of a fallen tree, I stepped down onto a branch that was wedged into one of the rock's crevices. Suddenly the branch gave way and disappeared beneath my foot. A wave of shock filled me as I fell sharply two or three feet. I lurched my body forward, reaching to grab any part of the rock's face. The entire front of my body finally made contact with the granite surface, but I was still sliding down. The incline was now much steeper than before. I had no idea what was below me. There could be more rocks and trees, or a hundred foot drop-off. Like a straining hand with its fingers stretched out wide to grip the surface of a globe, I molded myself to the round wet surface.

Slowly, I continued to slide, my feet searching frantically for any crevice or ledge, my arms and legs reaching out as far as they could. I clung to the massive stone like a child being pulled from its mother in despair. My fingers clawed wildly at the slick hard granite, frantic to find even the slightest crack or hole to dig their way into. I pushed every part of myself into the rough stone as my face painfully scraped the harsh surface, my mouth biting savagely to grasp anything that came in its path. I was sliding off the edge of the world, and I was sure that there was only a great black emptiness below me.

Just then I stopped sliding. My fingers had found a solitary crack traversing the face of this sphere. I held as still as possible, my fear gripping madly to the massive rock with only one or two joints of my fingers able to penetrate the merciless wet surface. I could feel my heart beating against my chest as my lungs rhythmically betrayed me over and over, pushing me out away from the stone with my every breath. My feet dangled helplessly, feeling only the torrent of rain that was now shelling me like endless gunfire. I wanted to cry out, but I was too frightened to move.

I could feel my clothes and backpack steadily being saturated by the rain, making my body heavier and heavier. A layer of water flowed over the surface of the rock. Like a waterfall it streamed underneath me and around me. I could feel my fingers weakening, and I knew the inevitable: In a very few seconds I would be forced to let go.

I wanted to turn my head and look down to see what, if anything, was beneath me, to find out if there was to be any hope of survival. I also knew that moving to look was a luxury I couldn't afford. In this closing moment, time was precious and, one way or another, I would find out soon enough. Perhaps it would be better if I didn't know.

I had never experienced this kind of overwhelming fear before. Nor had I ever been brought to look at the face of my own death.

Desperation seemed to fill every cell of my body. I felt my fear slowly consume me, washing away my passion for life, drowning my dreams of the future. I hated this feeling of terror, and I despised that it had now come to own me. If my death was at hand, I wanted to die taking in one last triumphant breath, not crying out in fear, never to be heard from again. If this was my last moment, then let it be one of passion, an explosion of emotion greater than any I had ever known. Let this *not* be some tragic fate that was thrust upon me because my helpless fingers had finally given up, but let it be a moment of my choosing, to be the beginning of my next adventure, not simply the fearful end of this one.

The rain, as though having heard my thoughts, gently began to subside as did the frantic pounding of my heart. Trying not to move, I carefully took a deep breath and then let it out, hoping to rid myself of some of the fear and desperation that, like the hand of death, reached for me, grabbing at my life. As my body relaxed I felt a kind of euphoria come over me, a peacefulness I had never known before. I knew that this was it, the moment of my choosing.

I closed my eyes and took another long breath, breathing as much of life as I could. Then letting out an exhilarating bellow, unencumbered by any word, I relaxed my fingers and let go.

10

One Lone Pine

How long had I fallen? I couldn't be sure, for time truly does stand still when there is only you and the infinite air space around you. With no reference to any physical reality, it's as if there's no reality at all. The ultimate freedom I was experiencing in the here and now transcended physical reality. It was pure feeling, pure emotion with no mental perception attached to it. The first cognitive thought that finally intruded on my experience was my total disgust that I was again *having* a mental thought and that the experience of pure emotion was about to be over.

My second thought was the mental identification of tree branches and how harsh they felt sliding along the more tender parts of my body. Not to mention an even faster recall of what a rather large branch feels like when it is thrust up between my legs, connecting most unmistakably with my buttocks, my tailbone, and my groin. Beyond any doubt, reality had returned as my body was unexpectedly consumed by the long wet needles and the rough scraping branches of a very large pine tree.

Having made contact again with the physical world, I began an immediate inventory of which part of my body hurt the worst. Then I realized that *this* reality was still moving as the top of the pine tree in which I was now perched swayed back and forth. I grabbed on to any and all parts of the tree, resembling a well-worn flag that had wrapped itself around a pole so tightly that it could only be retrieved by the courageous *someone* who might climb up that pole and rescue it. I swung back and forth until the momentum of my weight subsided, bringing the tree back to its silent stance.

Just how long I clung to the top of that tree was difficult to know. It must have been a while though, because the rain had long since stopped and it was dark by the time I climbed down.

I remember staring blindly at a soft white glow above me, wondering if it was the moon or something more hiding just beyond the thick layer of haze. Then quite miraculously, the clouds pulled apart. Like the fingers of two hands that had been woven together, they slowly divided, unveiling the luminescent sphere. This most compassionate moon, which followed so soon after the storm, was like a beautiful maiden who now searched the dark misty terrain for her lost and fallen lover.

Lost and fallen, so was I, but very much a survivor of this storm. I felt humbled and grateful. . . . To whom, I wasn't really sure. Perhaps to God?—whatever that is. Or maybe to this lady of the moon who had so graciously lighted the way for me to climb down out of that tree and find this sheltered alcove in the rocks. Within this solitary refuge, I felt safe and very honored to be alive. I was in awe of what had just happened. From the moment of my greatest fear, I had slid off the side of this cliff into the vast nothing and fallen some twenty feet. Then I was caught by a single tall pine, a noble tree who chose *not* to grow next to all of the other trees just below, but here, alone, pushed up against the side of this rock wall, looking down on the others.

The moon, having climbed high enough to clear the nearby branches, beamed down on me filling the alcove with a white-blue light. Life had never seemed so precious to me as in this instant. My whole being felt more content than ever, as if it were now filled with a soothing bell-like sound that resonated throughout me. I wanted to gather in every nuance of this scene that I might remember it on some less auspicious night. The sky had never been so clear, nor had this lady of the moon ever looked so bright. She moved carefully across the indigo sky, as though waiting for some response as to what she might have whispered to me, more than likely a question that could only be felt but never really understood. I stared into her white light and allowed a medley of thoughts to gather for our silent conversation. Like prose the words fell from my mouth. Spontaneously and without effort, they blended with music I had written some time ago— a melody that had been waiting for just such a moment.

My lady . . . of the night sky.
Sister to the sunrise.
Guardian . . . of the mountain.
Companion to the sea.

My lady . . . dressed in white light,
Won't you talk with me this night.
Tell me of all . . . that I've forgotten.
Tell me all the secrets . . . that I long to know.

My lady . . . how I've wondered,
of the sparks that dance about you.
And of the voice . . . that calls unto me.
Whose face I've never seen.

My lady . . . send them to me.
All the secrets of my dreams.
Light the way home . . . so I'll remember.
How I long to be there.
Tell me . . . tell me everything.

Tell me when the whole of life began . . .
was there such a fear that life could end.
And is to bring an end to such a fear . . .
to know the end . . . is to begin.
And rise above illusions.
Creations of our own.
And soar into your twilight.
My lady of the moon.
Twilight . . . dark night . . . moonrise.

A cold calm chill pulled me from my trance, reminding me that my clothes were heavy and well-soaked from the rains. Opening my backpack, I took out some matches and a few half torn pages, which I crumpled beneath some twigs and branches that had been sheltered by the overhanging rocks. I struck a match and blew gently on the dry tangled nest trying to coax a little fire to join me in this darkness. As the paper began to catch, the small flame illuminated the tiny intricate writing on the burning pages.

Suddenly, I was jolted by the realization that I had just set fire to the professor's story. I dove forward, placing both hands over the fire. Frantically, I pushed on the burning mound until all signs of the flickering light were out. My heart pounded rapidly in its attempt to nurse me back from the momentary shock. My hands, warm and blackened by the soot, were still shaking, leaving me unable to tell whether they had actually been burned.

Carefully, I retrieved the charred pages and unfolded the creases as best I could. From what I could tell in the dim light, there appeared to be little damage, that is to the story. My nervous system was not so easily repaired. I sat back with the pages in my hand, breathing steadily to calm my rattled bones. I felt panicked, not just from the burning pages, but from a pressing need to read this story immediately. I could not put it off any longer. Something was telling me that I had to take it all in before morning.

I scavenged through my backpack to find some less valuable scraps of paper, which soon caught fire, igniting the twigs I had gathered. I fed the fire with what I could find until it began to thaw my cold fingers and dry the edges of my wet beard. I placed my damp jacket on a nearby rock and slid my backpack underneath my head laying myself as close to the fire as I could. The tiny flames could warm only one side of my face but gave out a soft glow across my chest and hands lighting the now ragged pages I was about to read.

11

Grrrr . . .

It was most apparent within the first few lines that Professor Talon, although presumed to be mad, was also an accomplished writer. Unlike what I'd expected, this account of his experience was not jotted down as notes or ideas. It was actually a well-defined story. The circumstances under which the events took place, or how they began, would at least for now remain a mystery. Whether his journey had been an illusion, a dream, or some kind of conscious reality, its secret would be well kept on the missing piece of the opening page burned in the fire just minutes ago. Therefore, his story begins mid-sentence:

. . . so too did the soft mist reflect itself in the water affording no clue as to where the water ended and the mist began. Without the courtesy of any friendly moon, night's darker shadows roamed freely upon the silent mountain lake. Had it not been for the occasional rippling sound of his paddle's rhythmic dive, I might not have seen him coming at all, for the smooth contour of the sleek canoe created less than a whisper as it slid effortlessly through the invisible water.

Like a ghost he appeared, his luminescent white hair and beard floating weightless through the soft gray haze as though his head needed no torso to carry its mass. Then with the swirling motion of his slow even strokes, the ghost came to life as a giant of a man, who calmly guided his wooden vessel in the direction of my camp. Perhaps it was my fire burning close to the water that drew him out of the dark empty nothing. But whoever he was, or whyever he came, there was no fear to be found in any part of me. You might say he'd been expected by some *better* part of me, and the rest of me quite warmly received his company as well.

His shirt was of a common flannel, patterned dark green and red, his mountain-man's attire complete with thick trousers, boots, and a fringed leather pouch that hung long from his belt. He gathered himself on an old log, drawing close to the fire and its bright amber glow, which lit up the blue and the white of his eyes as well as the white hair gently feathered around his face. Like a statue of Zeus, he sat strong and tall, with one knee raised high to support his arm and his chin. Occasionally his fingers would wander about, slowly sculpting the contour of his mustache and beard. The depth of his eyes stared not at the fire, but were fixed solely on me. He had a look and smile possessed only by kings and the greatest of those who had traveled the world as their means to an end.

It appeared that no words were meant for this moment, as though thought and feeling far surpassed any verbiage. Yet the silence seemed crowded with my anticipation and wonder . . . and my longing to remember why he felt so familiar. It was the lone cry of a wolf that finally entered the stillness, calling out hollow and distant in search of an answer. My visitor replied with a soft blink of his eyes and the hint of a crescent moon smile.

"Perhaps he will join us," he said as a jest, smiling gently again, staring into the fire. And then with such ease, as though we'd spoken for hours, he gave me these words that won't soon be forgotten.

"There was once a time here, in this your world, when there was no human. There was no hatred or greed, no deception or sorrow. There was what your scholars call evolution, and there were the animals, the creatures of the Earth running rampant and free. They were wild and chaotic and in total balance with all that had been created. Each was a reflection of an unlimited thought, a nuance birthed by the Creator to be the character and the glory of the essence that they reveled in. If it was the jaguar, the nuance was that of power and cunning, while the deer savored the passion to be gentle and compassionate. The wolf favored loyalty, and the bear was forever sovereign, while the otter found play in each and every adventure.

"Each living thing flourished as some aspect of the ongoing passion of life. Each was a nuance in the purest of form expanding into the forever of the Creator's vision. All was unlimited. Endings were mere beginnings, and the flow of change was the order of a more refined balance. And when it was done and all had been set into motion, it was you who volunteered to explore the nuances, to become the fingers, the hands, and the body of the Creator itself in an adventure called human."

I readily became lost in the poetry of his words, my mind being called into total attendance. I had never thought of myself of having volunteered to be human or some physical aspect of that which he called the Creator. These thoughts stirred a thousand questions bombarding my mind: *Then who are you, and for that matter, who am I? Why are we here? Where did it all begin?*

He again smiled patiently as though waiting for my

questions to subside and then graciously answered them one by one, with no words from me, without any asking.

"I am called Iyokipiya, though I have been known by many names, and I am much like the wind. This you will notice when I am gone. You . . . you are a prophet, the seeker of the truth, and the truth is why I've come in this hour.

"For eons you have been taught that you were separate from the Creator, that God was outside you, above or beyond you. Even the word God has become the cause of a kind of social strain, seldom finding a place where it is politically correct. Through the control and dogma of humankind's altered thinking, many of you have been convinced that God is a judgmental figure, someone who toys with and tests those not already damned for their adoration, their loyalty, and their fearful love. In truth, the Creator is the essence of all that is, moving and flowing through an energy called love. You are a physical expression, the embodiment of that Creator, ever expanding in an adventure called life."

I could feel my brain rowing madly as though caught in some turbulent storm. And once again he waited patiently for that storm to calm. Then he continued, answering my silent questions, like they were part of an ancient story he longed to tell. His speech became light and playful as if telling the story to an inquisitive child.

"Like tiny probes you travel in a multitude of directions, through the color and splendor, with the freedom to embrace a billion different perceptions however you choose. Through this endeavor you are constantly enhancing and expanding the infinite mind of the Creator into a even greater awareness. In the human body, you are the explorers, the physical senses of a divine being who allows you to feel and experience the passions and emotions of every creature, every animal, every expression."

From a distance the wolf suddenly called out again, slightly louder than before.

"Yes, and what about this friend of ours, the wolf?"

As though in response, the wolf howled a lonesome cry. My visitor paused, allowing the slightest chuckle to rise up inside him. Then he continued, trying to suppress his private grin.

"The animals—which are rather unlike all humans—are very simple and quite pure in their existence. They have no mental judgment of humans nor any of the other creatures and most importantly," he hesitated producing a gentle smirk, "they never ask *why*. They simply stay in the moment where they thrive and evolve wholly balanced with the world and all that is around them.

"For instance, a jaguar, or a great tiger, runs after its prey and on the day it strikes, it feeds. And on the day that its powerful strike misses, it does not sit down scratching its head and ask in some helpless and despondent manner, 'Why did that happen to me? What did I do wrong? Perhaps it was from my childhood, from something that my parents did to me. Or maybe it was from the karma of that other lifetime. If only I could have had therapy when I was younger, none of this would have happened.' Instead, the jaguar or the tiger sort of stretches and considers that swing a bit of exercise for the morning. The incident is quickly forgotten, without ever asking that proverbial question . . . *why*. Animals have no agenda or judgment attached to their memory. They do not remember and say, 'Well you know . . . that other lion over there really pissed me off the other day, and I'm not only going to think of a way to embarrass the hell out of him tomorrow, but I'm going to tell all of the others lions exactly what an idiot he *really* is.'"

The unexpected play of his jest caught me completely off guard and threw me into a fit of uncontainable laughter. It seemed to bubble up inside me like a fountain of pure bliss that I simply allowed to flow out of me, without restraint. It was in the following moment (and just for a moment) that my visual perception of him changed dramatically. Through my giggling outburst and watering eyes, I saw him dressed in a luminescent blue and white coat that draped over his knees and to the ground. His whole being seemed to glow in a translucent light, like a hologram projected into the dark night.

As my laughter and bliss began to subside, so too did this image begin to fade. When I had at last regained my composure, the reflection was gone leaving me with the original image of him. He smiled and paused for a time as though he was aware that my joy may have allowed me a glimpse of his true appearance. Then he continued with a more earnest tone, leaving me with the impression that this small episode of bliss was to prepare me for the seriousness of what was to come.

"You are a part of the purity of these animals, co-creators of them and of all that is and ever shall be. This is your birthright as children of the Creator to co-create your future, your every adventure, with the assistance and grace of that unlimited being. You have always had the freedom to choose every moment from the garden of possibilities that surrounds you. Whether you choose to be in sorrow or bliss, triumphant or defeated, tomorrow is yours to dawn as you wish.

"For ever so long, you have surrendered your ability to manifest because your passion to be of spirit was not an accepted or popular fate. To again believe in the magic that anything is possible is to know that all is changeable, that a miracle is what you create. It is also to take responsibility for all that you have already brought to you in the here and now. Be it poverty, bliss, illness, or love, it is always of your choosing, no matter how helpless you believe or have been told you are."

Now, closer than ever, came several cries from the wolf, much more desperate and mournful than they had been before. The howls seemed to accompany whatever sensation I was feeling, although I knew not what to call this lost and starving emotion. It was as though what he had said was mysteriously familiar. These words, both sweet and sorrowful, somehow rekindled a clouded memory, some simple truth that had long since been buried by the stale beliefs through which I had been living.

"The lone wolf, he calls for you," he said softly, still harboring a noble smile. As I contemplated his comment about the animal's ghostly cry, my eyes found his. Then slowly he pulled me into the warmth of his expression, the floundering chatter of my mind dissipating like stars at dawn.

"This wolf and you are one and the same," he said, "with the spirit of your lives so caged by the ways of this world. For you, the snare is simply the programming of your mind. But the wolf, on this night, has fallen prey to the jagged jaw of a man-made trap. It is a deadly grip that now threatens the pure essence of his life. Calling out in this hour he attempts one last cry, one last echo for the wind to carry to whoever might hear. Maddened by the pain and the desperation of his capture, he sends out his sorrowful message to his family and to all of the Earth's creatures. He tries to warn them of the destructive and unconscious song that is sung by humankind, day after day."

Lowering my eyes into the blur of the fire, I felt like a shadow that was wishing it, like this wood, could be burned into some clearer place of reason. My emotions seemed crowded with futility and sadness about my life, my culture, and the world around me. Yet as the result of his words, all of my woe was for this forgotten truth that I shuddered to hear and yet welcomed home so dearly. I stared without purpose into the fluttering yellow flames as he continued on with his weighty words.

"In the days to come, if the children of the planet do not heed this message, the dance of the human experience will soon be over, and the music of the wind around the world will play no more. To save the dance, the children will once again have to sing the original song, the song of the Earth, that of the Creator."

I looked up again into the promise of his eyes, their light blue-gray color penetrating the darkness. Then, with his voice softened to nearly a whisper, his reassuring manner somehow slowing the pace of his words, he spoke directly into the confusion of my saddened heart.

"Go to the wolf . . . and let your compassion be like a river. Be with him. Honor him. Restore the loyalty that was once birthed in him long ago. Know him. Become him. Convince him through your passion and your love that the divine spirit of humankind is not forever lost, not completely fallen. Free him from the steel entrapment that a corrupt and unconscious humanity has destined for him. And if he snarls and lashes out at you in his fear and mistrust, then woo him with your humility. Seduce him with your compassion. Renew his trust in the creature called human. Become one with him in the totality of your being. Through this union, he will give back to you the life force, the fire, the original nuance of that which he is, that which you have lost through the disharmony and degradation of the human ego. Find the spirit of this animal that is inherent within you, and you will embrace the purest essence of that which you once reveled in as God. He will remind you of who you are, that you are truly the children of the Creator and that it's now time for you to remember this wisdom and to begin your journey home to. . . ."

As abruptly as the professor's story had begun, so too did it end, its profound words leaving me hooked like a fish caught on a now abandoned line. It appeared that the professor had been interrupted, leaving his memoirs unfinished (and my curiosity unfulfilled). I searched through the pages, front and back, to see if there was more. Had he gone to free the wolf? And why did he end up at the psychiatric ward?

To my despair, there were no more words within the papers' folds and creases. I put the story aside and found more wood for my struggling fire. Lying down close to its warmth, I closed my eyes, secretly hoping to return to the mystical adventure I had been reading. I thought about the wolf, about its suffering and how defeated it must have felt, caught in the jaws of the trap. The feeling reminded me very much of an experience I had once encountered at the local zoo, a simple event that has somehow stayed with me for all these years.

I remembered seeing a pair of Siberian tigers that had given birth to two cubs. Although the larger cats generally kept themselves hidden behind the cement walls, their cubs were well-displayed as the pride and joy of the zoo keepers. I recalled thinking, as I watched them play behind the steel bars, that these incredible animals would never know their freedom. They would never hunt game or run across the tundra unhindered.

Completely exhausted, I could feel my body beginning to fade, trying to inconspicuously sneak off into a well-deserved slumber. But, as my eyes closed, my mind was still rotating. It slowly turned, repeating all that I had read, the prophetic words of the professor's mysterious visitor, be it my uncle or someone else.

I could still imagine his voice so clearly, the phrases churning in my head. Like an animal caught in a maze, my mind kept repeating his last sentence as though it were trying to find the way out, trying to find a means to finish the sentence, the thoughts that had ended so abruptly. He had said, *Find the spirit of this animal that is inherent within you . . .* and *. . . it is now time for you to remember this wisdom and begin the journey home to . . .* to where? I thought. *And begin the journey home to . . .* to what? I wondered, my thoughts slowly fading. *And begin the journey home to . . . and begin the journey home to . . . and begin the journey home to . . .* **"to the truth of you . . . of course. To the powerful and creative fire that is but dormant inside you. To the purity and the wonder of the primeval force that flows through each and every cell of your magnificent body.**

"When you hear the cry of a wolf that is caught in a deadly trap, you feel its suffering. You ache for it within the whole of your being. It is more than just emotion, more physical than any feeling. When you see a beautiful bird sadly jailed inside a cage, never allowed to stretch its wings and soar into the heavens, you feel its mournful bondage, its longing to take flight. For cocooned within your memory is your own ability to fly, of how to soar and spiral with the spirit of your being. When you see two newborn cubs in the essence of their frolic, unaware of their captivity, the confines of their future, you anticipate their journey that will take them back and forth, pacing in a cage as a spectacle for view.

Even now you still remember and can see them as you did
in their innocence and play, pawing one another, rolling and
grabbing with the ferociousness of babes.

> They growl and they roar
> with but a squeak inside a yawn,
> soon distracted by an ear,
> or a tail, perhaps their own.
> Precious is this moment
> as you see them once again,
> longing just to hold one
> in the cradle of your arms.

Then there comes a feeling,
deep in the hollow from inside you.
It's a sad, sad feeling and you look
to see where it comes from.
 You gaze all about the concrete cage,
until far off in the back, lying against a cement wall,
you see a great and beautiful beast stretched out upon the floor.
 The animal lies on its side,
its massive head resting and rolled back
with eyes half-open, caught in a daze,
appearing to be dead . . . but perhaps not so.

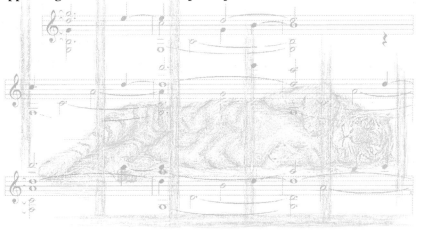

You gaze into the sadness of the half-opened eyes.
And your heart feels the pain of this great and noble giant
that now lies lifeless, empty of hope.
An animal that once ran so powerful and free,
now caged . . . silent . . . forgotten in its life.

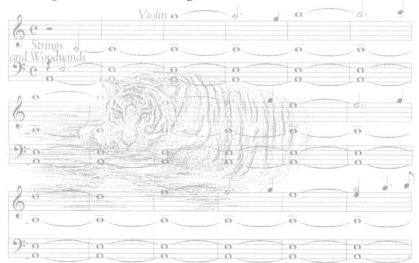

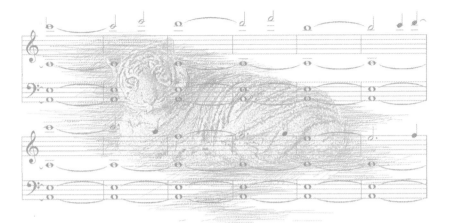

Then suddenly, he lifts his head to see you.
His eyes frozen upon you, open wide, staring through you.
You have touched him with your thoughts,
and he has felt you in this moment.
You stare into the dark eyes that now mirror your own.
He knows that you know, that you feel his pain inside you,
the cold, dark entrapment that forever will surround him.
You long just to touch him, hold him in your arms,
to reach out unto him with all that you are.

So with all of your thoughts,
with all of your love and compassion,
you go to him through your feeling,
allowing your consciousness to enter the cage
and drift to where he is, to the far side of the shadows.

He slowly stands to greet you,
fully aware that you are there,
fully aware that only he can see you
and feel you entering his sadness.

    You reach out to caress the strength and beauty that he is.
Wiping the sweat and pus from his sad and broken eyes,

you hold his massive head
in the cradle of your arms,
as he rolls himself into you,
so aware that someone knows
how much he longs to be free.

You hold him in your arms,
bathe him with your touch,
and love him with all that
you have ever known of love.
You drape yourself around him,
with your passion and your love.
You promise him that somehow you will free him.
Yes, somehow, if only you could climb down inside him,
together with your power and your knowledge you'd escape.

So gently with your love, you mold yourself into him.
Loving him, every part of him, every cell that he is.
Moving so slowly, down into the essence of his being,
Lying down within him, into the spirit of his life.

A thunder of drums begins to boil beneath you.
Pounding harder, and faster,
you breathe into the feeling, distant and primeval.
Your cells begin to churn and stretch inside you.
You feel it now igniting.
Your shell is turning inside out, there is change in all directions.

You breathe into the feeling that molds you and births you.
You surrender to the wildness that explodes from beneath you.
A ferociousness, a freedom, tingling and vibrating.
It crawls up your spine,
up your back, out your hands.
You claw at the ground,
and growl with your breath.
You rise up
into the power of a roar.

You roam about the cage, pacing back and forth.
Behind the bars that trap you, that hold you and bind you.
You feel the fire raging, building up inside you,
the power, the fury, the beast all about you.
You claw at the bars, and you pull at the steel,
the strength within you growing stronger and stronger,
until with one breath and all of your might,
you break out of the steel cage that no longer can hold you.

Then you run into your freedom,
and you run, and you run.
To the rocks, to the trees, to the forest . . . home.
Over the terrain and through the brush,
to the hills and the mountains.
And you run, and you run,
to your freedom, you run,
and you run . . . and you run . . . and you run. . . .

12

Wild Awakenings

Although my body was still numb and frozen in slumber, my mind had begun to awaken and was now scrambling to decipher the dream from which I was now returning. It was unlike any dream I had ever known. More real than my clearest memory, and more passionate than any fantasy, this night's excursion had a life of its own, stepping far outside the boundaries of my well-educated reality.

Within the dream there was a cage with steel bars that confined a tremendous cat, a Siberian tiger in the prime of its life. My discovery of this great animal, who was filled with such sadness and pain, compelled me to free the beautiful beast. Through some miraculous means, some dream-able cellular metamorphosis, I entered not only the cage, but also the body of the tiger. For a short time I actually became the great cat. By uniting our strength and our passion, we broke out of the entrapment and ran into the freedom of the mountain forests. I could still detect within the lower parts of my torso the rawness I experienced through the power of this animal. Bounding over huge rocks and logs, I climbed and stretched, completely wild within the motion of my inner flesh. I had been totally engulfed in this physical expression that had no human perception, no mental comparison. Like an instinct, or a force that was primeval in origin, this was pure feeling, pure animal, pure claw, growl, and roar.

Even now, in this waking moment, the accelerated energy flowed within my being, my fingers wanting to knead with their claws, my throat continuing to breathe a partial Grrrrrrr. From beneath me, the warmth of some massive stone was tickling and sensitizing the fur on my belly and rib cage. From above, the sunlight saturated the hair on my face and paws. I didn't want to leave this in-between world, where dreams and conscious reality share a brief passing in time. It felt incredible to *be* the dream of such a passionate wild animal that was stretched out naked on a rock, basking in the warmth of the first rays of morning.

My linear mind was relentlessly pulling me back to an awakened perception. I finally took a deep breath and surrendered the last of my dream with a long even sigh. Keeping my eyes closed to the harshness of the sunlight, I raised up into a yawn and scratched at the hair on my chest and arms.

It was then, in that very first second of conscious reality, that I became aware of the rough rock beneath me, pressing against the soft nakedness of my human body. As I opened my eyes, I found myself unfurled like a great slumbering feline, atop a giant boulder wearing only my own fur and skin and some newly found scratches. My clothes were strewn about the rocky hillside, each garment perhaps symbolic of the specific site of an exuberant stretch or roar. A boot here, a sock there, a shirt now caught in a bush, all marking the trail of my mysterious night's journey into the magnificent kingdom of the animal. My fleeting shock and fear were quickly consumed by the excitement of my joy. So content I was here and now to laugh at myself; to find myself spun in the play of such wonder; to know that at least by some count or measure, the experience I gleaned through my union with the tiger had indeed been real.

I stood naked in the midmorning sun, my legs spread apart, my penis dangling in the wind. With my arms stretched wide, I savored the last of this feeling that was steadily fading. It was very much like the flicker of euphoria I had experienced when I released my fingers and fell from the cliff. It was the same purity, the same rawness, only this time that spark of life had taken hold and run wild within my being. It left me strong and alive and hungry to know more.

That which I had presumed was a dream had taken a new form, leaving me with only glimpses of tangible memory that seemed to be held more within my flesh than within my mind. Nothing would I trade for the experience of the pure essence of this animal churning fervently inside me. If ever I had crossed the line into the wonderful world of madness, it had to be now, although I cared *not* in this moment. Surely it was the modern world that had bolted and gone mad, staggering so far from the power and knowledge of these magnificent animals.

Nestled down below, some hundred yards past the last of my abandoned apparel, was the reflection of water, which sparkled here and there where the tree branches allowed it to be seen. With the stretch of my eyes, and several squints, I could make out the shape of an old roof and pieces of board that reached out over the water, the remains of perhaps a dock or a boat. The lake looked like a miniature of the large body of water I remembered. As a child I was sure that its depths hid enormous monsters. It seemed comical now to picture my uncle fishing here, his boat able to cross the lake with a few dozen strokes. But it was definitely the same lake and undoubtedly the same cabin, which in itself gave me the feeling of having achieved some success.

Finding my original camp, I gathered up my gear and tossed it into my backpack. Then I began traversing down the mountain. Scampering like a small child, I collected my garments along the way, stopping occasionally to redress. Having gathered all but my wrist watch and one renegade sock, I made my way through the last of the undergrowth to the edge of the lake.

The cabin looked tiny in comparison to the one in my memory, the half-sized logs still framing a crooked doorway and one large boarded-up window. The porch, with its few remaining planks, was a challenge to navigate, as I stepped from creaky board to creaky board. Inside, I found an abandoned home with a display of old broken tables, chairs, and boxes, still arranged as if my uncle intended to return that very afternoon. The furnishings were completed by a few cracked dishes, a bottle or two, and a small stack of wood that had never found its way to the fire. Even my childhood memories seemed to have been left here amidst these antiques as though they too had been forgotten with the years.

Now only generations of dust resided here. The soft thick layers covered everything except one old rocking chair that was missing most of its slats and all of its right arm. Surprisingly, its contoured seat was somewhat polished. Evidently, someone had sat there, and not that long ago. Any trace of the occupant's footprints must have been erased by the higher volume of debris encouraged to come in through the open door. Whoever had been there, there was no way of knowing.

I jokingly said goodbye to the ghost in the rocking chair. Leaving the door open, I retraced my steps across the porch and headed back towards the summit. Glancing back one last time to perhaps better remember the place, I could see the old rocking chair still swaying from my disruption.

Although my excursion to the lake cabin had revealed no clues as to my uncle's whereabouts, the journey had brought me into a new perception about my life. Somehow I felt guided by these strange occurrences. Therefore, my next task was to find out what had happened to the professor, to learn about his encounter with the wolf, and to understand more about my own experience with the animal.

I made my way back up the hillside's rocky face knowing that the sunlight would fade early in this small hidden canyon. I wanted to make it back over the ridge and down the other side before darkness claimed the mountain for its own. The wind, having picked up in rhythm, seemed to grow stronger and steadier the higher I climbed. Like a companion it led me, or perhaps it followed, the trees whispering back and forth with the brushing of their pine needles. The sun before its setting had waited patiently for me at the summit. It dressed the rocky horizon and the surrounding terrain in shades of orange, pink, and lavender.

I sat for a time to witness its splendor, the sun's sphere of fire slowly falling behind the jagged crest of the plateau.

I would always remember this hour and the events that had brought me to it: my fall from the cliff, the professor's story, and my wild majestic run within the animal. I knew that through it all somehow my life had been changed, the vision of my own future ignited once more. Trying to seize some of the magic and mystery of this place, I played with these lyrics, blending them with music I had written long ago.

Winds along the canyon.
Oh legendary breeze.
Your elevating rhythms . . . have captured me.
Echoes of a memory.
When all of life knew harmony.
You've awakened such a feeling . . . that still lives in me.

So catch the wind . . . it's the soul's desire.
Climb aboard the spark of life, it . . . catches fire.
Ride the fire . . . the journey's into forever.
. . . Like the winds along the canyon.

By the time I found the welcome sight of my jeep, the air was chilled and nightfall was around me. The ragged winding road required a much slower descent as my headlights swung back and forth spraying the tree branches with a splash of light now and then. I felt younger and more alive having been on such an adventure, although I had no idea how to tell anyone about it.

For several miles my question remained unanswered. How *was* I going to explain what had happened? Was I simply going to say that *I fell off a cliff and was caught by one lonesome, friendly pine tree?* Of course this explanation seemed boring compared to *losing all of my clothes and scampering throughout the woods naked all night like a wild animal.* Maybe I would just start out with something like, *I was reading a story, the main character of which eventually left the written text and spoke to me directly in my head, guiding me into the body of a tiger.* Yes, that should just about do it. Then I wouldn't have to go and look for the professor at all. Why, they'd take me right to him and give me the padded cell just across the hall.

Hearing a voice in my head had to be the most incriminating part of this adventure, although I can't say for sure that such a phenomenon actually occurred. Perhaps it was just a dream that caused me to do a little . . . primal sleepwalking. Besides, how is someone supposed to tell the difference between one's own thoughts and a voice in one's head? After all, I have a whole smorgasbord of thoughts bouncing around in my noggin all of the time. For instance, if I were to take a mental inventory of the sentences that went through my brain within the next thirty seconds, (starting right about now), it would sound like this.

Who am I having this conversation with anyway?
There's no other road down off this mountain.
My cat is pissed again because I forgot to feed him.
I'm a complete failure as a composer.
There are no purple dragons anywhere.
We're going to have an earthquake.
The young woman at the mailbox is no stranger.
No one is ever going to believe what just happened.
Is there a climax to losing your mind?

Now . . . which one of these, if any, should I consider to be a voice other than my own? Which one is not just a part of the chatter that accompanies me in every minute of the day? I paused for a second, perhaps to see if someone might actually answer (. . . . .). Although the empty space I just experienced supported my original belief that, when put on the spot, those shifty voices never say a word, I knew that this particular discussion (that was with whomever) was far from over.

My old mountain highway had now found its way into the smatterings of a small town, which except for the very busy local tavern was somewhat deserted. The tavern (I thought) would be the perfect solution to my mental dilemma. *Just stop and have a beer!* I was sure *some* voice had said. I pulled into the parking lot full of dusty and well-worn pickups and found a place next to an old red Ford. Above the tavern door was a painted sign in chipped flakes of green and brown.

THE BEER BEAR BAR AND SALOON
(Growlers welcome)

At this time, I chose to fully ignore this coincidence, although I felt reassured to know I would be in familiar company in this tavern . . . that is if they accepted *lions and tigers as well, Oh My!*

Striding through the traditional saloon doors, I was soon reminded that this was Saturday night, and the entire town (of wherever I was) was right here and in full bloom. Rock and Roll music, disguised as Country and Western, was being played from the ever-so-small-stage by what I presumed was the more-than-local-band. Their music and antics had drawn the undivided attention of everyone in the place, including the loud and overgrown bartender who, by his size and his looks, *had* to be the head grizzly in residence.

The men outnumbered and outweighed the women by about three to one, so the place was alive with the scent of liquor, smoke, and an abundance of hormones. The three-piece band accompanied a lady singer, who had no desire to be considered a lady at all. The silver snaps of her tight western shirt strained to contain her. And, her blue jeans *had* to have been stretched by the tanner just for this occasion. The beer I ordered came without delay, making me feel right at home amongst the unmatched chairs, the small round tables, and the half-filled mugs of frosty ale.

As one song ended and another was about to begin, I could tell by the brewing excitement that I was about to experience one of those classic moments—one of those beer-bear-bar-and-saloon moments. Coming up was the song they had all been waiting for; the one that the band had played every night for the past decade; the one everyone knew—words and the melody—by heart. Beers-in-hand and attitudes ready, they watched as the lady rawhide singer began her traditional rap.

"Now . . . if some of you ladies are out huntin' for bear tonight—and some of you men as well . . . who you kiddin'—then there's only one thing that you've got to know. One very important thing that you must never do. Regardless of all that sniffin' and pantin' and pawin' at the ground—even if they is on their knees—you got to remember these fine words of wisdom."

A triple tumble of drums and one solitary cymbal crash set up the opening line, which was followed by a foot stompin' beat that put the whole room in motion.

(Thump . . . thump, thump, crash)
 Don't feed the bears . . .
 In the heart of a pale moonlight.
 Don't feed the bears . . .
 Or they'll follow you home at night.
 You'd better take care . . .
 If you got one in your sigh——hights.
 Cause they're hungry for lovin'
 and a kissin' n' huggin',
 and they'll be rubbin' on ya all night long——hong
(Thump . . . thump, thump, crash)
 Don't feed the bears. . . .

The entire building shook with the rhythm of the clapping and stomping, the rafters straining hard to keep a lid on the place. It was because of the thunderous uproar and the loudness of the band that it was difficult to decipher exactly when the real earthquake began. I suppose it was when those pesky whisky bottles finally rattled off the shelf, followed by the female singer who slid off the stage onto a table full of beers and bears, that I reckoned Mother Earth had decided to shake a little for herself. There were some folks shouting and others rushing for the door. Still others stood there trying to ride out the motion.

It was not until this precise instant that I realized the uncanny similarities between a bar full of drunken dancing bears and a wooden shack full of people experiencing an earthquake. Actually, from my observation (other than the slant of my chair) not much had changed. In fact, I was quite sure that several of the patrons had not noticed the quake at all. I could tell by the few who were still clapping to the music, which had long since stopped, and by the old timer who was sitting in the corner calling for a beer. Within seconds the shaking was over, although the personal renditions about the quake would probably go on for hours.

Having already had the Earth move beneath my feet once tonight, I decided it best not to finish my beer and to simply head for the door. Slowly I made my way through the now stationary furniture, but somewhat staggering commotion, and out into the parking lot. By the time I reached my jeep, the music had resumed and "Don't feed the bears" was once again echoing out of the wooden shack into the local streets.

As my jeep climbed back onto the old country highway, I knew that I would not soon forget my visit to this particular watering hole. Nor would it be easy to forget the list of thoughts I had contemplated while wondering which one could be some other voice in my head—especially the thought that said, *we're going to have an earthquake. . .* or something like that.

13

The Getaway

The knocking at my front door was no more welcome to me than returning to the city had been the night before. My bedside clock, insisting that I had slept in, displayed 11:40. The obtrusive rapping was soon joined by my doorbell's pathetic rendition of a chime, making it more than obvious that whoever it was had no intention of giving up. Unable to contrive any miraculous means for a spry bedside escape, I finally surrendered to my unavoidable fate. I had to get up, get dressed, and answer the door before *whoever* came climbing through my bedroom window.

I could easily tell by the puffy cheeks and tightly squeezed mouth (which now filled the peephole in my front door), that the early morning caller was none other than my neighbor, Mrs. Nurple. Prying my second eye open, I tied up my nakedness with my robe and begrudgingly answered the door.

"Good morning!" she chortled with an early morning smile. She held a small manila envelope in her hand.

"Good morning, Mrs. Nurple," I replied.

"Now Jared, you're not going to tell me that you were still in bed when here it is almost noon," she said, scolding without a shred of guilt for having gotten me out of bed.

After a slobbery, "No," I added with squinting eyes, "What is it that I can do for you, Naomi?" I was instantly brought out of the last of my sleepiness, realizing that Naomi was not her real name, but one I had bestowed upon her. Swiftly I moved past the mistake by asking, "Is that a letter or something for me?"

"Yes," she said excitedly. "This came yesterday morning. The postman left it in my box by mistake. It must be important having come all the way from Nepal." She reached out her hand, hesitant to release her grip on the poor helpless envelope and clearly starving to know what was inside.

Fully intending to cut this scene to the quick, I said politely, "Why, thank you so much, that was very thoughtful." I slowly squeezed the door shut, adding, "And give my regards to your husband Ted." This of course would have all been well and good, except that as the door latch clicked I realized that her husband's name was Fred, not Ted.

The letter was from an old college friend, Clyde Hendersen, a glorified archeologist who boastfully sent me letters every couple of years to let me know that he was once again exploring some other exotic place in the world and I (of course) was not. The envelope was marked Kathmandu, Nepal, with a whole slew of multicolored stamps across one side. I opened the letter and read:

Dear Jared,

Greetings from Kathmandu. I've been working in Nepal since last August. Ran across something that I thought you ought to know about. You might have already been notified. Anyway, we've been trying to excavate an old ruin here on the Gandak River. There've been a lot of problems because the dig is situated in the middle of a funeral site.

As part of the ceremony, the mourners carve the name of the deceased on one of the walls, sort of like a memorial. I've spent quite some time looking at the names on these stone structures. Some of them are recent, others are very old. At times I see one written in English.

That's why I'm writing to you now. I found a name that we both knew rather well, especially you, Jared. The name was Katherine Mason. Perhaps it's just a coincidence or some kind of mistake. Maybe you've already heard, I don't know. I do remember that you and Katherine had a parting of the ways many years ago and that she moved to Nepal.

Anyway, I just wanted to let you know, for what it's worth. The carving of the name looks recent, probably within the last couple of years. I asked around about it, but nobody knows anything else.

I'll be returning to the States for a few weeks in July. I'll try to connect with you then. Hope all is well.

Sincerely, C.H.

I knew there was no mistake; it had to be my Katherine. I didn't quite know how to react; after fifteen or twenty years of not seeing someone, just how grief-stricken was I supposed to feel? I did feel a kind of sadness. Yet, more vivid in my emotions was the letter from her I had run across just days ago, the one that referred to Shankara. I probably hadn't even thought of her much for the past decade, yet here was the old letter telling of her departure from me, and now a new one, telling about her departure from the world.

Placing these puzzling notions as well as the letter in my desk, I began to shuffle through my morning routine. I was anxious to start my expedition to the mental hospital, feeling a great urgency about locating Professor Talon. What I was going to do after I did find him, I had no idea.

I threw a little breakfast together and grabbed the entertainment section out of the morning paper. Plopping myself down in front of the television, I sifted through the channels as well as the paper to see what else might be going on in the world.

Clicking on several of the local stations, I found little satisfaction with the Sunday morning programming—that is until a somewhat familiar face appeared on the screen. It was the woman I had seen at the hospital, Jessica Williams, the TV evangelist. She looked quite different, her hair and makeup perfectly masking any sign of her more ragged self, or at least the self that I had previously witnessed. Like a bouquet of plastic flowers, she stood properly erect behind the glass podium, every detail precisely arranged to satisfy the camera from all angles. Her lacy blouse appeared to be embroidered to her bosom, while a small string of pearls lay nestled in her cleavage. "My God," I said to myself, "a pair of breasts never had it so good." I reached over and turned up the volume to catch the tail-end of what she had been saying.

". . . and that is why I have decided to end my work here and discontinue my Sunday morning broadcast. I know this may seem rather sudden, but I feel it's for the best."

There were a few slight gasps from the audience, followed by an uncomfortable silence and a sniffle or two. Jessica then lowered her head, staring down into the podium. The camera, zooming in for a close-up, revealed the tears that had begun to make trails with her heavy makeup. With blurring, watery eyes, she looked out at the audience one last time and said, "I'm so sorry." Then she slowly turned and walked out of the camera's view as the focus then moved to pan the shocked and spellbound audience. After a few close-ups of assorted sad faces, and a second of network confusion, the station went to a commercial.

I turned off the television and sat there somewhat surprised myself, and more than slightly curious as to the full explanation for her leaving. Although I knew very little about her, for some reason I felt great compassion for the disruption and confusion that she must be experiencing. She was obviously going through some serious changes. Strangely enough, I felt a twinge of excitement for her, a feeling that seemed to have no real point of reference for me.

As I scarfed down the last of my eggs and toast, I finally found the article I was looking for in the entertainment section of the paper. It was the review for John McDowell's production of *The Time Keeper*. As I had expected, the review was extremely favorable, its author not hesitating to expand on McDowell's ability to, (I quote) *cultivate new and undiscovered talent.*

Part of me wanted desperately to call and try to reschedule my appointment. However, having bungled the first meeting so badly, I was still too embarrassed to even consider it. Although this personal disaster felt like a bad twist of fate, I couldn't help but remember what my uncle (or whoever) had said to the professor in his story: *Everything was of our choosing, no matter how helpless we believe or have been told we are.*

I could not fathom how my uncle's emergency—which destroyed my chances of working with McDowell—could have been something of my choosing. It was just a stupid accident, the bad timing of which created total havoc in my life and altered my future forever. And what about the strange events on the mountain, my falling off the cliff and all? I had to admit that I was still excited about *some* of what had happened, but like my lost meeting with McDowell, I didn't set out to make any of it happen. All of it happened purely by chance. It just happened.

I closed the paper, attempting to do likewise with my unanswered questions. Perhaps if I could find Professor Talon, he could help explain or at least shed some light on this dilemma. I grabbed my coat and headed for the door, when all at once I realized what I was about to do. With my mind full of confusion, I was going to run down to the hospital for the mentally ill, see if I could locate one of the committed crazies, and ask him for advice about my life. What a swell idea! I think I'd better hurry.

South Providence State Hospital was on the other side of town. The long drive gave me time to think and perhaps formulate what I was going to say to Professor Talon, if I did find him. Most of all I wanted to know about his encounter with the wolf. Did he actually find a wolf in a trap, or was it more like what I had experienced with the tiger? For that matter, I was also intensely curious about the mysterious, but strangely outspoken, visitor that he had written about. Was this person a tangible being, with a body, arms, and legs, and if so, was it my uncle or someone else?

I also wanted to ask him about the young woman I had seen in the elevator at the hospital, the one who may have visited my uncle with a spray of rose petals; the one who also appeared parading through the war zones in my dream. I wondered if he knew her or anything about her. Was her name Sharee, and did she really know my uncle as someone now called Shankara? And what about the other names—Iyokipiya and Raha Muumba— did they refer to my uncle as well?

Pulling onto a newly blacktopped street, I maneuvered past the manicured lawns, watching for any sign of the hospital. Just ahead were a few clinic-type buildings encasing a large area of well-kept grounds. In the center of the complex was an old four- or five-story building painted a kind of muddy rose color. The structure, built probably in the late Forties, had all the carved trimmings and architectural spurs of a historical edifice. Its poor maintenance though, as well as the thick wire mesh that covered the majority of the windows, gave it a haunted appearance in contrast to the precisely groomed lawns that surrounded it.

A sign at the corner of the grounds verified my hunch that this was indeed South Providence State Hospital. Slowing down, I followed the streets circling the place, plotting my entrance. Completing one pass around the estate, I found myself once again approaching the front of the building. The tall double doors of the main entrance looked very uninviting and impenetrable, but there seemed to be no less formal way in.

Then, to my great surprise, those doors burst open, expelling a woman in a light flowing dress and a man in blue hospital clothes with a black mustache and long straight black hair. They swiftly danced down the front steps and then bolted as strands of clothes and long hair streamed out behind them. They were pursued by two rather stout and somewhat slower runners who were dressed in white hospital uniforms. The pursuers, who also wore scowling faces, barked out an array of muffled shouts, which soon drew the attention of everyone on the grounds. Like two graceful collies being chased by a couple of persistent bulldogs, the runners continued along the sidewalk and away from the building.

I slowed down, trying to see between the row of trees and parked cars surrounding the grounds. As the escapees came closer, I was able to get a second glance, confirming my suspicion—the man running beside the woman was indeed Professor Talon. My heart began to pound faster, my driving becoming more and more reckless. When I looked again, my heart nearly stopped. The person running with him was the young woman from the elevator, the woman I had also seen in my dream. To my complete disbelief, they were making a run for it.

To make matters worse, I soon realized that the long sidewalk down which they were running was going to pour them into the street on which I was driving. In fact, I could see by the speed of my jeep and the haste of their flight, that *jeep* and *people* would collide at precisely the same place. That is, of course, if I floored my gas pedal for the next 20 yards. It was obvious to me that they could easily escape if I sped up and became their getaway car.

I was presented with a profound opportunity for an incriminating act that could either land me in jail or land *into* my jeep the two people I desperately wanted to find. I was also aware that if I did nothing, they both might keep running off into nowhere, never to be seen again.

Half of my mind was excitedly screaming, *You've got to do it! You must help them! They will know where to find your uncle.* While the other half was sternly screaming, *No you can't! You can't get involved! You'll get yourself in trouble.* The mental volley went back and forth while the window of opportunity was slipping away, the excited runners coming closer and closer.

Finally, my right size-ten foot made the decision itself and slammed the gas pedal to the floor. The jeep shot forward, speeding to where the sidewalk and street joined. Trying not to think about just how much this reminded me of a scene from Bonnie and Clyde, I screeched up, stopped at the curb, and threw open the door of my jeep. I was met by the startled and wide-eyed faces of the escapees, who spontaneously followed my panicked instructions, "Jump in!"

Without hesitation the woman sprang into the passenger's seat, while the professor catapulted himself into the back open half of my jeep. I stomped on the pedal. The tires squealed and spun, jetting us down the lane, leaving the two panting bulldogs staggering in the street.

Shaking my shoulder by tugging excitedly at my shirt, the young woman shouted, "You were great! You were just great! Oooh-wee, it was perfect!" Releasing my shirt, rolling her eyes to the sky, she said, "Thank you Shankara. Thank you, thank you, thank you. Oooh-wee, that was great!"

The professor, who was just as excited, was standing in the back of my jeep holding on to the roll bar. He gave out a bloodthirsty victory cry, followed by a "Yip! Yip! Yip!" and a lot of other sounds I couldn't begin to imitate. I fully expected to look back and see him with slashes of red paint across his cheeks, waving a tomahawk above his head. To my relief, he was just smiling and laughing as though it were all some great game. In fact, they were both carrying on in a chorus of such commotion and laughter that I couldn't help but be caught up in it myself. Then the woman blurted out, "Pull over here, this is where I left my car."

I spun into the curb with the help of her tug at my steering wheel and came to a halt. She gave me a sudden kiss on the cheek. I blinked at her impulsive action only to find an instant later she had disappeared from the jeep and was crossing the street. She walked briskly into the adjacent park. Looking back, she waved and shouted, "I'll be in touch. You were just great . . . both of you." She then turned and went on her way.

The professor, having climbed into the passenger seat, turned toward me with a blank and bewildered expression. I quite blankly returned the gesture, the both of us wondering why she had hurried off so abruptly. Turning our heads we looked again out through the park at the now small figure of the woman some fifty yards away.

Totally taken back by my experience of her, I finally mumbled,

"She is *so* incredible . . . who is she?"

The professor, slowly turning back toward me with a puzzled look, said, "I have no idea."

"What?" I exclaimed.

"Not a clue," he said. "Never seen her before in my life, but I do have to agree . . . she is pretty incredible."

In total disbelief, I went on, "You mean to tell me that you just escaped from a mental hospital with someone that you don't even know?"

"No," he said calmly, putting on his oval wire-rimmed glasses. "I have just escaped from a mental hospital with two people that I don't even know. Who the hell are you?"

After we laughed, I finally asked, "You are Professor Michael Talon, aren't you?"

"Well, yes," he said, scratching his head as though he were questioning it himself.

"My name is Jared Grayson, I'm the nephew of Ben Grayson . . . the man you were trying to see at the hospital."

"Oh yes, you're the one," he said with a pleasant, but curious, expression. "You're the one that ended up with the pages of my story."

"Yes, that's right . . . how did you know?"

"It's a long story, but I'd better tell you on the way. Right now, we'd probably better get out of here." I agreed wholeheartedly, pulling back out into the street and pointing the jeep in the direction he indicated.

Professor Michael Talon, at least from my perception, was sort of a contradiction in terms. On one hand, he was the very image of a true scholar, occasionally putting on his wire-rim glasses when he felt the need to scribble something down on any scrap of paper. He was obviously well-educated and devoted to not only his work as a teacher, but to the constant expansion of his own knowledge, a true explorer of wisdom for its own sake. On the other hand, if you were to dress him in piece of hide and moccasins, and give him a buffalo to chase after, you would soon find him immersed in such a vision, probably pulling you into it as well. How he had been sculpted into his current life and circumstances, I was yet to understand.

I told him I had come to look for him, and merely by accident happened to pull up during their great escape. I said I had seen his lady accomplice in the elevator at the hospital.

In turn, the professor told me that this same woman had mysteriously appeared in the commons area of the institution and just happened to know of a door that had been left open. He said he probably would have stayed where he was, as he was likely to have been released very soon anyway. However, the woman had told him that he might be in danger. Feeling a bit uneasy himself about how the institution had been able to keep him, the professor took advantage of the situation and fled. Apparently he too had some suspicion.

When I asked about his experience with my uncle, Professor Talon said he had been in the Echo Ridge mountains on what he called a vision quest. The man, my uncle, was indeed a real person who came to him in the midst of his quest. He said it was a very beautiful, but somewhat haunting encounter, quite true to the description he had given in the story. When I asked what had happened with the wolf, he became rather quiet as if he wasn't sure this was something he wanted to share with me. The pause though seemed to accompany a shift in his emotional state, an acceptance of vulnerability, as he gave an accounting of his intense encounter with the animal.

"The wolf's left foreleg was caught between two jagged strips of steel. The trap had already torn the flesh, and the leg was bleeding badly when I first approached him. As he saw me, he flew into a rage, further injuring the leg. I immediately fell on all fours in a desperate attempt to calm him. With my face still in the dirt, I could feel his frozen stare fixed on me watching for the slightest movement. As I slowly raised my head, I was met by a pair of fierce yellow eyes with round black pupils and a snarling mouth that gripped and trembled with traces of white foam and saliva. His cunning eyes seemed to burn into mine, holding me in a kind of trance. I could feel him probing my emotions, especially my fear, searching deep into the most vulnerable parts of me. Through this emotional link I could also feel *his* fear, as well as the intense pain that sabotaged his ferocious stance.

"The jaw of the trap was fastened to a metal stake by a long heavy chain. As I tried to maneuver myself toward the stake end of the chain, the wolf again went wild, thrashing about. He was unable to move very far, for the trap was caught among some small stumps and tree branches.

"Then I recalled the words of my mysterious visitor, about becoming one with the wolf, of finding the spirit of this animal within me. Slowly I crawled to the stake end of the chain and wrapped it around a bare part of my leg. I cinched down on it until I too began to feel the pain of the hard steel biting into my flesh. Wrenching down on the twisted chain, I gave out a cry.

"The wolf reacted immediately to the sound of my pain. Gazing nervously at my leg, he whined and cried, his whole demeanor becoming more calm. To my amazement he seemed to recognize that we shared the same suffering, and his rage became a kind of compassion. The wolf's behavior now resembled the tameness of a domestic dog.

"Once I had gained his trust, he actually allowed me to pry open the jaws of the trap. As he dragged himself away, I could see that his leg was completely mutilated, his foot hanging twisted and limp from the break. I knew there was nothing I could do and that he had very little chance of surviving. Helplessly, he staggered to a nearby tree and lay down beneath it in a bed of dry grass and leaves. He remained there, panting and staring at me with what were now very soft eyes; so content he seemed in light of his pending death. He whimpered but a little; I responded by lying down with him. This action came purely out of instinct, from an overwhelming passion that now guided my every move.

"The wolf died sometime during the night. His lifeless body lay beside me when I awoke the following morning. It seems strange to me now, but at the time I felt very honored to have been there, somehow becoming more sensitized with the passing of his spirit. It was as though I were no longer alone, but accompanied by some feeling constantly churning and moving inside me. As I surrendered to the feeling, I found myself wanting to stretch and run, seemingly driven by a kind of rawness that I've never known before. Fully aware that all of my senses had been heightened, I began to wander the forest exploring what was a whole new world, one far more delicate and balanced than I had ever imagined.

"It was during this exploration that I was disrupted by the turbulent roar of a forest service helicopter. It crested a nearby hill and then landed in the valley below. I followed the sound to find out what was happening. That's when I saw him again, the man who spoke to me at the lake, the man you call your uncle. He was lying unconscious on a stretcher the rescuers then placed into the helicopter. Once he was secured, the chopper lifted out of the valley and vanished over the trees heading toward the city.

"I needed to discover who he was, to find out what had happened to him and if he was alright. I hiked down the mountain and returned to the city as rapidly as I could. I figured they had taken him to the nearest hospital, Saint Anthony's. Once inside the hospital, I found myself using my newly enhanced senses, tracking him like an animal, roaming the halls of several floors until at last I found him in room 417.

"Because it was late, I had to sneak past the security guard, who apparently picked me up on one of his monitors. It was not long before he found me in your uncle's room and startled me by grabbing my arm. As he attempted to force me against my will, something inside me suddenly erupted. It was as big a shock to me as it was to him, but as the power of his grip cinched down on my arm, I experienced a sensation that felt like the sharp teeth of a steel trap cutting through my flesh all the way to the bone. Every cell of my body seemed to explode into a kind of rage that was not propelled by anger, but was fueled purely by an instinct for survival. The more the guard tried to restrain me, the more the rage engulfed me. I recall thinking how strange it felt to be filled with such a ferocious fire, and yet not wanting to actually hurt anyone. All I wanted to do was get free. The next thing I remembered was waking up in a locked room."

The professor looked down as though he were concerned about what I now thought of him and his story. Then he raised his eyes again with sort of a nervous smile and said, "I know that all of this sounds totally nuts, but. . . ."

"On the contrary!" I interrupted. "It not only sounds totally believable, but actually quite familiar as well."

He replied with what was now an inquisitive smile. "Really?"

"Well, let's just say, I'm still missing one sock and my wrist watch from the last time I was overcome by the deep need to growl."

This, of course, opened a whole new conversation about my own experience with the animal. As we drove to his house, I told him what had happened during my sojourn in the mountains, which now felt far less disturbing and somewhat less incriminating. It was comforting to know I was not the only fur-bearing lunatic in the city. It felt good to have found a comrade, someone who had stumbled onto the same path as I had. Perhaps I was not alone in this adventure after all.

14

The Blissmaker

Professor Talon's home was very much a replica of my own. A 1950's one-and-a-half stories, pretending-to-be-colonial house that was far too small for its original grandiose design and far too large for the lot on which it sat. Unlike my light green abode, his home wore a mock redwood color with teal trim on the windows and porch. The yard supported a substantial number of overgrown shrubs and trees that were probably planted when the house was built. An assortment of lavender and red petunias, along with other complacent annuals, completed this picture of a watercolor life. It was just what one would have expected for an underpaid yet overeducated college professor. But as Michael Talon turned the key in the front lock and pushed open the door, we were about to enter an abstract painting that no one could have expected.

A loud gasp, followed by the clatter of my comrade's keys dropping to the floor, sounded an alarm inside me that set my heart racing. As I peered over the professor's shoulder into the room, he spoke in a tone of unbridled horror, "Oh, my God, no."

The main room was a devastation of paper and debris blanketing the floor and antique furnishings. The bookcase wall that once held a library of literature was now barren, the books and other contents lying beneath it like a pile of discarded bones awaiting a communal grave. His large roll-top desk sat in shambles, stripped of its many drawers, its intricate compartments raped of their belongings. A computer and a telephone had somehow remained in place. The television, a stereo, and other equipment were untouched; this assault appeared to be motivated by pure maliciousness. The Professor took three steps into the rubble and slowly dropped to his knees. His head fell forward as his body collapsed into defeat.

"My God," I said. "Who could have done this . . . I mean, why?"

I waited in nervous silence for an answer, the long pause accentuating the suspense. The professor, with clear conviction, finally replied, "It's because of the book."

"What!" I said. "What book, what are you talking about?"

"I believe that they were looking for a book that I am writing."

"What could you have written that would have provoked this?"

"It's a long story," he said, "and a difficult one to tell."

"Did they find it. . . I mean did they take what you were writing?"

"No. It's right here." He said laughing slightly through his sadness and disdain. "It's all right here." Pointing to the disarray of pages surrounding him, he knelt helplessly as though in sorrowful prayer.

"I don't understand," I said. "If it's right here, why didn't they take it?"

"I don't think they were here to steal anything. I think they were trying to find out how much I actually know."

"Know about what?"

"Well . . . several months ago I received a package from Kathmandu, Nepal."

Right then I remembered the letter from my friend Clyde Henderson about Katherine's death. It was also from Kathmandu.

"Do you know someone who lives there?" I asked.

"No," he said. "I have never had any correspondence with anyone in that part of the world. Anyway . . . a note in the package was from someone by the name of Sharee—"

"That's her!" I shouted.

"That's who?"

"That's the woman who was in the elevator at the hospital.

That was the name on the card with the roses, and I believe it was *she* who brought them."

"You mean the woman who helped me escape?"

"Yes, at least I think so."

The professor scanned the room's literary rubble. "So this is what she was warning me about—that there may be people who don't want me to publish the information that she sent me in the package. This would seem to confirm that the information I was given—even though it is a bit hard to take in—is probably true. I mean if somebody is this nervous about it, nervous enough to be so destructive just to find out how much I know, well, no wonder she was warning me."

As the professor wandered off into his own silent contemplation, my own frustration provoked me to grab his attention.

"What the hell information are you talking about? What did this note say?"

"Well," he continued, "this person named Sharee, the one we are presuming is this same woman, sent me a large manila envelope. It contained a note from her as well as a letter, some current world event-type information, and what she called a journey. The journey is like a walk into one's own consciousness, sometimes past, sometimes present. In her note she said that I had been chosen by some spiritual guide, an elderly man by the name of Shankara who—"

"That's the name!" I blurted out. "The other name that was on the signature card of who was to receive the roses. That's the name that I assume referred to my uncle."

"Really. That *is* interesting. But how can it be the same man?"

"Perhaps it's not the same man but just the same name."

"That may be true, but then why did he call himself Iyokipiya when he spoke to me that night at the lake?"

"There was another incident with the maintenance woman where he referred to himself as Raha Muumba."

He paused for a second and then spoke as if to himself, "But why so many different names?" Addressing me again he asked, "Do you know what nationality she is, this maintenance woman?"

"Well, she's a Black woman, and I recall hearing her say that the name Raha Muumba might be Swahili or something."

At this the professor simply said *hmm*. His eyes started shifting back and forth as though mechanically connected to his brain, which was systematically chewing on this new information.

Far too impatient to wait for his superior brain to tick through the possibilities, I anxiously blurted out, "SO WHAT WAS IT?"

"What was what?"

"What were you chosen to do?"

"Oh," he muttered, stumbling back from his thoughts. "Well, I don't know if one would say I was actually chosen. I think it was really more a case of, I was afforded the opportunity."

He smiled a little, lightening the tension of the situation before he went on. "Anyway, the note from this woman Sharee said that the main letter and the rest of the information was from this fellow Shankara. He apparently had dictated it to her from his deathbed. In the letter, it was, let's say . . . suggested that I use the information to write a book. It was to be like a novel containing this information as well as stories and personal experiences of others that would somehow be dropped into my hands. These stories would also pertain to and help validate the information."

He briefly examined my questioning expression and then added, "Yes, it was all a bit strange when I first heard it too but—"

"No, no," I said, shaking my head, "please, go on."

"Well, the old man related that, although the essence of this information would best be written in the form of a novel, its contents and all of the events had to be true. They had to be occurrences that someone actually experienced in this dimension. Sort of like *the stories are true, but the names have been changed to protect the innocent.* The truth of these events would energize the book and allow it to be carried throughout the world, resonating at a very high frequency. He said that no matter how strange the events were or how unbelievable the story line got, because of the truth employed in its creation, people would feel the frequency and embrace it through their emotion. They would know that it was the truth, even though it had been presented as a work of fiction. Oddly enough—and I have no idea why—the book is to be titled *The Blissmaker*."

"Professor," I said, "this whole thing sounds pretty bizarre to me. I mean, an energized book resonating at a high frequency? What the hell is that?"

"We think it sounds bizarre, I know. But how does it make you feel, I mean deep down, purely from an emotional place?"

"Well, in light of all the outrageous things that have been happening to me, it feels very real. It feels like—"

"Like the raw truth?"

"Well, yes, strangely enough, I suppose it does, but—"

"I know, I felt the same way when I received the letter, and that is why I went ahead and started writing the book. As soon as I began to really look at it all, a cavalcade of interlocking events began, like my encounter with Iyokipiya at the lake, and my incredible experience with the wolf. Not to mention our spontaneous meeting during the great hospital escape, and well . . . all of this that has just happened." He gestured at the room around us. "I mean somebody is pretty concerned about what I have been told or what I might put into print."

"But how does any of this warrant demolishing your house to find what you might have written?"

"I'm concerned that it's because of the information I was given. Remember, I told you that in the letter there was some very convincing evidence about world events."

"Yes."

"You see, most of this information would be very disruptive to the system, you know, social, government, medical . . . those kinds of systems, as well as a whole slew of religious traditions."

"But what exactly?"

"For instance, it told about some kind of secret world alliance that controlled the financial markets by controlling most of the money, or gold, as the case may be. It also talked about how this regime would promote the use of plastic currency like credit cards or debit cards so they could know just how much money people had and what they used it for. In time they would actually do away with all currency along with much of our freedom. There was even something about eventually inserting some sort of computer chip under people's skin so they could keep track of everyone and know where they were and what they were up to. The goal of this world alliance is to have complete control over the whole society with the ability to regulate everything. This would include monitoring populations and basically choosing who would live and who would not. It said that they have gained a strong foothold in our own United States government through certain high ranking members of the Republican party, and that they actually lost some of that control when a Democrat became president. He likewise warned about dynasties emerging within the office of our presidency.

"The letter also described how certain diseases, such as plagues that destroy the immune system, were not evolutionary quirks, but actual viruses created by an offshoot of this world alliance. They were developed in a laboratory for the purpose of diminishing the population. Unfortunately, their strategy was flawed because the viruses started mutating, infecting everyone. Many religious prophecies refer to a time when undiscovered plagues would ravage the planet. This apparently is what they were talking about. There was also something about how this same organization already had made major advances towards the cure for diseases like cancer, and yet they were keeping them hidden from the public for political and financial reasons, or perhaps for more population control."

I just stood there lost, my mind staggering around in all of the information. The professor, oblivious to my bewilderment, continued.

"The letter also described how during this period, the Earth would become very unstable with earthquakes, hurricanes, and a myriad of natural disasters occurring literally on a daily basis. This activity would be the planet's way of cleansing itself of all the destruction, war, and pollution of humankind to restore the natural balance. Eventually it would be just as the Bible predicts:

that the meek would inherit the Earth, the meek simply being the people in alignment with nature. These would also be the people who would know to leave the cities and move out on the land, storing food and other provisions for the pending disasters. The result of this great cleansing by the Earth would usher in a new era with a much higher state of consciousness, one that no longer focused on competition, power, greed, and other ego-based realities.

"There was also information about UFO cover-ups and communication with extraterrestrial beings. The book is not only to be written to teach people the truth about many of these things, but also to show them how to evolve beyond the kind of unconsciousness behavior that has caused our planet to be in such peril. Perhaps it's also to give them some warning of what's yet to come.

"In his letter, Shankara described how the consciousness of people in general has fallen into a kind of sleep, a comatose state where whole civilizations now slumber in what he called *the fall of integrity*. He said it is like a disease cultivated by altering the truth repeatedly, but only to a small degree. Like a snowball down a mountain, the convenience of one lie begets another, one person or generation passing on altered interpretations to the next, until finally the actual truth has been buried and forgotten.

"He wrote that we live in an ocean of illusions supported and perpetuated by people's fear for survival, of their desperate need to get ahead of someone else, to have more belongings, or to be more powerful. Many of these acts are done *in the name of truth*, or worse yet, *in the name of God*. That is, according to their own prescribed beliefs, whether the act was imbued with integrity or not."

"But don't you think that most of these people have only the best of intentions?"

"Shankara refers to this phenomenon as *the fall of integrity*, not because all of the people caught in this perpetually altered flow have bad or malicious intentions. In fact, he says that, as individuals, they're not even wrong, that the majority of them are good and profound spiritual beings willing to die for their beliefs.

The problem is that they have allowed themselves to become followers, to be controlled by rules that have long since wandered from the truth. He describes *the fall of integrity* as the fall of people's ability to feel, to reason for themselves their highest good as individuals or as a collective."

"But I believe that there are a lot of people, even within the media, who make great strides towards uncovering the truth about the world and about these kinds of social delusions. Don't you think that if you write that sort of thing they, as well as others, will personally take offense?"

"Only if it applies," he said. "Those who are a part of the solution and not part of the problem will surely empathize and agree. Perhaps they may even have some intuitive reaction and be motivated to do something about how it makes them feel. I believe that the ultimate truth about our lives as individuals comes from what we feel and not what we think. What we feel is instinctual. Most of what we think, we have been taught. If these words take a poke at someone's ego or cause them offense, then perhaps it will also provoke them to take a look at the system of rules they have been following instead of their own spirit."

"But how can you be so sure that all of what this Shankara has said is the truth? Especially on issues that have long been questioned and surrounded by controversy?"

"Don't you see, that's just the point. In his letter, he didn't ask me to believe him. He asked me to reason his words and to explore them for myself, through my own inner journeys. That way, when I do arrive at some truth about all of this information it will be something I know as my own experience—not what someone else has told me or how I have been brainwashed by the media, or some religion, or worse yet, some *popular conclusion* absorbed simply because I didn't have the gumption to experience and reason it out for myself. The journey that he sent with this letter is a good example. It's sort of a walk into one's own consciousness in order to gain a more experiential understanding of a situation. That's also why he suggested that I put all of this into the form of a story so that it would be more of an experience rather than just another sensationalized spiritual news bulletin."

Shuffling through a few pages of what looked like a letter, he then began to read. "In his message Shankara said, *Do not grab on to my words as though they are the unwavering truth. Test my truth in every way that you can, in every moment of the day. Follow not my ramblings the way that you have for eons followed the propaganda of other men. Follow only yourself into the truth that you find. Trust what you feel far and above what you think, for the mind will betray you in its desire to be a follower, while the soul and your feelings will forever propel you into the truth of your being.*"

My mind seemed to be questioning everything that I was hearing. It also seemed quite disturbed . . . disturbed, that is, as though it had been rescued out of a lifetime of complacent stumbling. Before I could form any conclusion about my once again ruffled existence, the professor continued.

"Jared, just stop for a minute and reason the circumstances. Here we have this very elderly man by the name of Shankara, a total stranger, who from his deathbed spontaneously sent me a package with all of this information. He encouraged me to be on a journey to find the truth and write a book about what I found, despite the fact that I have never written a book before. He wrote to me about some of the more political and controversial issues of our times, even though he probably lived in some monastery and had never been out of the country. I mean, you have to admit, he probably didn't watch afternoon talk shows or read *The New York Times*, and yet he talked about this information as if he were giving me his personal memoirs.

"Not only that, but almost *all* of it was written in a very poetic, very esoteric style that placed no more emphasis on political corruption than on the behavior of a butterfly. To him, it was as though one were no greater or lesser than the other. It was all just the truth. His sole reason for writing to me and giving me this information was because one afternoon he heard me shouting into the wind like some crazed lunatic about how distraught I was with the world and how confused I found myself to be in it. He said he heard me cry out for the truth, and so he wrote and gave me what he knew of it."

The professor stopped and chuckled at his own words. Then he commented, "The incredibly unnerving part of this whole thing is that I actually *did* that one day. I mean, I shouted at the sky as though someone were really going to answer. I know it sounds totally nuts, but it's exactly what happened."

"But how does any of this warrant demolishing your house? These are issues that people question and dialogue about everyday. And although its true that some of these conclusions are somewhat disruptive in light of popular beliefs, I still don't see what it is that you know or might write about that would be so disturbing, or revealing for that matter."

Then there was a brief pause in our conversation, one of those very long brief pauses that lets you know that you may have only heard part of the story and that, perhaps, you may never hear the rest. I watched the professor ponder whether he should go on with his explanation or stop and take advantage of this lull forever.

Finally, he turned to me with a rather shy and nervous expression. "Well," he said, "there was one other thing."

Slowly, I felt a great uneasiness creep up from behind me as though, in light of all I had already heard, maybe, just maybe, I didn't want to hear about that one other thing.

15

The Enlightened One

As the professor began to reveal his final disclosure, I could sense the caution in his voice. He was now being forced to trust me with what he was about to say. I knew this kind of voice for it had recently been my own. I could quite easily recall an earlier conversation with myself about how I would explain what had happened to me on the mountain with the animal or the coincidental events that followed. Revealing a small piece of my smile, I connected my thoughts with his doubting eyes, hoping to say without words, I *know, I know. It's alright, go on.* Slowly, his demeanor softened as he entrusted me with the rest of his story.

"In the letter," he said, "Shankara made several references to this period of Earth changes that would affect not only the terrain and weather of the planet but also the consciousness of its people. It would be the fulfillment of a thousand prophecies from a wide spectrum of spiritual beliefs and manuscripts, ranging from Egyptian hieroglyphics and Hopi prophecies to the Book of Revelations in the Bible. All of the prophecies would be correct, more or less, in their basic premises, even though many would still disagree on how the changes would occur and perhaps for what reason. In fact, he said that some would never witness the true splendor of this global event because of their ongoing confrontations about whose God was the real God or whose interpretation was right.

"Many of these prophecies tell of a divine energy, a profound being who would come in conjunction with this planetary shift. The most popular interpretation of this event is the second coming of Jesus. Interestingly enough, in his letter Shankara refers to this *expected one* as 'the Buddha, the Christ, the Enlightened One.' He conveyed that this being has already been born and now lives among us, walking around just like you or me. He said that for all of this lifetime this one has been totally unaware that he or she is indeed the one."

He went on. "After I heard all of these terms referring to this one person, I looked them up in their respective native languages. In a literary sense the name Christ was not anyone's specific name, but was actually a title given to a man named Jesus, or more historically, Yeshua Ben Joseph. It was believed, and still is by many, that after his death he ascended and illuminated his body.

"The term Buddha was likewise a title given to a man by the name of Siddhartha who was said to have mastered the human experience, changing his body back into light, becoming one with the flow of the Creator. He was not known as Buddha until after his supposed death. It is generally accepted that both Jesus and Buddha enlightened in their human lifetimes and evolved into a greater understanding of God or the Infinite. In Shankara's reference to these names, he implied there may also have been other such titles in other cultures, all referring to the same kind of event or enlightenment. He described this phenomenon as though it had occurred to a variety of people throughout human history who unexpectedly became aware of their true destiny. He implied that the very same thing is happening right—"

"Now wait, wait, wait," I said, stuttering nervously. "Wait just a minute. If you're about to tell me that my uncle just woke up last week from a day of fishing and discovered that he is the second coming of Christ, or Buddha, or whoever, then I'm—"

"No, no," he interrupted, "that's really not it exactly, although I suppose it's possible. I mean, in the world of truth, anything's possible. Actually, I get a stronger feeling that your uncle, (or whoever) is more of a guide, or mentor to this Christ, this Buddha.

Sort of like Merlin was to King Arthur; someone who is here to assist this one in the same manner that I was assisted when Iyokipiya and I spoke out in the wilderness. Shankara said that at first I wouldn't recognize this chosen one, but soon after our meeting I would begin to see signs, drastic events guiding this one into the awareness of who he or she truly is. He made it sound like it could be just about anybody, even you, or me . . . or maybe that woman Sharee, or perhaps some celebrity or other public figure. He said that before I was finished writing the book I would know exactly who it was and be able to reveal the name publicly in the writing."

Without hesitation he went on. "He also said that as always there would be people and elements of a dark nature who would try to destroy this person, and there would be several attempts made on this one's life before he or she were aware of such a divine heritage. Some of these occurrences might appear as accidents, even though they would actually be the polarity of the dark side drawing the incident to the chosen one's higher nature. In other words, the lightness of their spirit might attract disruptive energies that would naturally be pulled to the encounter to be neutralized or healed by the event."

For several seconds the professor waited, leaving me a space in which to grope helplessly and contemplate all he had said. The thought of my uncle, or perhaps someone who possessed him, as the savior to the planet, or even mentor to such a chosen one, was difficult enough to fathom, let alone the prospect of God calling down to me (or some other floundering human) to say, "Oh, by the way, if you haven't figured it out by now, you're the second coming of—" The thought was simply mortifying. I'm sure that the Supreme Being who started all of this has a great sense of humor, but this would be taking it just a little too far.

In addition, after the professor mentioned the accidental attempts on this chosen one's life, I was reminded about that short fellow (the Village Idiot) who was knocked into a coma by Jessica Williams, the TV evangelist. Now *that* was a comforting thought. A four-foot-tall enlightened one giving his messages throughout the world from atop of parked cars. Not to overlook (mind you) that my uncle, the presumed mentor, *did* wake him from a coma and guide him off to who knows where.

And what about the TV evangelist, who *is* after all a celebrity and public figure. She was already in a perfect position to be some sort of savior. She was also involved in that accident, which may very well have propelled her into some drastic changes, provoking some new spiritual awareness in her own life. Maybe *she* is the enlightened one. Not to mention my uncle's accidental fall, as well as my own brush with death when I slid off the rock face and was nearly skewered by a pine tree. Slapping myself repeatedly on the side of the face, I chanted over and over as I shook my head, "*No* no *no* no *no* no *no.*"

My thoughts having stumbled into an obscure reality of their own (and the professor now watching me, as I stared off into space), I attempted to put my brain into reverse and return to some recognizable form of dialogue.

"So, Professor, who do you think ransacked your house?"

"Actually I'm not sure, but I believe it occurred because of a meeting I had with some men just a few days ago. I had spoken briefly about the letter to a colleague of mine at the university. He's not really a close acquaintance, but he is an expert on government and world economics, which is what he teaches. I wanted to see his reaction to some of this information. At the time he just sort of scoffed at it, but then about a week later he said he'd encountered some people who were very interested. In fact, they wanted to set up a meeting where they could talk to me about it at length. He insisted that the meeting take place at my house for privacy, and he was very vague as to from where these people had originated.

"Three days ago, he and two other men met with me here. From the moment they entered my house I had an uneasy feeling. It really put me on my guard, so I shared only smatterings of what they had already heard from my colleague. I also added some nonsense, hoping to steer them off course.

"Apparently my deception didn't work, because I suspect that they are the ones who broke into the house. I took the page with the information about the World Alliance and this enlightened one with me to the mountains. I didn't feel comfortable just leaving it lie around."

"So are you saying that all of that information is true?"

"The correlations between the information and our present day situation made it all seem not only quite possible but even probable. And after this plundering of my house . . . well, yes, I'm starting to believe that this most definitely is true."

I thought about this and then asked, "And what about what this Shankara told you, I mean that part about the Earth and how there was such a strong warning for people to be in alignment with the planet and nature. It sounded so doom and gloom. Like the world was going to end tomorrow. Do you really think that we're in that much trouble?"

"Let me tell you what happened to me about a month ago. I attended an environmental conference that brought together a variety of scientists and environmentalists from all over the world. It was hoped that by uniting them, sort of joining their common wisdom, that the outcome might draw some needed attention to the problem, giving a little jolt to the governments of all nations, as well as informing the general public of just how bad the situation on the planet really is."

"So just how bad is it?"

"Well, while I was at the conference I heard a lot of different people speak, but there were two men in particular who had a profound impact on me. It was not only what they said but how they said it, as though a few rays of raw truth streamed out of a gray fog of technical monologues.

"One was a young oceanographer who specialized in ecological studies. After several minutes of relaying his collection of microbiological data, he summed up his speech by blatantly announcing, 'The bottom line is that, approximately 70% of the ocean floor, which produces the same percentage of the planet's food chain, is dead.' A somewhat generic murmur seemed to travel throughout the room as though he had simply announced that lunch was going to be served a half hour later. Then, to everyone's astonishment, he lifted the microphone from its holder and slowly pushed the podium off the stage sending it crashing onto the main floor. The entire room promptly came to life with nervous jitters and disbelief. He then politely said thank you, gently laid the microphone on the stage floor, and calmly walked out of the room. I'll never forget it.

"The other speaker was more of an unexpected guest who came all the way from the Amazon Rainforest. He was introduced as the *Curandero*, or shaman of his people. He stood about five foot tall with straight black hair and dark olive skin. Clothed in his native dress, he spoke through an interpreter, although his intense expression and manner of speech left little doubt about his message.

"This shaman said he belonged to one of a very large family of nations that had once inhabited the Rainforest, a land where the trees were many generations elder to the humans who walked beneath them. Since the beginning of time his ancestors, his children, and his children's children, had been called The Keepers of the Air. They were the people who had watched over and lived among the great Rainforest trees that provided the wind—that is the oxygen—for the Earth and all of its inhabitants to breathe. Now, he said, much of the Rainforest is gone, either burned or destroyed by what he called *the peoples of profit*, and many of the tribes have been forced out of the Rainforest with thousands dying, whole generations being destroyed by foreign diseases.

"The shaman's last words were spoken first without translation, his interpreter caught up in his own emotions. Finally, from a shaking voice the translation came, and as close as I can remember, he said,

I have not come to ask you to save my children. My children are dead, and my family is gone. My people and all of their generations shall sing no more. I have come to ask you to save your children, for without the forests that give breath to the Earth, it is your children who will die next. The wind is a gift from the lungs of the Creator and no amount of gold or profit will create such a gift again.

"I remember being so moved by what he had said, that he'd traveled such a long way with his plea for the children of other nations, knowing that his own children were gone forever. Something in me changed that day, some part of me that was once numb and sedate began to curdle, festering an uneasiness, a restlessness that could find no peace, no satisfaction. It was a melancholy unlike any I had ever known; his words hung about me like a mesh of cobwebs, smothering me with hopelessness about a world beyond repair.

"It was not until the morning I received the letter from Kathmandu that I found some reprieve and peace of mind. That morning life seemed to shift into fast forward motion. I'm sure that much of it had to do with the content of the letter, but there was also something more, some internal fury that even now I am unable to describe."

The professor handed me the few surviving pages of the letter, the delicate paper now in my large awkward hands.

"Here, read it for yourself," he said. "In fact, take it out to the back porch where there is more light. I'm going to see if the computer still works and look up these names that your uncle has collected. If I can link up with some language libraries on the Internet, I might be able to find out how Shankara, Iyokipiya, and Raha Muumba translate and where they originate."

I took the pages and found my way out to the back porch, which was like a greenhouse where several happy and very healthy plants resided. I planted myself in a wicker chair and prepared for the information. I longed for some clarity about the recent events in my life, including why I was now about to wade into this pond of prophecies once again.

16

Ancient River

The word Tuesday had been written in the margin as though the letter were a diary or perhaps a series of messages dictated at different intervals for someone else to compile later. The number 3 appeared in the top corner of the page. Midstream, I stepped in and read the professor's private letter from the persona, the enigma, named Shankara.

> . . . it is not for you to believe that you have been chosen to write a book because of some mysterious prophesy, some pending destiny that now must be fulfilled. It is *you* who have indeed chosen yourself because of a desire and a passion for the truth.
>
> I write you this letter because in your own thoughts and words you have reached out for the truth. Within the last of your seasons you have called out to the wind, with the whys and the wherefores of a despondent world. Laying aside your ego's desires, you have searched for the answers, with a hope and a prayer for a play-of-possibilities that perhaps could arise. I, I am a madman who plays in the wind and it was there that I heard your cry for the truth.
>
> And so I have penned through these cumbersome words all that I know of the truth in this world, with

parables of governments, politics, and strife, with the plagues and corruption, of a wounded world. I've woven tales of tomorrows, of beginnings and ends, and of a balance and harmony that once governed that world; a place where magic and wonder now play as myths in the hearts and souls of the imaginaries.

Life after life you have returned to this dimension to try again and remember. Caught up in the adventures of your revolving dramas, most of you follow the trail of your own limitations. You wander lost through a reality known to the spiritual realm as the Gray World, a world of fear and judgment, competition and control, a place where the human ego is worshiped.

In the Gray World your heroes are the peddlers of violence; your gurus are the peddlers of the evening news. Your saints are the myths of the movie screen, and your God is a box called the television. In the Gray World you kneel to the social order and dance to a calliope of advertisements. And that which is outside this programmed world, that which is the mystery, the essence of your spirit, is rebuked and called an illusion.

In truth, my friend, there is but one illusion, a time and a place called the Gray World, where you the immortal spirits now lie in slumber, longing to awaken and remember.

For eons it has been prophesied, in all of your cultures, that there would come an era when the chaos and darkness of such an age would find you in Armageddon. Today, you now live in the early days, in the throes of such an epoch, for your Earth can no longer survive the abuse of an ego-based humanity. For thousands of years darkness has reigned on this planet, propelled by competition, control, greed, and fear, but now comes a time when this polarity will shift and light will come into power.

Change will become the word of the day as the Earth begins to cleanse itself of all the neglect, the rape, and the pollution that has destroyed the natural order. Like a desperate mother protecting her young, the Earth will do whatever is necessary to cleanse this world of its destructive ways and restore the sacred balance. Wind and rain and the purity of fire will become the tools of change, to shape and rebuild the fragile shell that once covered the blue-green planet.

Earthquakes, hurricanes, fires, and floods will become common occurrences, and all of the inhabitants who trod this plane will be brought into this awareness. Your weather will spin in erratic turns, and your seasons will change their cycles. And all will be lifted into a higher vibration through a very arduous birthing.

During this period, all of humanity will feel a great acceleration where every life of every being will find its journey amplified. At this time, the forces of a darker side will spawn a decade of tyrants, while elements of a lighter side will birth an Age of Spirit. Every soul will find its way to one side or the other, and the polarity of these opposing sides will become your Armageddon. Across the globe every bastard king, every warlord of this planet, will rally in their holy war and spend their final hour. Death, disease, and an array of disasters will dominate your headlines, and living for a brighter day will become your one desire. You are among the progressive souls who will walk into the future, and that is why you have come to ask for the truth and all its wonder.

As for me, I am but words to be scribbled on a page, the rhythm of a poem, the chant of a song. I am an old, old man in the winter of my life, savoring only a breath and a glimpse of the sky before I begin, and journey again, and walk again past the shadow of my life.

Such is the cycle that you have also lived—birthing yourself again and again, dreaming again, trying so hard to remember. But for lifetimes here, you have been caught on a wheel reliving every fear, with complacency as your daily bread and slumber as your ally. The Gray World has hardened the flow of your life. Like a column of stone you've become a monument to a history of sordid beliefs.

Even now you can imagine
the features of your own solemn face,
etched in a rock on the side of the cliff,
your soul yearning to fly down to the ancient river below,
        that bends and turns on into forever.

From this rocky perch,
you watch as a hawk takes flight.
It free falls into the depths of a beautiful gorge.
Bowing to its descent, it catches the air currents.
Effortlessly, it glides into the wind, leaving you imprisoned
within the wall of stone that has completely entombed you.
You contemplate the hours, the days, the years,
all of the choices that have brought you to this hard reality.

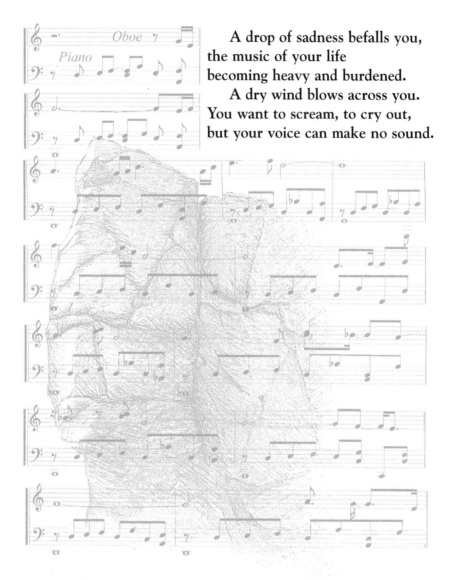

A drop of sadness befalls you,
the music of your life
becoming heavy and burdened.
A dry wind blows across you.
You want to scream, to cry out,
but your voice can make no sound.

Unable to move, you are hardened in the clay of your life.
All of sorrow is trapped inside you, inside your shroud of stone.
You reach for tears to relieve the pain,
but none can seem to find their way
through the statue that's become you.
You surrender to the helplessness that patiently awaits you
and cast your eyes out toward the vast canyon.

Then, from within you,
from where you know not,
comes a silent simple voice,
so familiar . . . so forgotten.
It lifts from inside you,
from somewhere beyond you,
and you allow it to speak
the words you cannot.

Great spirit.
Sweet life that flows through each and every living thing.
Find me inside this massive stone.
Renew the life force that once flowed through me.
Tell me again how to walk without boundaries,
how to dance for no reason, how to sing unbridled.
Show me how to fly beyond the grasp of my mind,
that rallies to tell me *I cannot . . . I cannot.*

Slowly, you watch as the breath of your words
becomes sparkles of dust carried off by the wind.
The silent vibrations fall into the canyon's shell and disperse.

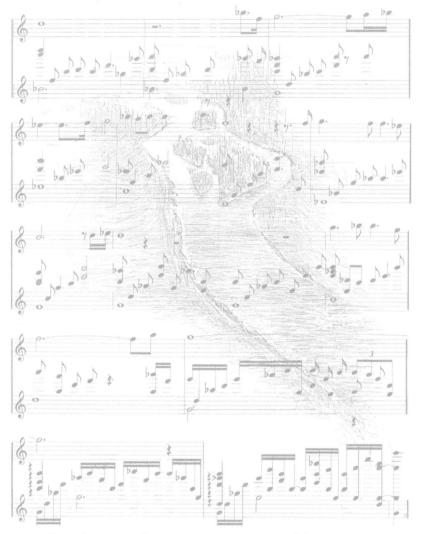

Somehow you know your presence is felt.
Your words have been heard by the ongoing life below you.
The birds, they pause. The grasses wait to bend,
and the ancient river below turns in your direction.

Then there is a trickle, the slightest sounds of water.
You hear it from behind you . . . perhaps from above you.
At first it's illusive, as a memory outside you,
but it finds an open crack . . . it finds a way inside you.
You feel the liquid seeping down, into every painful crevice.
Pouring over every edge, it's a waterfall above you.

Your shell begins to break apart. Your statue starts to waken.
With water splashing all around, crashing down through you.
You know the fall is coming as you hang on to the edge.
You surrender to the water and let go!

You fall like a stone, even faster than the water,
knowing you must fly now or crash into the canyon.
You twist and you turn, trying to be born
into the form of a great winged bird.
You stretch with your spine and reach out with your arms.
Arch your back now and spread into your wings.

The raging wind catches you,
pushing you out away from the stream of the water.
Without effort you glide upon the air currents.
You feel yourself resting on the wind.

You soar along the edges of the canyon's ravine,
just above the mirror of the
winding ancient river.
You ride above the water.
Freedom's become you
as you see yourself
reflected in the water's
window pane.

Classical guitar

The wind from your wings creates
ripples on the river, crystal trails
that go in each and all directions.
You follow these tiny streams
of water with your eyes.
First there and then there,
and then there . . . and there. . . .

. . . I had never noticed before how unevenly water makes its
way down a glass pane. It bends and turns and, seemingly for no
reason at all, creates icicle-like patterns of every design. Yet unlike
such frozen shapes, these clear trails of rain, which now glazed

this window, were alive, resembling a trillion small rivers. The blurring shades of greens and blues, making a watercolor mural that encased the professor's porch, disguised the shapes that had once been trees and sky, clear and distinct before the afternoon rain.

To my surprise, a steady downpour had begun, completely slipping past me while I had been lost in the reading of the letter. It now streamed down the surrounding glass making me drowsy and content, and a bit out of touch. How long I had been staring out through this veil of water I could not be sure, for the sky had grown dark covering all signs of daylight. I felt dazed by the letter and the journey I had read, unsure of how I was to react or where I was to have ended up. I stretched to rouse and collect myself before I left the porch and entered the main house.

Inside, the professor had apparently been busy for quite some time, picking up most of the books and papers that had blanketed the floor. "So you're back," he said, as though perhaps he was aware that I might have dozed off during my absence.

"Yes . . . I guess so," I mumbled, still trying to clear the hoarseness from my throat.

"So what did you think about the letter?" he asked.

"Well, I have to admit that this Shankara fellow does have a strong way with words, and those words do seem to go just about anywhere. I think what impressed me the most though was that story, or journey I guess you called it. I never thought that reading could be so mesmerizing. When he talked about breaking away from the cliff and free falling into the flight of a bird, it was so tangible, so vivid."

"What?"

"The journey," I said. "You know, where you take flight and soar along the winding river."

Another moment of silence, only this time his eyes smiled.

"Well, Jared," he said, "that's quite fascinating, especially since when I handed you the letter I didn't give you the pages with the journey. I found them here on the floor just a few minutes ago. He picked up several pieces of paper from the desk, put them into

164

a nice neat pile, and handed it to me with a wry smile.

Taking the pages, I said pitifully, "Oh no. Don't tell me it's happened again." I gripped a large handful of my hair and whined in protest. "How in the world does he do that?"

"How does he do what?"

"How does he get his voice inside my head?"

The professor, trying to suppress a grin, attempted to explain.

"If you mean on a scientific level," (which of course was not at all what I meant), "I believe that when someone, like you for instance, reads or experiences something that radically stirs your emotions and imagination, it's possible for your mind to spark an opening, causing dormant brain cells to awaken and start functioning—you know, that two thirds of our brain that scientists say we never use. If our passions are invoked to consciously reach for some dream-able expression, the reality of an imagined concept, then our brain, in an attempt to satisfy the desire, opens to receive more possibilities."

Spellbound by his explanation, I muttered under my breath. "Ya don't say."

"Yes," he quickly answered, his excitement building. "For instance, just a short while ago you were reading this letter from Shankara." He took the pages of the letter from my hand. "On this last page you read the first few lines of the journey that *I* received, but you were missing the rest of the story. Yet while you were reading you became so engrossed in the experience, that it triggered your pituitary gland to secrete a hormone flow thereby activating some dormant portion of the brain. You were able to turn on higher brain functions because, on an energy level, you were feeling and experiencing something for which your memory had no linear or mental data. There was no way to satisfy the need, to satisfy your desire to know. Therefore, your brain activated new cells to explore what it had never encountered before."

"You mean, I wanted to go on that particular journey, so through my desire my imagination took over and created some kind of an ending while I sort of fell asleep?"

"No, that's not at all what I mean. Your imagination is just a spark, the catalyst in the process. I believe that the experience you just had was very real. And wouldn't you agree that you were also not alone?"

"Well, yes, I guess—"

"You see, Jared, I believe that we all can travel and explore far beyond our physical reality. Through utilizing our imagination, we can perhaps convince our programmed mind to embrace something just beyond its learned knowledge. Sort of blowing open the door into a higher state of consciousness. Then, through pure feeling, and a sensitized use of breath to oxygenate those newly awakened brain cells, we can experience a whole different reality. This new perception may involve an enlightened being like this Shankara, who can communicate to us directly when we are open to receiving it. So there's no need to panic my friend, it has happened to the best of us."

"You mean this has happened to you?"

"Well, not exactly in the way that it seems to happen to you, but lately I *have* been known to lose track of a little time and space while chatting with the wind."

I tried to laugh through my frustration and confusion, knowing full well that there was nothing else to do but stumble along. Reaching for even more, I asked, "So, you think that what I just experienced with this Shankara was his communication to me through a higher brain function, even though he just happens to be dead."

"No. I'm quite certain that just because Shankara no longer has a human body of his own has no bearing on how well he communicates to you through unlimited thought."

I stood there puzzled by his answer, then I continued questioning.

"So what about my uncle? Could this same thing be happening to him? Is he talking and acting so strangely because this Shankara is communicating to him? Or is he actually possessed by this voice? I mean, is this like that bizarre channeling stuff I've heard so much about?"

"Well, if *that stuff* you're referring to was something that you simply *heard so much about* (which probably came through the media or some challenged religion), then it's also probably something that somebody wanted you to think, even though you, as well as they, likely had little or no real experience of the matter. I would strongly suggest, Jared, particularly in this area, that you trust only what you experience, not what you have been told or read about in some overdramatized analysis. Spiritual understandings, based on people's very pointed and subjective opinions (which are then graciously peddled to the public), are how paper religions and their dogma are born and breed. Follow your own feeling through what you find, and you will always be guided into higher understandings, especially about spiritual matters."

Dissatisfied with his response, I argued, "But I believe that there are many religions that promote a lot of good, ones that create fine communities and give aid to a wide variety of people."

"That's absolutely true," he said. "Indeed there are. There are also a lot of others that would gladly pluck out any and all of your newly-found feathers if they heard even a single notion about this very natural and innocent experience you just shared with me regarding your acclaimed flight over the river. Jared, trust me on this one."

I felt stunned, imagining all too clearly a vision of myself, fully plucked, standing knee deep in the down of my own plumage. As big a chicken as I was (especially when it came to exploring my own spirituality), I knew that in the future I had to proceed with great caution and devout discretion.

"Jared," he added, "I'm not talking about people's good intentions or right actions. I'm talking about all of the judgment and dysfunction that may be attached to it, thereby fueling the illusion that any culture or religion is superior to another."

The professor then sat down at his computer.

"Give your mind a break from that for a minute and take a look at this," he said. "I think you might find it to be quite interesting as well."

My mind readily shaking off all images of molting poultry, I looked into the computer screen hoping to focus on something more linear and less fowl. Staring into the blue glow of the monitor, the professor began to explain.

"Through the Internet I was able to contact several different language libraries that gave me definitions for each of the names your uncle has apparently been using. I entered the name Raha Muumba in the Swahili dictionary. It came back with *Raha* meaning joyful, or blissful, and *Muumba* as maker.

"In Lakota, my Native American dialect, the name Iyokipiya translates as one who makes happiness.

"When I entered the name Shankara in a Sanskrit dictionary, I got a direct translation. It simply said *The Blissmaker.*"

A kind of clarity seemed to capture the next moment as though we had stumbled across a fine jewel, a gem strategically left by someone for us to find.

The professor interrupted the silence. "A lot of other information appeared with the name Shankara. It gave references to a half a dozen men who had used that same name. Most of them lived out their lives in the regions of India and Nepal, somewhere between the first and the tenth centuries. A couple of them are described as members of a holy order, and that name, Shankara, was part of a hereditary line or lineage.

"One of these men, who was called Sri Shankara, was apparently quite a scholar and well known for his compositions about Vedic wisdom and its traditions. I actually found several of his writings, as well as a few stories others had written about him. There was one in particular that I thought you might find very interesting.

"The story described him as a holy man, a teacher or guru who had several students in his charge. They lived in what was called an ashram, sort of like a monastery, I presume. It tells how, at that time in his life, this Shankara had attained the ability to place his body into a meditative state, which allowed him to lift his spirit, his soul, from his body and travel to other places. It said that, while this was happening, his physical form remained dormant in a kind of sacred posture until he returned.

"One day he was challenged by one of his students about comments he had made in regard to mastering the human experience. He had talked about overcoming certain physical and material desires that might conflict with one's spiritual path. The students confronted him, wanting to know why it was that he was such an expert on mastering such desires when he had spent his entire life within the boundaries of a sacred and cloistered environment.

"He apparently accepted the students' challenge and agreed that he should go and explore the material world. He said he would indulge in it for several months and then return to discuss what he had found.

"As it was in those times, there happened to be a wealthy king in a nearby land who was dying. Sri Shankara, taking advantage of the opportunity, decided to put his own body into this dormant meditative state for a period of time, lifting his soul out of his own physical form and placing it into the body of the king at the moment of death."

"What?" I protested in total disbelief.

"I know, Jared, it sounds pretty crazy, but to tell you the truth, I have heard stories about similar incidents in other cultures where spiritual beings have stepped into people's bodies when they died. Sometimes they are referred to as Walk-Ins. This doesn't mean that it's something dark like being possessed. It is more like an exchange that was prearranged by both parties to serve a higher good.

"Anyway, as the story goes, this Shankara was able to temporarily rejuvenate the body of the king and use it to explore material desires. So he began the experience of living in a grand palace with an abundance of great food, fine wines, and beautiful women. Since he was surrounded by everything a man could ever want, he was able to fully indulge in all of the delicacies of the human experience and to find his answers.

"However, after several months of partaking in this lifestyle, he became so engrossed in this material world, that he started to forget who he actually was and why he was there.

"It's like what Shankara has said about all of us, that we came to explore the physical world, and in the process got so lost in the adventure that we fell asleep in our consciousness, forgetting who we are and why we came."

Not really knowing what to think of all of this, I asked, "So what happened to this Sri Shankara?"

"Well, long after he should have returned, his students finally started searching for him. One day they heard about a dying king who had a miraculous recovery. Figuring out what had happened, one of the students decided to go to this king. He requested an audience with him masquerading as a poet or singer. When he was allowed to perform, he sang a story about a holy man, a teacher, who had taken the journey into the density of the human experience and fell into a slumber there, never to return.

"At hearing the story, Sri Shankara remembered who he was and why he had come. He then lifted his soul from the body allowing the king to die as had been anticipated. He returned to his own body and to the teaching of his students."

The professor waited for a response. Then in an attempt to pry a reaction from me, he said, "So, Jared. Pretty amazing story, don't you think?"

"To tell you the truth," I answered, "I don't know what to think. But I do wonder about my uncle. If this is what is now happening to him, then does that also mean that after Shankara is done here, he will leave and Uncle Ben will just die? I mean, that's what the doctors told me in the hospital, that it was unlikely that he would come out of the coma, at least of his own will. Maybe he is already gone."

"I don't know, Jared. I just don't know."

I felt a wave of grief thinking that this was what may have happened to my uncle. The professor, seeing my uneasiness, pulled at my attention, "Jared, things may not be as out of control as they appear. There are no accidents in this life. Everything happens for a reason, perhaps exactly the way it was intended. That includes everything from the journey you just experienced to my running across this story."

Feeling totally bewildered, I looked down and began a thorough examination of the tops of my shoes—as the professor, of course, continued on.

"You on the other hand, have probably been out of the flow of your own truth, living an adventure that someone chose for you and not what you truly wanted. More than likely, you've been plodding along in a very programmed life, surrounded by a very programmed world that left you empty, frustrated, and asking yourself, Is this really all there is to the human experience?

"What you are experiencing now is not necessarily distorted and out of balance. On the contrary, it's the world that is, in and of itself, distorted and out of balance. Perhaps today, you have simply climbed off the wheel in order to find out what happened to the passion. What happened to the truth? To ask the same question that a lot of people are asking these days, Is this really all there is?

"Several years ago the same thing happened to me. I found myself surrounded by a socially ordered life of—buy and sell—got to get ahead—keep up with the latest fad or you'll have to double your dose of Prozac. I finally had to stop and say, Wait a minute! This planet is suffering and falling apart. Which is only recognized as a problem when it's not interfering with somebody's selfish desire to make an even bigger profit. It just wasn't enough anymore to have my material needs satisfied by another trip to the strip mall to scavenge after some bargain sale, where prices are slashed—hurry it won't last—buy one get one free—and don't forget your rebate."

I chuckled, partly at what he had said, and partly at seeing myself robotically rummaging through the shopping mall just so I could fulfill my deep need to be a consumer and have exactly what all of the other sheep had. I knew that he was right, and I also knew that what he had described was precisely what I'd been feeling. It was the very reason that I had taken my leave of absence, to find the dream that had been lost in the shuffle.

Turning back toward the professor, I asked, "So, this is why you went ahead and started writing the book, because you felt this way?"

"Well, yes," he replied. "I'm sure that had a lot to do with it. In addition though, throughout my own personal exploration, I have also bounced myself into a few other dimensions, and I know that there's a lot more going on in this reality than what has been spoon-fed to us on a daily basis. And after my encounter in the wilderness with your uncle, or I guess we should say Shankara, well, I think I'm beginning to find some other answers."

Excitedly I raised my voice, "But that's what I want to know too. Who am I in all of this, and what is—"

"No, Jared," he interrupted with a solid but reassuring tone, "this isn't just a lot of confusion for you. It's where you begin, that is if you choose. It's where you start to find out for yourself, without asking me or anybody else, without relying on old dogmas and concepts that you never questioned before. This is your own path now. And although it's true that you may also have to admit that this is a journey about spirit, it might be one that brings you back to the truth, back to your passions. Because that's what spirit is. It's your desire to feel and explore everything."

"And what about my uncle or this Shankara? What is that all about for me?"

"Only you can find that out, just like I have to find out for myself. That's why when you read the letter you went on a different journey than I did, because you went where you needed to go and so did I."

"But what about my uncle's health? He's a walking time bomb, and he doesn't even know it. And you—you might also be in danger. Maybe somebody doesn't want you to reveal the identity of this Buddha or Christ person in your book."

"Don't worry about me," he said. "I'll be fine. But I think finding your uncle would be a good idea. He should definitely be warned about his condition. And if my assumption is correct, that he is some sort of mentor, he will probably lead us to this chosen one. Until this enlightened one truly finds out who he or she is, he or she may be in danger, or apt to attract some kind of accident."

I wallowed in the silence for as long as I could. It was difficult for me to understand how the professor could talk with such ease about these notions, as though it were actually quite possible, and even conceivable that the second coming of a Christ or Buddha could be walking around the city having a friendly chat with my long lost uncle. Perhaps it was a notion that I would have easily forgotten had he not reminded me of it through his own anticipation and excitement.

In addition, I had no idea if my long lost uncle was even my uncle anymore. Instead, he might now be some dead swami by the name of Shankara who had deemed himself mentor to this chosen one—not to mention that this chosen one might actually be a four-foot-tall street urchin known as the Village Idiot. Intriguing or not, the whole thing was insane, but I had to admit that I was standing right in the middle of it, and it appeared to be convincingly real. At least it felt that way.

My mind fully exhausted from the situation, I suggested we exchange numbers, and then I gave the professor several generic reasons why I had to be on my way. He accepted them graciously, as did he my phone number and address. As we walked out onto the porch, I turned to say my goodbyes.

"You know, Professor Talon . . . "

"Please" he interrupted, "just call me Michael."

"Well, Michael, one of the things that I'm most puzzled about is this young woman Sharee. I mean, where does she fit in? What part does she play? She acts like she knows exactly what's going on, and yet she also seems to act totally out of impulse. I have even had dreams about her."

"Really," he responded.

"Yes, it was a couple of nights ago. I dreamt about several scenes from very bloody battlefields. They ranged from as early as the Civil War to World War II. I saw things like the swastika and Japanese flags as well as uniforms and equipment from every war imaginable."

"That's amazing, but where did this Sharee fit in?"

"She was in every scene. She wore a kind of white buckskin dress, and she wandered calmly through these battlefields spreading some sort of leaf or herb from a small bundle in her hand. It almost looked like she was planting seeds or something."

"Sage."

"What?"

"Sage, she was spreading handfuls of sage. You know, like the brush you find in the desert. To the Native Americans it is sacred, and they use it to purify and bless things—like a hallowed place or an object like a prayer pipe. I use it myself. Many times it is burned and the smoke is used for the same purpose, to purify or to raise the frequency of something. That is what I believe she was doing in your dream; purifying the battlegrounds by raising the frequency of that time and place."

"She looked like a saint," I said.

"She was performing a very sacred act. That was a great dream, Jared. I would feel very honored to have had such a dream."

"Actually, Michael, it's more than just that, I mean about this woman Sharee. I know this may sound a little out-of-bounds, but I am incredibly drawn to her. I don't even know her, yet every time I see or hear something more about her, it completely entices me. The feeling reminds me of the first time I ever fell in love, and that was a hundred years ago." I immediately felt foolish.

Michael, only adding to my embarrassment, commented, "I know exactly what you mean, she is truly an amazing young woman. And that is why it is also fortunate for me that you, my friend, are just way too old for her. While I, on the other hand, am more than eligible and most available." He patted me on the back affectionately as we both laughed. I knew that he was joking, and even though he was probably right, I still had to play along.

"That may be true, but don't forget that after I rescued her from the mental hospital she gave me a kiss on the cheek before she ran off."

"Ah, that's nothing," he replied sarcastically. "When I was inside the hospital, before our great escape, she gave me a full-blown kiss right on the lips."

"What!" I said.

"That's right. She came in, pointed across the room at me and said, 'That's my husband over there.' At which point she walked over, put her arms around me, and gave me an affectionate kiss."

"And you just went along with it like you knew her, this total stranger kissing you right on the mouth."

"Are you kidding?" he replied. "I'm in the looney bin, and a beautiful young woman comes gliding across the room like a flowing vision and gives me a very sensuous kiss, and you think I'm going to protest? On the contrary, I played along with her as best I could for as long as I could. Besides, in a room full of people who are supposed to be crazy, I really didn't think that anyone would notice, let alone mind."

I shook my head, chuckling as I walked along the wet sidewalk. "Keep in touch," I called. He waved and went into his house.

Hastily, I stepped out into the rain-drenched street, the heavy drops of water bursting against the dark concrete. I glanced back towards the house one last time when suddenly there was the explosive blare of a horn and the sound of tires squealing. I turned around frantically, my body anticipating a devastating blow. Shock erupted inside me as my hands slammed onto the hood of an oncoming car. My life, so unprepared to be consumed by the car's forceful metal, collapsed in on itself from overwhelming fright. The next thing I felt was the hard cold pavement beneath my knees as I realized that there had been no crushing blow. The car had stopped inches from my body and any critical impact. I knelt breathless and trembling between the glare of two headlights, face to face with the roar of an engine and the spray of hot steam.

"Jared . . . my God . . . Jared, are you alright?" came Michael's distant shout.

It appeared that I was, alright that is, although my heart pounded rapidly in spite of the news. I struggled to my feet trying to play down some of the drama of having fallen of my own accord without even being struck.

"Yes, I'm fine," I called, waving in his direction. "I just slipped and fell." Motioning to the panicked driver of the car, I said, "I'm alright really . . . it was my fault. I'm sorry, I wasn't watching."

I crossed over to my jeep and dove into the driver's seat, waving one last time to Michael before I shut the door. As the other driver pulled away, and Michael disappeared once again into the house, I was finally left alone with my own fear. My hands shook uncontrollably as I stared out of the rain-beaten windshield, my body still in shock and stiffened from its sudden brush with death.

I hated this feeling, and I was disgusted and humiliated that I had fallen without even being hit. I was angry with myself for having been so careless, as once again my life passed before me into the reality of my world. In the solitude of this moment I was reminded of Shankara's words, which seemed more confusing and abstract than ever, that *in this life everything was of our choosing, no matter how helpless we believe or have been told we are.*

17
Chasing the Chase

The next morning I found myself enrolled at the espresso stand waiting patiently with a herd of restless city dwellers, none of whom had any time to lose as they scurried to their jobs. Coffee reigned in this early hour. The ritual played out time and again: a customer waltzed to the counter; the clerk gallantly attempted to recall which unique caffeine blend had been requested the day before. I was the drone in this jittery scene, for seldom did I venture so prematurely into the buzz of dawn's downtown flurry.

This particular morning I felt an unfamiliar urgency as if my own rather mundane life had been put on hold and would agree to move forward *only* after I'd found my misplaced uncle—or some facsimile of him. Somehow the need to search for the enigma Shankara seemed redundant. As I walked the awakening streets, I was sure there was a *Shankara* waiting to peer out of every tiny window that loomed above me. I fought the urge to look up and focused on the patterns in the sidewalk and the more tangible task at hand.

I had decided to canvass an older district of the city, a place where Mohan (the other Village Idiot) had been known to reside. If the short fellow had left the hospital with my uncle that evening, there was a chance they might still be together. I knew that my random search was no less than a toss in the wind, which made me even more conscious of the internal force driving me forward into the unknown.

As I scanned the panorama of the avenue, I began to notice a wide range of characters inhabiting the same street corner. There was the Chinese merchant, who sold his morning newspaper to the waitress, who had crossed the street from the cafe, saying an impersonal hello to the flirtatious old banker, who had ignored the crippled beggar, who had now managed to scuffle his way over and plant himself directly in front of me.

I had no choice but to stop, unless I was willing to catapult over him like some crazed dressage horse. His interception had been timed perfectly despite the fact that he had no legs and his arms were his only means of propulsion.

The sight of him was a ghastly surprise. And although I was probably one of a hundred people who passed his way that morning, I was undoubtedly the only fool wearing one of those new and naive faces. Such a mug must have glowed like a beacon amid the gray, not-to-be-bothered city dwellers.

The paper cup he held out at arm's length barely reached my waist. The lower portion of his body appeared to be bound to a small wooden block. The bottom of his chassis was contoured like a rocking chair, giving him the ability to shift his weight back and forth so he could scamper among the hasty walkers, all of whom did their best to ignore him. I would have done the same had I not been singled out as a target for this uncomfortable encounter. My sadness and compassion for him, mixed with my selfish disgust and pomposity, made for an interesting blend of feelings that left me speechless. I did my best not to make any direct or meaningful eye contact with him.

I knew that the quickest solution to the problem was to give him some money so I could be on my way. Rummaging through my pocket, I pulled out a handful of change and reached for his cup. Abruptly, he snatched it away, receiving the money directly into his gray and calloused hand. He spun around and hurried off, disappearing among the walkers.

Through my feelings of pity for him, and embarrassment for myself, the words of Shankara came back into my mind. Once again I was haunted by the phrase: *In this life everything is of our choosing, no matter how helpless we believe or have been told we are.* This thought was echoed by the professor's words, *there are no accidents; everything happens for a reason.*

I couldn't begin to imagine how this irritating confrontation with this beggar could be of any significance to me. It was just a brief moment in time, and I reacted as most people would. More than likely this sordid fellow examined a thousand faces every hour, sifting through them to find that one unsuspecting pigeon who— who if he had any sense would realize that a vagabond who patrols the downtown streets all day would probably know every detail and habit of every person who was ever common to the area— including some homeless character named Mohan.

"Shit." I blurted out. "What an idiot I am." This man would surely know Mohan, or at least would know of him.

I turned to look, but there was no sign of him. Sidestepping the oncoming pedestrians, I hastily made my way, tracing the path he had taken through the stream of people. Surveying the situation, I bobbed up and down looking over the heads of the human traffic and combing the lower landscape of the sidewalk and stairwells. I stopped after only a few minutes, having already jostled angry pedestrians who didn't hesitate to voice their objections. I stood at the corner like a lost child. Tottering on my tiptoes, I scouted the adjoining streets. Slowly I surrendered, sinking back down onto my heels. Then, just for an instant, I caught a glimpse of him crossing the street two blocks away.

Giving up my chase on the sidewalk, I leapt into the street running alongside the slow moving traffic. I darted through the DON'T WALK intersection, ignoring the occasional honk of the cars I had dodged. Then I caught a second glimpse of him, as did he of me. Realizing that I was now running after him, he panicked and hastened his pace. Moving with quickened stride, he scampered around the next street corner and vanished from view.

The fact that I had probably now frightened him into thinking that I wanted my money back only added to the absurdity. How bizarre it all felt. Here I was, a relatively successful and somewhat together individual, who was now desperately chasing after some handicapped person who five minutes ago I could barely even look at and was hard-pressed to cough up a dime for. How interesting it was that my own selfish need had so easily overridden all that nasty uncomfortableness. Once again my ordered life turned upside down as I found myself irrationally clamoring through the downtown streets.

Running full tilt, I finally turned the corner where I had seen him disappear, only to plunge into a puddle of pigeons, which immediately exploded into flight. They dispersed in every direction in a symphony of fluttering wings, leaving me the sole survivor to all of the commotion. Breathless and staggering, I stumbled to a stop.

To my surprise, the street on which he had turned was actually the entrance to an old cobblestone square, one I had not wandered through in years. It was about a block long—a canyon carved out from the surrounding brick buildings. Numerous large oak trees canopied much of the scene, accompanied by a scattering of iron benches and street lamps that appeared to have been standing since the turn of the century. In the center was an aged concrete fountain that had probably not plumed water for quite some time.

There was no sign of the beggar. My abrupt intrusion into this placid sketch seemed to go unnoticed. I leaned against an ornate lamppost, trying to catch my breath and better blend into the sedate surroundings.

The square was filled with a smorgasbord of characters playing the same parts that they had likely played in a daily production of the same scene. There were the coffee drinkers huddled over their cups of caffeine, as well as their smoking comrades trying to squeeze in that last cigarette before those confining hours at the office. Then there were the assorted individuals disguised as transients, who attempted to share the park benches with the invisible people, those well-dressed men and women who had disappeared behind their newspapers, which fanned out here and there throughout the park.

On one bench, just beyond the stagnant fountain, I noticed a

Black woman who looked vaguely familiar. I didn't actually recognize her until I witnessed her playful antics. It was good ol' Emily from the hospital, and what she was doing only added to my morning's bewilderment.

She was sitting between two men, neither of whom acknowledged her presence. This was probably to her advantage however, as she appeared to be, quite inconspicuously, exploring them using her nose. Sniffing about like a curious canine, she carefully probed the man on her right, who was well-groomed, wearing patent leather shoes and a fine gray suit. His face, like his awareness of her, was completely screened off by his morning newspaper. Her wide-eyed reactions left no question as to the aromatic appreciation she had for the mischief she was up to.

Unable to believe the irony of it all, I started to laugh. Perhaps purely through instinct, I knew she was experiencing her union with some form of animal. The excitement of it all, as well as my own memorable panic, seemed to gurgle inside me with a continuous stream of chuckles. To know that she was experiencing something like I had with the animal was an exhilarating thought. It also made my own experience feel more real than ever, which filled me with an emotional mixture of fright and jubilation. Careful to not give away my position, I peered like a cat around the side of the lamppost as she continued her sensory prowl.

The man on her left appeared to be Native American with dark skin and long tangled black hair hanging down around his shirt pockets. He was sound asleep with a brown paper bag tucked between his legs, giving the impression that he had probably been camped on that bench for quite some time.

As she picked up the scent from his head and shoulders, a questioning look crossed her face. This was followed by a slightly more disturbed expression as she examined his hands, which lay open in his lap. Sniffing directly around the area of the brown paper bag, her face utterly bloomed with an expression so foul that I couldn't help but erupt with laughter.

Hearing my outburst, she spotted me. Instantly our eyes made contact, exposing my snickering grin, which promptly made her *fully* aware that she had been caught in her canine exploration. Realizing how it must have looked, she too exploded with laughter, doubling over on the bench, making little attempt to contain herself. Her own outburst caused both of her seated companions to abruptly awaken as one newspaper was quickly folded for its immediate departure, and one brown paper bag fell helplessly to the ground disgorging an oversized beer bottle. Clanking loudly, the container rolled over the rough cobblestones and into the center of the square, spilling the last few sips of its precious ale. Spontaneously, Emily lost the last of her composure. In a jubilant flurry, she sprang from the bench and headed in my direction.

"Mr. Grayson, whatever are you doing here?" she whooped, trying to suppress her mirth by covering her mouth with her hand. For several seconds we were caught up in this comical scene. As our short episode of hilarity subsided, she continued with a fast frenzy of words.

"It's not funny, Jared," she giggled. "I don't know what has gotten into me lately. Ever since I ran into that uncle a yours why I've been feeling the strangest things—which is why I came down here this morning, to see if I could find him and to figure out what's going on. Do you know where he is?"

"No," I replied, "I've been looking for him, my—"

"I mean to tell ya," she interrupted, "just the other night, I was dreamin' this wonderfully disturbin' dream when—" seeing my puzzled look she stopped momentarily. "Jared," she asked, "don't you know what a wonderfully disturbin' dream is?" I smiled and shook my head in true dunce fashion, awaiting her sure to be colorful explanation. "Why, that's one of those dreams that is so marvelous, I mean just so heavenly, that you're just sure you probably shouldn't oughta be havin' it.

"Anyway, I was dreamin' one of those dreams, and in it I was dreamin' that I was a coyote—sort of—and I was runnin' with a whole pack of other coyotes. Well, it was simply amazing 'cause we was all woofin' and yelpin' and howlin' at the moon, we was, like there weren't gonna be no tomorrow. Well, it was the best time I think I ever had, in dreams that is. The whole experience was so real, so physical, that it wasn't until my husband finally woke me up (beins that in my furry frolic I just happened to bite him on the butt) that I realized it was a dream."

"You did what?" I interjected.

"Bit him right on the butt, I guess. I didn't know it at the time, but mind you, he didn't take no offense." Shaking her head she went on, "Oh no, in fact he got so excited by the whole thing that he still gets out of control. He simply saw it as some sorta invitation to be totally wild and now he's wantin' to have sex all the time. Why Jared, I've had to close all of my poor old ratty Venetian blinds, and keep um closed on account a his runnin' around naked all the time, with that big ol' shlong of his waggin' back and forth. Why, what will the neighbors think, and you know those kinda neighbors, Jared, why they're always looking on, even though it's none of their business what he be doin' with his—"

"Oh my God," I said, wincing with both embarrassment and laughter.

Finally she stopped her vivid explanation, only to add an instant later, "Oh heavens, I am carryin' on, aren't I. Must be all this animal stuff I'm feelin'. Whoa! I can still feel the chills from it. And—oh dear, Jared, you must think I have lost my mind."

"Well, not really," I said. "To be totally honest I have—" I stopped midsentence having caught a glimpse of the beggar on the far side of the square. Excitedly, I finished by saying, "I think I have probably had quite a similar experience." Starting to walk in the direction of the beggar, I hastily added, "But I've got to go now."

"But Jared," she said, "what actually do you mean by—"

"Sort of an emergency," I shouted as I ran off, "Sorry!"

"But Jared, what about . . . "

Her words blended into the noises of the city as I found myself once again running after a glimpse of something or someone that I could no longer see in front of me. In short order, the small figure of the man had vanished as swiftly as it had reappeared.

My spontaneous sprint left me at the corner of Fifth and Washington, in front of Saint Martin's Cathedral, the main Catholic church for the central district. I recognized it from a handful of visits I had once taken with my parents. The large concrete columns guarding the granite steps seemed just as intimidating as they did when I was a child. The massive wooden doors were hanging idle and open, as though the last person out had simply forgotten to close them—an invitation for just anyone to peer in. Perhaps I would be just anyone, as I found my curiosity urging me into the archives of times past.

Inside, the aisles and pews were abandoned, leaving only the light from the stained glass windows to wander about in the shadows. Silently I walked down through the center of the church and slid into one of the pews where I could again be anonymous. The professor's words about corrupt religions with their hierarchies and rules seemed to have followed me into this place and settled in next to me on either side. I felt surrounded by that stifling dogma remembering how much, as a small boy, I believed in it all and how much I wanted it to be true. Perhaps all of it was truth when seen through the eyes of an impressionable child. I couldn't help but be witness, here and now, to the emotional duality I was experiencing. My memory stumbled around within all of the guilt and fear that for me had become the rules of such a religion. And yet my body and my soul felt reunited in this place, a place of innocence and wonder, where every alcove, every corridor seemed filled with spirit as though pure faith had prevailed through the decades.

In the midst of my contemplation, a woman came in from one of the side entrances. She wore a dark maroon pantsuit, which accentuated the highlights of her blonde hair. Her expression and the way she carried herself led me to believe that she was probably in her mid-thirties. She noticed me immediately and began to walk toward me as if she intended to ask why I was there or to flush me out of the place entirely. Drawing nearer she tilted her head to one side and then the other like a curious bird, trying to decide if she recognized me.

As she came closer, her inquisitive manner gave me an eerie feeling, as if she might actually be some overwrought spiritual seeker and I, on this day, might be her mid-morning apparition. Cautiously, she slowed the pace of her last few steps. In an almost reverent tone she spoke. "You're the one."

A chill ran through my veins, my conscious mind scrambling for some comic relief from this unsettling announcement. Sarcastically I thought to myself, *would that be, your own personal messenger from God that you requested today? Or perhaps you were looking for that good ol' Messiah himself.*

At this, the professor's words flashed through my thoughts: the second coming of Jesus Christ was here now, and it could be anyone of us. Reaching for any means to squelch that idea, I spit out an abrupt, "What! What did you say?"

"You're the one."

"What do you mean?"

"You're the one, the one with the melody line."

This answer only enhanced my nervous confusion. Whatever she was talking about, I had no idea.

Shaking off her initial stare, she finally said, "I'm sorry, I mean, you're the one from the hospital. Your uncle was in the bed next to another man who was hit by a car—the other man who was also in a coma. I'm Jessica Williams. I was driving the car that hit that other man."

Even after she said it, I couldn't imagine this was the same woman, the television evangelist I had seen the other morning. The transformation was extraordinary. She was truly an attractive woman, without the bouffant hairdo and the overworked makeup.

Trying to cover my astonishment, I offered an answer. "Yes, I remember you from the hospital. I think I also may have seen you on television a few Sundays ago." At that she lowered her eyes and smiled the saddest of smiles. Interrupting her melancholy, I added, "In the hospital, you were with the priest . . . Father O'Brien."

"Yes," she replied. "In fact, he is the reason I am here. He told me he had spoken to a friend of his here at Saint Martin's, Father

Mathews, who knows the homeless man. Father O'Brien told me his name is Mohan. He said he might be able to help me locate him. I want to find out if he is alright and to see if there is anything I can do for him. In truth, I know that he is not alright, that he is not well. Aside from the complications from the accident, Father O'Brien says that Mohan is terminally ill, some kind of cancer that is in and around his brain or something. Although he is still very active now, the doctors don't give him long to live. That is why I wanted to find him."

"No," I said, "no, I didn't know that. Actually, I don't know anything about him, other than that he apparently left the hospital with my uncle. I have been looking for both of them myself, but no luck so far."

With a small sigh, she slowly sat down in the pew in front of me and briefly stared out one of the stained glass windows. Disturbing her trance, I asked. "You said something about my being the one with the melody line. What does that mean?"

"You'll have to forgive me," she replied. "In my desperate need to find Mohan or your uncle, I asked Father O'Brien if he knew how I could get in touch with you. He gave me your phone number and said that you were a teacher at City College. He also warned me that there might be something strange, something evil going on with your uncle. He said your uncle was in need of an exorcism. When I told him that I didn't understand what he meant, he sat me down and had me listen to a recording of your uncle, something Dr. Schultz had given him at the hospital.

"Contrary to the reaction that Father O'Brien expected me to have, I found it to be extraordinary and quite compelling. It seemed to take me back to a place in my childhood that was very pivotal for me. It was a time when I was being sexually abused by my stepfather, a time that up to now I had always done my best to shut out of my mind. Now I remember leaving that field of wild flowers and being called back into the house where it all happened . . . where I wasn't allowed to be a child anymore. I was told that all of the abuse was because I had been bad and that I wasn't to tell anyone about it . . . ever. I never did, till now."

Then she stopped, realizing that she had wandered off into her own emotions. "I'm sorry," she said, "I didn't mean to—"

"No, really, that's alright. I think I understand, but what about the melody line. You said something about a melody line."

"Yes," she said, "in my experience of it, when I came in from that field of wild flowers and entered the house, I heard in my head this haunting melody line mixed in with your uncle's words. I know it wasn't on the actual recording, but I heard it just the same. It played throughout the most fearful and most painful part of that journey, almost as though it were guiding me through. I am a singer, Mr. Grayson, and that melody line has stayed with me. I can remember it even now.

"After leaving Father O'Brien, I tried to call you. When there was no answer I decided to go down to the college and see if you were there or if I could find out anything more about you. My search brought me to the library, where I found an audio file of music that you had written. When I listened to the recording, I couldn't believe it. There it was again, the same melody line."

I immediately became uncomfortable at the coincidence of this woman hearing my music during her journey and my also hearing one of my compositions while I read the professor's mysterious letter. To blot out my discomfort, I tried desperately to focus on what she was saying next.

"Perhaps," Jessica continued, "I'm just remembering that particular melody from having heard it previously. I don't know for sure." She stopped for a second and then asked, "Has this music been recorded and made available for purchase? Or has it been performed somewhere that I might have heard it?"

My nervousness about the coincidence was immediately overshadowed as her questions about my music seared through me like a sharp razor. The music she found was a digital recording I had made and provided for the library. I had forgotten that it was still there. It had been written some time ago in an era of my life when I was still working so diligently to be noticed. I knew exactly which piece of music she was talking about. It was the same piece of music that had filtered through my own head when I listened to the recording of my uncle at the hospital. With great embarrassment I answered her question. "No . . . no, that music's never been produced in any form."

With a puzzled and almost frightened look she said, "Then how did I know it, that one melody line?"

Her question was indeed perplexing, but no more perplexing than the two dozen or so that I had been struggling with in the last few hours. After a short pause (as she noticed my slight departure from reality), Jessica spoke in a very sensitive voice saying, "Your music, it's beautiful. People should hear it. It really should be played somewhere."

I thought about my missed meeting with producer John McDowell. I pictured the stack of compositions still tucked away in my brown leather satchel. Through my sunken emotions I responded to her with the unspoken words caught in my throat, *it almost was*.

Just then a shuffle of noise came from the back of the church. The frame of a large man appeared as a silhouette in the open doorway. For a time he just stood there watching as though he had no intention of actually coming in. For a moment I had a wisp of anticipation that it might be my uncle, but as the man finally entered the foyer I could see he was wearing traditional black clothes and a white collar. Obviously he was one of the resident priests, a man about my height with a medium-sized build, straight black hair and olive skin.

"Jessica," he spoke to the woman, "if you're still looking for your friend, that short fellow Mohan, I think you'll find him out on the front steps of the church."

Jessica immediately hurried to the entrance. I wanted very much to follow her, but the priest delayed me by stepping in front of me for a proper introduction.

"I'm Father Mathews," he said, extending his hand.

"Hello, Father, my name is Jared Grayson."

"Oh, yes," he replied, "Father O'Brien told me about your situation. Have you had any luck finding your uncle?"

"No," I said, "but that's what brought me down to this part of the city today. In fact, I've also been looking for this Mohan for quite some time myself, so I think I had better try and catch him before he—"

Plainly blocking my attempt at a quick getaway, Father Mathews held on to the conversation and his own agenda. "Mr. Grayson, I know it's difficult to understand, but there may be some validity to what Father O'Brien has said about your uncle. There are things in the spirit world that are far beyond our understanding. An exorcism can bring no harm to your uncle, and even if it's not the appropriate action, it might still make things clearer, regardless of the outcome. Father Angelo, a priest here at Saint Martin's, is very knowledgeable on these matters and has performed exorcisms for many years. Father O'Brien has spoken to him, and they are convinced that this is indeed what is happening with your uncle; that someone or something has intervened in his life."

Feeling cornered, I replied, "I really don't know about any of this. And the one thing that I would truly *like* to know is why everyone is so sure that what's happening with my uncle is something bad?"

Surprisingly, he smiled a little and said, "Well, to tell you the truth, that is pretty much my position as well. In fact, that's exactly what I said to Father O'Brien and Father Angelo, but I don't have much experience with these matters. Perhaps I naturally would like to think that it is something good instead of something evil. But like I said, even if an exorcism is not the appropriate action, there would be no harm in doing one."

Hearing his remark surprised me and, but for the fact that he was standing in the way of my pending departure, I probably would have found several reasons to like him. I smiled politely and answered, "Well, regardless, the first thing I need to do is to find my uncle, and perhaps then I'll know better what is truly going on with him."

He smiled at me agreeably and then graciously gave me his salutations so I could be on my way.

At the entrance to the church I found Jessica standing in the doorway like a shadow, watching a human circus of activity being performed around a massive concrete column outside. For a man who had just come out of a coma and was dying of cancer, the one called Mohan was no less comical than an elf and no less animated than a Disney cartoon. It was difficult to tell what he was actually up to, but it appeared that he was doing an extensive and somewhat theatrical exposition of something he was writing. At first he walked clockwise around the column, and then counterclockwise, all the while speaking to himself, gesturing with both his hands and feet on the content of his private dialogue. Intermittently he would squat down with his elbows between his knees in true hunker fashion and scribble something on a small piece of paper. A second later he would jump up and begin his ritualistic dance again.

"What do you suppose he is doing?" I asked Jessica, who wasn't smiling as readily as I, but looked as though she were in some kind of hypnotic trance.

"I'm not sure. I think he's writing something, dictating to himself." Nervously she asked, "Do you think he's alright?"

"For him," I said with a slight chuckle, "yes, I think this is pretty normal."

"What should we do?" she asked, as though she had become emotionally short-circuited by the scene.

"Well, whatever we're going to do we need to do it *now* because I think he's finished his writing and is headed off down the steps."

Moving without hesitation, Mohan was up and briskly on his way with an abundance of short-legged steps.

"Come on," I said, "let's catch up to him before he disappears."

As I turned to follow, Jessica grabbed my sleeve and said, "I can't . . . I can't speak with him."

"What?" I said. "What's the matter?"

"I'm not sure why, but I just can't. Not right now."

"Alright," I said. "But I have to." Hastily I started down the granite steps, looking back to see if she was alright.

"Jared," she called, "tell him that if he needs anything, anything at all, I can provide it. Money is not a problem."

Stepping off the curb into the intersection, I faintly heard her voice call out one last time, "Will you do that, Jared?"

Crossing the street, I moved into the commotion of the busy sidewalk. I looked back to give her a reassuring wave, but by this time she had turned away and was picking up some pieces of torn pages that were on the steps where Mohan had been parading. Unable to get her attention, I focused my sights on the departing Mohan, trying not to notice that for the third time (this morning alone) I was chasing after a total stranger through the downtown streets. I thought about how humorous this would all be if someone were watching me, following me this morning as I galloped like a 205-pound camel from here, to there, and then to somewhere else. Then I thought about Shankara, and all of those tiny windows looming above me. Then I tried to think really, really hard about absolutely nothing and just kept running.

18
Library of Graffiti

This time my frenzied chase was not in vain. It lasted about a block and a half and led me down an alleyway that must have been somewhere behind the buildings surrounding the cobblestone square. Old brick walls towered on either side, massive structures with few windows and only an occasional door framed by several garbage cans. The sun, having found its highest place in the sky, shed rare streams of light down into this dark dreary canyon. It lit up the trash and debris on the ground, defining the sculpture of wrought iron fire escapes above me and a cobweb of black wires strung between the buildings. Panting hard to catch my breath, my nostrils filled with the stench of furnace fumes and rotting food, for it was my luck to tour this particular passageway a day or so before the garbage would be collected.

Some fifty yards away, I could see Mohan perched on top of some sort of trash containers. He stood with his back to me, facing the solid concrete wall where the alley had come to a dead-end. Nearly two stories high, this wall had no doors or windows, yet it was not a blank slate. Its gray face held a library of graffiti, adorned with stanzas and lines written by one hand, one poet, one artist, who had to be Mohan. With a block of chalk held like a paint brush, he scrolled out his words, perhaps the phrases he had been composing in front of the church. With a closer look, I could see he was standing on two very full garbage cans stacked on a large wooden crate. This balancing of box and cans raised him some six to eight feet into the air, where he continually tested the integrity of his platform by reaching out far to one side to finish each sentence. He seemed to take no notice of me, staying focused on his writing, even though I was sure he knew someone was standing behind him. The piece he was working on read thus far:

Desperation is the kindling
I will gather for my fire . . .

There had to have been some forty of his creations, each three to five lines in length, covering the entire wall. Written with the same pale yellow chalk, they were well-defined against the dark sooted concrete canvas. A few resided as high as twelve feet or more, even higher than the one he now composed. Some of the sayings had been partially washed away by the rain, making room for others to crowd into the usable space. It was a collage. It was a story. It was no less than an extraordinary work of art. It was also quite likely that very few people even knew it was there, which I'm sure had no bearing on why it had been written.

As I read some of his verses, these carefully preserved thoughts, I soon lost touch with where I was. My mind wandered drunk through these words and this unfamiliar territory.

I thought I'd learn to fly,
but they say I'll forget how to walk.
I guess I have too many shoes anyway.

What is it that makes me stumble,
when my feet don't touch the ground.
You would think I was all but human.
Well, that's what they told me anyway.

Alright madness,
I am all out of fear.
I dare you now
to dance in the light of my flame.

I thought time was my shadow,
until I couldn't see him anymore.
After all, who lights the way for the light?
Perhaps we should just dance in the dark.

I touched the face of nothing.
He laughed at me.
He said, hardly anyone
comes here anymore.
Then he opened the lavender gates.

I thought the Earth was home,
until I noticed all the stars.
It seems no one is really asking anymore.
Maybe they already know.

I wondered what happened.
I thought I saw me crying.
It must just have been the wind,
airing out some of my moments.

Helplessness,
you follow me like a shadow.
So I will breathe in a thousand suns.
Then where will you hide?

Laughter...is for the tasteless joke that
you wish you had never told.
Bliss...is your laughter at you for having
told it.

Each time I come to the edge,
I have to wonder where I've been.
It's funny how time makes court jesters
of us all.
Besides, is anyone really watching?
Who cares, let's get blissed.

All of me can never seem to come together.
Yet none of me can see everything.
Without the darkness,
how would light ever shine?

Shadows...are rainbows in disguise,
for in time even sadness has
a sense of humor.
Divine Spirit...Do you play some great jest
upon me?
Or perhaps, do I?

Without breaking the stream of his writing he called out, his voice echoing off the brick walls, his alleyway having the acoustics of a fine amphitheater.

"Good Pilgrim!" he said, as though he were reciting lines from Hamlet. "What manner dost thou come hither upon my counsel? What is the why and wherefore of it?"

I remained silent and dumbfounded by his question; a question I did not understand. Realizing the true measure of my ignorance, I grunted, "What?" and then added my own question, "Uhm . . . I'm sorry . . . What did you say?"

Breaking the flow of his writing, he turned and spoke in the driest, most common street dialect I had ever heard.

"I said," he exclaimed, "what . . . ever . . . do . . . you . . . want?" Then he turned back and resumed his writing.

"You're Mohan." I waited for an answer. "You were in the hospital. You shared a room with my uncle Ben Grayson for several days." He just kept writing. "I saw you there. They said you were in a coma. So was my uncle."

Then he rallied back sarcastically, "All of humankind is in a coma. How could you tell the difference?"

I waited, almost spellbound, not knowing what to say. Then I again attempted to extract some information. "I was told that you were with my uncle when he left the hospital. I have been trying to find him. He has an arterial condition that could cause him to have a stroke at any time. He may not know about it. I wondered if you had seen him."

It was as though my words had fallen on deaf ears. Reaching one last time for an answer, I said, "I'm his nephew Jared Gray—"

Suddenly, he turned around totally animated, his eyes wide with discovery.

"You're the one!" he exclaimed, my own statement sliced in two by his excitement. Turning back to his writing, he placed a period at the end of his last sentence, jumped off the crate and garbage cans, and walked up to me with an unmistakable clip of enthusiasm in his step.

"You *are* the one," he said again as he scanned me with his eyes, noting every detail of my appearance.

"What!" I said nervously. "What do you mean?"

"You truly are the one."

"Why are you saying that?" I persisted.

Scratching his chin, he said, "You're the one the elevator kept dropping off at the psychiatric ward." He chuckled and began to walk around me in a circle. "You're the one who sat on that big rock and roared like a tiger and left your underwear all over the woods." Still circling, he laughed even harder. "You're also the one who fell off the cliff and nested your ass in the top of a pine tree. Now that was funny. That was really very funny." Smiling broadly, he added, "You . . . you are even funnier than me!"

Hearing all of this information played back to me, I felt a wave of panic run through my body, not to mention a splash or two of embarrassment. I couldn't imagine how he could know these things. No one was there when they happened. And then an even more frightening thought occurred to me. Perhaps *he* was the enlightened one and that's why he was privy to all of my antics.

Desperately scrambling for some better explanation, I asked, "How do you know . . . about all of those things that happened to me?"

"He told us," he said.

"Who is he? Who do you mean?"

"He tells stories about you all the time." Giggling, he said again, "You really are very funny."

"Do you mean my uncle?"

"Call him what you like, it doesn't much matter to him."

"How does he know . . . I mean, how does he know about all of those things that happened to me?"

Doing a double take, he seemed to snicker at my ignorance. Then he said, "No doubt about it. You're definitely the one."

Then I yelled through my frustration, "What is that supposed to mean?"

Finally, he quit circling, slowly walked back to his graffiti, and picked up the chalk he had left sitting on the garbage can. He returned to stand next to me. Now more serious and compassionate, he said, "In the evening, when the rest of the city has gone to sleep, come to the East Bridge . . . underneath. Sometimes we gather there at the fire. Sometimes he comes to the fire and talks to us." Looking directly into my eyes as though probing my confusion and fear, he smiled softly and said, "Don't worry, there is only good for you here . . . nothing else." Then he turned, repeating what he had said. "Look for the fire. You will see it under the East Bridge." Slowly he skipped away leaving me to stand alone in the alley.

Then he stopped, looked back and shouted, "The woman who was with you at the church, tell her thank you . . . thank you for hitting that parked car and sending me flying into the air. It's been a great flight." He took a few more steps and then turned back again and added, "The best."

I stood there and watched him disappear, feeling totally bewildered by what it all meant. I glanced back at the last verse he had just completed:

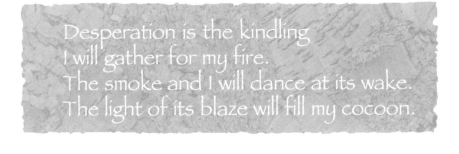

Desperation is the kindling
I will gather for my fire.
The smoke and I will dance at its wake.
The light of its blaze will fill my cocoon.

The essence of these words poured into me like rich honey, clear and golden, and unmistakably pure. This by no means meant that I had gleaned some great comprehension of them, but somehow it felt like they belonged to me as well. Perhaps they were of understandings yet to come. I was no less confused about having discovered all of this information, but now there seemed to be a guiding force behind it, a momentum that lessened the exasperation.

As I walked out of the alley and re-entered the streets now filled with human commotion, I felt a strange twinge of excitement. It was as though I was unique amid all of this human bustle, special somehow through these unusual events and personal encounters. I wondered if it centered around my quest to find my uncle or if maybe, just maybe— And then I had the strangest thought, that perhaps . . . **these small events had been happening around you all along, but until you actually started paying attention, you never bothered to notice them.** "Right," I said out loud to myself. "No—Wrong!" I bleated. "Wrong, wrong, wrong, wrong, wrong . . . wrong grammar, wrong voice, wrong use of the pronoun *you* in that last sentence! Wrong, wrong, wrong, wrong!" **But an interesting idea, don't you think?**

"Eeeah!" I screeched, desperately looking over one shoulder, then the other, wanting to find a face to go with the intrusive commentary. I then unconsciously stepped off the curb to jaywalk across the street. Suddenly horns were blaring and cars were swerving as I found myself surrounded by a war party of savage motorists. Making my way to the safety of the other side, I heard the final cry of one bloodthirsty old woman in her BMW, who shouted, "Are you out of your mind?"

As I leaned over one of the city garbage containers to gather my senses, I found myself asking that very same question: Are you out of your mind? Are you finally and unmistakably out of your mind? Then cautiously I stopped, looked in both directions, and listened very anxiously to see if someone might actually answer.

19

Note of No Return

Voices or no voices, informing Michael about the meeting under the bridge seemed to be of the utmost importance. Returning home that afternoon, I checked my phone machine, where I found a message from Jessica Williams. She must have left it not long after our encounter at the church.

> Hi, Jared. I just wanted to apologize for this morning, for not being able to pursue Mohan with you. I hope you found him and learned something more about your uncle. Please let me know if he responded to my offer to help him. I would sure appreciate hearing from you. I wish we'd had more time to talk. After hearing your music I feel that I . . . well, I just wish we could've had more time. Thanks. Good luck.

I did need to call and tell her what I found, but my call to Michael had to come first. I pulled his name out of my wallet and dialed the number. There was no answer. Nor was there an answering machine, which seemed strange, for I was sure that I had seen one sitting on his desk. At the very least, I wanted to leave him a message. Then I tried his office number. The line was busy. I had no choice but to try again later.

I shuffled about my house preparing myself both physically and emotionally for my evening expedition down to the East

Bridge. In the kitchen I found a sink full of dirty dishes waiting ever so patiently, as was my cat Mouzzer, who was peering through one of the lower squares of glass in my back patio door. With my having left so early for the city, he had been locked out all morning. This had undoubtedly put him behind schedule for his eighteen-hour snooze, which he was now diligently reminding me of with his willfull and woefull stare.

As I opened the door to let him in, I instantly realized that my back door was unlocked. This gave me immediate cause for alarm because the door was always set to lock when it closed. From numerous cold and embarrassing incidents of being locked out, I knew that the only way to alter this pattern was to use a key from the outside, which I kept hidden under the steps. I was sure I hadn't used that key in over a month.

I scanned my house to see if anything was missing or disturbed. Upstairs and down, everything seemed to be in order. I went back out to the porch to check for the key hidden under the steps. It was there, but not in its normal spot. It was obvious someone had used the key and been in my house.

I did a more thorough examination of the place, remembering how Professor Michael's home had looked with his books and papers thrown about. Moving into my office, I carefully checked my desk to see if any of my own literary rubble had been taken or tampered with. I searched through the many articles I had been looking at in the last several days. There were the scraps of paper with Michael's story, as well as the music I had resurrected from my attic. I racked my brain trying to remember what had been there. There was Clyde Henderson's letter from Nepal about the possibility of Katherine's death, along with the junk mail I had received that morning.

Finding that nothing was missing did not relieve even a morsel of my anxiety. I gazed helplessly around the room trying to think of anything that should have been there that was now gone. As I walked into the living room, I noticed through the front window that my neighbor Mrs. Nurple was making her daily visitation to the mailbox. It reminded me about the young woman she had seen going through my mail that morning. Then it dawned on me. There was something that I didn't see in that stack of papers.

Quickly, I stepped back into the office and scrambled through the disarray of pages. Reaching the bottom of the stack, I went through it again. It wasn't there—the letter I had received some twenty years ago from Katherine telling me that she was moving to Nepal and that she might be pregnant. It was missing. I distinctly remembered that it had been attached to the piece of music I had written in honor of that particular emotional upheaval. The song "Sail You Home to Me" was also gone.

It was baffling. Why would someone want my music or the letter that had been written so long ago by my first love saying she had left me to follow some guru to Nepal? I tried to remember the letter in my mind, seeing the words, the writing, and then the name, Ramya, Shankara . . . something or other. That's when it struck me that maybe the name was what someone was looking for. Perhaps he is the enlightened one after all and that is what they were trying to find out.

A small wave of anxiety churned in my belly. I picked up the phone and dialed the professor's number. Again there was no answer. It was urgent that I find him now to let him know someone had been in my house and taken the letter. I tried his office number again. As before, it was busy.

Rummaging about my home, I gathered what I needed for the evening and then stashed the back door key in my woodpile in case I had any return visitors. With my house secure and my cat asleep, keeping his usual watchful eye on the place, I passed through my front door and out to the porch.

As I fiddled with my keys to lock up, I noticed a man getting out of his parked car. I couldn't help but think he looked familiar, even though he appeared to be headed up the adjacent sidewalk to the house of my neighbor Marshal.

I hurried down the stairs and stealthily made my way around the bushes in my front yard so that I could continue to watch him without being seen. The more I saw of him, the more I was sure that I had spoken to him somewhere. As he disappeared behind the trees, it came to me: the big blonde mustache and the dark tan, which had looked so out of place at the hospital, belonged to the doctor, Sam Stiltson. He must have stopped by to give me some more information about that woman he had seen or about my uncle's medical condition. He came by to personally give me some message, but was headed to my neighbor's house by mistake. With all that had been going on, I surely didn't want to miss him or anything he had to say.

Swiftly I made my way across the two front lawns and past the tall shrubbery, hoping to catch the good doctor before he had actually disturbed my neighbor. Charging around the corner I leaped up the three steps and onto Marshal's front porch.

Abruptly, I stopped, nearly colliding with a situation that was not at all what I had expected. Although it was indeed Dr. Stiltson, it was somewhat of a surprise to find him locked in a warm, affectionate kiss with my neighbor, the grizzly-of-a-bear Marshal. Erupting with embarrassment, I stood there like a gawking preschooler, inches away from their private moment.

"Oh God," I blurted out, "I'm sorry. I didn't realize that you were . . . I mean, I thought the doctor was—"

They laughed at the awkwardness of my verbal stumbling. Endless seconds seemed to pass until finally Marshal intervened saying, "Jared, it's alright . . . really. Sam and I just haven't seen each other in a—"

"No," I nervously interrupted. "No, that's all okay by me . . . I mean, what you were doing . . . really."

With all of my mumbling, I was sure they must have thought I was a true closet case. Dr. Stiltson, in a gracious attempt to rescue me from my floundering, reached out to shake my hand saying, "So Jared, it's nice to see you again. How have you been?"

With the confidence of his handshake and reassuring tone of his voice, I soon found the courage and the wherewithal to laugh at myself as though I were simply being recognized as the court jester in this particular scene.

Marshal then joined in saying, "Sam has been keeping me filled in on what's been happening with your uncle. Have you had any luck finding him yet?"

"Yes, Jared," Sam added, "there were several sightings of him before he left the hospital. Have you heard anything at all?"

"Well, actually, yes. Earlier today I was able to locate Mohan, the man who left the hospital with him, the other man who was in a coma. Mohan apparently has seen my uncle several times since then. In fact, he told me about a gathering that is supposed to be taking place tonight somewhere under the East Bridge. I have no idea what it's really all about, but he said to go there this evening and look for a fire under the bridge."

"And what about your uncle's health?" Sam asked. "Did he say anything about his condition, how he was getting on?"

"No, not really. At least he made no reference to it."

"And what about this Mohan character?" Sam continued. "He was also a patient of mine. I don't know if you are aware of this, but he not only has sprung out of a coma, but he is also dealing with terminal cancer. Robert Benson, the oncologist on the case, said that it has spread through parts of his brain. He also said that, due to the advanced stage of the disease, Mohan elected not to have chemotherapy. This is not uncommon for someone with his diagnosis, and it's probably why he is still able to be so active. Did you get any indications about his condition?"

"I did know about his cancer, but he didn't mention it. I spoke to him only briefly, though. Perhaps I'll be able to find both of them this evening, and I can ask more questions."

"Do that, Jared. And bring your uncle into the hospital if at all possible. We weren't able to run all of the tests necessary to give a real clear diagnosis. There are several medications that he should be taking right now, ones that might help ward off a stroke or an aneurysm."

"I'll do what I can. I was actually on my way out the door when I saw you drive up, so . . . I guess I had better get myself back on track and be on my way."

"Well, keep us informed," replied Sam. "There is something quite extraordinary about this one, your uncle. As strange as it sounds, every time I checked on him, it was always like being in a room full of music, even though the place was completely silent."

I stood there mesmerized by his comment until Marshal broke my trance by saying, "Oh, and Jared, speaking of music. We really enjoyed hearing you play the piano the other night. I mean, we always enjoy it, but a couple of nights ago it was pretty late and you were working on something that was so full of passion. It was really wonderful."

"Oh, God," I said, teeming with embarrassment for more reasons that I could count. "I hope I wasn't keeping you up?"

"No, not at all," Sam replied. "Play at all hours of the night; it's really not that loud, and we enjoy it."

With that comforting thought, we said our final goodbyes. I headed back across the lawns toward my jeep, wondering just what else might have been heard in the late night hours through the walls of my house. It was a little disturbing to discover that some of my more private moments at the piano were perhaps not so private after all. I also had to admit that the image of two rather furry and robust men lying together in a passionate embrace during one of my more passionate preludes was a new and different concept, although it was inspiring to know that at least someone in the world was listening to and appreciating my music. Driving away from my house, I probed my memory, trying to recall just which piece I had been working on that particular night. Desperately I was hoping that it wasn't something lyrical, which would have had me howling off-key at an undoubtedly cringing moon.

As I pulled up to the professor's house, everything seemed to be as passive as a postcard. I went up to the door and knocked once, and then twice, but, as with the phone, there was no answer. I waited for another minute or two, peering into the windows and then calling out his name. Still there was no response. Then looking first to see if his neighbors were watching, I opened the screen door and tried the front door knob. The door was open.

"Michael!" I called out. "Are you here? Is anyone home?"

Slipping into the living room, I noticed that everything

appeared to be as I had last remembered it. The place was silent.

"Michael, are you here?"

Carefully, I moved through his house. Nothing looked out of the ordinary. Then I walked out onto his back porch, where I had drifted off reading his letter from the guru Shankara. This time the window pane was dry, and the room light and airy, completely unlike the illusive atmosphere I had experienced the night before. It made me feel as though *that* journey, *that* episode in my life, had never really happened.

Then I noticed an envelope that had been carefully placed on the seat of the chair. It was a note from Michael for me. With a nervous chill, I sat down in the chair and began to read.

Jared, I am leaving this note strictly as a precaution. I would have called, but my phone isn't working. In case I don't return this evening to remove this, or if I don't return at all, you will know something has happened. Shortly after you left last night two men came to the house. One of them had been here several days before with my colleague from the university and was asking all of the questions. This time their questions gave me concern that they might be searching for the enlightened one. That is why I'm going with them as they requested. They will be back in an hour to pick me up. If by chance you are reading this, and it is the following day, then there is a problem and I have made a very bad decision.

There is one other thing. Something that I can't put in this note. I now know who the enlightened one is. Be careful with yourself, Jared.

Michael

I collapsed into the chair, my heart pounding. I had no idea what to do next. He had left me no clue of where to look or even where to begin. Desperation swarmed around me as though the professor's walls were echoing out the helpless calls of a thousand voices.

I couldn't fathom why he would go with them, especially now that he had identified the enlightened one. I was frightened for him, very frightened. Whether his going with them was an act of courage or stupidity, it was a dangerous one. He was taking a hell of a gamble, and I prayed it was a wager he had not already lost.

Surveying the premises I walked around one last time to see if there was something that could help me to know where they had gone. There was nothing.

I thought about calling the police and filing a missing person report, but since it had been less than twenty-four hours and I wasn't actually any relation to him—not to mention the fiasco that I had already experienced with the police around my missing uncle—I decided to just wait. Checking to see that both of his doors were locked, I then returned to my jeep, feeling totally frantic about what I was going to do next.

Returning home, I found everything as I had left it. The newspaper was on the front porch. The cat was asleep on the couch. The back door was still locked with its key stashed in the wood pile. The phone machine and mailbox were idle and empty. Even my uncle's pants and plaid shirt, which I had been given at the hospital, were resting peacefully on the fireplace mantle, as if waiting for his return. Had it not been for the fact that my entire being was pulsating with fear and uncertainty about what to do next, one would have thought that the world was good and all was well.

I wanted very much to step out of my own head and into this tranquil scene of my living room and have all of the turmoil and confusion be gone. My linear mind rallied to agree with this, reminding me that, after all, I didn't know the professor very well. I also knew very little about this guru Shankara, not to mention the supposed enlightened one. Perhaps it was just a big story, a hoax. Maybe I was just dealing with a bunch of spiritual fanatics. Besides, it was unimaginable to me that I, some bookshelf composer, would be engaged in a situation of such importance that it would involve someone referred to as the enlightened one, savior to the world. This was madness. The more I thought about it, the more insane it all seemed.

It was quite possible that, because of the accident, my uncle had simply lost his senses and was now wandering the city with amnesia. He may even have a stroke and die before he ever knows who he truly is and what actually happened to him.

I slumped to the floor cross-legged, letting out a deeply exhausted sigh. What in the world am I doing? Why am I involved in this, and why am I believing all of this stuff that is being handed to me? It doesn't make any sense at all. It's all crazy. Why don't I just stop and go back to my normal life?

Somehow, I had to rid myself of this spiritual nonsense by finding something more familiar to focus on. The television—what could be more distracting than that?

I turned it on and pulled myself up to the screen, perhaps in an attempt to saturate myself with whatever would appear. Surfing through the channels, I finally stopped on Oprah Winfrey's afternoon talk show. This, I thought, would instantly draw my mind into something outside my confused reality. As Oprah returned from a commercial break, I promptly noticed the three words in large lettering that made up the entire backdrop of her stage: it read REMEMBERING YOUR SPIRIT. "Eah!" I yelped, jumping back from the TV tube. "Oh my God," I said, shaking my head in total defeat, "*Et tu, Oprah, et tu?*"

I clicked off the television and took a deep breath. Letting out another big sigh, I tried to release my anxiety. But to my surprise, what actually came out of me wasn't a sigh. Instead, I let out a sound that felt totally natural and yet totally inappropriate in spite of its spontaneity. In that moment I breathed out a long, decisive "Grrrrrrr."

I felt divided, as if my body and spirit could no longer tolerate the turbulence in my mind. My soul wanted to run like a wild animal and explore this new and uncharted territory, while my brain desperately held on to everything that was logical, that was tangible and familiar. My spirit wanted to breathe, but my mind cried out for me to give it all up, to walk away, to go back to the predictable life that I knew so well.

It was that very thought that caused me to shift, to make the decision about what I was going to do. A predictable life was where I had come from, and there was no going back. One thing was certain. In the last several days I had felt more alive than I could ever remember. Regardless of how it all looked or how out of control it all seemed, somewhere inside me my spirit was pressing me forward. Something was calling for me to take yet another empty-handed leap into the void. I was compelled to go on, no matter how frightening it appeared.

I sat quietly for a while just trying to feel myself breathe and bring my body, mind, and spirit back together into the same space. I could detect my throat and belly wanting to sneak in a partial growl, and my arms and legs constantly wanting to stretch. Reaching up to the fireplace I took down my uncle's clothes. I put my face into the soft flannel and breathed through the warm cloth as though I might find a clue there, perhaps a scent that I could use to track his shadow like a baying bloodhound. This crazed idea was mad with fantasy and yet rich with possibilities. The smell from the shirt was human and natural. My actions felt both insane and outrageous as though I wanted to crawl down into my body, down into pure feeling, something that had no mental data, no mental confusion attached to it. I wanted the pandemonium inside my head to be gone without losing all of the wonder, the passion I had been feeling.

That confusion seemed to walk by my side as I returned in the evening to wander the downtown streets. I retraced the path from my journey that morning, through the old square and past the church. The sun had already disappeared behind the tall buildings, and all around me people were finding their way back into their lives, commuting home after a long day's work. For me it seemed like the work, the challenge, was just beginning on a day that I thought would never end.

I meandered about until I found myself back where I had met Mohan, the alley where he had recorded his prose. This time the brick canyon appeared even more cluttered with dumpsters and garbage than before. Facing the concrete wall, my eyes drifted over his many poems and came to rest on one particular phrase.

> Helplessness.
> You follow me like a shadow.
> So I will breathe in a thousand suns.
> Then where will you hide?

The alley's only occupants were early evening shadows, which had driven all signs of sunlight out of this manmade quarry. I tried to breathe deeply into my body, to find a sprig of new life, but my efforts only filled me with the scent of garbage and rotting food. I felt helpless and depressed about my future, a destiny that, like this wall, seemed impossible to climb. It was ludicrous to me now that earlier that day I stood in this same spot with just as much confusion, and yet I also sensed a kind of excitement about what I was facing.

What had changed? Why did it all feel so different? There seemed to be no answer to these questions. I wanted to flee this place and free myself of this confusion and anxiety. I felt trapped inside some ongoing work of fiction for which the author could find no ending. There was nothing left to do but to go to the bridge and look for the fire. Perhaps there I could find some answers, or at least find a reason to stop.

20

Fireside Arena

On the west side of the river, the area next to the bridge was an industrial graveyard of boarded up buildings and abandoned cargo containers. Some twenty yards from the shoreline stood a ten foot high chain link fence with a few strands of barbed wire strung across the top. The fence seemed to run indefinitely along this side of the river as if keeping out unwanted intruders as well as keeping in the rubble of these industrial ruins. Tracking beside the water's edge, I soon came to a place where the old brick two-story structures appeared to move and sway, their walls softly lit by what was perhaps a fire somewhere on the ground.

Eventually I could see down through the buildings at what looked to be an old alleyway that serviced several of the adjoining warehouses. In that same spot, I also found a convenient opening pried in the fence, an entrance to a path on the other side. It was a trail much like animals would make in a forest by stepping only where it was necessary, leaving other obstacles to be maneuvered around. Carefully I made my way through this jungle of dumpsters and discarded machinery, the walls of the buildings closing around me, their incandescent glow growing brighter as I walked along.

Faintly, I could hear traces of several people talking. I slowed my steps, becoming more cautious as I drew nearer the sounds. Then just ahead was an open space surrounded by numerous boxes, an assortment of crates, and a few old automobiles dating back to the Forties and Fifties. The fire that I had been seeking was in the center of this shanty arena. Two transient-type fellows sat nearby warming themselves. One was a small man with Latino features and coloring while the other was a much larger Black man with short tightly-curled hair. Neither of them seemed to notice me while I unsuccessfully tried to stay hidden.

As I stepped closer, I could see as many as thirty people gathered, none of whom appeared to be concerned about my presence. The most noticeable aspect of this group was the dress of these various characters. Sitting on the ground facing the fire was a rather scruffy fellow with a scraggly beard and a well-worn set of rags. Next to him, seated on a box, was a clean-shaven gentleman, probably in his fifties, with a herringbone suit and a briefcase on his lap. Standing not far from him was a very tall, thin man with blond hair wearing some kind of uniform or maintenance clothes. An Asian woman, dressed like a shopkeeper, was just to his right. Camped out directly behind her was a woman reminiscent of a typical bag lady, rummaging around in a shopping cart. Next to her was a fellow who looked East Indian and resembled a cab driver I used to know.

Within this kaleidoscope of characters, there were those who looked familiar to these surroundings, while others seemed totally out of place. I could find no rhyme nor reason to the odd combination of appearances and nationalities that had congregated in this scrap yard of an arena. They all appeared quite reserved, some talking softly to one another, while others milled about as if waiting for something to happen. A few looked to be somewhat lost as though they had simply stumbled in by mistake and then forgot how to find their way out.

I walked around the outer boundaries of the crates, camouflaging myself as best I could, looking for my uncle within this Twilight Zone community. Then to my surprise, I noticed a man who looked like young Father Mathews, the priest I had spoken to earlier that day at St. Martin's Cathedral. He was standing on the opposite side of the open space, but gave no sign that he recognized me.

I began to make my way in his direction, when all at once I saw the face of a woman—soft delicate features that filled me with delight. I almost forgot where I was . . . and who I was. Her expression was lit by the firelight, which burned as though in honor of her being there. As ridiculous as it seemed, I was smitten with the moment. The flower in my vision was the young woman I assumed was named Sharee, the one who had kissed me on the cheek after my semi-gallant rescue of her and the professor from the psych hospital.

She was wrapped in a soft gray blanket, standing on the far side of an old rusty Packard sedan at the edge of the opening. Seated just in front of her, on the flared fender of the car, was the silhouette of a man with his back towards me. In the midst of her conversation with him, she spotted me and smiled almost as if she knew that I had been there all along. Her expression felt flirtatious to me, and yet I had to question my own ability to even recognize such a gesture. As I crept around behind some crates, she discretely followed with her eyes, never losing track of me or of the conversation she was engaged in. I continued this subtle dance hoping to get a better view of her and to perhaps catch a glimpse of the fellow with whom she was conversing. I felt like a giddy schoolboy, tripping over my own feet, trying to keep my sights on her and still make my way along the parameter of the wooden boxes.

I broke my stare to maneuver around a large metal container to get a better view of her. Abruptly, I stopped dead in my tracks. The man seated on the car was Uncle Ben.

The sight of him filled me with an explosion of memories and emotions, as well as a kind of awe at his ragged but noble appearance. My mind struggled between this perception of him and glimpses of how I remembered him from my childhood. I just stared, trying to take in this majestic image as though time had gone back a thousand years to an age when knights were yet destined to be celebrated in fables.

He was washed in amber tones from the fire's embers, which flooded the scene like a theatrical stage. With one knee raised high, supporting his arm under his chin, he leaned to one side, very calm and sovereign. The old discarded vehicle on which he sat was no less royal than a throne. He wore the robes of a pauper, a tan poncho that draped past his elbows and across his lap, ragged, torn, and frayed about the edges. It was tied at the waist with a belt, which gave him a very heroic bearing. This accentuated his size and shape against the collapsed sedan beneath him.

His white hair and beard seemed luminescent, his skin tone bronze from the firelight. He sat very relaxed, observing the scene, his eyes slowly scanning the people. With his right hand cupped in toward himself, he used the back of his fingers to slowly brush his beard, back and forth in a silent hypnotic motion.

Then he made direct eye contact with me, and I was sure he absolutely knew. Of course, what it was that he absolutely knew, well, *that* was never really the question—because I couldn't get past the look in his eye so my mind could formulate a question. His intense stare held me captive. For a brief time it felt like everything had slowed down, taking all of the signposts of my reality and carefully placing them into the bottom of an empty jar.

My trance was broken by the intrusion of yet another familiar face belonging to a short fellow who had stealthily climbed up the backside of the sedan and onto its well-rusted roof. It was Mohan, who undoubtedly was of the impression that he had cleverly crept up to his new perch unbeknownst to my uncle. The reason for this activity—why he was seated there like some mischievous monkey—soon became apparent as he artfully posed himself in the same heroic posture as the giant-of-a-man seated just below him. In a semi-serious portrayal, he began to mimic my uncle's gestures. Sitting with his arm draped over one knee, he stroked the pretense of a beard with the back of his fingers.

This quickly drew the attention of the crowd as people began to chuckle, not only at the fun that Mohan was making of his much larger counterpart, but because it was quite obvious that my uncle was well aware of Mohan's presence. Slowly a suspicious grin appeared on the big man's face. It was as if he were allowing this charade to continue, waiting for the one perfect moment to squelch it by surprise.

With the sly motion of a very large snake, he carefully reached up with his hand and grabbed Mohan's lone dangling foot. At this Mohan's expression went through a flurry of cartoon faces like a surprised cat with a mouth full of feathers, who was about to become the afternoon's exercise for a very big bulldog.

Mohan totally surrendered to the circumstance, the only signs of a struggle being his wide-eyed expressions. He played the scene for all it was worth as he was slowly pulled down into the waiting arms below. Tumbling like a child, he finally landed on his rump on the ground.

My uncle smiled and shook his head back and forth, saying, **"Yes . . . well . . . when you can mimic me well enough to consciously lift your spirit from your body and soar into the heavens where we can sit down and have lunch, then I will truly be impressed. . . . And one day you will, my friend, perhaps sooner than you know, for your time here grows short."**

At this Mohan playfully produced the saddened smile of a circus clown. Silence filled the space until my uncle addressed Mohan again.

"You have heard me speak of this before . . . and now you would ask, *But why, Shankara, would I want to leave this human experience now? You have only just arrived, and I have been waiting so long for your coming.* In truth, my friend, my time in this human form also grows short for not long after you walk away from your earthly shadow, I too will leave this physical expression."

Casting his eyes to the rest of the people, he made brief contact with a few, giving the impression that he recognized each of them. Leaning back he raised his chin slightly and began to speak to the crowd as a whole.

"You see . . . that is the only difference between myself and all of you. I know that my walk with this human body is but an illusion in time and space, and you, as of yet, do not. You believe that the conscious hours of your daily existence mark the beginning and end of you. You believe that I am some awakening

prophet whose enticing words cause you to wander into a dimension of fantasies.

"In truth, *you* are the prophets and these journeys are creations of your own. I, I am but the wind; this you will come to know on the day that I am gone. On such a day you will scramble to know whether I was ever really here at all, with only the echo of my words as intangible proof of our human dialogues. For you see, I did not come to this experience to rally you into some earthly reaction where you would then follow me the way that you have for eons followed your man-made religions. I came to stir you to remember the splendor of who you are; to remind you that you too are the wind, and that you once came from the stars. I came to invite you to dinner, to a great banquet where the table has been set to celebrate your homecoming.

"Presently, these ideas seem foreign to you because you cannot see past your everyday thoughts, thoughts that keep you very focused, spinning in the perpetual cycle of your everyday lives. Yet this is how powerful you truly are. Through your thoughts you have the ability to create every moment of that reality called your future.

"Some of you have heard me say that *everything is of your choosing, no matter how helpless you believe or have been told you are.* You cringe at such an idea because you cannot imagine why you would create all of the negative experiences of your lives."

A slight smile gently creased his face as he facetiously added, "And it's true . . . sometimes it's hard for me to imagine as well. After all, why would you create yourself to be frustrated or embarrassed . . . or to perhaps fall from a cliff, thereby nesting yourself into the top of a pine tree. Why indeed would you do such a thing?"

Without warning, I felt my attention pricked as though one of my most cherished feathers had been strategically plucked from my tender behind. Taking no notice of his satirical assault on my fragile persona, my uncle continued on.

"I will tell you why . . . because as a divine spirit, as a whole and infinite being, your experience—whether deemed negative or not—was exactly what you wanted.

"Of course . . . when you are performing your daily duty as a helpless human, using only one third of your brain capacity, well, then undoubtedly it would feel as if such an event was the last thing you could have wanted."

There was a murmur of laughter throughout the crowd.

"But let us suppose that you are indeed not just a floundering mass of human cells, but an immortal spirit connected to every living thing through your emotions and your heightened ability to feel. Could it not be that through your own brilliance you might actually be pursuing a much higher plan in the scheme of things—one that encompasses every event of every lifetime so that your spirit, your soul, might learn and expand into an even greater understanding?"

A hush fell over the crowd, which appeared to be hypnotized, wearing an assortment of numbed expressions.

"So then," he continued, "now let us suppose that in this lifetime you chose to be a four-foot street urchin, with a flair for Shakespeare. You have been stumbling along in a slightly frustrated and distorted life, which now includes an adventure with cancer in your body. Because of the cancer, you know that you do not have much time left to awaken from the illusion of the human experience. Therefore, as the brilliant immortal spirit that you are, you manifest the following scenario.

"From the top of a parked car you antagonize some poor woman until she finally rams her Rolls Royce into the car you are standing on—totally by mistake. The impact sends you flying into the air, landing you head first onto the hood of *her* car, thereby sending *you* into a coma. Naturally, they take you to a hospital where you just happen to be placed into a room where I, an illumined spirit, just happen to be hanging out. I also just happen to take your own spirit for a little walk outside your comatose body, which gives you proof that you are not merely a human body at all, but an immortal being, who at any instant can become the wind—if you choose. Henceforth, you no longer fear your own death, and are now very much looking forward to your next adventure, whatever that might be."

All at once, Mohan jumped up and turned towards the gathering of people with his chin in the air and his eyes closed. Grinning smugly, he bowed in several directions, triggering a wave of chuckles and giggles within the crowd. My uncle reached down and picked up a small stick. Lightly tossed towards an unsuspecting Mohan, the tiny piece of wood struck him gently in the back of the head, quickly restoring the short fellow's humility, bringing his comical curtain call to a close. At this, I and many of the people laughed again.

My uncle then commented, **"Yes, Mohan . . . a very enlightened scenario indeed . . . and it only took hurling yourself into a coma to finally figure it all out."** Then he added, **"Clever, but not what I would call . . . particularly conscious."** He waited for several seconds until the crowd's mirth had subsided. Then he took up his monologue midsentence.

"Or," he said, **"let us suppose that you are the unhappy woman who actually hit the parked car on which the small man was standing. Deep within your being you also have the desire for your spirit to be as free as the wind. In your infinite wisdom though, you know that for an entire lifetime you have been mentally programmed by a religion that is partially based on guilt. Therefore, you create the scenario of putting some poor homeless man with cancer into a coma, which engulfs you with an enormous amount of guilt. This particular manifestation allows you to have a very close look at this self-inflicted judgment that has been a guiding force throughout your life. To your great surprise though, in the midst of your wallow, you just happen to run into this little fellow again. One fine evening, you not only find out that he came out of the coma, but now he is very ecstatic about the bliss and joy that he has discovered—because you put him into one. In fact, he is even thanking you profusely for taking the time to *land* him on his head. You perceive that you have been indulging in a tragedy**

that never really existed at all, that the guilt was simply an illusion created by a program in your linear mind. This incomprehensible set of circumstances causes you to do a 180-degree turn in a direction that has brought you to a new understanding—that there is undoubtedly a lot more going on in the spiritual realm than you were previously taught.

I knew he was talking about Jessica. Slowly I turned my head to inconspicuously examine the crowd for her face. It took but a moment to find her.

"Or," he said pressing on, "perhaps you are a man who unwillingly went to the hospital to identify your long lost uncle, which in turn caused you to lose your chance to become a rich and famous composer. You did this because within your infinite wisdom you knew that what your spirit really longed for was . . . was simply to know the truth of who you are."

There was a long pause, as I became emotionally stranded, wondering if everyone knew that he was talking about me.

Once again he took up his familiar posture with one knee raised high and began to rhythmically stroke the edge of his beard. Looking out over the people, he added, "When you come to know the absolute truth of who you are, to know the divine part that you are actually playing, then flowers will bloom in your pocket and the wind will long for your commands."

He looked directly at me, a belated acknowledgment of his previous comment. With a satisfied smile, he spoke, "How brilliant of you." He looked out around the people gathered and said, "How very brilliant of all of you."

Standing up, he slowly paced back and forth in front of the sedan like a Harvard professor about to launch into a lecture. "And so now, he began, "so now you are asking yourselves, *Well, if I was so brilliant in all of my stumblings, then why didn't I know it at the time, and why does being so brilliant always have to be such an arduous experience?*

"It doesn't," he said, answering his own question, "and if you lived your life in total bliss and joy with no thoughts of desperation, lack, fear, hatred, or the judgments of yourself and others, you *would* create only brilliance and nothing else."

"An impossible task you say— No more impossible than the turmoil and frustration you create on a daily basis. In fact, on an energy level it actually takes more effort, more expelled life force to create chaos and negative congestion than it does to create balance and bliss. Therefore, let us approach this through a more scientific understanding, one that will give your linear mind proof of why I would say that, indeed, *everything is of your choosing*. And, if you are a quantum physicist with a refined knowledge of polarities, or a Tibetan monk with a refined knowledge of auras and the many layers of emotional bodies, then you will soon realize that the explanation I am about to give is a simple diagnostic of how a very intricate system actually works.

"So let us begin with the premise: *Every thought that is embraced with emotion will in time manifest into an event or a third dimensional form.*

"*Thought* is the beginning. It is the essence of what you call God or spirit. It is the catalyst, the first cause of all that is. It is infinite, ever changing, and ongoing. Every thought that is embraced and fueled by emotion becomes a comet of energy that travels into the void. Its mission is to become a tangible form of its original ideal so it can then return to you, its creator.

"Thought is a kind of impulse, which in the moment of its creation, is divided into a positive and negative (or neutral) charge. Here the positive aspect of the thought moves throughout the universe forming and gathering molecules and atoms and all that it needs to become physical matter. Thought works much like a boomerang with the negative charge, or ground, waiting for the positive charge to make its circle into the void and then return to reconnect as a new form.

In the third dimensional world, where there are already so many physical forms in motion, a thought may take an even shorter journey where it simply uses the positive and negative pull to draw back to its creator an event or tangible form that already exists. Be it the manifestation of a love affair or a car accident, both are readily available as possibilities for you in the physical realm on a daily basis.

"*Emotion* is the essence that propels the thought and fuels it on its journey. When you contemplate a thought, and then embrace it with your passion, it is ignited throughout your body by energy centers. There are seven of these energy vortexes, which are in an ethereal realm, not visible to the human eye. In some cultures they are called the seven seals or chakras. They resonate within the human structure resembling round discs that start at the base of the spine and are then stacked like plates up to the top of the head. Each seal is similar to the shutter of a camera lens that opens and closes, allowing energy to be dispersed into your cellular structure and then out into the universe. These seven seals also correspond and work with certain glands that are arranged in this same fashion within your human structure. For example, the fourth seal is the heart chakra, which works in conjunction with the thymus gland, or the sixth seal, which is an energy opening that corresponds to the pituitary gland just behind the forehead.

"These seals or chakras work as a system. When thought enters and flows through this system it resonates with some of the chakras more than others according to the kind of thought that it is and the kind of emotion that it invokes. As the seals open, the thought expands and divides into its positive and negative charge. The positive charge is sent out into the universe to evolve into some sort of tangible manifestation.

"The negative charge emanates into the cellular structure, assisted by water and oxygen. Each seal activates its corresponding gland, which causes hormone flow in the body. Both aspects of this process cause the body to become like a reservoir of negatively charged frequencies acting as a lightening rod. The human structure and the aura around it become magnetized as a negative or neutral ground in third dimension. Hence forth the body will act like a magnet drawing to it the positively charged event or object that has now manifested into some form of the original thought."

At this point I checked to see if I looked as lost and dumbfounded as some of the people sitting around me. Assured that my jaw was not hanging between my knees, I tried to focus again on the abstract concept about which he was speaking.

"So now, let us suppose that what I have spoken is true, that you are indeed the creator of your own reality and that you do so by having a thought fueled by your emotions, which eventually manifests as an event or object. What kind of thoughts do you contemplate and what sort of emotions do you fuel them with?

"Do you have the thought of falling in love and then embrace it with your passion? Or do you have the thought that falling in love never happens to you, and then embrace it with futility? Or perhaps you *do* have the thought of falling in love, but then embrace it with futility, or any other combination you might explore. Everything counts, every thought, every emotion, and every union of the two that you have melded together since the beginning of time.

"With this in mind, contemplate all of the thoughts and emotions that you had today, and then try to think about how many you have had in just this lifetime alone. Now, add to this very long list of your own pending manifestations the thoughts and emotions of all of the other people with whom you are currently sharing the planet. Just imagine it. The list is enormous, is it not? . . . It is also your reality."

Returning to the automobile's fender, he slowly looked out over the crowd of people as though taking a psychic inventory of every person's thoughts.

As for myself, I was still struggling with the idea of how I had been put into the driver's seat of *this*, my own reality. I had always felt that I possessed some sort of free will to choose right or wrong, good or bad. But he was talking about having chosen every thing that ever happened. What about all of the innocent people who are killed by natural disasters or car accidents? And what about my own life? Why would I choose to be an unsuccessful composer whose music had never been performed? I loved music; it had been my life. Or why would I, at the age of thirty-eight want to be single? These choices didn't make sense to me. And what about this thing called God, what happened to the Supreme Being who was supposed to be in control of all of this?

"Yes," he said to the people, **"and what about this thing called God."** I jumped at the possibility of such an intrusion into my personal thoughts. **"Or perhaps you refer to this idea as the Isness or the Great Spirit.**

"The only way to speak about this one is to speak of an enormous act of love that took place at the birthing of the immortal spirits. All of you who walk about with this infinite ability to choose do so because you are indeed the offspring, the children of a divine being that created you out of an energy called love. For centuries, many of you have called this one God or the Father, and this is a fairly precise description, for you truly are the flesh and blood, that which was born of such a Creator. Your spirit is liken unto a handful of light. It was once pulled from the light body of this divine source, who then tossed your spark out into the universe and said, *Create from me, so that I might become all things.* So great was the love of this one that you were given the ability to create from your every thought, so that you could explore every adventure.

"That which you call your free will is not merely a discernment of good or bad. Right and wrong is a human judgment, the perception of an event in time. Free will is the essence of total freedom with the ability to create anew, on behalf of this Divine Spirit. So great was the love of this supreme being that you were allowed to become whatever you desired, be it a saint or a tyrant, a king or a pauper. Every adventure was for the expansion of wisdom, so that you, the immortal lights, would become all things and expand the knowledge and greatness of the Creator.

"You were birthed as an act of great love. You were sent out as a stream of light, which was a flow of love, energy that would always be connected to the Creator. Your journey was to go out

into the void and expand this love into every sound, every shape, every color, every nuance that you could imagine. Love was the source. Love was the intent. Love was the motion. So what happened?"

Total quiet reigned over the next few minutes as though the people gathered had suddenly gone into silent mourning for the words and the forgotten ideals of which he had spoken. Slowly, he stood and clasped his hands behind his back. He peered into the eyes of the people like an old school master waiting for someone to answer.

"So what happened?"

Then he became very still, his eyes opening wider, adding to the suspense, until at last he said, **"The ego was born."**

He paused for a brief second and then continued. **"It was never intended. It simply happened. It came about because as you, the immortal spirits, journeyed out into the density of third dimensional matter, you became totally engrossed in the human drama. You forgot that which you were and the source of love from whence you came.**

"Through this separation, an altered state of consciousness was birthed. In some of your cultures you call this event *the fall from grace* **and perhaps you have created parables to try to tell the story.**

"This altered state, which from now on I will simply refer to as *the ego,* **also separated you from each other. As a result you soon found cause to be in competition, for all had the power to create and yet all were still expanding in the same universe. This motion of competition would soon spawn other unexplored elements of hatred, vengeance, jealousy, and greed.**

"It has taken you eons to evolve into the kind of humanity that you are now. Lifetime after lifetime, century after century you have seeded your dimension with the thoughts of war, persecution, abuse, death, lack, and an array of ego-based judgments that are beyond count and number. You are caught on a wheel of evolving dramas—manifesting preprogrammed thoughts that now hold you captive—propelling you forward into

the future of your self-destructive probabilities. And the fact still remains *that everything is of your choosing, no matter how helpless you believe or have been told you are.*"

He stopped for a few seconds and glanced into the night sky as if he were contemplating the direction of the wind or perhaps waiting for it to change in response to his thoughts.

"**But let us begin with just you,**" he continued, "**which will have the illusion of being a little less overwhelming. As you walked through this your day, did you have thoughts of greatness and miracles? Or did you think about how difficult your life has become and how unfair it all seems. Did you think about world peace and how beautiful the human experience could be? Or were your only real thoughts of the day fed to you through the television, pondering political double-talk and sex scandals or the repeating commercial that had you spellbound by the thought that you would be so much more if you just owned that new automobile.**

"**In the realm of your creative thoughts, where do you spend your day? Where do you spend your time? See within yourself and take an inventory of all that you have embraced with the whole of your passion; the desires that you hold as absolute truths of this particular day in your life.**" After a slight pause, he said, "**Contemplate this for a moment.**"

21

Burning the Shadows

Contemplating the many thoughts of my own life required a very tedious biographical inventory at the mental five-and-dime. There was a little of everything and what now appeared to be an awful lot of nothing. I was hard-pressed to find any thoughts of greatness, and the idea of a miracle was totally out of place. The cerebral drivel that did come forward to be noticed came conveniently categorized by the emotion that had undoubtedly fueled it into being.

There were numerous thoughts of feeling frustrated and defeated, as well as a mental cavalcade of not feeling good enough, smart enough, or young enough. In addition, there was a closet-full of *not* feeling handsome enough, sexy enough, or desirable enough. The despairing phrases of *how will I ever pay the bills*, *how will I ever find a relationship*, and *how will I ever be discovered as a composer* rang out like church bells on a bright Sunday morning.

As far as my thoughts of the world in general, well, like most people, I thought whatever the television told me to think, and that, too, was a scary thought. I couldn't even fathom what we, as humanity, had created out of our ego-based consciousness—or unconsciousness as the case may be.

To begin an accounting for just myself, for all of the thoughts that had already swelled up in this lifetime alone, was to edit the *Jared Grayson Dysfunctional World Book of Encyclopedias* with the world's smallest eraser. The task seemed impossible. In addition, I had no idea how to stop the destructive thoughts ingrained in my head.

There was also *this* thought to deal with—the one I was having right now—this desperate thought of total confusion. Currently it was just a thought, but what would it manifest in the future? More of the same feelings of desperation and confusion? Or perhaps a whole slew of wonderful little tangible events to prove just how desperate and confused I really was.

Then I had a thought that was even more terrifying. If emotion is what fuels the thought into becoming a tangible event or object, then does more feeling, more emotion make it manifest even faster or create it to grow even larger? And if that's the case then it means that right now I'm in the midst of creating— Oh, my God. . . .

"**So now,**" he began, interrupting my cognitive overload, "**now, as you begin to take an inventory of your lives, you can see just how powerful and creative you have been—not to mention just how much you have to look forward to in the future.**" He chuckled at his own words.

Finding very little humor in his conclusion, I tried again to focus on whatever else he could possibly have to add.

"**All are children from the divine source with the power to create through their thoughts. Most everyone currently existing in this dimension is in a cocooned slumber. If this is indeed the truth, then how can it possibly be changed? If the accumulation of negative thoughts has grown to such overwhelming proportions, how could anyone override such a flood of ego-based intentions? How can one change the destiny of one's own life let alone the destiny of the planet?**"

He hesitated briefly and then added, "**There is a way.**" His words hung like fresh bait longing to be cast.

"**There is a great sword, an Excalibur of truth that can cut through all of your self-fulfilling prophecies. There is a means of changing your destiny, and there is no greater wisdom than the essence of the two words that I speak to you now— *to know* . . . that is all—*to know.***"

"*Knowing* is the final step in the creative process. To have a thought, to have a desire, is to set the manifestation into its circular motion. To embrace that thought with your passion and emotion fuels it toward its destiny. *To know*—is to know beyond all doubt, reason, or fear that the thought of what you desire will indeed come to pass. The power of this can change what is already in motion. When it's created as an act of love, its force is multiplied.

"To believe . . . is not to know. To believe is conjecture. To know . . . is absolute. It's a frequency as unwavering as the truth.

"To believe is to leave room for questions and for an unlimited number of intervening probabilities. To know is to enact pure wisdom, which is the culmination of body, mind, and spirit.

"To believe is to ask for more reasons. To know is to envision and then create.

"This same understanding also holds true in all perceptive realities. Let us suppose you are a devout Christian who is praying to that which you call God. Do you pray because you *believe* that God will answer, or do you pray because you *know* that God will answer? Which prayer is more powerful? Which prayer envelops the abundant love and trust that a divine source would have for all who would pray?

"I say unto you, that I am the wind. But I too have personality and history. I have also told you stories of my many lifetimes. So what is the real difference between you and me? The only difference is that I *know* who I am, and you are still struggling just to believe in anything at all. I was once like you, caught on the wheel of my evolving dramas. Then one day I simply got the joke. On that day I gave up everything in my life just to know the truth of who I was. I surrendered all of the judgments of myself and others to finally gain the wisdom of this dimension. Through an act of great love, which gave me the ability to recognize in totality the light of the Divine Spirit within myself, I was able to consciously lift my soul, my spirit, from my body. Leaving my physical form poised in a state of grace, I learned to travel beyond the human experience until one day I did not return. I chose to exist in a different reality, at a higher frequency. There have been those like myself in every one of your cultures who have mastered this experience and moved on into other dimensions.

"The human experience is a most beautiful and magnificent adventure indeed, but it was never intended that you be entrapped in this physical form. To have the choice, to come and go at will, is the truth of your birthright as children of the Creator. To regain this kind of freedom is simply to know it's within you; to *know* this beyond even the slightest shadow of doubt.

"This act of knowing, fueled by your passion and your love, can open any doorway. It can unlock any heart. It can cause warriors to lay down their swords and lose their desire for all war and competition.

"In the times of your past, there was a woman known to many as Sister Mother Theresa. She cultivated thoughts that healed the sick and provided homes and food for a nation of children, as well as shelter for thousands who were destined to die in the streets. She did not simply believe in her God, but had abundant knowledge of the love that came from this divine source. Her thoughts and prayers were not feeble pleas in the night, but sure and solid words to be said, *knowing* that the answer would come.

"In your history there was also a man by the name of Adolf Hitler who had the thought of ruling the world. Through his passionate thought, he would nearly destroy an entire culture causing a siege of death and persecution that would affect the whole of humankind. He accomplished this reign of terror, not because he *believed* he was right; he rose to his power because he *knew* it was within his reach—he had no doubt.

"Now . . . does this mean Hitler was correct in his actions? Of course not. His passion to control and persecute humanity was based purely on his altered ego and could not have been further from the source of love that was his origin. It *is*, though, an accounting of why he was allowed such an adventure. As the love of the Creator had once promised and set into motion, all immortal spirits would have the free will to create from their every thought, whether they desired to be a king, pauper, saint, or tyrant.

"There was also a man who lived in your world who thought that through the divine love and support of his Creator he could walk upon the water. His thought was so sure and his knowing so strong that one afternoon he actually strolled out onto the sea. He was in such perfect alignment with the flow of nature that when he asked the water to support his weight, the water responded. He too was considered a madman indeed— a madman who knew that a miracle was not just something mystical. It was something that you create.

"What you call a miracle is simply one pure thought— created out of a divine love—fueled by unwavering passion— held in the flow of pure knowledge. Simple. In fact, it is so simple, a child could do it. Perhaps as children you did."

Returning to the fender of the sedan, he sat back into his familiar posture. Again he seemed to probe the minds of the people, waiting for an appropriate time to continue.

"I want to tell you a story . . . about myself. It is a tale about one of these simple miracles, one that is perhaps from half a dozen centuries ago.

"In that lifetime, the event of which I speak happened when I was a young boy, nigh three or four. My mother had died during my birth, and although my father raised me, he was always a little angry about that. This was also why my father sought the advice of a holy man in a temple far from us. He wanted to know why had his life taken the turns that it had.

"So one day he packed us up and we traveled to a great monastery, a place well-known for its natural spring. It was thought by some that the water came directly from God. There were many stories of miracles and mystical events that had happened to its visitors.

"So we went to the temple and waited for several days because it was not easy to see this holy man. I was always told to stay outside the gate, but my papa would enter and sit with the others who were waiting. Time and again I'd sit and wait for my papa's return.

"One day, as he went into the temple I decided I had waited enough. I knew how long it would be before he returned, so I went for a little walk myself. I wandered around the massive wall surrounding this temple, which was a huge fortress, at least for a toddler.

"Eventually I came to a crack in the wall, a hole in its stone face. It was down very low and next to the bushes, where only a child would notice. Squatting down, I peered through the opening. Inside there was a beautiful garden. As I looked more closely, I could see a pool of water surrounded by stones of varying size and shape. Sitting up high in the center of the pool was a great stone, and it appeared that water poured directly out of the stone.

"Well, I was a young child. I had never heard that a spring might pour naturally from rocks. I thought the stone was magic.

"I had to see more, so I pulled some rocks away and climbed through the wall. As I approached the magic stone that poured water, I noticed an old man sitting next to the pool. The crown of his head was wrapped in a cloth and several layers of robes draped about him. I could also tell by the way his white eyes stared into the sky that he was blind.

"Quietly I snuck by him, hoping he would not notice. As I got close to the pool, he startled me by saying, 'Did you come for a drink of water?'

"I thought, well, I'm not in trouble or anything. He's talking to me and offering me some water. I replied, 'Is the water alright? Can you drink it?'

"He told me to come a little closer, so I sat down with him on the edge. He said, 'Yes, this water is very good.' Reaching down with his cupped hand he made a scooping motion, except he did not touch the water; his hand moved above the surface.

Then he raised his empty hand to his mouth, closed his blind eyes, and tilted back his head to drink.

"Well, I thought, this old man was far more than blind. That is until I saw water pour out of his empty hand, into his mouth, and down the sides of his beard.

"Without a doubt, this was an amazing thing, even for a child. I thought this pool was magic, and I was sure that I could create such magic too. If this feeble old blind man could do this, then surely so could I.

"So I reached down with my hand cupped and grazed just above the water as he had done. I brought my small empty hand up to my mouth to pour the water in . . . and nothing happened. There was no water.

"Then the blind man asked, 'Did you like it?'

"I pondered earnestly, should I tell the old man that I did not taste the water? After all he could not see. Then, being completely honest with myself, I finally thought, no, I wanted to taste the water and pour it directly out of my empty hand, just as he had done. I wanted it more than anything, and I knew that I could do it.

"An instant after that thought, before I could speak, he said, 'Let us try again.' Then he again reached down with his cupped hand, grazed the top of the water, closed his eyes, and drank from his empty hand.

"Well, I was a very clever young lad and this time I noticed that just before the water poured, he closed his blind eyes. I thought, *that* must be the magic, that was the trick. I was sure of it. All I had to do was close my eyes before I drank. It was simple. I became very excited.

"So I reached down, scooped over the magic water, and in total joy pulled my hand up to drink. I closed my eyes to the world, to everything that I had ever known, to receive the water. By no surprise, the water poured from my hand.

"As it poured into me, I saw in my mind a black void with stars. Then I saw an old man with beautiful eyes that smiled at me.

"I was a young child, and I thought the stone was magic; I did not know any better. No one had yet taught me that miracles and magic were only from myths and fables.

"So after some time with this old man, I crawled back through the hole in the wall and went back to the gate to find my papa waiting for me. He was angry—not only because I had wandered off, but also because he had not been given an audience with the holy one.

"As we walked down the road he grumbled and shouted. He told me that he had gone into the temple and commanded one of the monks to take him to see the holy one immediately.

"The monk had said, 'I cannot. He is busy right now with a young boy.' My father was very angry at this young boy. . . . I did not make the connection at the time.

"Later when I told my papa that I had poured water from my empty hand, he beat me for creating such a story, for telling such lies."

My uncle then rose up and began to meander among the people. Presently, he said, **"You are not unlike the child I was or the madman who thought to walk upon the water, nor the one who sought to dictate the world. You are a sparkling gem, lost in the ashes of your past, longing to be found and remembered. This knowledge and wisdom I speak of, is not that which I give you. It is something inside you, a fire you already possess."**

He continued to walk, very sovereign, throughout the crowd, until he stood before the fire. He kicked gently at the smoldering logs causing the flames to rise and send a flurry of sparks up and around his towering figure. Staring into the fire he said, **"Close your eyes. Shut out the world that is around you, and drink from within. Find the *you* that lives inside that hollow shell.**

"Feel yourself surrounded by the blackened empty nothing where only a handful of stars dare to walk the night sky. See with your thoughts tall trees standing all around you, their branches heavy with golden leaves. See how some of the leaves have fallen to the ground in a carpet of yellow, gold, amber and red.

A sweet wind blows through the trees.
It breezes through your clothes sending a chill up your spine.
You look all around . . . for what . . ? You're not really sure.
Then, with your imagination, you envision a great fire.

You set out to gather wood for such a fire,
a kindling you know to be found only inside you.
You know as you forage for each and every branch,
that you gather in the very sordid parts of you.

You notice a stick of hopelessness, and then a branch of defeat.
Heartache lies in chips and bark, lying at your feet.
You see the faces of your past molded in each piece,
the memories that you gather for a glorious
and brittle burning.

You pick up a bough of desperation,
and those twigs, a handful of hesitation.
You search through the reflections of your life,
until at last, you have created a brush pile
just longing for the blazing.

You bow unto this wood because you know it is you.
And you honor every moment of its making.
Time now stands still, and the wind holds its breath,
watching for the miracle to awaken.

And then, ever so carefully,
you take your hand and touch it to your heart.
With all of your passion, you reach in through your body,
past the flesh and bone, into the spirit of your being.
You find within your soul a flame forever burning,
a flicker that has longed for your return.
Gently, you reach into the flame,
and pull forth a handful of your light.

You bring this sacred fire out of your body
and hold it in the palms of your hands.
The light pulsates like the beating of a drum.
It illuminates your face and burns bright in your eyes.
In total awe, you gaze into its wonder.

You stand before the gathered wood,
tall and bright like the blade of a single candle.
Then, without thinking, you breathe into the private words
that somehow have found you.

This is the truth of who I am.
I am the fire.
I am the flame of creation.
Let the shadow of my life
burn into the blaze of my freedom.
Let the fire of spirit now fill my cocoon.

With a rush, you throw the flame down onto the wood.
It flutters and explodes into fire.

The blaze crackles and flames,
growing brighter and brighter,
flooding your vision with a radiant light.
Burning and blazing,
it's a wildfire before you.

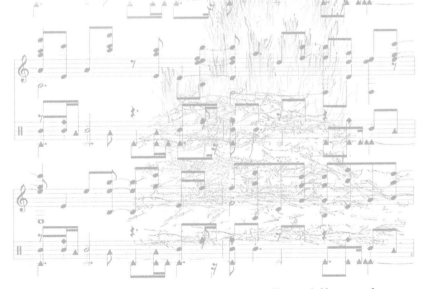

The smoke comes to join you in a trillion different shapes,
to dance, and swirl, and celebrate your wake.

The sound roars about you, the warmth passing through you.
You spin and turn in circles around the flame.
Sparks from the fire trail into the air,
to mingle in the night amongst the stars.
With a wave of your hand the fire bows before you,
then rises again at your command.

Like a native to the dance, dressed in fine regalia,
you twirl in the spiral of the flame.
You bow and you turn, then rise up with the fire,
stepping to the rhythm of your heart.
You dance through the memories. You dance through the night,
until at last you can dance no more.

Gently, you allow the flames to settle into the bed of hot embers. You lay yourself beside them in the purity of their heat. The power of their light emanates around you. In this you are infinite, filled with the clarity of a divine truth. It all seems so simple, so clear, so unlimited. You are wrapped in the blanket of your spirit.

You close your eyes and stretch out into the vastness of your creative thoughts—into any kind of fantasy you desire. You imagine your head resting in the lap of a beautiful lover whose fingers delicately comb your hair, and who sings a sweet melody, one that you wrote yourself for just such an occasion. You are ever so content and mesmerized by the touch of this lover who quietly whispers your name . . . Jared . . . Jared. . . .

"Jared . . ." she called out in the haze of my awareness. "Jared . . . can you hear me. Jared . . . are you okay?" I felt her fingers running through my hair. Slowly I opened my eyes and gazed into a face, a face that suddenly became—

"JESSICA!" Hastily, I sat up leaving the comfortable cushion of her caressing arms and soft bosom. Swiftly her fingers slipped out of my hair. "Jessica! What is it? What happened?"

"It's alright, Jared. Everything is fine. Don't get so excited. I think you just dozed off. You were lying here with your head on the hard ground so I propped you up in my lap until you woke up. Everyone has left, and I didn't want to leave you here by yourself."

"Oh God," I said, rubbing my eyes, "I'm sorry, I must have fallen asleep."

"It's fine, Jared . . . really, it's alright."

"Where did everyone go?"

"I'm not sure. I was kind of like you. When I opened my eyes, most of the people had gone, including your uncle." Then she asked, "Are you okay?"

"Yes, I'm fine." I said, even though I felt vulnerable and disoriented, having just awakened in her arms.

Then a strange lull formed in our conversation. We remained in the glow of the fire's last embers, neither of us knowing quite what to say. I glanced around at the empty arena with its old automobiles and wooden crates, remembering faintly how it had looked earlier with the people gathered.

I clambered to my feet trying to gain some sort of composure. Then from out of nowhere she said, "I have been asked to appear on AM America, the morning TV talk show."

"What?" I said, having not a clue about what she was saying.

"They have asked me to be on their program. They want to interview me about why I left my television show."

Dodging Jessica's attempt to convey her innermost thoughts, I bluntly suggested, "May I walk you to your car?"

She stopped short and, with a hint of embarrassment, answered, "Actually, I came by cab. Father Mathews called and told me he had heard that your uncle might be here. Apparently this gathering has happened before."

I could feel her anticipation, her deep need for some self-exposing conversation, which presently I had no desire to be caught in. Turning away, I gestured towards what I thought would be the way out. I began to walk back up through the alleyway, assuming there was a main street at the adjoining end. She did her best to keep up with me amid her desire to tell me these personal things, which I could feel her attempting about every third step.

Everything seemed to be moving far too fast. I felt out of control, like when I was sliding off the side of the rock that night on the mountain, exhilarated by what was happening and yet terrified by the possible outcome.

As we reached the street, she again tried to share her thoughts. "I heard it again tonight, Jared, the music in my head. It happened again as I started to doze off at the end of his talk. Jared, I think it was your mus—"

"Jessica! I don't know what to think about all of this. My life has been far from normal the last several days. A friend of mine, who was involved in all of this, is now missing and may be in some sort of trouble. I just need to slow down and spend some time trying to sort it all out."

As a taxi came around the corner, I whistled and waved,

catching his attention. He made an abrupt turn and headed in our direction.

"Jared, I just wanted to ask about your music, I wanted to know if I could—"

"Jessica!" I interrupted, slicing through her words. "I don't know what to tell you. I don't know where the music comes from. I don't know why we hear it or what just happened back there. Do whatever you feel compelled to do. Just don't ask me anything right now, please." Realizing how helpless my frustration sounded, I added, "I think that everything is alright, really. I just don't know where I fit into all of this."

At last the taxi pulled up allowing me to end the conversation. As I opened the car door for her, I felt Jessica gently squeeze my hand.

"Thank you," she said. "Thanks for everything. Good night."

"Good night, Jessica." I closed the taxi's door and watched it drive away.

For a few seconds I could see her face in the back window. Her expression was confidently hopeful. In that instant—she scared the hell out of me. She seemed so strong, so together about all of this; that is compared to when I saw her sobbing at the hospital. Somehow it felt like we were both on the same path, especially with both of us hearing my music during our sojourns to—wherever. The only difference was that she walked through all of this like the gallant and beautiful woman she was, while I appeared to be some honking gander running around the city streets with my feathers falling out.

Trying to gather myself together, I looked around for a street sign that might tell me exactly where I was. I had no idea about the time. It must have been fairly late; the storefronts were dark, and the streets were deserted but for an occasional passing vehicle. On the corner, the white letters illuminated on the green background read JESPER BOULEVARD.

I had never been on that particular street before, at least not that I could recall. The name, though, was more than familiar. I remembered it from a piece of paper I had placed in my pocket on that fateful day I was called to the hospital to identify my long lost uncle. Fame and fortune lived on that street, for it was the street where John McDowell's office resided.

I couldn't help shouting like a madman, my words echoing out into the darkened air. "So here I am, Jesper Boulevard!" Then in a more subdued and rather feeble tone, I added, "Yes, here I am. Standing just a few steps from McDowell's door, in the middle of the night, with not even enough money to catch a cab out of here." I chuckled at the insanity of it all. "Yes," I said with a kind of satisfying sarcasm, "now this is one of my more interesting manifestations."

It was a long walk back to the bridge. At this time of night I really didn't feel safe strolling along the river, the way I had come. It also appeared that Jesper Boulevard veered north before it got to Broadman Street and the bridge. Behind Jesper Boulevard was an alleyway that ran parallel to the river and would eventually end up at the same place.

As I entered the alley, I began to think about Michael Talon. Here I had been lying around in some sort of psychic adventure with fire and bliss, and who knows what else, blazing. Michael, on the other hand, was in trouble. It was also possible that I was the only one who cared or was even aware of it. Through my involvement with Shankara, I felt like I was continually being pulled into some mystical daydream, when I should have been focused on what was a serious problem. Michael may have been kidnapped. He might even be tortured to reveal what he knows about the enlightened one. And why doesn't anyone else know about this? Why am I the only one?

I walked along the alley cobblestones becoming more and more lost in the endless questions flooding my mind. And although I felt quite submerged in all of this cerebral chatter, it didn't take me long to find myself again when I suddenly realized that two men had entered the alley from behind and were following me.

22

Eyes of a Jesus, Eyes of a Buddha

Glancing back revealed that the street lamps had created a surrealistic backdrop for the silhouettes of the two darkened figures who now appeared to be my predators. Stealthily, and with subdued haste, they made their way through the shadows, steadily closing the fifty-yard gap between the wolves and the lamb. Fear now walked along with my quickened pace, draining the confidence from my steps, causing my knees to weaken and falter. As my heart raced in twelve-eight time, I calculated the possibility of bolting to the lighted street at the other end before the ambush had occurred and the terrible deed was done.

Who these men were or why they were following me was a blur in my mind. Perhaps they had kidnapped the professor and came now to capture me in an attempt to discover the identity of the enlightened one. Or they might just be hoodlums who spotted my mindless meanderings and decided to take advantage of the situation by slitting my throat and robbing me of the thirty-five cents that now jangled frantically in my pocket. I dared not turn and look again to find out. In truth, there was no need. I could easily hear the cadence of rhythmic footsteps pursuing me. I tightened my fists and swallowed a deep breath, preparing to explode across the rough cobblestones and out of this desperate cave towards the lighted opening of my freedom.

Then, without warning, some forty yards in front of me, the

large shadowy frame of a man stepped into the path of my escape. His heavy army coat partially disguised the club-like object in his hand. There was no way out. The door of my cage had slammed shut, leaving me to twist and squirm in the throes of my helplessness.

Shock seemed to puncture my lungs, my breath blowing out of me, dissipating into the cold night air. The third man just stood there, guarding the opening, watching my every move. My mind grabbed at the faintest of possibilities, heroic attempts that reeled out like a fumbled spray of playing cards, falling one by one on the debris-strewn ground.

I needed a chance. I needed a miracle. But most of all, I needed the open space in the alley just ahead where the front ends of two delivery trucks protruded from an adjacent access. I slipped into the space hoping to find nothing less than the yellow brick road. To my dismay, I found an area just big enough for the two trucks to be backed up to a concrete loading dock.

Three or four closed doors were scattered along the surrounding walls offering remote possibilities of escape. I raced frantically to each one, turning and pulling at the knobs, whispering silent pleas through the cracks and peepholes. To no avail—all of them were locked, and no one came to answer them at this, my darkest hour.

For just a second I stopped, held my breath, and listened. The footsteps were still approaching, accompanied by a low murmur of voices. They had to be just around the corner.

Standing at the back of the two delivery trucks, I noticed one had a set of swinging doors that were unlatched. I pulled them open to find that the truck's cargo space was empty. Climbing up into the truck, I closed the doors, which caused a creaking and clunking sound. With any luck my stalkers would think that the noise came from my having gone through one of the service entrances.

Once I was inside, everything went black. My pupils quickly dilated, searching for any signs of light. The stench of rotting food filled my senses. Holding the massive doors closed as tightly as I could, I became very still and listened.

"So where'd he go?" came a muffled voice from alongside the truck.

"I don't know," someone replied.

"Maybe he had a key and ducked into one of these doorways."

"Could be, 'cause it doesn't look like he's here now."

"Check the back of the trucks."

I tightened my grip, trying with every ounce of my strength to keep the doors from opening. There was one tug, and then another, followed by a voice saying. "Nah, he must of went through one of these doors."

Once again I held my breath and listened. The silence left me wondering why it had become so quiet, so quickly. I waited for several seconds, paralyzed, until I heard a distant voice say, "Come on, let's go."

The jolt of one last surprising tug at the doors nearly caused me to lose my grasp. I began to pant uncontrollably, my nervous system rattled to the core.

"Yeah, alright, I guess he's gone," someone answered. "He probably didn't have any cash on him anyway."

I waited patiently this time, envisioning three evil toothless grins just on the other side. After several minutes, I slowly allowed the doors to part letting in a long stream of light and a welcomed breath of fresh air.

I climbed out of my premature tomb, carefully walked to the front of the trucks, and cautiously peeked into the alleyway. There was no sign of anyone in either direction. I let out a great sigh and leaned on the hood of the truck trying to decide which direction to take, guessing at which end of this treacherous lane I would find the least number of thieves, murderers, and kidnappers. The way I'd been going was now the shortest distance out. It was also the one running towards the bridge and eventually my jeep.

Guardedly, checking for any sign of danger, I moved out into the alley and took a good long look around. Just across the way, in an adjacent opening, I noticed an object that looked very much out of place. Lying on the ground, protruding from behind a large assortment of garbage containers, was a beautiful piece of fringed white cloth, like a scarf. It looked to be made of satin, and its texture and brightness seemed to glow amid the oily cobblestone and sooted concrete. It flared out from around the bottom edge of a trash can like a flag or marker longing to be found. As I got closer, I could see that it was embroidered at the end with a zig zag design in the shape of a W or M. Drawing nearer, I noticed part of a very expensive black wool coat or suit. Moving in closer, I caught sight of a highly polished black shoe and then a coat sleeve with a limp hand dangling from it. Nervously, I stepped forward to see more clearly.

There, at the base of concrete steps leading from an open doorway, was the stout figure of a man squatting down hunkered over himself. He had silver-gray hair and a long wool suit coat; a white scarf hung to one side, falling off his shoulder. Oh my God! I thought. Someone had actually been mugged or perhaps even murdered. He was probably dressed to attend a performance at one of the posh theaters up on the main street. More than likely he was attacked while returning to his car.

By the way he was hunched over, it was difficult to tell whether he was sitting or unconscious and propped up by something underneath him. He wheezed softly and swayed slightly, confirming that he was at least still alive.

After the scare I had just experienced, I was enveloped in compassion for him. I wanted to do anything I could to help. As I leaned over to see his face, I noticed the flicker of a small candle, which sat burning between his feet. It was now obvious that he was actually squatting over the flame. His facial features were frozen and, although his eyes were open, his vision was caught in an impenetrable stare. He appeared to be an attractive man, although it was difficult to tell within his lost expression. He was clean-shaven, except for a gray mustache that was well-groomed and slightly turned up at the ends. I wondered if he might be in shock, or perhaps so defeated by whatever had happened, that he was unable to move.

With great sensitivity, I reached out my hand and gently touched him on the shoulder saying, "Are you alright? Have you been hurt. . . ? Do you need some help?"

The physical contact seemed to bring him back to life, but his movement was slow and hypnotic. Turning his head, he looked directly at my hand, now resting on his shoulder. His expression was notably soft with an inquisitive smile as though he were perhaps imagining that it was not my hand, but a small bird that had landed there. He then reached over as if to pick up that bird and hold it for a closer look.

As he carefully took my hand, I couldn't help but notice his intense and very beautiful eyes, light blue gray in color, and vast as an ocean. They were both amazing and haunting, reminding me of eyes that belonged to actors whom I had seen play the part of Jesus in numerous movies. Then he turned to look directly at my face, until *his* eyes were all that I could see. They truly were the eyes of a Jesus, the eyes of a Buddha. I felt washed by the presence of his sight, my empathy for him somehow being mirrored back to me. The feeling mesmerized me. Even the sensation of his holding my hand seemed almost angelic. These eyes that I now witnessed were enlightened eyes, benevolent eyes. For an instant I couldn't help but wonder if by some strange set of circumstances I had been led here to find the Jesus, the Buddha, the Enlightened One.

Delicately, he lifted my hand and brought it up to his mouth as though it were a perfect rose and he now wanted to smell its aroma and touch its petals to his lips. Ever so gently he pulled my hand in closer, and then to my complete surprise, he slid the ends of my four fingers between his lips and into his mouth. In total shock, I froze.

Then he began to gently suckle my fingers. My mind exploded into sheer panic as I reared back and tried to pull them out. This mortified reaction caused him to bite down on my fingers, digging his teeth into my tender flesh and bones. He cinched down into a grip so tight, I was sure that any attempt to retrieve my fingers would surely sever them completely.

Fear seemed to rip me in two; my whole being wanted to escape, for I now stared into the dark and demonic eyes of a Satan, of a Lucifer. I felt like a helpless animal with my paw caught in the sharp jaws of a steel trap. All too clearly I could envision my hand with small bleeding stubs, fingers that had once played the music of Beethoven, Mozart, and Chopin. So great was my fear that I had to force myself to breathe. My terror seemed to feed his malice, his treacherous bite producing a partial grin with his mouth full of my own fragile extremities.

His eyes looked completely through me, down into my soul, beyond my innocence, snaking in and around my hopes. My God! I thought. If there is a Supreme Being, please save me from this horrid act.

Moving with the rhythm of his raspy breathing, his watery dark eyes pulsated, expanding and contracting. I tore my own eyes away, pulling from this evil trance, sure that if I did not I would be devoured by it.

Looking away, I caught sight of drug paraphernalia on the step behind him, a needle and syringe beside a bent spoon, which held a melted white substance in its bowl. I now knew what I was dealing with. This was chaos beyond insanity. This man was trapped somewhere far beyond reason; a rabid animal out of control, having surrendered his own will to the poison of some narcotic.

As I looked back into his ferocious and distorted face, I thought about Michael's wolf, caught in a trap, consumed with rage, snarling and lashing out. I thought about how he had described his own pain, revealing his compassion to the fierce animal.

Could it be that this man before me was not unlike the wolf? Could he be the victim of some abstract rage or dark force that had now come to possess him? After all, where were the beautiful eyes that I had seen just seconds ago? Where was the affection? Was that not still a part of him? Trapped by the circumstances of this terrifying event, I could think of nothing other than to approach it with some kind of compassion—

With that single thought, his demeanor changed, his clenched vise loosening slightly. Quickly, I tried to free my hand, frightened that if I could not release my fingers in that brief second that I would lose them forever.

Instantaneously, he reacted to my fear by clamping down with his lethal bite, his hideous eyes peering back into mine. The timing of this event was so precise I couldn't help but wonder if he was simply reacting to my emotions, the emotions on which he so successfully preyed. If that was the case, then it was possible that to free myself completely, I would have to be both courageous and compassionate, even though I would be hard-pressed to find either of those virtues.

It was difficult to fathom how I was going to change my thoughts and feelings into a loving act. With my position so vulnerable, my emotions so attached to his, I dared not be superficial. My compassion had to be genuine.

I closed my eyes and contemplated Michael's story. I remembered being so moved by how the wolf was calmed by his caring presence. Like a blind man, I carefully reached out my other hand into the black empty nothing until I was able to touch the man gently on the side of his face.

He responded immediately, changing into the feeling I was sending him. Like a chameleon whose color is altered by its surroundings, he once again became soft and angelic, possessing the eyes of Jesus, the eyes of Buddha. He was but a reflection of me, of my thoughts and emotions, my caring and compassion. It was as if he possessed no will of his own.

I needed to know if what I had found was the truth, that such a phenomenon existed and that I indeed had the ability, with a single thought and a handful of compassion, to change my reality as well as someone else's. I took a deep breath to prepare myself. Then once again I imagined the demonic eyes I had seen. I remembered my fear and the vulnerability I had experienced.

Within seconds, he became my thoughts, reflecting back to me all of my worst fears, my vision of demons. Even with the understanding I had just gained, it was difficult to change back, stepping past the pain of my fingers being devoured by such a monster. Then, just as suddenly, I realized who the monster was. This was but a reflection of my own emotions; the dark and desperate creature really . . . was me.

This revelation caused me to stumble over my own identity. Who was I? Was I some horrible monster? The best part of me was good and very talented. I had composed beautiful music that could tame even the darkest creature. These new and redeeming thoughts soon accompanied the sound of my own music, which I began to hear in my mind, a composition I had created not so long ago. It was a positive and triumphant piece called *Opus For a New World*. In this instant, it heard its cue to rescue me from the darkest corners of my mind.

With the music now sounding in my head, this ferocious creature, in the image of a man, slowly loosened his clenched jaws. He released my hand completely, letting his eyes roll back, his facial expression filling with a kind of awe and wonder. He carefully laid himself back against the concrete steps as though he were newly enchanted and I was the pied piper who had seduced him with my melody.

I hummed pieces of the music as I came to my feet, the man still listening, so content with where he was. I left him there, in whatever reality he had found, and made my way back into the main alley, continuing my journey toward the open street. Passing in front of the two delivery trucks, I thought about my close call with the three malicious characters who had attempted to corner me. I could not imagine why I would have created such a drama. Currently though, the whole event felt somewhat less threatening, presuming that there indeed had been some great purpose behind it, some wisdom that I was yet to understand.

The entire evening had been quite remarkable, filled with adventure, intrigue, and magic. Oh yes, there was definitely magic, more than I had experienced in a decade. I was amazed by all of the strange events that had been happening, almost as if I were being groomed for some profound purpose, some extraordinary task. I felt powerful, almost majestic, with the ability to imagine and create anything in the world . . . absolutely anything. Then I had the most preposterous thought of all. Maybe *I* was the Enlightened One.

Uncontrollably, my laughter burst out of me in whoops and hollers, echoing between the tall brick buildings at the sheer absurdity of my momentary madness. If I had never been in touch with my ego before, this was indisputably a close encounter. In fact, I was quite sure that my ego must have just sprung forth into full bloom . . . for me, myself, and I to adore.

With a flare of sarcasm, I chortled out loud. "Yes . . . Yes, that has to be it. I'm the second coming of Jesus Christ, and they simply forgot to tell me. How rude of them." Again I let out a bellow of hilarity. "Or better yet, maybe I'm the reincarnation of Buddha. Maybe that's it. Just put on a little weight, learn to sit with my legs all tangled up, and there you have it. Not a problem." I chuckled again as I took my last few steps out of the alley and into the lighted atmosphere of the open street. About two blocks away I could see the entrance to the East Bridge. "Yes!" I shouted into the empty street. "At last . . ! Take me to the bridge!" Then I added, "Oh hell, never mind the bridge, I'll just walk across that water." I hammered at myself in total joy, knowing full well that as *this* night had been unfolding I would be lucky to get across the bridge and find my way home at all.

As I spotted the twenty-four-hour convenience store across the street, coffee seemed like a good idea. Dodging a couple of slow-moving cars, I jaywalked the four lanes. Then I promptly stifled my glee having noticed two scruffy-looking characters who had posted themselves at the front entrance. Their slurred speech and jovial manner likely resulted from spending the better part of their evening drinking the contents of whatever was stashed in the paper bag that sat between them. One of the men had shaved dark stubble for a haircut and the other straight black hair slightly longer and ill-kept. They had perched themselves like a couple of parrots on several wooden milk crates that had probably been left outside by mistake. Their exaggerated and philosophical dialogue rallied around a conversation that I did my best not to acknowledge. My instincts told me to make no eye contact with these inebriated fellows; I had no desire to be pulled into their dissertation.

As I slipped past them and through the doorway I heard one of them raise his voice and say, "Hey man, did you see that guy? Did you see him, man, he looked like Jesus Christ or something."

Promptly, the other answered, "Are you kidding, man!"

"No shit. Come on, I'll show you."

Panic, my now familiar comrade, joined me as I quickly scouted the small store for another exit or at least some inconspicuous place to hide. I darted into the nearest aisle as I heard the slurred but excited deliberation now being projected very loudly from the open doorway.

"Yeah, he had the beard, and the mustache, and the hair, and everything."

"Reeeally!" expounded the other voice, "Whoa, just like Jesus Christ, huh . . . I wanna see this guy. Where'd he go?"

In that instant I couldn't help but picture myself being chased through the streets by an enraged mob, with clubs and torches blazing. With my luck, they probably also had a wooden cross stashed somewhere, along with a couple of spikes and a plentiful supply of long prickly thorns.

I scampered around the corner display of cookies and into the next aisle, which was empty and furthest from the door. Hastily, I grabbed a product off the shelf and pretended to be reading the back label. If I was spotted again perhaps my total non-response to this absurd outburst might squelch it before I had to deal with these lunatics directly.

The two men finally did appear at the other end of the aisle. To my surprise though, they gawked at me with astounded expressions and then with a few chuckles turned and disappeared into the next aisle. I waited a few more seconds, still pretending to be earnestly reading, just in case anyone else might have been watching.

Actually though, I did not truly grasp just how bizarre this particular scene was until I began to read the description on the box I was holding: *We will be a reliable friend where others might have let you down*— Post haste, I turned the package over to reveal the white and blue letters: TAMPONS.

"Eah!" I yelped, dropping the box to the ground. Then, of course, I had to pick it up again and spend the next several seconds trying to find where to put it back on the shelf.

Today, I thought, today perhaps would not be the best day to proclaim myself as the Enlightened One. In fact, in the future, I believe I'm going to be very careful about what I say about anything, not to mention choosing better neighborhoods to hang out in.

Making my way out of the store, I decided to skip the coffee and see if there was any possibility of locating my jeep and actually making it home before I just happened to turn myself into a pumpkin. Or maybe I already was a pumpkin, and this human body was the illusion. On second thought, just forget that first thought, the pumpkin thing. Perhaps for the moment I should just try to focus my thoughts on absolutely nothing, if that was possible. Is that possible?

23

The Visitor

It was amazing to me that in the three years I had lived in my house I could not remember having ever been disturbed from my slumber before I was at least partially awake and remotely conscious. In the last week, though, I was averaging about three out of six such arousals. Nearly fifty percent of my snooze-button-mornings had become slap-in-the-face-uprisings, which I greeted with a yawning mouth, half-opened eyes, and the stylish flair of my ratty blue bathrobe. It appeared that *this* morning was not going to be any different—a series of knocks sounded from my front door. I stumbled to the door and spied through the peephole at my uninvited visitor, to find out just how presentable I would have to pretend to be.

The face in the peephole sent an instant shock wave throughout my nervous system, my mouth gasping for breath. It was him! White hair, white beard, and all six-foot-four of him right here at my front door. "Shit!" I whispered, "What is he doing here?" I backed myself flat up against the door as though I were bravely attempting to keep it from falling in. Then the jarring DING! DONG! of my doorbell raised me completely off the floor like an electrified cat with its fur jetting in every direction. "Shit!" I blurted out again, the word seeming to find its own way out of my mouth. "Why is he here?"

Hastily, I tried to take a mental inventory. Here I was, in my own home, nearly face to face with the very person that I'd been in search of for the last several days. So what was the problem? Here *he* was, just a man, (or at least he appeared to be), and not really even a stranger. He was simply my Old Uncle Ben. Right? So why did I have this overwhelming urge to run out the back door, scamper barefoot down the alley and never look back.

I scurried to the front window to peer through the curtain for a better look. His attire was 100% pure rummage sale, beginning with a white cotton shirt that was a bit dated and moth-eaten around the edges. His pants, khaki in color, were reminiscent of the work trousers my father used to wear. An unmatched pair of socks complemented the ragged work boots, which were tied very loosely as if to make room for his enormous feet. The expression on his face was very alert and pleasant, much like I remembered him on those cold spry mornings when he used to wake me to go fishing. There was absolutely nothing at all unusual about this generic scene, except that it was taking place on my front porch and I was clambering about like a neurotic chicken trying to figure out what I was going to do.

The only appropriate course of action I could conjure up was to just step on into the scene and see what happened next. Slowly, I opened the door to be greeted by a content grin, smiling eyes, and big guttural voice that simply said, **"Good morning."**

"Good . . . morning," I replied with an enormous amount of hesitation.

"How have you been doing?" he asked, with a kind graciousness that (without a doubt) was also asking for the truth, the whole truth, and nothing but the truth, or so help me God he would know it. And what did such a question actually mean anyway? Was he asking how have I been doing this morning or how have I been doing since I was nine?

He waited patiently for an answer with his eyes fixed on mine; eyes that seemed not only to pass right through *me*, but throughout my house, up and down the staircase, in and out of my sock drawer, and circling the parameters of my toilet—his inventory at last completed. Totally paranoid, I was sure this moment of psychic probing had revealed every gruesome detail that could have been known about my grody little life. I felt like I was standing naked in front of a whole schoolyard full of smirking but well-mannered children. So, in answer to his question I muttered, "Uh fine. . . I guess," which of course was not at all how I felt. Finally my mouth just blurted a mishmash of words that my left and right brain had yet to agree on. "So, Uncle Ben . . . are you *really* my Uncle Ben?" I rolled my eyes at the ridiculousness of my own question.

"Uncle Ben?" he repeated like a question, chuckling slightly at my confusion. Then he added, **"Well, I have been called by many names, and . . . yes, I guess Uncle Ben will do for now.**

That did it. With a comment like that I knew that, without a doubt, we were definitely out of bounds here; this most certainly was not Kansas anymore, and Toto was as lost as hell. I had no idea who was actually standing in front of me, and I felt even more paranoid because I had no idea why he was here. I was in no mental condition for any tedious chitchat. I had to just go ahead and ask.

"So, Uncle Ben," I said, attempting to be nonchalant, "why exactly are you here. . . I mean, why now?"

"For the exorcism, of course."

"Yes, of course, the exorci—WHAT?"

"I was told that you thought it might be a good idea for me to have an exorcism, and so I am here."

"For the exorcism," I repeated.

"Yes . . . for the exorcism."

"You mean . . . you would agree to participate in something like that," I said, as though we were actually talking about a visit to the guillotine.

"Of course! I would consider it to be a great honor. An exorcism after all is really just a kind of blessing where darkness is abolished and the essence of light is evoked, and bringing forth light, in any sense of the word, is one of my most cherished ideals . . . so, without further delay perhaps we should go?"

"What? Where?"

"To see the priests . . . or whatever."

"Now! You mean, right now?"

"What other time would be better?"

"But I haven't even dressed, and I'll have to arrange it with Father O'Brien and that other priest. It may take some time and—"

"Very well," he said stepping off the porch. **"I will wait for you in your vehicle."**

I just stood there and watched as he climbed into my jeep to begin a patient wait that was going to be far more than just a few minutes. I was totally baffled by the scenario that had just unfolded, but I was sure he was up to something. The calculated spontaneity of this morning's visit made me feel like a chunk of well-seasoned bait that had been pulled from the bottom of a very old chum bucket. I didn't know what to think of it all, but I did know that the game was afoot. I would have to run like hell if I was going to keep up.

After calling the hospital to locate Father O'Brien, I was told he wasn't there and I should try Saint Martin's Cathedral downtown. At Saint Martin's, I found not only Father O'Brien, but also Father Mathews and Father Angelo, the priest who was considered to be the foremost expert on exorcisms. They were having a meeting, but were more than willing to cut it short and see us as soon as possible. The incredible ease of engineering this historic event made me even more uneasy. After hanging up I couldn't help but wonder if I should have mentioned that my uncle had volunteered, that the whole expedition was actually his idea.

Before I spent the day casting out demons, I thought I'd better check the phone machine for any calls or information about Michael Talon. The first message was from Jessica Williams.

> Hi Jared. I'm calling about the television show I told you about—you know, AM America. The interview will be aired on Tuesday at ten A.M., though it'll be taped the day before. They're giving me the opportunity to sing a song as well. I'd really like you to see this.

Oh, another thing. I forgot to mention it last night. It may not be important, but it happened while you were unconscious so I thought you might want to know. When I first opened my eyes that evening, I saw that young girl—the pretty one who sat near the front wrapped in the gray blanket—well, while you were lying there, she put her face right next to yours like she was examining your features or something. It may have all been very innocent, and she was smiling at the time. She did this for quite awhile until she saw me watching. Then she got up and left. You may even know her. It just seemed a little strange to me, that's all.

Well, I hope you will watch the show. Please do so, Jared. Bye now.

This was exciting news—she had to be talking about Sharee. Perhaps this younger woman had been taking a closer look that night. Maybe she was attracted to me after all. Maybe I did have a chance with her. Jessica's calling about the television show was a bit scary, though. I sincerely hoped she wasn't reverting back to her evangelical ways. Preachy I couldn't take, and I had no desire to be reborn or saved by anyone. Besides, I was far too busy being lost and dumbfounded. Where would I find the time for anything else? I was curious, though, about hearing her sing, and since this was a regular network television show and not something off the religious station, I thought it might be different. I jotted down the date and time and played the next message:

"Hi Jared. It's Sam . . . from the hospital. I was just calling to see if you found your uncle or had any news. If so, please try to bring him in for those tests we talked about. As you know, he's still very vulnerable and there are medications that might help ward off a stroke or aneurysm.

Also, you remember the woman who said she was

your uncle's wife, Clair Grayson? Well, she came back to the hospital to check on him. A nurse, who had seen her the first time, saw her getting out of the elevator. The nurse followed her down to the main floor where the woman stopped at the pharmacy and got a prescription. When she left, the nurse checked the name with the pharmacist to make sure she hadn't been mistaken. Her name is Adrian Anderson. The nurse didn't pursue the matter, thinking she simply had the wrong person. Later, she got to wondering if there was something odd going on, so she mentioned it to me.

Anyway, just thought I would pass that along in case you knew someone named Adrian Anderson. Good luck with your uncle, and do let me know if you find out anything or if I can help at all. Talk to you later.

I did faintly recall a woman my uncle had been involved with, probably when I was a teenager. I never really knew much about her. After writing down the name, I shuffled through the scraps of paper on my desk until I found Professor Talon's phone numbers. Dialing his home, I once again found no answer or answering machine. On his office line I got an answering service.

"Professor Talon won't be in his office today," said a woman's voice. "Would you like to leave a message?"

"Yes, my name is Jared Grayson, I'm a friend of his. Would you know where I might reach him today?"

"No, but I can give him a message when he comes in."

"Do you expect him today?"

"No, but I can give him a message when he comes in."

This was not going to get me anywhere. From the start I had the feeling the woman was more answering machine than answering service. She probably didn't even know Michael Talon.

"Miss, this could be a little more serious than that. He was supposed to contact me and he hasn't. I'm worried something may have happened to him."

This got her attention. "Well, that is odd," she said. "I also thought it was a little strange when he left a note on my door yesterday instead of calling me."

"What note?"

"The note saying he was going out of town for several days. Something about a document he went to see. He always calls in, but this time he just left a note. Do you think there's something wrong?"

I gave her my phone number and asked her to let me know immediately if she heard anything. There *was* something very wrong here. Michael was in some kind of trouble, and I had no idea how to help him. What felt even more wrong though was that all of this mystery around Michael's disappearance had something to do with this Shankara and that woman Sharee. If they were all so brilliant and enlightened, why didn't they know and do something about it? I had a lot of unanswered questions, and I was feeling hard-pressed to find out anything I could.

I decided to simply ask him . . . this alleged uncle of mine. To do what everyone had been telling me to do—ask about everything.

I grabbed my keys from the coffee table and pawed through my shirt pockets—looking for what? I wasn't actually sure. Before opening the front door, I peeked out to see what he might be doing. He was sitting up with his head leaning against the headrest. His eyes were closed as though he might have dozed off. As I closed the front door, I let out a healthy sigh in hopes of relieving some of my nervousness. Reaching my jeep, I jumped in and put the key in the ignition.

"Well," I said, trying to act very cool and controlled, "there are some things I need to ask you. It's about my friend Michael Talon."

My words brought no response. Not even a flinch. Trying to ward off the possibility of there being anything mortally wrong, I raised the volume of my voice and said, "I felt that you probably knew him and. . . ." Still no answer. Nervously, I waited for him to make some sound or open his eyes.

Then it suddenly hit me; he had an aneurysm. Oh my God, I thought. Maybe he's already dead. I reached over to shake his shoulder. "Ben!" I called out, "Ben! Are you alright?"

My jostling only caused his head to tip slightly forward. Startled, I shook him more vigorously and called out again. "Ben, can you hear me? Ben?" He rocked back and forth like a rag doll. "Oh no, it can't be!"

I sprang out of the jeep and ran to the other side. Throwing open the door, I put my ear against his chest. All I could hear was the throbbing pulse of my own quickened heartbeat. I felt the vein in his neck. The only movement I could recognize was the trembling of my own hand. I knew I had to get him to a hospital as soon as possible.

I grabbed the seat belt and strapped him in, tightening down the shoulder harness as best I could. Catapulting back into the driver's seat I quickly started the engine and slammed the stick into reverse. I lurched into the street and stomped on the gas pedal.

Roaring through the four way stop, I turned the corner to the main avenue and raced past the long row of maple trees that ran along the sidewalk. My uncle, now slumped over, was being held up by the fastened seat belt, his hands still carefully folded in his lap. I knew I had to hurry. Time was of the essence. I frantically tried to calculate the quickest route to the hospital, but in my hysteria the streets names became blurred and confused. I was terrified that I had at last been given this chance to know him, to speak with him, and now he could be gone forever.

I zigzagged across town going west and then north. I turned onto Alison Avenue, a main thoroughfare that would take me past Saint Martin's Cathedral and into the heart of the city. Speeding past the church, I made a quick left. I reached over and held on to my uncle's lifeless body so he wouldn't fall over, as my tires squealed around the corner.

Then, to my astonishment, my uncle abruptly raised up with enormous breath of air, the shock of which caused me to lose control of the jeep. It spun out, leaping over the center median.

Within seconds, we had climbed onto the adjacent sidewalk, devoured a white picket fence, and collided with a small tree in someone's front yard. We stopped with a terrific jolt as though the vehicle had run into a concrete wall.

The collision, although not at all devastating, did cause our seat belts to tighten, grasping us like a couple of wrapped rump roasts bound by a solitary string. The windshield wipers flapped back and forth as leaves quietly tumbled down in a steady shower from the small maple tree we had struck. I was stunned. As I tried to catch my breath, I heard the sound of my uncle's voice.

"I was wondering," he asked calmly, "exactly why is it that you chose to attack the tree?"

"What?" I said, in total disbelief.

"The tree," he said. "I was just wondering. Why did you attack the tree?" He waited patiently as if actually expecting a rational answer. "It is alright," he added, "that is, if you indeed had a great longing to do so, or perhaps found it to be fulfilling in some way, then of course, this would be fine. . . . But, rather destructive don't you think?"

"What? What are you talking about."

"The tree."

"We just had an accident—"

"No, actually, I believe *you* had an accident. Technically, I wasn't really in the body at the time. At least not until it was over."

"What do you mean?" I screamed. "Are you alright? I thought you had a stroke and were dying."

"On the contrary, I feel very well, thank you. Better than the tree, I imagine."

"WHAT! I can't believe this! I'm tearing all over the city trying to get you to a hospital and—"

"Yes, it was quite an extraordinary occurrence. I will have to ponder this one myself. But I am curious about the tree."

"What!" I shouted again, my word ushering in a brief span of silence.

I could hear the faint sounds of police sirens. Bystanders had begun to gather, gazing into the vehicle to see if we were hurt or just out for a little joy ride.

Seeing the police car about a block away, my unruffled companion then climbed out of the jeep and said, **"It looks like you are going to be tied up here for a while. I believe we passed the cathedral a few blocks back. Perhaps I will go on ahead and begin our meeting with the priests. We don't want to keep them waiting."**

He smiled and moved his eyebrows up and then down just once. Casually, he strolled through the multiplying onlookers, across the avenue, and onto the sidewalk. I was almost surprised that his parting words weren't, "Well, jolly good then, have a nice day."

My brain floundered, trying to understand what I had just witnessed. It was almost as if he were part ghost and part man, and periodically joined the two together when he wanted to be profound or rattle someone's cage just for fun. Besides, how was I supposed to know he had just stepped out of his body for a little cosmic stroll? And what about my uncle? Does this mean that my uncle is gone now? For a while it really didn't look like there was anyone in that body.

Luckily, the drama around this accident was negligible, there having been no real damage to either the truck or the tree. The fence on the other hand, which now resembled a small stack of kindling, would have to be replaced. I graciously offered to pay for all of the damages and told the police I had simply dodged an oncoming car—even though all of the nearby witnesses were hard-pressed to remember one. Once they were convinced I was neither inebriated nor insane, the officers sent me on my merry way to continue, and hopefully conclude, my meeting with destiny at Saint Martin's Cathedral.

24

The Exorcism

Arriving at the church, I wandered about the grounds trying to both vanquish the worst of my jitters and locate someone who would help me find the priests and, hopefully, my uncle. A small woman wearing an apron finally spotted me and took me into the complex. She guided me through a series of dark carpeted corridors that joined and turned like a maze. We passed several open doorways, the vacant chambers echoing the silence, making me very conscious of my noisy lumbering stride. The woman's tiny steps were birdlike compared to mine, which became even more apparent as she turned and signaled for me to stay quiet. She pointed to an open doorway at the end of the hall.

Entering the room, I could quickly tell that the exorcism had already begun. The modestly decorated sitting room, with one desk and several upholstered sofa chairs, reminded me of my last unplanned visit to Hansen's Funeral Home.

The space itself was well-guarded by a variety of sacred statues residing in the recessed alcoves of the surrounding walls. Each of the sculptured figures, which were about three feet tall, stared blankly with painted eyes. They seemed to be focused on the center of the room where my uncle was seated on a wooden straight back chair with his legs crossed at the ankles, and his hands palms up symmetrically in his lap. With his eyes closed, he looked very peaceful and contemplative despite the purpose of his visit. Draped around his neck was a cream colored cloth, which hung down to nearly his waist. The priests stood around him in a circle keeping a safe distance from their adversary. For a second, it reminded me of an execution by electric chair, lacking only the wires leading to the selected seat. Regardless, I was sure there would be no shortage of electricity.

All three priests were dressed in their traditional black attire and white collars. Cloths, similar to the one they had placed on my uncle, were draped around their shoulders. Father Mathews, the younger of the three, had been given the job of cross bearer. With a steadfast grip, he held on to a crucifix, the staff of which was nearly as tall as himself. He looked as if he were prepared to use the cross as an assault weapon if necessary. I could sense his nervous anticipation, his readiness to spring into action at any second. I had the distinct impression that, like myself, this was his first exorcism. The eerie pageantry I was now witnessing already made me hope it would be my last.

Father O'Brien stood far more at ease as he read Latin from a Bible lying open in his arms. He was as I remembered from the hospital, calm and sure of himself. Focused on his recitation, he glanced up occasionally to observe the other two men and keep a close vigil on the demon at large. His regimented Latin phrases revealed only traces of his Irish heritage.

The third priest, Father Angelo I assumed, was a stocky man of medium height with bold rounded facial features and a broad nose that accentuated his eyes. He supported a stout belly and was balding with a healthy patch of salt and pepper hair that reminded me of a Franciscan monk. In one hand, he balanced a large glass bowl of water. In the other, he held some sort of scepter, which was about the size of a gavel. Occasionally he dipped this instrument into the water and then shook it forward as if he were striking someone. I presumed he was blessing the room, and specifically the area around my uncle's chair, with holy water. He recited in whispers the same words that Father O'Brien was reading, creating a slight echo of the ancient invocation, which gave the place a haunting atmosphere.

It all seemed quite dreary and repetitive until I noticed Father Angelo taking a more solid stance, placing himself directly in front of my uncle. Almost shouting, he proclaimed, "In the name of our Savior the Lord Jesus Christ, I command you dark angel to begone!" As he spoke, he shook several doses of holy water into my uncle's face and lap. "Begone Satan! In the name of Jesus, I command you to begone!" Feverishly he swung his scepter, tossing the water in all directions. He showered everything in sight, including myself and the attending statues. In his nervousness, I was afraid he might strike his poor possessed victim over the head and dispense with the other rudiments of the ritual. He brought the scene to a climax by shouting his final decree, "In the name of Jesus Christ, begone!"

My uncle, who had been sitting somewhat erect, suddenly slumped down, his head falling slightly forward, his whole body going limp. He looked as he did when I raced my jeep toward the hospital, causing me to suspect this to be yet another of his ploys, slipping out of his body as he had apparently done earlier.

But as the seconds ticked by, waves of doubt started to filter in. *Was there actually some hidden secret about to be unveiled? Could it be possible that he truly was in need of an exorcism; that as my uncle, he had been possessed by something?* Still, he did not move. *Could it be that my uncle's own spirit had at last found a way to bring him to this place and these priests where he could get help?* His silence rivaled that of the presiding statues. *Or could it be that he had subconsciously come to me for help in the hope that I might bring him here so that he could free himself from the clutches of this demon?*

"Ouuuush!" came the sudden inhalation of breath, his body once again rearing up as though birthing itself anew, helping me easily answer my previous questions; the answer of course being— none of the above.

Initially, the three priests paced about like nervous game hens who had unfortunately discovered that the wolf was still in the hen house. Then Father Angelo turned again towards my uncle casting one last desperate splash of water commanding, "I said begone, spirit, begone!"

My uncle, slowly opening his eyes, responded by saying, "Actually, my friend—I did, but you did not say for how long. And in truth, I am not really a dark sort of anything, but I wanted you to have the tangible experience of witnessing how spirit can travel from one place to another." He then took hold of one end of the sacred scarf draped around his neck and very carefully wiped the holy water from the side of his face, as though the scarf had been put there for that purpose. He added sincerely, "And that, in and of itself, would be a good place to start, because if you *do* have the intention of tangling with a dark angel in the future, especially one as crafty as Lucifer, then you've got to be very specific about what you're commanding.

"Likewise, to command your heroic charge in the name of Jesus Christ . . . well, I will tell you straight away that you will find very little power in just a name. If you want your Lord Jesus to assist you in such an event as this, then I might suggest that you give some passage to your words and offer yourself to be a vehicle for his divine energy. Call forth that you desire for him to become your hands, your feet, your heart, your breath, and then truly give him your human vehicle to work through. Do this without reservation, allowing him to ignite all of the energy centers in your body, and I can guarantee that he will be there with you . . . and then some. Have the courage to offer up the totality of your being—to this ascended lord that you love so much—and then *know* . . . know that as you do, he will indeed come and stand up inside you to do war with your demons—if that is indeed how you choose to spend your time."

The priests appeared to have no idea what to do next, as if the instruction book had neglected to address this particular problem. They just stood there staring and listening as my outspoken uncle continued.

". . . But when you call upon this beloved Jesus Christ to come into your body, don't be surprised if he perhaps has a far more brilliant solution to the situation than all of the religious books have taught you. After all, he really is the lord of compassion and not the lord of war.

"You see, this one you call Satan, whom you so devoutly call the Master of Darkness, is really only the master of those who fear him. Without your fear and reverent belief in him, you would find him to be a spirit no different than yourselves. In fact, you would find him to be *less* than yourselves because he has never actually had the glorious experience of being in the human body, which is one of the greatest adventures of all.

"Deception is Satan's only game, a game in which he uses the flow of your thoughts, your passions, your energies, to fuel his own dark intentions. Without your constant vigilance to the terror of him, he would be nothing. Now, does this mean that he does not actually exist? Not at all, he's as real as you are. In fact, I am quite sure that at any given moment, in which you decide to contemplate your fear of him or your spiritual battle with him, that he will readily come and sit with you for the rest of the afternoon.

"But, just for the sake of argument, perhaps you might consider this. In light of your adoration and loyalty to this one you call God, do you truly believe that such a Supreme Being would bring into your dimension a dark entity that is nearly its equal, simply to torture and create mayhem for all of you?

"See this Lucifer's deception for what it is . . . an illusion; one that you have lived and proclaimed as one of your absolute truths since the beginning of your dated history. It is a learned understanding that has been bred into your culture through centuries of dogma. This concept has survived and evolved throughout your lifetimes because it has always been employed by your hierarchies and religions to manipulate and control the populace. The threat of hell and damnation is a profound tool for keeping the peasants in line, especially if you, the dictators of the dogma, have seated yourselves as the only stepping stone between the commoner and God.

"What has made this kind of degradation even more appalling is that as your centuries progressed, and the original dictators of this dogma died off, the old world concept of this Satan, lived on. Through pure ignorance you have made him the king of darkness, a title now most graciously accepted by his enormous and highly developed ego.

"Now . . . does this mean that you should just ignore him and pretend he is an illusion? On the contrary, if you have chosen to be in an adventure with him for the last few centuries, then he no doubt has a foothold in your life. You simply need to approach this from a more powerful perspective, and you will not only rid yourself of his interaction, but you will also become responsible for all of the negative aspects of your life that you have, up to now, been blaming on him. You know, those parasitic phrases like 'The Devil made me do it' or 'That was Satan tempting me.' To blame him is to empower him, which in turn gives him a permanent invitation to participate in your life.

"But let us suppose that you are indeed actually standing before a Lucifer as you thought you were a second ago. What do you say? Where do you begin?

"First of all, know him well. Know his game. Know his cunning and deceptive nature. Recognize all that he is in the darkness of his being, every scheme, every lie, every nuance of his foulness. Acknowledge and evoke his outrageous ego so that the wholeness of him comes to stand before you in the grandeur of all that he believes he ever has been. Dare him to show you the true essence of his vile existence so that you might give witness to the image of his true portrait.

"Before you will stand a spirit that was once like your own, a being now charred and burned from his loss; a spirit nearly unrecognizable because of his constant degradations into the frequencies of hatred and fear where at last he became them. Having lost the color of his blooming, the flow of his own life, he feeds on the lives of others who might stumble along his treacherous path.

"So see his fierce eyes and the twist of his mouth, and hear the snarl that clenches his throat. See him as a rabid and enraged creature, feverish in his anger, engulfed by his hatred. See him caught in the jaws of a trap, his flesh being torn from his ravaged bones. See him with no hope, no chance for freedom, condemned to an existence of pain and suffering. See him as a wretched beast in the stench of his horror, and then see him as yourself, as the darkness of you.

"And then . . . ever so sovereign in your approach, reach out your hand leading with just one finger. Touch him . . . touch one place on him, and as you pull your finger away, see a thread of color being spun from his blackened shell and extend it out away from him. Take that thread out as far as you can. Reach until this stream of color can travel out into the universe on its own. Then quickly touch him once again pulling forth another thread, of yet another hue from the darkness of his being; for cocooned within the blackness is the memory of every color, every nuance of a life that once bloomed as your own. Pull yet another, and another, and another; like the luminescent rainbow of a spider's silent web, weave a tapestry of color from the source of his darkness. Around and around, spiraling upward and outward, blues, greens, and lavenders, cast in all directions. Let him see once again the splendor of his being in a prism of every color, expanding all around him. Remind him of the palette, the hand of the Creator, that once birthed his spirit in the portrait of itself. Embrace him with your compassion. Find him with your love. Show him the colors of his birthing."

For several seconds there was a beautiful silent pause, like snow a moment before its falling. In this silence, any sound would have been an intrusion. But as Father Angelo wrestled himself from out of his private trance, he came forth with an utterance that was most offensive.

"Mr. Grayson?" he said, casting his eyes in my direction. "You are Jared Grayson, his nephew?"

I was taken back by his question; he spoke as if disregarding not only my uncle's words, but also my uncle's very presence.

Awkwardly I staggered out a reply, "Uh, yes . . . Father."

Then in a very businesslike manner he said, "Could you step into the other room with me for a minute. I would like to speak with you alone if I might."

My uncle turned and smiled at me with an affirmative nod that said without question, go . . . listen . . . learn. I followed the priest into the next room with Father O'Brien pressing at my heels. The double doors closed behind us, sealing in our presence, capturing our words. Father Angelo offered me a chair then privately took a pill bottle from a desk drawer and inconspicuously slipped something into his mouth. He then paced back and forth in front of me for a couple of seconds as though he were still forming his conclusion.

"Mr. Grayson," he began, "I have to conclude, after what I have seen, that your uncle is not under any kind of possession. I believe that he is just a man who has come here voluntarily because he knows that he needs help. I think that he has some very serious mental problems and that you should take him in for a psychiatric evaluation as soon as possible. Have him committed for a three- or four-day observation and get a clinical diagnosis from a good psychiatrist who can give you some idea why he is having these delusions. I suggest you get him some help, and soon, because he is very unstable and is definitely not living in this reality. I also think that—"

"Father Angelo . . . it is Father Angelo?" I asked. He replied "yes" as I continued. "I don't know exactly what to think right now, but I do know—" I cut my own words short. I could tell by the looks on their faces that my words were going to be given no more credibility than my uncle's. I concluded by saying, "Well, you may be right, but I think for now, I'm just going to try and take him home and see if I can find out who he is. I haven't known him for fifteen or twenty years. He also has some health issues that need to be addressed and I think *that's* where I am going to begin."

Rising from my chair and heading for the door, I said, "Thank you for your efforts. I will consider all that you have said." We exchanged our goodbyes and walked back into the other room.

To my surprise the space was empty, causing an emotional alarm to sound inside me, until I heard Father O'Brien say, "They're in the courtyard." He pointed out through the only window into a large garden area that surrounded a stone-laid patio about ten feet square. A planter box, made of the same rock and approximately the same width, rose from behind the area creating a long bench-like effect. A variety of evergreen trees and bushes had completely overgrown the structure, creating a very natural setting with streams of sunlight peeking around the buildings and into the greenery.

Father Mathews was sitting on the stone bench. Shankara was standing next to him with one foot on the seat, leaning over with his right arm braced on his knee. Even though they were both adults, there was a father/son quality to the scene as Father Mathews listened intently, and Shankara talked and gestured in what I'm sure was yet another impassioned monologue.

Interrupting my gaze, Father O'Brien touched my shoulder and pointed to a doorway next to the window. "That will take you out into the courtyard," he said. "I'm going back inside. I believe Father Angelo is not feeling very well." Shaking my hand, he added, "Good luck, Jared." He then went back into the office, shutting the doors behind him. I walked around to the courtyard door, opened it, and then paused for a minute to see if I could hear anything. Their voices were still faint as I crept around the grounds to an adjacent bench where I could secretly listen without interrupting. As usual, Shankara's voice *was* the conversation.

". . . There are many elements of your rituals, that you perform even now, which were once part of a scientific understanding of how to use these frequencies. For instance, there are times during your ceremonies when you use your thumb to make the sign of the cross over your forehead, your throat, and your heart. By this act you are actually blessing your fourth, fifth, and sixth seals or chakras, as they are called in other cultures. Presently, you do this primarily as a symbolic gesture, but there was a time many centuries ago when your founding fathers—who were really rather brilliant—did the same thing in full knowledge that they were activating these seals to provide a more direct energy flow to their divine source. There are those who practice Eastern philosophies who have always touched these identical seals in the same manner, only they first wet their fingers by touching their tongues to allow the moisture, which is a conductor of light energy, to help activate and open these centers. This is also partly why you dip your hands into holy water before you touch your forehead and make the sign of the cross. Water is simply a conductor of this light energy.

"Early on, when the forces of church and state had the desire to dictate over the populace, your popes and clergy conveniently misplaced much of this wisdom. By doing so they caused the common people to become ignorant and more separated from their God. This is also why the people were instructed early on to clasp their hands in prayer and kneel before the popes and clergy, because in this posture the flow of energy and life force is very low. Your scientists now have the ability to monitor and photograph some of these energies that flow in and out and around the physical body. If you were to photograph a pauper on bended knee with his hands clasped, his head bowed low in adoration, and then compare it with one of the chosen clergy, standing upright with his arms stretched out, palms open wide, you would see a great difference in the flow of electrum or life energies between the two.

"In the beginning, the common people were taught these postures to separate them from their own power. Now they are rituals being handed down from generation to generation; two thousand-year-old concepts that few have dared to question. The most unfortunate aspect about this is that there are many powerful tools hidden within some of your symbols and rituals. And this, my friend, is what you've got to get back, this is what you have to find again and renew for yourself, and all who would choose to explore such a faith.

"Your Jesus was an enlightened teacher, and if you could take your Bible and separate the words he actually spoke from the manipulative dogma that was added later, you would have a profound book indeed. But I will tell you forthrightly that he did not perpetuate elements of fear or guilt, nor did he rally around the idea of judgment. Judgment is a man-made concept birthed by the ego to control and manipulate others. Your divine source never judged you, nor will you ever be judged. It is only humankind that has stooped so low as to wallow in an attitude of such a low vibration. This idea of a supreme being who passes judgment over you has given you a place to dwell in the illusions of good and bad, while conveniently relieving you of the responsibility for having created either.

"If you truly want to know how great is the love of your divine source, and how truly loving and compassionate your Jesus was, then do the following. Take your Bible and a large black ink pen. Read through this book with feeling and passion. As you assimilate the words and phrases into your consciousness, mark out anything that has to do with guilt, fear, and the perpetuation of any judgment. Any emotion you have that reflects these elements, find the sentence that caused you to feel it and cross it out. When you are done, your book will not only be a lot shorter, but it will also be a true reflection of your divine source as well as a true portrait of a Christ called Jesus who tried to tell you of it. This will give you a pretty good idea of who you are, and of the abilities you have, and of the energies that are available to you.

"There have been numerous beings, courageous characters within the history of your religion, who have walked in the knowledge of these energies. Your Saint Francis of Assisi was an outstanding teacher, who attempted to bring forth the wisdom and knowledge of the animals. He explored nature and the simplicities of life, where he discovered a library of the nuances for this, your third dimension. The words he spoke then, about balance and harmony, are the same words that Native Americans and indigenous people all over the world try to speak to you now.

"Saint Francis was considered a madman of his time. His consciousness was a polarity to the control and oppression, which at that time was the genre of your religion. Surprisingly enough, they did attempt to adopt some of his discoveries, and with good faith in the beginning. Later they would find ways to use his simple understandings to invoke the poor and those who were of the simple life to stop their rebellion and return to the control of the church.

"Another being who is most profound in this understanding is the mother of your religion, Mary, the mother of your Jesus Christ. She is now a primary instrument for ushering in your new millennium. She steps forward with many different names and many different faces to bring forth a healing flow of feminine energies, which now come to suppress all war and violence. Through most of your human history, the dominance of male energy has caused a great imbalance in your evolution. Because of the competition and struggle for power—which is indeed a male attribute—you have brought your planet to near destruction. This beloved light, this virgin mother that you call the queen of peace, now comes with many others to restore the balance between the male and female energies.

"Your blessed Mary has been seen and experienced in visions all over the world and brings a message to all nations to pray for peace; a message to contemplate and envision a space and time without hatred, vengeance, neglect, and abuse. She rallies constant support for your mother—the Earth—which is now in the throes of these great changes. Through storms, floods, and fires these feminine powers now reach to cleanse and purify the planet of all its destructive energies, striving to restore the balance and harmony that was once the natural order."

I sat back and left their conversation for a while, leaning my head against the stone wall, contemplating his words about the Blessed Mary's warnings and the Earth changes. It was more than obvious that we were already in the midst of this planetary cleanse. All around the world erratic weather changes were causing an overwhelming number of natural disasters. Earthquakes, hurricanes, floods, and tornados dominated the world news. Yet amazingly, it seemed like the only people really paying attention to these planetary signs were those who had been directly affected, as if people had to have their houses blown away to notice what was actually going on.

I had to admit that, until recently, I had been much the same way, lost in a gray fog, a density I now saw as the hustle and bustle of the material world. I did remember there had been a time in my life, however, when I felt a deep need to assist our planet. I remembered the words to a song that had returned to me from the archives of my past. Once again I could hear the music and phrases of my composition *Save Us A Dance* as it played in my head, the last several phrases of the piece now sounding in my mind.

Black waters border the sand and sea.
Bathed by the sins of industry, an ocean sighs,
and the winged ones fly through an amber sky.
Lost to the greed of some selfish dream,
there's a dance to the rhythm of falling trees.
There's a dance to the sound of the ravaging rage,
of the money machine.

Swept by the storm of human desires.
Can't anyone here see the world's on fire?
Caught up in a blaze of abuse, with no end in sight.
Condemned by the words, "It'll be all right."
Oh I say, no . . . no . . . No!

Save us a dance.
On the crystalline waters.
Save us a flight, on the breath of the wind,
through a clear blue sky.
Save us a ride, through emerald forests.
Pilgrims of Earth . . . hear my prayer.
Save us a dance.

This—my history—written over a decade ago, had foreshadowed this very moment; the same profound purpose coming to the surface. I felt summoned once again to be witness to humankind's ambivalence, and rallied once again to do something about it. I couldn't help but wonder just how many others felt this calling. I thought about Professor Michael, Sharee, Mohan, Jessica, and all of the people who had gathered in the alley that night. And what about the rest of the world? Were there other people just now awakening to this feeling?

I had lost track of time. As I looked through the trees and into the open courtyard, I realized that I had also lost track of Father Mathews and Shankara. Hastily, I followed several stone pathways throughout the grounds until I found my way to the front entrance of the cathedral. With his tall stature dressed in its white hair and beard, it was easy to spot Shankara even at a distance. Some 40 yards away I could see him crossing the intersection . . . off to somewhere . . . somewhere I knew not. How he was surviving, when he ate, or where he slept, was a complete mystery to me—not to mention who he really was. Now though, I could no longer deny what I was feeling. I couldn't imagine him as anything but the Enlightened One. Perhaps that was what Michael Talon had finally discovered. Perhaps, because of it, some ill fate had befallen him.

I didn't know what to do except to let these thoughts flow through my mind. Any attempt to sort them out would only clutter the essence of what I was yet to understand.

As he walked away, I knew not to try and stop him. One thing was certain though, whoever he was, he was not my uncle. In fact, after all that I had seen and heard, I was sure, he wasn't anybody's uncle—

". . . Are you sure?"

"What?" I blurted out, apparently to the sky, for there was no one there to answer except for a few pigeons and a couple of stone columns. I looked into the crowded streets, only to find him standing amid a swarm of moving pedestrians, looking back at me and grinning as though waiting for an answer. It never failed. If I actually thought I heard his voice talking in my head, it was always with some extemporaneous comment that caught me totally off guard, causing the two lobes of my brain to collide like a scene from Laurel and Hardy. I was sure that every comment was cleverly constructed not only to help me question my sanity, but also to scramble my mind into believing *and* not believing in the same instant that *anything* had been said.

"**. . . Are you sure?**"

"Yes, I'm sure!" I shouted.

"**. . . Very good then.**"

I smiled and shook my head, speculating that by acknowledging such a voice, I was surely ushering in my own madness. With what appeared to be someone else's words sounding in my head, I couldn't help but wonder just how much of this play satisfied a secret need, some part of me that so wanted it to be true—for there to be this kind of magic in the world.

". . . Jared."

Though he was no longer in sight, I could still hear his voice.

". . . Excuse me, Jared."

Abruptly, I realized that Father Mathews was standing behind me, attempting to pull my attention from my cerebral void.

"Yes, I'm sorry Father Mathews, what did you say?"

"Jared, I'm glad I caught you. . . . Where's your uncle?"

"Oh, he went on ahead."

"Yes, I see." There was an element of doubt in his voice. Then he added, "I thought I would let you know, I just got a call from the police, and I believe they were calling from the city morgue. They asked if someone here at the church could come down and identify a man who was just brought in. Apparently he was found in the park near here. One of the officers, who patrols the park, recalled having seen this man several times in front of the cathedral. They thought we might know him. He was described as a small man with shabby clothes and no identification. Jared, I'm pretty sure it's Mohan. They discovered him early this morning, propped up against an old oak tree. When a police officer tried to wake him, he simply fell over. The coroner was hoping that we could give them some idea of who he is."

A strange kind of sadness seemed to reach up and take hold of my hand. I had no choice but to embrace it, realizing only in that moment the emotion I felt for this small fellow. "Do you really believe it's him?" I asked.

"Yes, the description they gave me was quite clear. I don't know if you were aware of this, but he also had terminal cancer. We have known that this day would eventually come."

"Yes, I knew about his condition."

"There is something else, Jared. Father Angelo is ill. Apparently, not long after you left the room he doubled over in discomfort. Father O'Brien helped him into the bathroom where he was sick. We've decided to take him to the hospital to see if it might be serious. Father O'Brien is bringing the car around now."

"Oh . . . I'm sorry," I replied. "That's terrible. Is there anything that I can do to help?"

As the words left my mouth, his answer was painfully obvious. Had I the power to turn back time I would have snapped those words back up like a sprung mousetrap. The last thing I wanted to do was to go to the city morgue, pull open a long drawer, and look at a dead person—especially one that I recognized.

"Well, Jared, you have seen Mohan several times and . . . there really is no one else. Could you, Jared? They just need someone to identify him. Once we have taken care of Father Angelo, I will call the morgue about what to do."

Every fiber in my body screamed Nooooooooo, No No No Noooooo! Which is why it was such a surprise to me when my mouth opened of its own volition and politely said, "Of course."

"Thank you, Jared. Perhaps we can talk later this evening."

It didn't take him long to be on his way, leaving me to sour in the brine of the task I had just been given. As I begrudgingly trudged down the church steps, I racked my brain trying to remember just how many times I had been to the morgue to perform this very same duty. As I rummaged through a lifetime of memories, the answer finally came back quite clear. None!

25

The Morgue

The reception area at the city morgue was far more congenial than I had expected. It resembled a hospital with the personnel wearing appropriate uniforms. Fortunately, the man behind the counter recognized my name immediately; Father Mathews had called ahead. To my great relief, it appeared that the formalities of this somber expedition were going to be minimal. With a signature here and a signature there, I was handed over to a woman with a clipboard, large orthopedic shoes, and glasses that gingerly hung on to the end of her nose. I assumed she had the simple, but difficult, task of escorting people to see their loved ones for the first time, to greet friends and family in their progressively pale and lifeless states. This morbid thought, along with the morose silence that accompanied our stroll down the fluorescent-lit hallway, quickly nudged me into the cold reality of what I was about to experience.

There was a part of me that sincerely wanted to feel some peaceful satisfaction about Mohan's death, remembering that he may have had the opportunity to choose his own moment, his own time to go. Grief, though, steadily weakened my position, leaving me to wade about in the dew of my own sadness. Trying to stay positive, my heart was doing its best to believe that Shankara had assisted him with a mortal departure that was serene, beautiful, and sacred in its event. I tried to envision him as he had been found, in a picturesque setting, lying under a wonderful old oak tree, showing no signs of pain or struggle. Maybe this had been the master plan all along and he was simply fulfilling his destiny. I wanted so much *not* to feel bad for him. But, in light of the joy and laughter I had seen him bring to me and others, it was difficult not to feel the loss.

Of course, it was possible that the unidentified man lying in the next room was not Mohan at all. Perhaps it was simply some other homeless person who fit his description and had also been seen around the cathedral. I clung to this hope, wanting some unfamiliar face to appear when the anonymous corpse was unveiled.

We entered one of the main rooms and were quickly submerged into an atmosphere that was both clinical and reverent in its terminal affairs. By far, the most uncomfortable aspect about the place was the subtle smell that ambushed its visitors from all sides. It was a mixture of chemical and detergent-like odors that was all but foreign to me. They unsuccessfully did their best to mask the overwhelming presence of death that, without a doubt, had an aroma of its own.

The long narrow space was basically empty, which gave it the dimensions of an enormous casket. Running the length of this chamber, the wall to my right was divided into a series of square wooden panels, around two-and-a-half feet in size and stacked three high and ten wide. I assumed they were the drawer fronts for the sliding trays that held the corpses. Their geometric arrangement reminded me of the small spice drawers my mother had in her kitchen when I was a child, the miniaturized compartments holding herbs or occasional candies or trinkets. It was always an adventure to spy into each, finding perhaps something surprising and wonderful.

Today though, I had no desire to pull open these drawers, for I knew there were no wonderful surprises to be found. Behind these drawers were the remains of fathers and mothers, sisters and brothers, grandparents and children, as well as a few friends and neighbors. And then there were the faces that no one had claimed, the homeless, the runaways, and more than likely a short fellow with a flair for Shakespeare.

Today, it appeared that Mohan was alone with no one to claim him, no one in the world except me. I was amazed at how melancholy I felt, at how much I was already willing to grieve for him, considering how little I actually knew him. For whatever reason, he had been a sprig of new life in the stagnant forest of my everyday existence, and that I would always remember. I wondered what would happen to his poetry, to all of the auspicious words he had so passionately collected. I also wondered how many people actually knew him the way I had.

As we respectfully walked along the rows of drawers, the attendant systematically read the names written on the small pieces of paper tucked into slots just below the large brass handles. Two rows from the end she paused and looked closely at the markings on the ID plate of the middle drawer. She told me where to stand and then stopped for a second and stared at me as if she might be giving me a space to prepare myself for what I was about to see. She asked, "Is this a relative of yours?" I surprised myself by answering, "Yes, I am his family." I don't know why I said it other than it was the answer that she might have been expecting.

She took hold of the large handle and with a great tug rolled out the long tray. On it was a sterile looking, clear-frosted plastic bag that, without question, held some sort of human form. A zipper ran down the middle of the shape. It was already partially unzipped, revealing a glimpse of shaggy brown hair, still unrecognizable to me as Mohan's.

I wanted so much for this *not* to be him, or at least for it not to be some morbid and horrifying picture that I would have nightmares about for the rest of my life. My mind, desperately attempting to avoid the inevitable, was creating the faces of several strangers who might be unveiled here instead. These images were soon followed by a vision of Mohan's profile in a luminescent glow that was nothing less than angelic. I even contemplated just keeping my eyes closed. Perhaps I could pretend that I recognized the face without even looking.

As she reached up to pull the zipper, I took a deep breath

trying to calm myself; my stomach likewise was doing its best not to betray me here and there all over the floor at this critical moment. Then, without warning, the unimaginable happened. The bag moved.

It was really just a slight disturbance. One that could have easily been excused as some postmortem spasm or the corpse redistributing its own weight after shifting when the drawer was pulled. The attendant hesitated with her hand on the zipper as if taking a time-out to convince herself that she had not seen any movement. I was hard-pressed to disagree with her, my own mind readily contemplating the infinite number of reasons for such an occurrence.

Then, quite unmistakably, the large plastic bag shuffled and jiggled. An electrical impulse streamed down through me all the way to my toes, igniting my body to rear back in total disbelief. The attendant dropped like a paper bag full of groceries whose bottom had fallen out, her arms and legs rolling out in every direction like so many cans of string beans or perhaps apples and oranges. I had not the coordination to catch her nor the faculties to even move. I just stood there trying to prepare myself for what was about to happen next.

All at once, the plastic cocoon split open, the zipper moving down of its own accord thereby birthing a very spry and awakening Mohan. Sitting up, shaking his head like a fleabitten dog, he exclaimed, "Whoa! Give me some air. Enough of the big Ziplock baggie. . . . Where am I?" Checking out his immediate surroundings, he spouted, "Whoa . . . looks like the morgue." Then, resembling a periscope, he rotated his head around until his eyes fixed on me. "Whoa . . . looks like that fellow Jared, visiting someone at the morgue." Then he glanced down to see himself sitting inside the bag on the long drawer. "Uh oh," he declared, "looks like Mohan . . . in a body bag . . . being visited by that fellow Jared in the morgue. Oh, no!" he moaned to himself. "Mohan, old buddy . . . you bought the farm."

He collapsed back into the bag like a falling tree, causing the drawer to rattle and shake on its rollers. Having regained but a handful of my crumpled composure (from this my second encounter today with what appeared to be the living dead), I cautiously stepped up to the bag and peered into the opening. Mohan was lying posed with his arms folded and his eyes closed. Still doubtful, I bravely offered, "Uhm . . . dead? I don't think so."

Springing back up with his eyes open wide, he exclaimed, "Really! . . . not dead?" Raising one eyebrow, he added, "I don't feel dead . . . don't sound dead." Leaning forward he raised back up and inhaled a long breath through his nose. As he let it out, he triumphantly proclaimed, "Yes! . . . I still smell bad! I *am* alive!

"Oh Jared," he spouted with great excitement, "it was incredible! One minute I was just sitting there under a tree, and the next thing I knew, whoa! I had completely lifted out of my body and was moving, soaring, going anywhere I wanted. Shankara showed me how to do it. It was sort of like a dream, especially towards the end. Of course, I guess you might call waking up in the morgue more of a nightmare, but when it first happened, when Shankara first guided me out, it was absolutely real, and I was totally conscious of the whole event. It all seemed so physical, so tangible just as Shankara described it. What he keeps saying is true, Jared, it's true. We do exist outside our physical bodies, and whoo wee, is it amazing, I mean absolutely amazing! I didn't want to come back, but he said that it wasn't my time yet, so I had to—"

"Mohan," I interrupted. "Are you alright? I mean do you feel okay?"

"I feel wonderful. Well, except for the part about being declared dead and sealed up in a body bag. That was a little gruesome, not to mention just a little insulting, but after the magnificent flight I just experienced, whoa! Who cares!"

As he climbed out of his plastic cocoon and down onto the floor, I detected a foul odor.

"Mohan, are you sure you're alright. That smell . . . what is that?"

Looking down, he slowly spread apart his pant legs, revealing a large wet spot around and below his crotch. Without hesitation, he said, "Must have had a little accident during re-entry." Giggling with the innocence of a child, he added, "Sorry dad, guess I forgot to go before I got in the car." He laughed out loud, even though my only response to his comment was a very sour face. "Well?" he whined in response. "What was I supposed to do? Its not like the big body bag has a lot of options, not to mention a certain lack of amenities." Then he noticed the attendant lying on the floor. "Whoa! Who's that!"

"She works here. She brought me in to identify your body."

"Eeeyuk! Don't even talk about that. . . . So why is she under there now?"

"When she saw you moving inside the bag, well . . . I guess she fainted."

"Uh oh. That's not a good sign, Jared, definitely not a good sign. Sounds like the precursor to hours of grueling interrogation, and that, Jared, is without question not on my agenda. Therefore, my fine fellow, in view of these unfortunate circumstances, I believe I will make this my closing line and my cue for exiting stage left." With an about-face, he set his short steps into motion heading in the direction of the door.

"But Mohan!" I said. "We can't just leave without saying something."

"Not a problem, Jared. You stay as long as you want. And by all means, *do* tell them what happened." He took five or six more steps and then added, "And don't forget the part about how the body bag unzipped *all* by itself, and how that little man jumped out and scampered away laughing, and then just *completely* disappeared. Whatever you do, don't forget that part."

"Oh, damn," I protested.

Still in a daze, the woman on the floor started to move. Reaching the door, Mohan stealthily peeked out, first looking one direction and then the other. He then slipped through the opening and disappeared. His antics reminded me of the afternoon I sprinkled rose petals on him at the hospital. I could clearly remember having imagined him rise from the bed, leap up on the reception desk to yammer with the nurses, and then scamper on out of the place. So reminiscent was it of the scene I had just witnessed that I couldn't help but laugh at the coincidence.

The only logical thing to do in this very illogical situation was to act in the manner suggested—exit stage left, and worry about the rest later. With great haste I followed Mohan's escape route through the door and out into the hall. At the other end, I could see my fellow fugitive almost reaching the double glass doors, never having bothered to turn around or look back. As I started to put myself into high gear, I was startled by a noise from an adjacent corridor that ran perpendicular to the hallway.

"Pssssst!"

I scanned the entire hallway, but could see no one.

"Pssssst! Jared, over here."

The second "Pssssst" was far more recognizable than the first, which is why it didn't surprise me to discover Emily's face sticking through the louvered doors of the telephone booth encased in the wall.

"Pssssst! Jared, over here," she insisted.

With the same dramatic hiss, I replied, "Emily! What are you doing here?" She waved frantically at me to come closer while trying to keep herself hidden. I leaned forward to hear better, but held on to my current stance for I had no intention of climbing into that cubicle with her as I had done on a previous occasion.

Bringing new heights to the projection of a whisper, she spouted, "Jared! . . . that was Mohan . . . and he's supposed to be dead. I saw him, Jared, and that was definitely not dead—I mean not dead, not even a little." Cautiously, I took a few steps closer as she continued. "He's supposed to be dead . . . but I just knew he wasn't. We heard about it down at the hospital and well . . . I already saw him come back to life once before with your uncle up in room 417 and somethin' just told me that—"

"Emily," I interrupted, "why are you hiding in the phone booth?"

"Well, because I came down here and asked at the front desk if I could see him. Ya know, just to take a look. So they asked me if I was a relative. I said, yes, I was his sister. Then they got real fussy and asked me what business it was of mine—this unidentified man—and I said, 'Well, frankly, I think it is everybody's business, because the man is still alive.'"

"What?" I gurgled.

"Well, I could sense it, Jared, just like I can sense all kinds of things now. But *they* surely didn't. Why they just up and asked me to leave, ya know, be on my way . . . no bones about it. So I've been holed up here in this phone booth ever since. I was hoping they'd all go off somewhere and cremate somebody or somethin' so I could sneak into that room there and look for myself."

"Emily?" I asked, trying to suppress my amused disbelief, "You were going to sneak in there and just start pulling drawers open until you found him?"

"Oh," she said, slightly taken back. "Well, I guess I never really thought of it that way."

Then from inside the room I had just left, we heard a low voice calling my name. "Mr. Grayson. What has happened here? Where is everyone?"

"Emily!" I blurted. "I've gotta get out of here. They're going to start asking questions and I don't want to be the one standing here trying to come up with the—" (SLAM)

Abruptly, she slapped the louvered doors shut as I heard the same voice from just a few feet behind me clearly say, "Mr. Grayson, what has happened here?" I reacted immediately by bolting into a full gallop down the corridor, hoping there would be an exit at the other end. The attendant gave no chase, but called out several times for a security guard. At the end of my long runway, I pulled open the door labeled stairs and flew down the steps and out into a lower parking lot. Within seconds, I was in my jeep and moments away from yet another successful escape.

Moving along the city streets, I was occasionally exposed to the wash of orange and lavender sky that appeared here and there between the tall buildings. Trying to calm myself, as well as control my driving, I rolled down the window letting in a blast of cool evening air. I took several deep breaths and began an inventory of what had just occurred.

First, I went to the morgue. Then at the front desk, I informed them who I was and signed something. After that I was taken to see Mohan, who apparently came back into his body and disappeared while I lollygagged behind until I was seen talking to a woman, whom they had already asked to leave, hiding in a telephone booth. Then I ran out of the building like a criminal being pursued by a security guard. Now . . . that shouldn't be too difficult a trail for the police to pick up on— (*SCREECH*)

Stomping on my breaks, I pulled over with the sudden realization that I had just become a member of the most-wanted . . . a member of the very-stupid-most-wanted. I banged myself on the side of the head, shouting, "What was I thinking? The worst thing I could have done was run out of there. Besides that, I didn't actually do anything wrong. How could I be so stupid?"

I had to turn around and go back. No—first, I had to find Mohan, and then I had to go back. I had to locate him and bring him with me so that I could prove I wasn't some kind of corpse kidnapper. No—wait! First I needed to call Father Mathews and tell him what happened. He might actually believe my story. I could dash over to the house and check the phone machine to see if they were looking for me, and from there I could phone him. If I hurried, I could be in and out of the place before the police or anyone else showed up to interrogate me.

I decided to drive down the alley in back of my house. If anyone arrived while I was there, I could still make a clean getaway without being seen. Turning off my headlights, I parked so that my garbage cans would create some cover for my vehicle. I jumped out and crept up to the small gate of my rickety picket fence. Just beyond it my yard and the nearby surroundings were quiet and relatively dark. My neighbor Marshal had a few dim lights on, while my other neighbor, Mrs. Nurple, had her porch light off. Finding my way up the sidewalk and onto the porch would be no problem. Finding the key to the back door, which was hopefully still in the pile of wood, would take some probing. I felt around with my hand like a cat burglar who was breaking into his own—

"Having trouble finding your key, Jared!" came Mrs. Nurple's loud and hyperactive chortle. My nervous system reacted as if I had just been drenched with a bucket of ice water. I panted for several seconds with my hand over my heart, trying to gather the remnants of my faculties so I could respond to her surprise attack.

"Mrs. Nurple . . . good evening. What are you doing sitting out here in the dark?"

"Oh Jared . . . call me Nadine." she replied, turning on her porch light. "Why . . . I was just sitting in the quiet, enjoying the evening sky."

"Yes it is," I stammered, "turning into a lovely evening."

"Did you find your key, Jared?"

"Yes, thank you, it's right here."

"Oh good . . . I told your young friend that she needed to put it back in exactly the same spot because you have a tendency to lock yourself out now and then." She giggled at her own words, it appearing that I had done just that.

Slightly surprised at her announcement of having witnessed or perhaps assisted someone in breaking into my house, I inquired, "So Nadine . . . which friend would that be?"

"Why Jared, that sweet young woman, of course. The one I saw at your mailbox the other morning. I mean really, dear, you ought to just give the poor thing her own key—and don't try to tell me she's your daughter—after all, these are modern times, age doesn't matter. That's why when I saw her wandering around your back porch . . . well, I knew exactly what she was looking for, so I just called over to her, 'It's under the second step, dear,' I said, since I've watched you put it there at least two dozen times, and I knew you wouldn't want her locked out until you got home."

"What?" I said, "you mean you—"

My words were interrupted by a muffled shout from inside the Nurple home. "Naydeeeeen! Where the hell is dinner?"

"Oh dear," she exclaimed bringing her hand up to her mouth. "I forgot to feed Fred his dinner. Oh my, I have to run, Jared."

She scurried around her screen door and headed into her house. Trying to grab her attention before she disappeared I interjected, "But what about—"

"Say *hi* to your friend for me. Gotta run. Bye!"

Like a cuckoo bird from a tightly wound clock she vanished into her box-of-a-home with both doors shutting behind her. She then turned off her porch light, leaving me completely in the dark, in more ways than one.

I had no time to stop and think about what it all meant. I had to keep moving and stay focused on my current plight. Inside, I left the lights off and carefully stumbled over the garbage can and the cat food dishes until I made it to my phone. I called information, and was put through to the rectory at St. Martin's Cathedral. A phone machine picked up and a woman's voice informed me not only that no one was there, but also gave me an infinite number of details about the quilting party, the rummage sale, and saint somebody's annual bake-off.

Feeling pressed for time I decided not to wait long enough to leave a message. I then checked my own phone machine to see if anyone had been trying to locate me yet. According to the blinking light, there had been two calls. I soon discovered, as I began to play back the first message that the volume on the machine had been left down very low making it difficult to hear what was being said.

Jared . . . It's Michael Talon. Listen carefully . . . I don't have much time to talk, I have—

Frantically, I pressed several times on the volume button to turn it up. Then surprisingly, his voice stopped completely, and there was dead silence. I waited breathlessly in anticipation of anything else that might follow. Looking more closely to see if the machine was still working, I quickly realized that, in my attempt to turn up the volume in the dark, I had accidently pressed the erase button, deleting Michael's message.

"Damn it!" I screamed. "What the hell is the matter with me!" My nervous system began to unravel, my pulse and heart rate accelerating in a footrace towards a stroke of my own. I had to call the police— No, the police might be trying to find me. First I had to find Mohan and straighten out the misunderstanding at the morgue, and then I would call the police. Hoping to find that the second message was also from Michael, I desperately pushed the start button on the machine again.

> Hi Jared, it's Jessica. Sorry to bother you again, but there is something that I really need to tell you. Several days ago when I went to the library at the college to find your music . . . well . . . I took the tape home with me and I wasn't supposed to. You know, the tape with all of your music. I'll return it in a day or so, but I just had to make a copy of it. It's so beautiful, I had to have it. I also really need to tell you something else that I have—(CLICK)

Hastily, I turned off the machine; there was no time to listen to any of her drawn out scenarios. I had to get out of this place and go back downtown to see if I could locate Mohan. I would go to the alley where he had written his poetry on the concrete wall. Surely after his mystical experience from this afternoon, he would have some small but profound dissertation to write about it. Hopefully I would find him in one of his more esoteric moods, one that actually required him to be in his body rather than somewhere else.

26

The Harlequin

A dim spray of light guided me down through the alley, past the night's darkened obstacles and over the jagged cobblestones. Though I had been down this path before, the journey still felt like a voyage into the unknown. I stumbled over the uneven bricks much as I had stumbled over the last several days of my life, never knowing where to step, stubbing my toe at every turn, tripping and falling for no reason at all. I seriously considered retreating, turning around and going back. But the need to *know* pushed me forward. Moreover, any doubts I had were outweighed by the thought of the police waiting at my front door or of Michael Talon tied to a chair being interrogated about the enlightened one.

In the past several days my life had turned upside down with an odd mixture of magic and madness, bliss and chaos. Emotionally, I felt as if I could crack at any moment. I was quite sure of this prognosis because of the accompanying euphoria that came and went amid the panic and confusion—not to forget the cavalcade of coincidences that seemed to be spinning me in a circle, spinning me inside a journey called Shankara. At first it had been a great adventure, intriguing and mystical. But the snowballing of events that were continuing to escalate pulled me over, forcing me into a corner, making me choose between that magic and madness even though I was not sure which was which.

So I continued to walk, moving toward the uneven light that

cast shadows here and there down through the open passageway. The darkened cavern grew brighter the further I traveled. When I came to the library of graffiti with stories etched in luminescent chalk, I was surprised to find it rather well-lit. A yellow porch lamp and an open doorway produced a spray of fluorescent shapes scattered over concrete steps and several garbage cans. This portal, appeared to be the service entrance to a restaurant. The faint sounds of conversations and the clatter of dishes filtered out from this opening and dissipated into the night air.

Sitting on top of several stacked wooden crates, a kerosene lamp produced an additional bright wash of warm light over of the wall of poetic words. As I had anticipated, Mohan was standing in front of this monument of graffiti, completing yet another composition. Diligently he scrolled, turning and twisting the chalk over the rough stone-like surface, shaping the words, letter by letter. Anxiously I waited like a fleeting apparition, watching silently until the last line was revealed.

> When I come to the edge
> and I . . . have become my own reach,
> then flowers bloom in my pocket
> and the wind longs for my commands.

As he finished, he turned in my direction and called out, "Good Pilgrim. Thou hast escaped from that morbid dungeon of death, decay, and unnatural sin. Ah yes!" he reveled. "Do come forth and grace me with your heroic tale of the event. For I long for adventure, and you are indeed one of the most audacious lords I have ever beheld. Tell me, Good Sir, of the caper and of the cavorting that did ensue after my expeditious farewell."

"Mohan," I eagerly shouted, "you have to go back. With you missing they're going to think I've hauled your body away."

"There, there, I think not, my friend . . . Mohan will stay here, where Mohan belongs, because Mohan is very content to stay where he belongs . . . wherever that is."

"But I'm sure that the morgue and the police will be looking for me, wanting to know what I did with you."

"Au contraire, my friend, au contraire."

"But Mohan! . . . why do you say that?"

"Simple logic, Socrates. I form this . . . my hypothesis . . . from the gasps and horrified expressions of the three morticians whom I ran into just outside the front entrance of that . . . chasm of abandoned brothers. I'm quite sure they recognized me, so don't worry, old friend, they definitely know I'm alive and well." Tilting his head down slightly and rolling his eyes mischievously, he added, "They just don't know why."

Cackling like an old witch, he tossed his head back, "Ah ha, ha." His laughter bounced back and forth between the dark brick walls. With a puckish jig he danced about on his platform, jostling the kerosene lamp. This tossed a spectrum of light all around the high walls, silhouetting his gnome-like self. He frolicked a lively and crazed step.

The turmoil now brewing inside me was not unlike his maddened antics. Once again the roller coaster of my life had held on through its dashing descent and was now beginning its slow climb back up the next waiting crest. I too wanted to laugh. I even tried to laugh. But the fragmented sounds trying to come out of me were more of a haggard combination of bliss and blasphemy. And then it actually happened, the moment I had long been fearing—that moment in time when sanity relinquishes control to whatever the hell would like to come next. Splitting open like a ripe melon, my emotions spewed forth, spilling out a jumbled stream of confused words.

"That's just great!" I shouted. "That's just sooooh wonderful!" Totally unhinged, I staggered about in a slow circle, wailing into the night sky. "Hooooow fabulous! I'm not being hunted by the police after all. Isn't that something! Well, that just simplifies everything, doesn't it. Why . . . now all I have to do is find the missing professor who's been kidnapped by—God only knows who— And why, you ask? Well, I'll tell you why. Because he's the only one who knows who the enlightened one is. And do you know what that means? It means that if I don't find him, the enlightened one might get killed in some accident. And do you know why? Because he's too dumb to know he's the enlightened one, which is also why I have to find him, even though I don't know who he is. And it would probably be best if I did this before somebody decides to kill *me*.

"Of course, in the meantime, I also have to find my uncle who has either lost his mind or is possessed by some eccentric spirit who enjoys popping in and out, creating total havoc everywhere he goes, even though he's supposed to be some kind of illuminated lord—an illuminated lord who (in my opinion) is actually of no help at all." Pausing to inhale a single breath, I continued, "And, if I have time left on my hands, maybe I'll consider turning myself into an animal so that I can run around and sniff out why I have fallen in love with a girl who is twenty years younger than I—why some crazy evangelist woman is hounding me because she thinks she hears my music in her head— and why all of this insanity has cost me the one chance I had of making my music a success—of having my music heard— OF HAVING THE ONE BLOODY THING THAT I ACTUALLY WANTED IN THIS STUPID LIFE!"

Clapping, cheering, and a celebration of whistles echoed throughout the chamber of brick buildings as Mohan stood, in a standing ovation, applauding feverishly from his platform.

"Bravo Jared! Bravo!" he spouted. "Drama, drama, drama . . . oh really, Jared, you absolutely have missed your calling. You should have been an actor . . . Reeeally! Or maybe you *have* been all along and you just didn't know it." Jumping down off the wooden crates, he walked up to me and playfully tugged at my clothes as if attempting to loosen up the rigid bones residing inside. "Bravo, Jared, bravo . . . That was top notch! By Jove . . . I think you've got it!"

Screaming, I swung at him with my words. "What the hell are you squawking about?"

"It's a drama, Jared. Your life . . . and everything that's been happening to you. It's just a drama, and it all appears very real, even though it's really just a big game. It's a game that *you* just recently started to play for real, and because of that, everything has sped up for you."

"What?"

"Sped up . . . things are moving faster now because you have started to pay attention to how it actually all fits together."

"What! You're crazy! It's not all fitting together. It's all coming apart . . . my whole life."

"No, no, no, it just looks that way, because you think that everything is happening *to* you, when in reality it is all happening *because* of you . . . because on some level you wanted it."

"I didn't ask for this to happen, for Shankara to come bombing into my life or for people to be missing. I didn't ask to have everything turn upside down."

"Yes, Jared, in the bigger scheme of things, you did. And as soon as you surrender to just how brilliant those choices were, all of those abstract pieces will undoubtedly fall into place."

"How do *you* know?"

"Because, I watched the same thing happen to me, and to a lot of people."

"NO! . . . No, it's not the same at all, because you . . . you're just plain nuts. You're totally insane."

"No, no, Jared, insanity is something very different. Insanity is . . . insanity is when you make violent movies and peddle them to the public for money that you then hide behind saying, *Oh that doesn't affect children or how people behave on the planet*— Now *that*, Jared, is insanity. Besides, my friend, your sanity or mine is not really what you're having trouble with. What you're having trouble with is that you feel out of control."

"I *am* out of control!"

"No, you're not. What you really are . . . is fascinated, intrigued, and excited about the adventurous turn that your life has taken . . . and perhaps maybe just a little overwhelmed."

"Yes, I'm definitely out of control."

"Well, actually, you think you're out of control, and you also think that the big guy, Shankara, is causing or allowing all of this stuff to happen to you. In addition, you think he does absolutely nothing to help the situation and, most of all, that he enjoys the hell out of watching you crash into yourself."

Stepping one foot up onto a nearby wooden box, he continued. "Now . . . listen up, my friend, 'cause this is really the truth of it. Shankara is an enlightened being, a great teacher, who like all great teachers will give you every clue, every premise, every tool that he can think of, to bring you home to the truth of who you are . . . but he will not interfere in your adventure. He will not override your free will, or your desires, and he will not alter your destiny. And as far as, does he enjoy the hell out of watching us crash into ourselves? Yeah, I think he does . . . with all of the love and grace that we in this dimension have yet to imagine."

I took a few steps back and collapsed, my rump coming to rest on the top half of a wooden barrel. His words seemed to hang me out like a basket of wet laundry. I knew he was right. I just didn't know why. I also didn't know who I was, where I was, or what I was doing there. But as I looked back into his honest eyes, I had to come clean about what I was feeling. I did want the magic . . . that is, without all of the confusion. And I did want to communicate with Shankara and not just hear his words in my head for a brief second, especially after I had just run myself into a wall. I wanted the answers to a billion questions and more of the same experiences. I wanted to *not* feel so out of control and to know if the professor was alright. But most of all, I wanted to know if all of this was real.

"Jared," he said, interrupting my thoughts, "just because a spirit like Shankara doesn't interfere, does not mean that he doesn't intervene. To put it simply, he will be your rocket fuel, if *you* want to be the rocket. That's how you got to where you are now and were able to have those experiences. He's already hanging out with you, and *will be* in the future, if you want."

"But what about my friend the professor? I think he has been kidnapped because he knows who the enlightened one is."

Excitedly, Mohan asked, "He knows the name of the

enlightened one?"

"Yes. At least I think so."

"Really! Shankara has alluded to the identity of this one, but as of yet, he hasn't told us."

"But does this mean that my friend might actually be in serious trouble?"

"Jared, it's a difficult concept to understand, but there *is* a master plan here that we, on some level, are creating and designing . . . and sometimes that includes for bad things to happen. Hopefully, as we evolve, we will learn how to create only good things. And that is why a being like Shankara doesn't interfere. He doesn't want to take the learning away from us, not at any cost."

Mohan's understanding seemed to wash over me, soothing the rough edges, giving me permission to be more vulnerable and hopeful. "So what do I do now?" I asked. "I mean, where do I go from here?"

"It's simple," he replied. "You ask."

"What?"

"You ask . . . you know. Ask! *Hello out there. I know that you're listening, so I would like this or that, please—* You know . . . ask."

"Well . . . what do I ask for?"

"Chocolate donuts!—I don't know! Ask for whatever you want."

Briefly, I pondered this infinite question. If I could ask for anything, what would I ask for? Perhaps, a second meeting with producer John McDowell or, better yet, an encounter with Shankara or the enlightened one. And of course, the whereabouts of the professor. Maybe a chance to be with my uncle again, or . . . how about a rendezvous with Sharee for a candlelight dinner. . . .

Realizing that my mind had begun to wander, I turned back and asked more seriously, "So Mohan . . . what about you? What do *you* want, I mean . . . what do *you* ask for?"

"Ahhh, that," he said with a satisified smile. "Mostly . . . I just ask for the truth. You see, I've found that the truth is everything I could have ever imagined. The truth is always leading me, zooming forward—faster and farther. The truth is as sweet . . . as sweet can be. And the truth . . . the truth is my ticket home."

A reverent pause followed his words; neither of us wanted to break the feeling of such a thought. I knew I wanted this as well, and once again I wasn't sure why, but I could feel the flow of it swimming around inside me.

Then Mohan playfully shattered the silence. "Aaaaand! . . . I want to go to lunch at Shankara's. You know, that big banquet in the sky."

"What?" I asked chuckling.

"You remember. He mentioned it the last time he spoke." Trying to impersonate Shankara, he said, "*When you can mimic me well enough to consciously lift your spirit from your body and soar into the heavens where we can sit down and have lunch, then I will truly be impressed.* That, my friend, is what I want, to have lunch with the big guy in the sky."

"And what does that really mean, Mohan?"

"Well, if it's anything like what I experienced this morning while I was sitting under that oak tree, then what it is . . . is everything. It's the freedom to come and go. The freedom to be anywhere you want. It's having the choice of leaving your body because you want to, not because the body dies of cancer and you are forced to. Jared . . . I want to leave this life on the breath of the wind, not with one last gasp of air."

"So what *about* your cancer? Are you in any pain?"

"No, not really, I guess I'm one of the lucky ones. It's up inside and around my brain, sort of the silent creeper. The doctors gave me nine months to live, and that was about nine months ago. They said I would be fairly normal until the last few months. Of course, I have always had a little difficulty knowing just where my abnormality actually begins."

"So where will you go? I mean, what will you do?"

"I live here," he said, pointing proudly to the open door leading into the restaurant. "I live right here in the rear-end-suite of Wang Chong's Chinese Cuisine."

"You're kidding."

"Nope. I've stayed here for a couple of years. Wang, the owner, lets me live here in his old office in exchange for sweeping and hauling out the trash at night. Basically, I just sort of keep an eye on everything. In the early hours I have full run of the joint, including access to the kitchen, and I'm telling you, life is good in Wang Chong's kitchen." I laughed as he exclaimed, "But lunch with Shankara is the *real* banquet for me."

Playing along, I asked, "And what would you do there, Mohan? I mean if you actually went to the big luncheon in the sky. What would you say when you got there?"

"What to say, my good fellow, has never been my problem." Briskly climbing back up onto his platform, he stood illuminated by the kerosene lamp at his feet. As if stepping into a different character, he bowed from his stage and said, "Good Socrates, the difficulty lies in not what one should say, but in what one should *wear*, when attending such an *affair*. After all, with Buddha seated at your left, and Jesus seated at your right, what fashion would compliment these lords of such *flair*."

For just a second, he became completely still. Then he abruptly turned in the opposite direction and with one hand raised in a gesture, and one finger apparently counting the idea, he expounded, "I will ask Shankara." Stepping to the edge of the platform, he reached down and grabbed what looked to be a leather skullcap. It was a diamond patchwork of burgundies, tans, and browns, with a droopy cone that flopped down to one side. In this Harlequin-style hat, he stood boldly directing his words towards the sky, or to Shankara I presumed, as he began his theatrical performance.

[Enter character Mohan, stage right]
Mohan.

　　　"And oh sweet friend, my dear Shankara . . . to such a banquet . . . I do pray tell. What attire could I have, that would honor the grandeur of such lords and such kings? For long I have known and worn only my fear as I have waded through each lifetime for the coming of you. And though it be true that your invitation of bliss be but half of my reason for craving the truth, it is likewise my fear, hanging worn and so tattered, that now too longs for a closet to at last be found missing in."

[*Turning to one side, he contemplates*]

"And so I must face that I am left to come dressed in but the sweet naked light of the lord of my being."

[*Unfurling his arms, he pronounces*]

"Adieu to the words that I have spoken so well, now that all thoughts betray me to the feelings of I. For light is my shadow when spirit casts its hue. Leaving only the wind to give way to the secrets of how a fool among fools caught fire and then blazed . . . with a lavender flame . . . in the quiet of a mind."

[*Stepping about, he continues*]

"Now I'll paint with but one hair of my infinite brush and insist that the candle stay up all the night as to witness the fall of this human veil. For hence no gait will follow nor footprints trail me as 'tis only the chimes at the window who'll tell . . . as I gently brush by . . . on my way to the wind."

[*Turning his sights back toward the sky, he speaks*]

"And so my sweet lord, you dare see my dilemma. For what manner of fashion could be such the array that would embrace all the love that I feel towards your grace. And how will I bring, as a gesture of thanks, my sweet bouquet of roses for such the table you've set. For with not one hand to hold them, less two hands would take, to deliver the count of the sum I would bear."

Then, he slowly pulled the drooping hat from his head and paused, as though the silent emotions of Mohan had somehow slipped back into his contrived character. With great innocence, he gazed upward into the empty night and allowed a collection of more serious words to come from a place I would now recognize as the well-spring of his heart.

"And, will you be there, my friend . . . at the end of tomorrows . . . as I pull from my shadow and awaken its wonder . . . . For to catch me by swift in the palm of your grace, 'tis the wish . . . and the only true wish I could long for."

A light blue glow seemed to flood his expression as he stared passionately into the starlit night. And even though I could not hear the response, I was sure he was listening to his beloved friend, an answer perhaps to the question he had so easily asked.

I left him there in that scene, like a child at a window staring at the moon. I took myself home in my own silent way, my mind at last having quieted with nothing more to say. For a very long time I just listened to nothing, and then I stopped and listened some more. By the early morning hours I found myself seated at the piano, rambling through a collection of chord changes and abstract words that were being tossed about by my restless emotions. The music rolled inside me, each note, each word belonging to me, being birthed by me. My soul held the pen, and my heart turned the pages as the truth of that epiphany struggled out in the dark. I sang without inhibitions, without constraint, for I knew that such a time had finally come. A time for the taking of chances. A time for the asking.

27

"I'm Asking, I'm Asking"

KNOCK, KNOCK, KNOCK.

Having recently been subject to numerous abrupt wake-up calls (which had indeed plagued me since the beginning of my sabbatical), I had already surrendered to the conclusion that being pulled from the soft and fuzzy flannel of my bed sheets was going to be one of the more unavoidable aspects of my evolutionary growth. Now, however, through my blurred vision of the dial on my clock, I was already having doubts about such a progressive concept. If I was not mistaken, the long hand was on the twelve and the short hand was on the five. The dim light that floated about the room seemed to confirm this, as did the lethargy within the rest of my body, which had not yet bothered to respond at all.

I pondered momentarily whether the obtrusive rap, rap, rap, might have actually been part of a dream—someone banging their knuckles on the door of my subconscious mind. I waited and listened for a few seconds, allowing the warm peaceful silence to seep back in. The nothingness swiftly seduced my senses, convincing me to leave behind the rap, rap, rap, and surrender back into my comfortable slumb—*KNOCK, KNOCK, KNOCK.*

Abruptly, I sat up in total disbelief that someone could possibly be beating on my door at this hour of the morning. Rage punctured my sleepy demeanor as I ripped back the bedding, stepped into my slippers, and threw on my robe. I charged ferociously toward the front door, the rumble of the floorboards sending out a thunderous message to that courageous someone who had dared to awaken me before the sun was up. "Alright!" I snarled with my last few steps, "let's see who has taken it upon themselves to wake me at this hour." As I gripped the knob and began to pull open the door I shouted, "Do you have any idea what tiiiiiiiii—"

A virtual angel stood before me. She was wrapped in a cream-colored shawl that was draped all around her, with long delicate fringe trailing off the end of each elbow. She wore loose-fitting jeans with a pair of woven leather sandals on her dainty feet.

"Hello Jared," said her innocent voice. "It is Jared, isn't it?"

"Um . . . a. . . ."

"We haven't actually met yet, but I have seen you several times. My name is Sharee."

"Um, yes," I mumbled, noticing a taxi waiting at the curb. "Of course . . . Sharee."

Just then, I realized I was standing there with my ratty bathrobe hanging open, which meant that any number of other things could have been hanging out as well. I also knew, without a doubt, that my hair was hanging in all directions, and I could only hope that there was no sleepy drool hanging from my mouth.

With a few swift motions, I gallantly attempted to crochet myself back together by tying up my robe, brushing my hand through my mop of hair, and inconspicuously catching any visible slobber. With any luck she hadn't noticed my slippers, furry replicas of bear paws that had been given to me as a gag by a friend. Desperately trying to hide at least one of my animal appendages, I lifted the oversized slipper behind me, balancing on the other foot like an overgrown flamingo.

She smiled trying to suppress a chorus of uncontrollable giggles. "I'm sorry if I woke you," she continued. "Shankara . . . I mean, your uncle sent me here to give you a message."

Trying for a quick rebound, I focused on trying to appear slightly more coherent. "Yes, what is it?"

"The people will be coming for another gathering . . . . It will be at the same place by the river, probably just after the sun

307

has gone down."

"Really . . . and he said it was important for me to be there?"

"Well, sort of . . . yes."

Feeling as though I had gained back a morsel of credibility by having been sent my own messenger, I expanded on the importance of this idea. "Well, if he sent you by taxi all the way out here to tell me, he must really want me there. Did he happen to say why this was so important?"

At this, she lowered her eyes and smirked a bit. Staring directly at my pedestal-of-a-foot, she giggled a little more, and finally said, "Actually, he said something about . . . that he tried numerous times to communicate to you about it telepathically, but . . . you were still a little too dense to be able to hear him, you know . . . dense, like too caught up, or too busy to notice."

She allowed me just a few seconds to squirm in my embarrassment before continuing. "It will be starting fairly soon, so if you are going to make it in time you will have to hurry." Looking back toward the taxi she added, "I better be heading in that direction myself."

Slowly, she took a few steps backward in a subtle dance that became her departure. Before she slipped away, I said, "So that means I'll see you there?" Appearing slightly embarrassed, she said "yes," then turned and walked down the sidewalk.

"I will be there," I blurted out.

Then she stopped and looked back rather sheepishly. "There was one other thing," she called out, "I'm not sure if you are aware of this . . . but it's not morning. It's late afternoon, around five I think . . . see you there . . . bye." Skipping out to the end of the sidewalk, she climbed inside the taxi and was gone.

Throughout my pubescent life, my mother had always told me that, when it came to courting young women, first impressions were of the utmost importance. Today, I thought, I had truly outdone myself: the ratty bath robe, the scraggly hair, the bear foot slipper, the slobber; and let us not forget sleeping all day and answering the door in a state of total rage. Why . . . this truly had to have been one of my finest hours, and without a doubt, this courtship was off to a splendid start. In fact, maybe for a finale I ought to just put a potted plant on my head and do a little jig for the entire neighborhood.

"Eeeah!" I screeched, slamming the front door behind me. For several seconds I banged my head on the closed entrance hoping to rid myself of the reality of what had just happened. Rather quickly I realized that my self-abuse wasn't helping matters and that there was nothing else to do but swallow the embarrassment and move on to the next upheaval. I could think of only one thing that could be worse than what had just occurred—missing the gathering that she had come to tell me about and an opportunity to see her again.

Posthaste, I did a slam-dunk version of pulling myself together, attempting to do a mental inventory of the last twenty-four hours as I went along. One thought kept surfacing in my mind—one piece of the puzzle that seemed drastically out of place. What had happened to Michael Talon? It felt as if all of the recent events were just clues or trials that revolved around his disappearance. I couldn't help but wonder if my muddled approach toward finding out more about him stemmed from my fear of knowing who the enlightened one was.

Before leaving, I tried both of Michael's phone numbers. Again there was no answer. Then I phoned my neighbor Marshal to tell him about the meeting. He said he would find his partner Sam and they'd come if they could. There seemed to be nothing left to do but follow the trail of my destiny back down into the heart of the city.

By six o'clock, evening had begun to find its way through the city's tall brick buildings. The streets, swarming with cars and buses moving about in every direction, were almost unrecognizable to me. The wide concrete sidewalks, once silent and deserted, now teemed with human traffic, every street corner spilling pedestrians into the crosswalks as the signals gave out their permission to WALK.

I parked my jeep near Jesper Boulevard, about four blocks

from the Regency Theater. This would not only put me just a few blocks from where I thought the entrance to the alley was, but it would also give me an opportunity to stroll once again past the theater marquee beaming with producer John McDowell's name. I couldn't help but wonder if on this night, had things turned out differently, I might have been strolling down the aisle of this posh theater instead of stumbling down a darkened alley into the great unknown.

I walked down Jesper Boulevard strategically dodging the oncoming city dwellers. Peering into each alley, I strained to remember how they might have looked deserted and in the dark. The presence of people and delivery trucks diluted my memory with splashes of confusion, reminding me that I had not payed much attention during my last expedition here.

Three . . . four . . . five alleyways passed until I finally came across one paved with old cobblestones. That much I did remember; I'd walked on cobblestones from the gathering to where I hailed Jessica a taxi. Entering the alley I narrowed my eyes to blur my vision, straining for a mental picture of how this scene might have looked dark and empty. Halfway through the alley, I found a junction where two other alleys connected. Picking the one that looked vaguely familiar, I moved past several garbage containers, thinking I was headed towards the river. After about 30 yards I came to a fenced parking lot full of delivery trucks. Painted on the side of each vehicle was a little baby in diapers and the large brown letters spelling out DIAPERS WEE DOO, DOO. This was definitely not the place.

I retraced my steps back to the cobblestone junction and pondered the four directions. With some of the trucks having come and gone and it now being slightly darker, everything looked very different than a short time ago. In fact, I couldn't remember which passage I had come down in the first place. Frustration began to swell inside me as I remembered all too well that time was of the essence. I was sure it was now long past sundown as darker shadows had begun to shade in the nooks and crannies of my cobblestone choices.

I stood there examining the tops of my shoes and the geometric designs in the red clay shapes, contemplating which pattern of tiny squares I should follow. Dazed by my dilemma, I began to detect a taunting little melody jingling inside my head. *Follow the yellow brick road . . . follow the yellow brick road . . . follow, follow, follo—* "Grrrrrrrrrrr!" I growled at the thought of it. There was nothing at all funny about this predicament. I had no idea which way I was supposed to go, and it was starting to make me just a little angry.

Briefly I thought about Mohan. He would have the perfect solution to my problem. That short fellow probably knew these alleyways better than anyone. Then I suddenly remembered what Mohan had said the last time I asked him a question about my life. That question being, *"So what do I do now?"*

Clearly I remembered his reply. *"You ask,"* he had said, *"you know. Ask! Hello out there. I know that you're listening, so I would like this or that please— You know . . . ask."*

These words sorely reminded me of what I'd so readily forgotten—that I had spent the latter part of the previous evening writing a composition about this very subject. That piece of music was now turning in my head, the lyrics finding their way back into my confused thoughts: *A time for the taking of chances. A time for the asking.* I had only been out of bed for a few hours, and here I was standing in the same place, a place where everything seemed to be pointing in the same direction . . . *asking.*

In this instant, I had to admit that I was irritated. One might even say I was agitated and perhaps more than slightly perplexed that, once again, I found myself lost in the middle of this city, stranded somewhere in the middle of my life. But to put it quite frankly . . . I had no intention of *asking* the ethers for anything. I just didn't feel like it. I guess every man has his limit, and this was mine. Besides, what was I supposed to do? Just shout up into the sky, "Here I am . . . the dense one . . . the one who's not only too dense to hear you talking in his head, but who is also now lost out here in cobblestone-land and can't find his way out."

"No, no, no, no, no," I said out loud, "that would be stepping just a little too far outside my comfortable boundaries. I will find my own way to the Emerald City, thank you very much, and I don't need your help, Shankara, or anybody else's! After all, that is probably exactly what you want. You want me to act like some nut case, running around shouting at the sky when there's nobody even there. "WELL FORGET IT!" I shouted at the sky. "I will just go this way," I said pointing in front of me, "or maybe that way!" I said swinging my arm around like a scarecrow.

As I turned to my right and began stomping across the cobblestones, I realized that I was walking downhill. That wasn't right. That direction was where the dirty diaper trucks were parked. Doing an about-face, I began to march in the other direction. But now I was going up hill. That couldn't be right either. I turned to the left. No, that didn't feel right. So I turned right. Or was it left. I turned again, and then again. And then I turned all the way around in a complete circle.

"ALRIGHT!" I shouted "I'm asking, I'm asking. How do I find my way out of here?"

I waited for several seconds, but there was no answer, only the sounds of the city and a barking dog at the end of one of the cobblestone lanes. "Just like I thought," I said to myself. "There's never any answer. Ya' go ahead and make a complete ass out of yourself, and still there's no answer."

I felt spent and twisted inside, sure that the strain of this adventure had at last taken its toll. Bending over with my hands braced against my knees, I stared down at the cobblestones, my mind swirling of its own accord, madness seeping in, filling the idle spaces. "Well, Toto," I said to myself, listening to the dog's constant barking in the distance, "I guess maybe we won't be finding that Emerald City after all—"

I stood up and looked over my shoulder toward the direction of the barking. At the end of that alley there was a dog prancing about, an absolutely beautiful white and brown collie with long silky fur that seemed almost luminous under the first glow of the night's street lamps. This angelic vision of an animal jumped around and called out as if trying desperately to get my attention, "Come this way . . . *woof, woof* . . . come this way . . . *woof.*"

"WHAT!?" I shouted into the sky. "You sent Lassie to rescue me?" I broke into an unfettered cackle of laughter. "Oh-my-God, and you expect me to believe that!" I chortled. "Not even maybe. I might be completely out of my mind, but Lassie to the rescue . . . you've got to be kidding!" Bellowing out, I exclaimed, "Don't you think that's just a little too Hollywood for an act of divine intervention?" I laughed and laughed, my deranged clatter echoing off the brick walls until the collie barked no more. Magically it disappeared from the opening as if it had never been there at all. "But. . . on second thought," I said, "I do have to find my way out of here, and that direction is as good as any."

I made my way back out to the main street. To my great relief, it *was* Jesper Boulevard. Then I noticed that the collie had crossed the busy intersection and was now continuing down the alley on the other side. I jaywalked across the street and followed the dog into a new section of the alley.

After about ten yards, the animal turned right and vanished. As I turned the corner myself, I immediately saw the glow of fire. Its golden blaze lit up the surrounding buildings. Although still some thirty yards away, I could see a crowd of people seated on the ground near the fire, perhaps as many as a hundred. I could also see the dark silhouette of a figure walking slowly toward me. About half the distance between myself and the fire, the figure appeared to be draped in a poncho or blanket and, by the stride and the manner, I was sure it was a man. He was heading right for me, but the back lighting prevented me from making out his face. I slowed my pace, straining to discern the facial features, anticipating what I was going to say if it was indeed Shankara.

The closer I got, the more I was sure it was him. He must have gotten tired of waiting and was now coming to look for me. Even before I could see his face I could imagine his expression, those mesmerizing eyes and that half moon grin. Then like magic, the face materialized in a spray of light. . . .

It was Michael Talon.

"Michael!" I exclaimed in a loud whisper. "What happened to you? Are you alright?"

Before answering, he motioned for me to walk back into the adjacent alley so our voices wouldn't carry to the rest of the people.

"Yes, Jared . . . I am very well. I had a fabulous trip and I've got so much to tell you."

"What are you talking about! What happened to you?"

"Well, I met these two men," he said excitedly, "very interesting people, and we hit it off just famously, in fact we—"

"Michael!" I shouted.

"What?"

"Weren't you interrogated or tortured or something?"

"Well, the Peruvian food was a little treacherous at times," he said, chuckling slightly, "but I wouldn't consider it torture."

"Michael!" I blurted out, "You were kidnapped, right, taken hostage or something."

"What? . . . What are *you* talking about?"

"You . . . being kidnapped."

"When?"

"When? . . . Anytime, a few days ago . . . whenever!"

"My God, Jared, you're serious. Where did you ever get such an idea?"

"The note you left. I found the note at your house. It said you were in trouble."

"Oh no . . . Jared . . . I had no idea. I came back later that evening and threw that note away. It was still sitting in the wicker chair where I left it. I never dreamed that you actually saw it."

"But what about the men that you went to meet with? I thought they kidnapped you."

"No, on the contrary. They asked me to help them decipher a drawing, a rubbing taken from an Inca artifact. We think it may give the whereabouts of an undiscovered chamber in one of the ancient cities. It was a very sacred place known as the Room of Knowledge, a repository for all of their knowledge saved for future generations in case something happened to their civilization, which

314

is, of course, exactly what happened. The artifact gives evidence there may even have been early space travel from other galaxies, which was how such advanced cultures started here in the first place. That is why I went to Peru. To see if we could find an entrance to the chamber, to the Room of Knowledge."

"But what about the people ransacked your house?"

"I believe they were looking for the drawing. I also believe they're working with some, you might say, enemies of mine from the university, people who would very much like to discredit me as well as get their hands on the Inca rubbing. That's also why I left with my colleagues for Peru in such a hurry, why we had to keep it a secret. But I called you twice Jared. Didn't you get my messages?"

"I only got part of one message, something about . . . 'I can't talk now, so listen—'"

"Yes, I know. I was trying to catch a plane out of Lima and they had already called for boarding. I said, 'Jared, listen carefully. I don't have much time to talk. I have to catch a plane in about two seconds . . .' et cetera, et cetera."

"So you were never kidnapped?"

"No," he said, chuckling.

"So there never were any bad guys?"

"Well, there's always Wilkes from Stratton University. He's the one who convinced the hospital to have me committed in the first place. I'm pretty sure he is also the one who ransacked my house looking for a copy of the Inca map. But as clumsy as he is in his destructive efforts, I think he is more of a threat to himself than anyone else. So, I guess I would have to say, no Jared, I don't think there are any bad guys in this situation."

"What, no bad guys?"

"No . . . why?" He paused for a second staring into my distraught expression. "Jared," he finally asked laughing, "did you need for there to be bad guys in this situation?"

"What?"

"Bad guys, did you need to have some bad guys in your adventure?"

"What . . . no," I said trying to shake off my confusion. "So this whole thing was just some big illusion I cooked up to be on some stupid adventure?"

"Well, yes," he said chuckling even more, "I guess so."

For an instant, I couldn't move. I couldn't even think. Then Michael put his hand on my shoulder. Still laughing gently, he said, "Are you alright, Jared?"

Helplessly, I blurted out an explosion of emotions that had been building up inside me. "What are you laughing about? What could possibly be so funny? I have been running around like a total lunatic since this began, and you think it's funny."

"It *is* funny, Jared," he answered, "but right now you just can't see it that way."

"And why are you still laughing . . . laughing at me?"

He paused, and in an effort to calm me down he said, "I'm not laughing at you Jared, I'm laughing for you. Because right now you aren't able to. But soon you will, and then we will both laugh about it. We'll both laugh like crazy. I promise you."

"And what about the enlightened one?" I asked "Do you know who it is? Is it you? Is it Shankara? Who is it?"

"You mean Shankara hasn't told you yet?"

"What . . . who. . . no . . . when. . . ."

"Jared, come . . . let's join the others. I think that's where you will best find your answers."

Weary from the chase, a chase that now more than ever appeared to be me chasing after my own tail, I surrendered to his suggestion and turned to walk toward the gathering of people. As we strode along, Michael put his arm around my shoulder. His understanding in that moment helped me more than he would ever know. I admired the calmness with which he seemed to approach all of this, and I appreciated his support as we rejoined the group and stepped back up to the fire.

28

The Gathering

As Michael and I merged into the crowd, I couldn't help but notice the wide spectrum of people assembled. But for the significantly larger group, it was as I remembered from the first gathering. There were men, women and children from every walk of life, from every ethnic group. Had these people not been congregating around a campfire in an old industrial alleyway, I would have thought it to be a meeting at the United Nations.

There was also a sense of pageantry, as here and there individuals wore clothing or accessories reminiscent of their heritage. I saw a Black woman with ebony hair braided in long strands, woven with beautiful beads. I noticed a man with a French beret and an East Indian woman dressed in a sari with a sheer white cloth draped about her head. Sitting next to her was a bearded man wearing a yarmukle who looked as if he could be a rabbi, while standing next to him was a woman wearing a fringed leather poncho with several large gray feathers hanging down with her long dark hair.

I was also surprised at how many people I recognized. The young priest Father Mathews was there, as well as the small crippled fellow I had once chased through the streets. Dr. Sam and his partner Marshal had found their way, as did Sharee, of course, who was seated near the old Packard sedan, wrapped in her grey blanket. Mohan was situated center stage, perched on top of a large wooden barrel that rose up like a periscope within those gathered around. I also saw my friend the collie, who was curled up next to the fire as if it were her living room.

The ring of people, the fire, and the ruggedness of the surroundings brought to mind a scene from the Bible. I half expected to see Moses himself, standing with his white beard and long wooden staff, proclaiming his words to the masses.

It was amazingly quiet. All were trying to hear the private words Shankara was speaking to a lady seated near the front of the crowd. I could see Shankara down low, his broad frame balanced on one knee, his face only inches from her teary-eyed expression. I leaned far to one side and strained to hear their distant voices. Then suddenly, I realized it was Jessica Williams.

"There are no mistakes," he said to her in a strong but compassionate tone. **"There is only wisdom learned. And after all, how does your strategy about performing this music make you feel . . . just the thought of it?"**

"Wonderful. Excited. Fulfilled. All at the same time."

"Then follow your bliss."

"So you think I should do it?"

"Of course . . . and so do you.

"Pursue your passions. They are your natural instincts. Go . . . and sing. You have come a long way in the last of your days. Speak your truth and let it be heard."

Jessica giggled as she dried the last of her tears.

Affectionately, he asked, **"Alright?"**

"Yes," she replied.

"There really was no problem, was there?"

"No," she chuckled. "I guess everything was just moving along so fast, I got scared and started to doubt myself."

"My beloved woman, when your life begins to slow down and look once again like the Gray World, that will be the time to be in doubt. This . . . this is now your time to sing, and you will find that the people will begin to welcome your song." He kissed the palm of her hand; she smiled joyously in response.

Then Shankara stood, rising above the people seated around

him. He was wearing the same robe-like attire I'd seen him in before, a poncho folded about his torso and arms, pulled tight with a belt around his waist. The back of the poncho hung like a cape, draping off his shoulders to his knees. The firelight accentuated the whiteness of his hair and beard, giving him a luminescent quality that held me spellbound. Silently, and with an air of majesty, he strode toward the edge of the crowd to stand directly in front of Father Mathews.

For no apparent reason, the priest lowered his head and, with one hand covering his eyes, began to weep. Shankara took a step closer and reached under the priest's chin to lift his head. As their eyes made contact, Shankara gently spoke.

"You feel that the truth has divided you in two." Father Mathews nodded slightly. "But there is really only one truth you see . . . only one truth to go with each moment.

"This, your journey . . . is not about discarding anything. It's about gathering everything. Throw away nothing of your religion. Instead, gather it all up, every symbol, every cross, every bead and hold them close . . . so close inside you that you can no longer see them. Gather them into the center of your being and then courageously move forward and step beyond them into your future.

"In this way you arm yourself with the truth, because part of that truth is what has come before. You see, the truth needs no set of reasons, no doctrine, no dogma. Truth is the poetry of the unspoken word. So, tell of your truth by how well you live, and not by the bravado of how well you speak."

At this Father Mathews stood a little straighter and seemed to embrace these words with a slight smile.

"Remember that, on this your journey, if you choose to be a guide of the people, you are not striving to see who can get to the highest mountain. This time, travel down into the valley. Because you have already been to the Tower of Babel where your differences became your creed. That is where you dwell now. Let tomorrow be a journey to reunite the tribes, letting the differences, and all thoughts of separation, fall behind you on the trail homeward."

Graciously they bowed to each other and as Shankara moved away he said to those who had been listening, **"When the religions of the world begin to have a deep need for peace, rather than a deep need to be right, then you will have it— peace, that is."**

He then walked over and sat down on a large wooden crate next to none other than Emily. She squirmed and giggled like a nervous child as for several seconds they exchanged expressions but no words.

"So," he began, causing her to start just a little. **"So you have been running with the animals, I hear."** Emily grinned and nodded her head with approval.

"And you have discovered that by exploring all of that . . . animal energy, you have greatly heightened your senses and your natural instincts."

"Mm hmm," she replied, her smile growing larger exposing most of her ivory teeth.

"And you have also delved into a realm of sexuality beyond anything you could have ever imagined. In fact, it is so profound that you are hoping for the day when one of these orgasms will lift you out of the human experience and send you zooming into your enlightenment."

At this Emily burst out laughing, dipping forward several times as if attempting to contain her joy. Then she sat up straight with a Cheshire cat grin and playing along, she nodded saying, "Mm hmm. . . . Mm hmm." Throughout the crowd, many people laughed. Even Shankara showed signs of a smile.

He then stood up, patted her gently on the head, and spoke, **"You may be right."** He began to walk away, but then turned back toward her and said, **"But perhaps for the time being, you had better keep your blinds closed."**

Immediately the crowd broke into a rumble of laughter. As for myself, I was still trying to get past that he had spoken to Emily and she had hardly said a word. That in itself had to have been some kind of miracle.

It felt good to see the people laughing. I took the liberty of letting out a few chuckles myself. In fact, I was actually starting to have a pretty good time; that is, until Shankara turned suddenly and began to walk toward where Michael and I were seated. My laughter was quickly replaced with nervous tension as he came directly over and addressed my comrade.

"So then," he began, **"have you found the entrance to the Room of Knowledge?"**

"Well, not just yet," Michael replied.

"Are you looking in the right place?"

Smiling he said, "Why, yes, I think so. We have trampled all over those ancient ruins, and we know that it has to be there. We just can't seem to find the opening."

"So you are looking for a doorway into the ancient Room of Knowledge." Shankara leaned forward putting his face closer to Michael's. **"I will tell you a great secret. This doorway . . . well, it has no door, no hinges, no knob, no sliding stones, and no secret passage. That is why it has never been found. So perhaps you need to start looking for a different kind of doorway, a different kind of opening. Something that is a little less tangible. Perhaps a little more spiritual. . . . What do you think?"**

Michael smiled sheepishly, as Shankara playfully rapped with his knuckles on Michael's forehead, as though knocking at a door.

"Oh, and by the way, this book you have been writing, I would not be too concerned that this your work of so-called fiction does not have enough sex, violence, and murder to be a bestseller." Michael chuckled. **"After all, that is why we titled it *The Blissmaker*. You may discover that people will find the simple truth to be a lot more provocative. You may also find it necessary to go undercover for a little while after it is first published."**

Shankara turned to walk away, but then abruptly made an about-face. The next thing I knew, he was standing directly over me. As I looked up into his face, his clear blue eyes burrowed into mine.

"So how have you been doing?" he asked, a question that I'd heard him ask me before. And as before, my rattled brain was hard-pressed for a reply. Did he mean—how have I been doing since we had demolished a picket fence? Or—how have I been doing since I was lost in the alley, shouting into the sky?

Before I could answer, he said, **"Well, you probably better hang on to your hat, because really, we're just getting started."**

With these profound words he turned and stepped toward the front of the crowd, leaving me to fish for my tongue, which I had undoubtedly swallowed. There was a certain relief, though, at having been addressed with such a short stint. I knew it could have been much, much worse; I could have actually opened my fumbling mouth and had a go at saying something.

Returning to the old Packard, he planted himself on the fender and for several seconds gazed into the many faces, looking into their thoughts, calculating his next unpredictable remark.

Then unexpectedly, he raised his voice and said, **"Mohan!"**

"What say you?" replied Mohan in a quick and jovial manner.

"So it is your passion to be able to consciously lift your soul from your body. Correct?"

"Indeed, my Lord," he answered with both playfulness and nobility in his tone.

"Then tell me, my friend. When I lift this . . . my own spirit from this human body, where is it that you think I go?"

Thinking for just a second, Mohan replied with great certainty, "Anywhere you want."

Shankara laughed and said, **"Good point."**

As spurts of laughter cropped up here and there, Mohan playfully stood up and bowed to the group, a comical and not unfamiliar response. Yet this time while displaying his antics, he pivoted around and stalled his spin giving the impression that some other more serious emotion had intervened. Rising up into a kind of slow motion, he scanned the faces, awestruck, as if discovering them for the first time, or perhaps seeing them for the last. Then, he stood perfectly still, with the most heartfelt smile I had ever seen. The people quieted in response.

Shankara also waited momentarily before interrupting the

calm. Rising before the assembly, he placed his hands together in a prayer-like manner and bowed to them as though to signal for what was about to happen next. Mohan slowly slid back onto his wooden barrel surrounded by those seated on the ground.

"**Good morning,**" Shankara said, his bold voice breaking the silence, "**I say good morning to you for it is the morning of your lives. It is the beginning of an era in which a handful of you have begun to awaken the truth; a truth that forever has revolved around the simple premise that:** *everything is of your choosing, no matter how helpless you believe or have been told you are.*"

For a few seconds there was a subtle murmur. "So what happens when you begin to embrace this concept?

"What happens . . . is that your spirit rapidly commences drawing to you every adventure possible to provide you with proof that this is indeed the truth of your reality. Your daily occurrences become amplified and coagulate more quickly because, from within this truth, you are projecting from your spirit, and not your ego.

"So there you have it . . . you now have an answer as to why many of you feel that your lives have been turned upside down in the last few weeks. Although this is probably not the answer that you were looking for, it is, nonetheless, still the only answer." Again there is a soft rumble across the gathering.

"**And you especially don't want to hear that these events were really just illusions in time and space**—a mere handful of the multitude you have created throughout your many lifetimes in the human adventure—a human adventure that was also of your choosing.

"So let us begin with that first incarnation, the first time you decided to walk in a physical body and why you did so.

"Imagine yourselves at a great cinema where there are literally hundreds of individual theaters to choose from, each playing a different movie. The supreme being, creator, and overseer of the complex has given you permission to explore any one that you want.

"On one of the theater doors, you see the poster of a beautiful blue-green planet. Just above is the title: *The Human Experience*. Having heard stories all over the galaxy about this place, you quickly sit down and begin to watch.

"The movie is incredible, with images and sounds of rivers and waterfalls. Thousands of amazing animals roam all about the beautiful land, a terrain that supports creatures unlike you had ever seen.

"You soon realize that in your excitement you have seated yourself at the back of the theater, so you move forward to the middle where the screen appears much larger causing the movie to become even more real. Now the mountains and the trees are nearly life-size, and when the lion roars, it fills your being with a wild and powerful sensation. You can't help but want to experience even more.

"You sit in the front row where you can almost touch the screen. This paradise saturates you with the nuances of sounds and smells so refined that you know you must go deeper. You see other spirits who were once like you, who have now taken on human forms to explore this wonderland. They play and dance, sing and make love. You want to taste the fruit and feel all of the sensations, so you step up to the screen as close as you can. The hologram of light penetrates your being. Color and sound come streaming through you, giving you a shape and a form you have never known.

"For a moment you turn away from the screen and look back toward the projector to see the source of this splendor . . . and with a flash of light you are in it . . . you are on a great adventure called the human experience.

"In actuality, your scientists will agree with me wholeheartedly, and they will tell you that there is no such thing as solid matter—that everything, including your human body is just a mass of dust particles called quarks spinning in empty space. They will even tell you that the images of physical forms, of color and shape are the result of how light reflects off the spinning particles.

"So if the human experience is just a great illusion where everything is just a hologram of light, then who are you in this adventure?

"You are a whirlwind of sensations and emotions held together in an ever changing form by your own thought frequencies. Such was the enormous love of your divine source that you were given the freedom and the ability to be whatever you wanted. And since God is in reality the essence of all thought frequencies, then such an infinite light is with you every step of the way.

Once again Shankara allowed the quiet night to infiltrate his words. It was a most welcome pause in which my mind wanted to hide. This desire was short lived though as he spoke once again.

"And who am I in all of this?" he asked.

"I sit in the front row of the theatre. I call your name. And sometimes in your prayers, or in the quiet of your mind, I feel you turn and look back up through the veil and into the theater, back toward the idea of the projected white light. That is when I chant but a single word . . . remember . . . remember . . . remember.

"All of you have had death experiences where you stepped toward the white light and away from the human hologram. This event was generally not a conscious choice, but one enveloped with fear. And even though you had stepped from the screen and through the veil toward the white light, the cavalcade of emotions that propelled you there caused you to turn back to look at the screen. There you saw your old life, the illusions of your past. You saw your unfulfilled dreams and all of your regrets. Perhaps you saw that you were murdered and robbed of that life. Or perhaps you saw what was a simple death, and a lover who weeps, with arms embracing a closed casket. You saw your friends, your family, and the tears of your children . . . and then with that thought you were back. You reincarnated again, and started again, to fix it, to change it, and to make it all right—to correct the life that only you had judged was wrong. And that is why I will always say to you, *that everything is of your choosing, no matter how helpless you believe or have been told you are.*

"For lifetimes you have been submerged in the flow of third dimension so that you could explore this reality and discover a few simple truths. At the core of these truths is that age old and festering premise: *that everything is of your choosing no matter how helpless you believe or have been told you are.*"

He paused and then added, "Perhaps I should repeat the phrase just one more time? What do you think?" Some of the listeners laughed. "Yes . . . you have heard this adage come up time and again, and every time you hear it, you want to tear it in two. You want to run away screaming— *'It can't possibly be so. After all, look at all of the bad things that happen to me and to all of the other innocent people.'*

"This premise I speak of is not a reason or an excuse for why things happen the way they do. It is simply a law of the universe, one that explains how you, the first offspring of the divine source, have functioned and created throughout infinity. It truly is the natural order of how it all works whether you find it palatable or not.

"This concept, which is a very simple understanding, is one with which you have a great deal of difficulty. It is incomprehensible because such a universal law makes you responsible for everything that you have created in this lifetime and all that has already played out.

"So what does this actually mean when I say that you are responsible for everything? Well . . . it means you are responsible for all of the beautiful experiences of your life, as well as your illnesses, your misfortunes, your bad luck, your failures, and every destructive thing that has happened to you or to *this*, your beloved planet, since the beginning of time."

He glanced down at the ground as whispers and shuffling noises fluttered through the audience. As for myself, I found his message cut me to the quick. What if we truly were responsible?

The possibility left me dumbfounded. His words seemed so futile and my mind heartily rejected this notion that there were no victims. I couldn't help but take refuge in the idea that bad things did happen to good people. People were murdered. Babies were born deformed or retarded. There was a part of life that was just unfair, and a lot of innocent people were the victims of this unfairness.

"Sort of a tall order to assimilate, isn't it?" Looking back out into the crowd, he continued. "And that is why for eons you have not been willing to look at this colossal dilemma. It is unimaginable that everything has been of your choosing, because you see so many victims in your world. You say to me, 'But what about the children who are born deaf or blind? That is so unfair. How can it be that such a future is of their choosing? And what about the innocent souls who fall peril to a flood or earthquake. How unfair.'

"Really?" he questioned. "You feel these events are so unfair? Well, then for just a moment try picturing yourself as a prisoner. Your husband or your wife has just been murdered in front of you. In addition, three or four of your children have been raped and taken from you never to be seen again. You are standing in a line of people walking into a building to be executed—your final destination, a communal grave."

He waited a second or two and then said, "Indeed, how unfair. You're absolutely right, how terribly unfair. And if the truth be known, I could recall for you the events of my own lifetimes with personal accountings of an overwhelming number of scenarios even more hellacious than this. I could tell you of tragedies that would surely rally you to cry out on my behalf, how unfair! How terribly unfair."

Shankara then took several steps, pacing and turning in front of the crowd. The people became absolutely still.

"As for many of your Christian religions, they would respond to this unfairness by saying, 'Well, God must have had a very good reason for allowing all of those people to be the victims of genocide.'"

For a second he shook his head. He finally said, **"Believe me when I tell you that a Supreme Being, who is the source of all love and grace in this world, does not sit around contemplating which thousand or more of you will be allowed to be massacred before the day is done. Such an atrocity as the genocide of any part of humanity could only have been conceived by a human ego, an altered state of consciousness that has the free will to become any sort of monster that it chooses."**

Folding his arms, he waited expectantly for a reaction from the people.

"But just for a moment, let us look at the monster. Because after all, you are so sure that the monster is not you. This is also what spurs you on to judge that everything is so unfair. Perhaps even now, in this very lifetime, you live in a scenario where you are totally convinced you are a victim. Therefore, see if you can imagine this.

"See yourself as a parent, an innocent victim because your child has been murdered by one of these monsters. Would you feel any different if I were to tell you that in the lifetime before you were the murderer of that monster's child? Or perhaps you mutilated someone else's child, and now you have created this event to process your own guilt and gain the wisdom of such a senseless act.

"This sort of cause and effect, multiplied by numerous other variables, other creative thoughts, is what makes life unfold as unpredictably as it does. It is the game, the volley of recycling events, that you perceive as the chaotic accidents of your lives; thoughts and events that have been colliding and regenerating themselves since the ego was born. And the most difficult part for you is that you are all in this adventure together. Be you a tyrant or saint, king or pauper, you are all a part of the human experience that is moving forward of its own volition, a momentum that for a long time has been out of control.

"Humankind, through a culmination of collective creative thoughts, has manifested a future that is in a perpetual flow of judgmental, hateful, vengeful thoughts that far outnumber the struggling thoughts of peace, love, and compassion. Since the beginning of your history you have set into motion a multitude of probable events. They have become like a rock slide down a mountain, one thought reacting to another; then in a chain reaction more are affected. That is why the frequencies of war are so prevalent on your planet. Because someone always has the need to carry the torch of retaliation, a torch carried from generation to generation.

"In addition, *time* is not, nor has it ever been your ally. Time is the shadow—the shadow that follows along behind delivering all of the manifestations of your past thoughts. It does this without bias, rhyme, or reason, without correlation or sequence, completely out of the realm of logical linear understanding—or so it seems. You, who act primarily as an ego-based humanity, feed this fire of negative thoughts and keep it burning by judging nearly every event that rolls past you, keeping the torch of retaliation in motion, passed from injustice to injustice.

"For eons these disjointed occurrences have fallen in a continuous motion forming lakes and pools of confused and disruptive consciousness. Time was once created to perpetuate a place that was intended to be a garden. Now, time is but an hourglass full of a billion perpetual human events that fall like grains of sand into a place that is today called the Gray World.

"So when we speak of those captives who are standing before a gas chamber, having been stripped of their lives, their hands and feet covered with the blood of their spouse or their innocent children—and the reason for this particular event is simply because they were born of a different heritage or because they have different spiritual beliefs—then I will tell you that I agree with you wholeheartedly. That it's just not fair. That it's horrible and mortifying, and just not fair." Lowering his head reverently, he said again with a shadow of his true voice, **"Just not fair."**

Then he lifted his eyes slightly, his expression so very intense, and said, **"But is that not why you came?"** For several seconds he waited and then began to once again stroke the edges of his beard. "Is that not why you came and walked the night streets to find an alley where people had gathered . . . for what reason, you weren't really sure? Is that not why you followed an instinct, an impulse . . . like an ancient star searching for an answer, some possibility that could make it all more palatable, that could make it all more believable, or bring the injustice to an end? Is that not why within the last of your days you have stopped to listen to the wind . . . wanting to hear something . . . wanting to know . . . wanting to remember?

"You live in a world, in a consciousness, where slumber and ignorance are prevalent. And among you, amid this thwarted flow of humankind, there are but a few who know, beyond any doubt, that this futile recycling of human lives and attitudes was not what was intended.

"You see . . . that is who you are. You are the beginning, the awakening life. You are the seekers of the truth. You are the simplest of people.

"As for myself, I did not come here to interfere in your journeys. I came to invoke you to remember. I came on behalf of the child who is deaf or the one who is blind. I came on behalf of the noble father and the sweet mother who have lost their children and now stand in line to be exterminated, who call out for the reason why they are to be slain. I came on behalf of a billion lost souls who cry out in their pain, who may never hear the simplest of words that I share with you now."

Slowly, he took several steps back toward the broken-down automobile and sat down on its fender. "In the early morning hours," he said, "I have heard some of you pray for a savior. *'Jesus come save us . . . Buddha, Shiva, come save us.'* Many of you wait for such an enlightened one, for the second coming of the Christ perhaps. You think this one will save you. All that you have to do is wait and not murder too many more of your neighbors, and pretty soon that savior will come and fix it all—punish the *other* heathens and make everything right.

"There are also some of you who have actually heard me speak of such an Enlightened One, a Christ, or a Buddha who will come to uplift the whole of the world and all of humanity. And it is true. Indeed this one has arrived.

"In fact," he said raising his voice slightly, "this one sits among you here and now, nervously awaiting the announcement—who will be unveiled as the Christ."

An excited murmur rolled around the arena as all eyes began to scan the gathering, examining each other, speculating the possibility of being seated next to the enlightened one.

I too looked about, wondering if it was perhaps Mohan or Sharee, Jessica or Michael. I juggled these thoughts with a continuous rhythm, partly because I wanted it to be one of them, but mostly because I was trying to avoid the insane notion that kept surfacing in my mind—that the enlightened one . . . actually was me.

Standing up, he paced in front of the crowd. "In truth," he continued, "that is why some of you came out at all . . . to this audience this evening. You came to find your Christ. You came to find your Savior."

He wandered out into the middle of the crowd until he finally said, "So . . . do you want to know who it is?"

There was a rumble of talking with a few thin voices echoing out, "Who is it? Which one?"

"Are you sure that you're ready to know?" he said, toying with us. "Perhaps we should have a little more murder and mayhem on the planet, maybe a bit more ethnic cleansing, some more human genocide . . . just for the effect. What do you think?"

The crowd immediately grew louder; anticipation and anxiety blended together. Throughout the gathering people began calling out. "Who is it? Tell us. No more waiting. Tell us who it is."

The chant grew louder and louder until Shankara raised both of his hands to quiet the crowd. "So you think that you're ready?

"And what will you do with this Enlightened One when you know who it is? Because the last Christ who came to this human experience, your Jesus . . . did not fare very well at all. If I'm not mistaken, I believe that you, as humanity, pierced his hands and feet with spikes and hung him spread out on a cross where you watched him bleed to death.

"Not a very lavish reception for a Christ. Not to mention that you then rewrote most of what he came to tell you so that it might serve you better in your ego-based desires."

The agitated crowd grew still, as though the silence itself were a call to Shankara to reveal the one . . . to reveal the name. He turned and began to walk back toward the broken down sedan at the front of the crowd. In a motion of contemplation he stroked his chin, pondering his dilemma, his muffled voice repeating his own words, **"So you really want to know."**

Then with a rush, he turned around and looked directly at me. There were a few seconds of impenetrable silence until at last he spoke, **"It is you."**

Panic exploded inside me, my heart pounding, my head racing. Then he looked out into the rest of the crowd and calmly said, **"It is all of you."**

For the next few minutes I tried rather inconspicuously to catch my breath as Shankara, of course, continued on.

"That is why you came. That is how you knew to be here. You . . . are the awakening Christ. You are the second coming . . . the second coming of a higher state of consciousness, an energy, a frequency that in other realms is known as the Christus energy. The name Christ or Buddha is really just a term that describes the transition whereby a soul or spirit, having mastered the human experience in third dimension, evolves into the Christus energy—into the fourth dimension— into an understanding where the seen and the unseen become one. It is a state of awareness available to all in your reality. It is what your Jesus and your Buddha spoke of so long ago when they said, '*You are the same as we, no different. You are children of a divine source, and one day you will come home to this truth and perform miracles just as we have.*'

"When you have evolved into the understanding of a Christ, you will live in an awareness where the lower frequencies of fear, hatred, competition, greed, and guilt will no longer be

experienced. In fourth dimension you will be able to perceive your reality on an energy level, with the ability to see thoughts and emotions as tangible forms. You will begin to use thought frequencies rather than speech to communicate and to spontaneously manifest events and tangible matter from those thoughts. You will live in a place that is purely an evolutionary advancement for you, where science and spirit have melded as one. You will live in a world that is very different from the one you know now. And some of you will call it . . . heaven.

"Some of you will call it Nirvana. Some of you will call it Enlightenment. And all of you . . . will know that you have indeed arrived there because for the first time in your ardent evolution, you won't have the overwhelming desire to fight over who was right and who was wrong."

There was a brief frozen silence, followed by low laughter that trickled throughout the crowd in a kind of chain reaction.

"You see, in this your third dimension, your perception of humanity is like one of your Western cinemas where there are the good guys and the bad guys. . . . You, of course," he said smiling, "being the good guys. Now . . . contemplate a reality where there are no bad guys. Would that still make you the good guys? Without this—your current identity as the good guys—who would you be?

"I will tell you a great truth about this, your current reality, a reality that rallies around the act of judging with the third dimensional polarities of good and bad, right and wrong. For any of you to be able to stand up on your podiums and proclaim that you are the good and the righteous, well, then someone else in the vicinity has to be the bad and the unrighteous, otherwise the game doesn't work.

"As you evolve into the Christus energy, the polarities of right and wrong will become a thing of the past and the act of making a judgment will be pointless. That is why I have said that it is not likely this Divine Source whom you call God will ever judge you for your sins, because the act of judging is a very low frequency thought, an idea that was born, bred, and peddled by the human ego and indoctrinated by your religions. I would doubt very much that a Supreme Being would stoop that low. Besides, you have already spent lifetimes judging yourself and others, so perhaps it is now time to move on.

"But what about our Jesus? you say to me. *He said he would come, and we have been so long in waiting for that coming. If we are indeed the second coming of Christ, then does this mean that he will not come?* Of course he will come, and it will be as he has promised. Besides, so many of you have been contemplating his return, forever so long, at this point," he said chuckling, "he really has no choice. Now, he has to come whether he likes or not. That is how powerful your creative thoughts and prayers can be.

"But if by chance your Jesus comes to you as a great winged bird that you hope will sweep you up and soar you into the heavens, do not be surprised if he says to you, '*Stop tugging at my tail feathers. Spread into your own splendid wings and fly with me.'*"

Laughter danced about the gathering as Shankara once again relieved the crowd's tension with unexpected wit.

"Likewise, if your saviors and enlightened teachers arrive all together with an armada of what you will perceive as aeroships—transparent forms of light and color—it would be best not to flee in terror. After all, your world is merely one thread in the tapestry of all creation. For you as humanity to believe that you are the only life forms existing in a multitude of universes is certainly a pompous notion that has been induced and supported by your religions since the beginning of their short existence. For you to imagine yourselves as the most evolved species, of any of the Supreme Being's spiritual creations, is truly, and I say again truly, an ego-based reality.

"This self-serving reality, which has been perpetuated through so many of your lifetimes, has not only taken its toll on your planet and your environment, but it has also created for you an arduous future, full of possible events and probabilities that are a part of the story that I have yet to tell."

29

Prophets and Probabilities

The gathering of people, who had taken a myriad of pathways into this arena, now waited patiently, silently for the rest of the untold story. It was difficult for me to imagine what could have been left unsaid with so many impressions already swimming around in my head, trying to spawn their way into some fertile understanding. Yet within my contemplations, I still harbored the feeling that all of my recent experiences and profound realizations were preparing me for what I was about to hear.

"You live in a world," Shankara began, "that is foreshadowed by probabilities, creative thoughts that have accumulated and evolved into the reality that we will now call your future. Many of these events are occurring while others are still pending. Regardless of this historical blueprint, the fact remains— nothing is predestined. Everything is still of your choosing.

"All prospective thoughts and perpetual events exist in a constant flow of consciousness that is moving and changing like a great river through a mountainous valley. Humankind is the river, and your Earth is the mountainous valley.

The direction of the river is unpredictable and unlimited because the motion that propels it is still creative thought. The destiny of the river is based on probabilities, or the accumulation of all thoughts.

"Within your world, within the fabric of each culture, you

have had prophets who since the beginning of time have foretold of the great change, the Armageddon, the fall of humanity. This wide range of predictions encompasses the Book of Revelations, the Hopi Prophesies, the writings of Nostradamus, the Mayan calendar, and countless more. The time frame of these prophecies is as varied as their origins. But no matter the culture, they were all based on the probabilities of that particular moment in time.

"Many of these prophesies have come true and continue to manifest. This is *not* because the events were predestined, but because humankind never changed the elements of the probabilities. Today you are in it. You are in the throes of this Armageddon, even though much of the population has still elected to be immune to the collapse, living out their preprogrammed existence. You will see this unconscious approach begin to shift as your arduous future starts to play itself out.

"But let us first begin with your Earth, for she too is in forward motion, executing her own probabilities of tomorrow. The great upheavals you are beginning to experience in your Earth's terrain and in your erratic weather patterns are part of a great cleanse. It is an attempt by Nature to realign the energy forces and restore its ecological balance.

"When life began on this planet, there was indeed a master plan. It was a blueprint in the form of an energy grid strategically laced around the planet. At the grid's intersections were energy vortexes, which were connected to and governed by the Earth's core and magnetic poles, north and south. This energy grid is what allowed your planet to become stable enough to support third dimensional life. It has provided you with an atmosphere as well as oceans and continents that were set into a very slow evolutionary motion, so that the whole of life could have a place to be expressed. It was to be a garden where humankind could come and explore, and hopefully master the elements of third dimensional matter.

"The only problem with this plan was that humankind has not been a very good gardener. As a collective, human beings have generated an enormous flow of ego-based energies. This is the result of eons of war, hatred, vengeance, competition, greed, and countless other such expressions. These elements, which are completely foreign to the flow of the planet's natural grid, have done serious damage to the original framework.

"In addition, your civilizations have developed crude forms of energy, such as electrical and nuclear power, that are like viruses to the natural order. Today, electricity has formed its own grid around the planet, which disrupts the *true* grid's natural balance. A huge dependency on these crude forms of energy have caused you, the children of a divine source, to forget many of your own inherent powers.

"Satellites can now photograph the electric lights of your cities at night. If you were to draw a line from one light to another, you would see the electronic cage, the static web that now entraps a living planet. As you well know, electricity cannot touch any life form without causing harm or even death. So it is with your ecological balance, which attempts to grow and propagate within this destructive force field.

"As far as your ecosystem is concerned, most life forms are now suffering abuse and sometimes extinction from the many poisonous chemicals that have been placed into the land, air, and water. Because of this you also are experiencing global warming. In many parts of the world, miles of forest land have been stripped, the very forests that produce the majority of your planet's oxygen. Numerous rivers have also been destroyed, not to mention your oceans, which have been polluted almost beyond recovery. These massive bodies of water are at the base of the planet's food chain, a balanced food chain without which the evolution of life cannot continue."

He paced hypnotically back and forth. Silence seemed to hold the crowd captive as Shankara's footsteps were the only sound that could be heard throughout the arena.

"So what is happening with your planet, with all of the erratic weather and the natural disasters?

"Well, your Mother Earth is fighting back. She fully intends to survive humankind's realm in some form or another. She is trying to shake off the cage of electrical and nuclear energies and disgorge the chemicals and pollution.

"In addition, she is causing your magnetic poles to shift. This is a learned understanding." For a second he hesitated producing a hint of a smile. "Ask your scientists. I did not just make this up. As a result of the damage by humanity, the Earth's magnetic poles are no longer where they used to be.

"Today, you are already experiencing an overwhelming number of natural disasters. Your daily news depicts a new one in the world almost every day. Often they are described as the worst earthquakes of the century or the most powerful tornados ever. The words *most* and *worst* will become common to your headlines, and all areas of terrain on the planet will be subject to this the Earth's cleanse in some form or another.

"The polarity of the north and south poles is what governs the magnetic pull of positive and negative charges on your planet. In third dimension, everything that exists as solid matter is made up of positive and negative charges. Therefore, any movement or shifting of these poles and their magnetic pull is going to affect everything, including all of you—the not so good gardeners.

"So what happens to you, the human, as the poles shift and the pull of positive and negative charges is altered?

"What happens . . . is that you will be drawn to one side or the other. You will either evolve with the flow, whereby the union of your body, mind, and spirit will become in alignment with Nature's new plan, or you will be consumed by the separation and the breaking down of the old form. This separation will literally be the fragmentation of body, mind, and spirit.

"Since male forces have been dominant on this planet, to be consumed or fragmented will be to fall totally into the realm of destructive male attributes. For a time this realignment will bring out the worst in your planet's warlords. Acts of competition, conflict, and genocide will fester until the consumption of the fire has burned itself out. In your communities you will see individuals go mad in the streets unable to cope with the flow of this new polarity. Now, does this mean that male energy is bad or destructive? No, on the contrary. In this, your third dimension, it is one half of perfection. But like so many chemical equations, if you have too much of one substance and not enough of another, the result may be a volatile situation.

"In your own societies you have already seen this kind of separation of body, mind, and spirit. In several instances you have witnessed your own children arm themselves with artillery so that for a brief span of time they could murder their teachers and classmates to experience the attributes of dominance and control. This is just one small example.

"These acts of uninhibited violence are birthed from an ego-based existence, propelled by the total imbalance of male energies. On a larger scale you have witnessed thousands murdered through ethnic cleansing by warlords who choose the same imbalance. You have always had such murder and mayhem on your planet, but not to the degree that you are experiencing now.

"So, that is a brief description of the effect that the shifting of the poles will have on you and everything that is around you. Unfortunately, that is not really the worst of your problems.

"Toward the end of your twentieth century, a collection of wealthy individuals on your planet decided to take it upon themselves to handle the evolutionary problem of . . . *too many people and not enough resources*. Through a series of self-serving and self-motivated actions, they have secretly set into motion plans for the restructuring of humanity so that one central system would be able to have complete control.

For our intents and purposes let us call this secret organization the new world alliance. The members of this new regime are wealthy individuals from countries around the world, including your own. In fact, wealth, and the power from wealth, is what they all have in common. This group now controls most of the world's money markets, which has given them a strong foothold in many of the world's governments. They have also infiltrated other organizations here in your United States including your military, your CIA, your Federal Reserve, and your IRS."

Within the crowd there was the interruption of a few unintelligible voices. In response, Shankara replied, "Yes, even your beloved IRS. After all, if you are going to stage a world takeover, you had better have some financial backing. Now does this mean that your U.S. Government is totally corrupt and that you should all gather up your firearms and flee to the hills? Of course not. That of which I speak is a worldwide system that is very refined and technologically advanced. Its objective is to produce a unified civilization, with a reduced population, one that will be able to survive off the planet's remaining resources. This, mind you, is a very fine idea if you just happen to have the right skin color, ethnic background, or sexual orientation."

"The format of this new regime is a concept that I will refer to as the Three C's—Cleanse, Consolidate, and Control.

"The *cleansing* process is meant to reduce the size of the world population. Close attention will be paid to making sure that certain undesirable groups are targeted for extinction. Since this alliance believes there are undesirable cultures or minorities in many countries, the act of ethnic cleansing will start to surface in numerous places on the globe—such as you are now seeing in Europe and some of your African nations.

"Recently, you have witnessed how sly and secretive groups can be in their acts of ethnic cleansing, executing hundreds upon thousands of people. In the future, it is likely that other organizations will be a bit more clever, embarking on methods designed to eliminate only those who have been infected by some particular plague or other genetic defect. In this fashion, they will be able to contaminate or infect certain undesirable groups, and then later dispose of them for a good cause.

"For the cleansing to be a success, half of the world population needs to be exterminated.

"As the cleansing proceeds, the *consolidation* process will come into play. In many of your countries this concept is already in effect. Its purpose is to keep track of where the money and resources are so that this new world alliance can have complete control over them. Their plan is eventually to do away with monetary systems in their tangible form and replace them with a single personal identification card that will act much like the debit cards you have now. In addition, home computer systems will become simply a keyboard and a screen where individuals store all of their information: their banking, bookkeeping, and personal records in a master system that they connect to through online services and the World Wide Web. Through a unified bank, which has already been set up, the central computer system can keep track of what everyone has, what everyone buys, where they go, what they do, and on, and on, and on. In time, the only way to obtain goods will be to have the ID card and be plugged into the master system by your computer.

"Once this scheme is in place, it will be rather easy to implement the final phase—control. By inserting a computer chip under the skin of every individual, the world alliance will be able to keep track of the entire population. Plans for a later version of the implant will include electrodes that can inflict pain if anyone has a problem with the new established order.

"Cleansing—Consolidation—and Control . . . for a happier and more obedient civilization. Quite an extraordinary plan, isn't it? In fact, for some of you it seems totally outrageous and completely impossible.

"Really. . . ? Then I will give you some examples.

"Currently, in your everyday life, how many of you have debit cards or credit cards that you use faithfully, seldom ever using money? Some of you use a computer to do your banking, your stock trading, and even the purchase of your groceries. You consult over the Web about your medical problems, your health insurance, as well as your most personal and private conversations. Some of you have already tied into a master computer system that you access with a keyboard, a computer screen, and a phone line. All of this you do knowing full well that every computer system is vulnerable to security breech.

"And what about this computer chip that they plan to insert under the skin? All around the world veterinarians are already doing this with pets for identification. The medical field is implanting chips in human patients to monitor particular organs and vital signs. Today, if you're afraid of your child being lost or kidnapped, as a safeguard you can have them numbered with a tatoo or have a chip put under their skin. In a similar fashion, the military already uses this procedure with soldiers who could end up missing in action, a kind of dog tag, if you will. In your holy book, the Book of Revelations, this identification piece is referred to as the Mark of the Beast. You might remember it as the three sixes.

Shankara then began to wander about the crowd, looking into the bewildered faces of some of the people.

"Still not convinced, some of you? Still not convinced that any of this is possible? After all, how would any one regime be able to take over so many people without them catching on and rebelling?

"Well . . . then just imagine this scenario: Several small nuclear warheads have exploded in different cities in your Americas. There is mass confusion throughout the country. People are missing and there are huge shortages of everything. Transportation systems have broken down, and all available supplies including food, medical, and fuel are rationed. Personal ID cards are issued in order to distribute the rations fairly. Because so many have been killed, everyone is marked and identified with an electronic chip. Then if there is more bombing, the people can be identified or perhaps found in the rubble by tracing these electronic tags.

"So then you ask how will they implement all of these systems? Through pure deception.

"In the days to come, when the world is in chaos and when your current and comfortable way of living is disrupted, you are apt to do almost anything to get it back. And this regime will tell you that one day all will return to normal, but first these new systems have to be put into effect to gain control of the current chaos. They will present this concept of a global alliance as the peaceful unification of all people for a higher good— Do not be deceived by this.

"Now understand me when I say that there are many people, leaders, organizations, and whole countries who are supporting this movement, who may be unaware that this regime is the underlying current of the cause they support. In fact, the number of people who truly have knowledge of this master plan are very few. In your country, most of them wear the cloak of the Republican party. Yet there are a multitude of individuals and groups who follow their lead, who follow an idea that will turn out to be a great deception. In truth, deception is the real platform for those of the alliance, and it is their intent to play with organizations, religions, and entire nations as though they were pieces on a chessboard. Their objective—to win the game and to have only a few pieces of just one color left on the board.

"So beware of early attempts to unite groups of nations for financial stability, organizations for world trade and unified banking—especially if they show little regard for the enviroment. The seed of treason has been planted in numerous places. Many who believe they are creating alliances for a cause may discover in the end that there was a great deception at work with the self-serving interests of this regime at the helm.

"Likewise, be cautious of early attempts toward global unification, at the core of which are corporate mergers and monopolies that conduct themselves like independent nations.

"The central system they have employed is like a pyramid scheme—first one deception splitting off into two, then two splitting into four and so on and so on down the line. In the end it is you, the common people, who are being deceived by other people, leaders, presidents, governments, and even nations who believe their actions are for some higher good.

"So that is the game, and it is already in motion. Those are some of the plans and some of the probabilities. There are also an unlimited number of possibilities surrounding them, and—*Everything is of your choosing no matter how helpless you believe or have been told you are.*"

Shankara then slowly walked out into the crowd, moving in our direction. He stopped, placing himself directly in front of Michael Talon, who now looked very distraught, with his eyes staring down at the ground. Michael's demeanor reminded me of that day when he fell to his knees after discovering his house had been broken into. Shankara just stood over him, pressing him into the moment, the space amplified by silence. To my surprise it was Michael Talon who spoke first.

Looking up he said, "By now Shankara, I have come to know you—I have come to know you very well. I know you as a compassionate teacher and also as a great strategist. And I *now* know what this is about for me. You have been spurring me to put all of this information into a book, a book titled *The Blissmaker*. You want *me* to be the madman who publishes this information and places it before the public—to be the town crier who tries to convince the entire world that it is the truth."

Shankara came down on one knee to look directly into Michael's face. **"Right now,"** he said, **"not all of this information is your truth . . . not yet. And you must not write it down until you know beyond any doubt that it is your truth. Then, as you publish your works, you will understand that you're not asking your readers to believe what you have written. You will simply be asking them to take a closer look, to see with better eyes, to look sharp, and be aware of the illusion that is all around them—to watch for the signposts of this your truth as the story of the human adventure unfolds."**

He then stood up, and as he walked back through the people, he raised his voice to the entire crowd, **"But did you actually** think that I was going to leave you here, floundering in this ocean of perilous probabilities, that I would just bid you farewell, wish you the best of luck, and then vanish, not having given you any kind of solution?"

He stopped and slowly scanned the faces in the crowd as though he were taking inventory.

"I have given you a mountain of information about your people, your nations, your planet, and your humanity. I have brought it to you because it is the ocean of probabilities that you are currently wading through. As for myself . . . do I believe that this will indeed be the tragic destiny for all of humanity? Not at all. If it were, I would not be standing before you now, nor would you be sitting in this arena. But the tragic outcome that I have spoken of is exactly where you are headed.

"So then . . . how *do* you step beyond the unconscious quicksand of the Gray World? How will you know where to be so that you are not swallowed up by some natural disaster? How will you survive a nuclear explosion? How will you live and eat without becoming owned by the deceptive plans of a new world alliance? How will you possibly enlighten within this probable future of misery, madness, and mayhem? How will you do it? How will you know?"

30

The Possibilities

We sat there, all of us, staring into empty space like so many lost sheep, silently bleating our most cumbersome fears. Shankara allowed us a few endless moments to ponder his words. His questions seemed to hang in the air as if time itself paid no heed as to whether they were answered or not.

Stepping over to the fire, he picked up several scraps of wood and tossed them onto the orange embers. All eyes turned to follow him, watching as the flames rose higher, mesmerized by the hypnotic firelight. Only his voice could have broken this trance as the people waited in silence for answers to the unanswerable questions.

"So here you are," he began, "snared in the clutches of the Gray World, surrounded by unconscious people, preparing yourself for flood, famine, persecution, and Armageddon . . . but for the most part you have no idea what to do.

"Or perhaps you do, and you *have* already begun to formulate a course of action. Perhaps you have decided to simply rally the people together and create an enormous army to rise up in the name of Enlightenment. You will then defeat this new world order, exposing their evil plans, setting things right once and for all. In addition, you will put the bad people into jails or concentration camps and convert everyone else into this new and more enlightened way of thinking. Of course, you will still have to deal with the earth changes and natural disasters. But you will persevere. You will burrow in and hold on to your hat until the whole thing blows over. Right?

"Wrong— That is what you have already been doing, and that kind of ego-based thinking is what has brought you to this predicament in the first place. This is also quite similar to the plan that the new world alliance has in mind for reorganizing you.

"Or . . . perhaps you have decided to steer a slightly different course. You have made plans to sit on your rump and wait for your salvation and that highly publicized Judgment Day. With any luck your Jesus or your Buddha will come and pull you from the mayhem, granting you redemption, forgiving you for whatever it was you thought you did. But as the root of this word salvation describes, the act will indeed be a motion of salvaging—salvaging of those humans who died in the process of waiting. Basically, this will be the rounding up of those poor souls who didn't have the wherewithal to stand up and step through the doorway of their own enlightened future.

"But now then . . . let us suppose that *neither* of these scenarios are your choices, and you truly *do* want to participate in the unlimited possibilities of the future. Then I say to you this—there is only one path you can take to go there: Stretch into your own blessed wings and *evolve*.

"You can no longer live for the old ways, following dysfunctional dogma, with a programmed consciousness tossed about by destructive probabilities. This is of course easy for me to say. After all, I'm not the one currently sinking into the quicksand of the Gray World. Nor am I floundering to stay conscious, faced with the overwhelming doom of Armageddon. But in truth, what you have to do is really quite simple. In fact, it is so simple that I can give you *all* that you need to know in three simple phrases.

Walk away . . . Stand on higher ground . . . Love beyond measure.

"First of all . . . *Walk away.* Recognize the illusion of

probabilities when it surrounds you. See the game for what it is and, if possible, don't participate in it. When countries are warring around you, perhaps your own nation, don't buy into the picture that you have been handed. If you rally up to be on the winning side, then someone else will surely have to be on the losing side, and then you are most definitely in the game. To participate, even on an energy level, is to feed the fire, to feed humankind's destructive probable outcome.

There is a river of deception winding its way through these world events. If the information comes to you through the media or your government, there may be an underlying current anonymously triggering these events. Now, does this mean that your governments and your media are deceiving you? Not necessarily. It means that they may also be caught up in this deception, at least to some degree. Have the wherewithal to trust your own perception and choose for yourself. Remember, one voice making a higher choice will have an effect on the whole of humanity's outcome.

"Trust your instincts. Trust what you feel about these situations far and above what you are told. Question everything that doesn't feel good to you. In most of these world case scenarios, everyone involved will have an agenda. Many of those agendas will be serving someone's ego.

"If you are feeling there could be a war in your own backyard, an earthquake or tornado, something that is going to break down your utilities and cause shortages of all of your survival needs, then *walk away* from the game of helplessness. Store up everything that you will need to get you through such disasters. Prepare now so you won't be forced to participate in the drama of desperate survival. A nation whose individuals are self-sufficient, with emergency power alternatives and a storeroom of necessities, is not going to fall peril to such disasters. They will not surrender to the control of a new world alliance or any of the deceptive plans of which I have spoken. Become self-sufficient in your everyday lives. Do whatever you can to *not* fall into the play of these probabilities. And if you have already done some of these things preparing for the new millennium—and the great collapse did not happen—very good, you have already had a practice run and are partially prepared for the probability of what is still headed toward you.

"If you are in the habit of only using debit cards and online computer systems for all of your transactions, then you are already participating in a system that will one day come to own you. Find your sovereignty in buying and trading tangible goods. Walk away from a life-style where your existence is just a series of codes and numbers catalogued on a computer network.

"You are living on a planet surrounded by an electrical cage. It's a crude energy that runs from the density of the cities, up to your house, and all around you. When at all possible, turn it off. If you don't need electricity for heat in the evening, shut it down. Find ways to disconnect it from your lives as much as possible. Feel the difference this makes in your perception of the world. Help Mother Nature and be a part of her healing process as she attempts to cleanse the atmosphere of this static energy. Your scientists have told you that people who live under power lines have higher rates of cancer and a myriad of other physical disorders. Under such conditions your livestock stop propagating and producing milk. This electricity is affecting you in the same way, far more than you realize.

"Want to be healthy? Place your body in an environment where it no longer has to compensate for the static electricity running through it, and you will renew your own natural energy flow. This flow is a life force that will gladly engage and aid your health back towards perfection. Likewise when you cook or warm your foods in your microwave ovens, you are drastically affecting their molecular structure—destroying their life force.

"For the most part, your television is an apparatus that brings a constant flow of static energies into your lives. It feeds you a stream of brainwashing commercials, programs, and movies that fill your living room and your physical bodies with frequencies of violence, destruction, vengeance, jealousy, competition, greed, abuse, hatred, and deception. Therefore, be exceedingly selective about what you watch and what goes into the consciousness of your being. The rest of the time— SHUT IT OFF!

"When your Earth is about to quake, it sends off subtle frequencies warning the animals and all creatures. You, like the animals, have the ability to feel these frequencies as well. I can guarantee—if you are sitting in a room, surrounded by a web of electricity, plopped in front of a brainwashing television . . . you will never hear the Earth's subtle warning that your house is about to be lifted off the ground. These kinds of warnings can also be felt before volcanic eruptions, hurricanes, tornados, floods, tsunami, avalanches, and whatever else your Earth is going to do in the near future that you will need to know about."

Without warning, I saw my life being rewound back to when I experienced the earthquake at the Beer Bear Bar and Saloon. Minutes before it occurred, I had a premonition of its coming. I remembered spending several hours prior to that romping around in the woods dressed in my own skin and fur. I also recalled Michael Talon's story about lying down with the dying wolf, later using animal instincts to find my uncle. Then, of course, there was Emily whom I witnessed sniffing her way through the city park one day. Now . . . what her animal senses were looking for—

"So," he said, interrupting my collage of beastly thoughts, "you may discover that in the instances where you have *walked away*, you have found yourself standing in a different place. Hopefully on somewhat higher ground.

"To *stand on higher ground* means—to step off the tracks as the train of probabilities roars by. It means to step towards the ground that is your highly-evolved future and away from the gully that was your probable past. It means that if your Earth is going through a great shift, move with her; align with her in every way you can. If you are a third dimensional being moving into fourth dimension, into what you call heaven or the Christus energy, then go there *now*. Walk in that direction. Devote your life to becoming a member of a more highly and spiritually evolved civilization. And yes, I understand that this might be a challenge when you are busy running away from a tornado or members of the new world regime trying to put a computer chip into your brain. But just imagine this. Suppose that you had already made the effort to move to higher ground in your life, only to discover that in such a place there was no tornado and no regime running after you.

"It is one thing to become steadfast in your truth and *walk away* from old beliefs and probabilities. It is yet another to have the courage to step forward into the unknown, beyond the methods you have used to survive since the beginning of your human experience. To *stand on higher ground* means that you have made the decision to be in constant forward motion— no matter what. It means that, as you step into the moments of your future, you do so by taking responsibility for every thought, every emotion, and every culmination of the two, including every lifetime that you have already lived. The most powerful part of this concept is that embracing your responsibility for everything in the past instills in you the knowledge that you can change or create anything in the future. Your survival in the days to come does *not* depend on how lucky, how adept, or how resourceful you are. It will depend on how brilliant you become.

"Since the beginning of your history, humankind has propelled itself through time judging everything as either good or bad, right or wrong. You have judged yourselves and each other to the point where now there is conflict and competition attached to almost everything you do. To *stand on higher ground* is to release all judgments of yourself and others, which will not only bring you into a place of higher understanding, it will detach you, on an energy level, from those of a denser nature who still choose to wallow in the elements of war, vengeance, hatred, and so forth.

"What this means is that when you see a neighboring country bomb and murder thousands of people, you will not judge them for being the worst of all humans, damning them to hell, whereby you take up arms to destroy them. Instead, you will see it through an act of right discernment, as yet another tragic episode in human history where a group of unconscious beings has altered the existence of numerous other beings who have now been forced to change their form once again. They will start again and be birthed again into yet another new experience.

"Now, does this mean that you should just allow yourselves to be bombed by someone and then act very enlightened and not worry about it? Of course not. But take heed to recognize that there is a fine line between self-defense and vengeance.

"I know this is a difficult concept for you to understand because you are very attached to each other's human lives, as well as to the injustices of your lives. But for an individual to finally embrace this recycling drama for what it truly is, is to uplift that individual into a higher reality. Such a realization propels one into a higher evolutionary state, therefore stopping the cycle once and for all. When you can stand in the higher place, a place of non-judgment, then you will no longer be submerged in this futile drama and you can climb off the wheel of the human experience. It will become a reality that you were once from, not one that you are in.

"That is when you begin to raise yourself into the frequencies of a Christ or a Buddha. From this higher ground, you will find it easy to walk away and not fall into the illusion of the human drama. You will begin to have experiences where you are literally passed over by the destruction and plagues of humankind's probabilities. Since your body is now vibrating at a much higher frequency, you will seem almost invisible to the density of the Gray World. This is because your body, mind, and spirit will be uniting as a whole, while denser humans will be experiencing fragmentation of their entire lives. There will be a separating of the two different dimensions into lower and higher frequencies, and you will be conscious of it.

"To *stand on higher ground* is to begin a serious quest towards the higher understandings of your enlightenment. It is a commitment to the self—on a journey to the self. In the process, you will not only raise your state of consciousness, but you will uplift the whole of humanity.

"This kind of path will lead you through many different realities where an act of loving will take on numerous facets. *To love beyond measure* is to see the sacredness of all things, to embrace how everything is a part of the whole and that nothing is lesser. It is to take each moment and then reach beyond it with your love. This adventure will be like ascending a stairway of white stone steps, each effort raising you into a higher understanding of what this life force called love is all about.

"Right now, such a lofty concept seems foreign to you. Perhaps you wonder, how will you ever have time to just wander about testing and exploring your ability to love. During this time of turmoil now beginning on your planet, you will be given innumerable opportunities to grasp hold of situation after situation to love beyond the measure of what you did a moment ago. With each act you will feel the frequency of your being rise into what is literally a new form.

"This is what your Jesus did after his death. He came back into this dimension, and from within a closed tomb he reclaimed his body. Through an act of total love, he slowly raised its frequency, changing it into a transparent form that you would perceive as light. Your Buddha did the same thing, only he did not die the body first. He simply sat under a tree one day and contemplated the wholeness of his Divine Source. Through his realization, that he was indeed *one* with this divine light, he raised his frequency to meet that great light and therefore moved into a new reality.

"For the most part, your experience of this will be a great transformation involving many people, and it will take place during the most arduous era of your human history. It will be the second coming of the Christ, the Christus frequency, a spiritual transformation on a planetary scale.

Shankara then allowed a peaceful lull to form in the arena. Making his way over to the automobile, he sat down on the flared fender. Looking into the crowd, he made contact with certain individuals, occasionally reacting by changing his expression ever so slightly, exposing an unexpected smile.

"Well, yes, Shankara," he said with a slight chuckle, "*that is all very wonderful. But now here I am, the blundering human, sitting somewhere with nuclear bombs exploding all around me. Some of my friends or family have already been killed. The cities and most everything are in shambles, and I have no idea which way to turn. Of course, then quite miraculously I remember those memorable words that Shankara spoke that last evening in the alley. That all I have to do is . . . walk away . . . stand on higher ground . . . and love beyond measure. Not a problem.*" Here and there people in the crowd started to snicker at his theatrics. "Impossible you say? No one could ever do it?"

He gave those who were laughing a brief time to quiet down. When it was still, he said, "A Christ would. So would a Buddha. And so will many of you, because in the days to come, the futile game of polarities—of right and wrong, good and bad— will become so obvious that you will begin to easily see that the only answer is to evolve beyond it. In this kind of transition, good will not win over evil. Instead wisdom will win out over both good and evil, and with that wisdom will come peace, love, laughter, unity, abundance, music, exploration, singing, fulfillment, grace, compassion, play, humility . . . bliss.

"So this is your path—the path to your enlightenment. In the future it will be a path taken by millions, a journey that in the past has been taken by only a few. Some of you have even asked about my own lifetimes. You have heard me tell stories about them and now you would like to know how it was that I managed to slip through this veil into a higher understanding."

He hesitated for a second touching his fingers to his chin, his head tipped slightly upwards. Having formed a conclusion, he finally said, "Perhaps I will tell you a story, a story of my last lifetime here in this your reality. It was the last of several lifetimes, even though it happened so very long ago, even before the time of your Jesus.

"In that lifetime, my father was a proud man and my mother a gentle woman. As ruler of the region, my father possessed great power, which is why he so wanted a son to be born to carry on his lineage. For years he had anticipated the day when he could celebrate the arrival of such an heir. But on the day of my birth, there was no joy to be found, at least not within the walls of my father's house. For the beautiful child that he had longed to see was to him nothing more than a monster.

"He thought that God had played the cruelest of jokes as he looked with horror at my form in the crib, a form with a voice that cried like any other, a voice that simply wanted to live. I was born with a terribly distorted face, with an oversized forehead and a curved brow that caused my eyes to be sunken and hidden, pushed back into the center of my face. My mouth was severely pulled to one side with most of my upper lip missing as well as most of my nose and part of one cheekbone. Except for one arm that was disproportionately smaller, the rest of me appeared to be quite normal. But the normalness about me was never to be noticed amidst the twisted and deformed features. And although no one knew why I had been birthed this way, everyone knew my fate.

"By my father's orders, I was to be drowned in the river, and yet all who were witness were to say that I had simply died at birth. All were forbidden to speak of the event.

"So I was taken away by one of the servants who said she would see that the drowning was done, but instead she hid me and waited for my mother who she knew would come for me.

"My father was devastated by my birth. With no hope of my mother ever giving him a son, he banished her to an old broken-down farmhouse on the far side of the valley. There she would live and hide me from everyone, including my father, who assumed I was dead.

"I grew up in a pen full of straw, and I shared this place with all of the animals, who became my brothers and sisters. There was a cow, three goats, a handful of chickens, and my best friends, two canine companions.

One of the dogs, the smaller of the two, was a female with tan and white fur. The other was a male, a giant of a dog who looked more wild than a wolf. They were my nurses, my friends, and the best of my teachers, without whom I would not have survived. They had no names, as I never learned how to talk, but I knew them by sight and smell. We always spoke in that feeling way or spoke the language of the dog. They saw me as my mother did, small and beautiful—one of god's unique creations. So much would I grow to love them all in the very short time I would be there.

"Five years after I was born, my father learned from one of his servants that my mother now cared for a child who was much like an animal. So he came to the farmhouse in search of this child, the child that he knew was his monster, with the intent to find and destroy the evidence that could shame him in front of his people.

"My mother died in her attempt to save me, as did my companion the small female dog. But the wild dog and I escaped the attack and made our way up into the mountains. It was there that we lived off of what we could find and what we could steal off the farmlands, but we were always careful never to be seen by the ones I saw as mankind. As time passed and we moved farther out, the wilderness became our home, until one day I had no memory of humanity at all.

"You see, I never really knew what kind of species I was, because there was no other creature like me. I was one of a kind, with no example to follow and only my wits to guide me. So I mimicked my friend the wild wolf dog, and the fish, and the birds of the air, and I learned that I was really a part of everything, that my spirit was shared by all.

"My life was the marketplace of nature's world, where I could choose from so many adventures, where I could become and explore the nuances of every form and creature. Life was a playground of frequencies with not one feeling greater or lesser. I never really learned how to judge anything or, likewise, to be judged by another. I never knew hatred, vengeance, jealously, greed, deceit, or anger. It was only when my wolf dog died that I would come to know of sorrow. I was never to be taught right from wrong or that good was different than bad. And the essence of an evil thought was something I had forgotten.

"I never really learned how to love anything, because I never knew what it was *not* to, and I spent much of my time feeling love for myself, because it felt so good inside me. It was through this act of loving myself that I came to know of my spirit and of the divine source that once birthed me here, with all of my wondrous choices.

"In time I learned, as a spiritual being, that the body was simply my shell, which I could leave in the shade of an old oak tree while I explored the spaces beyond. I came and went from the physical world until one day I met others—beings who had also stepped through the veil and realized their immortality.

"It was on that day that I returned to that place, to the shade of the old oak tree, and gathered up my human form to embrace the whole of me. I breathed into it all my love, the lightness of my spirit, till my body then became the light, the wonder, and the bliss."

The fire had died down, making the surrounding space darker than before. People now resembled shadows, their hazy forms blending together. But the night was given no time to seduce that particular moment, as once again Shankara's words broke open the silence.

"And what about you?" he questioned. "Are you so sure that you are incapable of such things? I was born wretched and deformed. Would you have me believe that you are less capable than I was? And for that matter, are you really so sure that you are alone in all of this, that you will have no assistance?"

Then he lifted his head, his eyes seemingly staring into a night sky, a sky now filled with an abundance of tiny white stars looking down on us. The crowd followed his gaze as all eyes turned upward.

"Yes . . . and what about the rest of your family?"

31
The Tapestry

So many stars, so many lights, like a billion tiny sparks filling up an indigo sky, just daring you to believe in the possibilities. At times it seems almost frightening to gaze up into the immensity of it all. And as always, it feels humbling to sit beneath galaxies upon galaxies, knowing, without a doubt, that you're not alone.

Tonight, I sat under just such a sky, a place where I most definitely was not alone—a place where others now convened, staring into the vastness of so many stars.

Shankara, having returned to his throne on the front of the sedan, kept a vigilant eye over the people. He watched as one by one they came back from their brief visits to the cosmos, from their lofty and private contemplations. And for a while it felt as if a collection of small prayers had been spoken, with words and phrases that only stars could understand.

"Well," Shankara began, **"quite a few stars, don't you think? Far more than anyone could count. Your scientists will tell you that there are a trillion more just beyond those. For that reason, it is really quite extraordinary when you stop to think about it . . . that *you* are the only intelligent life forms in the whole of this massive creation."**

With these words he stretched out his hands, as if receiving the entire night sky into his arms. This prompted small spurts of laughter. He lowered his arms with the hint of a smile.

"Yes," he said, facetiously. "that is really very funny, isn't it? What is even funnier is that at least half of the people on your planet actually believe that. Which then brings me to the other half, who when answering one of your public polls will be quoted saying, 'Yes, I believe there are extraterrestrials. I also believe there are intelligent life forms on other planets. Oh and yes, I believe there were early civilizations that in some ways were more advanced than us.' And that is probably what they truly believe. But for the most part, they would really rather not talk about it because they would then have to try and explain it to their children, and since their religion doesn't like them to talk about it at all, it would be best if they didn't.

"As for humanity, this is pretty much the way that you have decided to handle these kinds of situations—just leave out all of those nasty unexplained segments, which means that you will also be leaving out several sections of your planet's valuable history. Conveniently, these rejected segments also just happen to be the missing pieces, which, if inserted back into the evolutionary growth of your humanity, would have brought you out of the dark ages eons ago. But humans, projecting from a place of ego, would really rather not acknowledge that thirty thousand years ago there were highly evolved cultures utilizing space craft to move massive stones; while they, on the other hand, were still trying to invent the wheel. Of course, it has been a little more difficult to erase the pyramids in Egypt or some of the other ancient ruins that now stand as monuments to modern man's denial and ignorance.

"Often in our dialogues, I have asked you to remember who you are or where you came from. Some of you have glimpses of such a memory, shadows of a different time and place where you lived in a more advanced, somehow more harmonious culture. For the most part modern society tells you that such a remembering is not possible. But still somewhere in the back of your mind is a recurring thought that never really fades. You can't seem to put your finger on it, because it's more of a feeling than a memory. Today, in your time, you walk around observing and experiencing humankind, and you wonder what happened. How did it all end up this way?

"Spanning all of the continents of the globe, there are traces of civilizations that refute the established order. Today, they are but ruins. Yet even as they stand in rubble they hold the undeniable evidence that in the most ancient of times there was some very advanced technology being used to create some extraordinary structures, as well as whole cities. Not to mention several landing strips that date back to the time your own cultures were still rubbing two sticks together to make a fire.

"Long ago there was a time during your history when your evolution began moving out of its caveman era and into the beginning of early civilizations. At this time your planet was a beautiful garden with no asphalt, no pollution, and no electricity. It was a paradise visited by more advanced cultures, who were a few short light years away.

"These so-called celestial beings were and are the same as you, born the first offspring of the Creator, out on an evolutionary journey to explore and expand the essence of that divine source into every possibility. You see, as spiritual beings, you truly are all exactly the same. Through your journeys into the cosmos you have settled into different frequencies of physical and nonphysical matter. There you have taken on an outer form, a shell so that you could participate and experience that particular reality. Be you *Homo sapiens* or little green Martians, within the spirit of your beings you are the same. The only difference is that some of your spirits have gained a bit more wisdom than others.

"So it came to pass that some of these like-spirits, these celestial beings—perhaps even some of you—came to this planet, to this garden, and joined into the human experience already in motion. It was not only a romp through paradise, but it was also a grand opportunity to participate in a third dimensional understanding, which if mastered could bring one into the Christus energy. So some of you came here on aeroships of a sort and eventually birthed yourselves into the cyclical flow of human reincarnation. You planted yourselves into civilizations and geographical areas where now there are only ancient ruins to mark the event of your coming.

"That is why in places like Giza, Egypt, and Machu Picchu, Peru you have the remains of great cities, evidence of highly evolved civilizations who used the wisdom and technology from other galaxies. They built great monuments such as the pyramids employing a kind of engineering that was light years ahead of those primitive times. Even today your scientists cannot figure out how some of the massive stones were moved or how they would build such structures today. I speak to you now of these ruins because they are tangible evidence of when there was wisdom of a higher nature being used during humankind's early civilizations. It was a time of blending two vastly different cultures.

"Now, does this mean that all of you began your journey in the human experience this way, abandoned here by your extraterrestrial next of kin? Does it mean that you really did not evolve from apes? No, not at all. Many of the people in this adventure did take that evolutionary climb. In fact there are probably some of you here right now who evolved from apes. And you probably even know who you are, right? Come on, let us have a show of hands."

At this a rumble of laughter came up from the audience.

"But, let us not forget about your Adam and Eve. Some of you hold on tightly to this story as the truth of your origins, and to an extent, you are right. Early in your evolution the prototypes of humankind were very crude, because as science has told you the human prototype itself evolved from more primitive forms in a process that took thousands of years. It was not until this human form had progressed into a physical expression that could survive and function in an environment with so many other creatures that immortal spirits would have the courage to place themselves into such embodiments. And so it is true. There was indeed the *first* time in which a spirit, having housed itself into an etheric vessel called the soul, placed itself in a human body so that it could have a tangible exploration of the garden.

"Now, I will also tell you that these first embodiments were not quite like your biblical picture books have depicted. The first man and woman to take such a journey did not have beautiful smooth white skin with olive twigs dangling from their perfectly combed hair. Instead, they were very crude and rather animalistic. For the most part, they did very well to live and propagate in an environment with so many wild and outrageous creatures roaming around them. In fact, the early adventures within the human body were very hazardous indeed and ended up being a lot more than the immortal spirits had bargained for.

"Therefore, what some of you have believed about your origins with an Adam- and Eve-like scenario is true. The idea that the human form evolved through a series of primitive ape-like expressions that took thousands of years is also true. Lastly, that your earliest cultures were joined by other more advanced extraterrestrials who came to incarnate in the human experience is likewise true.

"You see, it is all true, because it all happened within the framework of your history. The only problem is that as time passed you decided to separate and throw out certain elements of that truth, which is exactly what an altered ego does. It separates out only what can serve it on a personal level and leaves behind the rest. Spirit, on the other hand, is compelled to unify all things, bringing everything back into the whole. This is why an ego-based humanity finds it so hard to believe that more advanced civilizations could have been here as a culture—why for centuries they have done everything that they can to discard that truth.

"At this time, I am not introducing this kind of celestial information in order to throw a monkey wrench into your very ordered history. It is meant to fill in the holes so that as a more conscious member of the human race you can at last have the truth. As you evolve into some of these understandings, you will discover that the actual truth will put you in a phase of the human drama that is a lot more hopeful and a lot less futile. Besides, what we are actually talking about is not something that is new for you, something that came from far away. It is that which is in your memory, something that you already know and perhaps have already done. Time and again I have told you that you are far more brilliant than you realize. The truth is, you are far more brilliant than you remember.

"So now you want to know, well, if there was so much wisdom and so much advanced technology floating around at that time—what happened?

"As some of these more evolved celestial spirits took a human form, they soon discovered that the human incarnation was a lot more cumbersome than they had anticipated. Yet through their spiritual knowledge about their life force, some of them actually lived for hundreds of years. Your historians and archeologists have given you information about ancient writings that tell of certain beings, pharaohs who were considered Gods of that time outliving many generations. These beings were soon to discover, though, that through their first death experience they would begin to forget their other origins. They would reincarnate as newborns and become lost in the illusion of mortality—fear, grief, blame, hatred, and so on and so on.

"The good news . . . is that the immortal spirit never devolves or loses the wisdom that it has gained. It merely becomes sidetracked now and again, trying to remember where it left off. It is important, though, for you to understand that to take the third dimensional journey into physical matter is an event where spirit takes an enormous leap in its evolution. It's precisely why you volunteered in the first place and why many came from the stars to do the same.

"And yes, it was exactly as I stated . . . you did volunteer. One afternoon, while you were floating around in the ethers, you suddenly proclaimed to your Divine Source, '*I will try an adventure into physical matter. I will go and give it a shot.*' And so you did, which is why you should also honor yourselves for having the courage to take such a journey. Only the most progressive of spiritual beings have even tried.

"Some of you came here from other dimensions with higher wisdom that right now cannot completely be remembered. But you knew that to come, and to master the world of physical matter, was one of the greatest prizes of all. Presently, there are beings like some of your extraterrestrials who watch you closely to see if you indeed master the event. You should also know that as you begin to gain some understanding about these extraterrestrial brothers and sisters of yours, they will begin showing themselves, dropping in to help you in your process. You might even recognize some of them as they arrive.

"That is indeed the real truth of it all, that you are all part of a very large family. And like most families, there was a time when you dispersed and went out to explore your own unique pathways even though you are all still immortal spirits created from a divine source. Today, that family is once again gathering and you may discover that you have relatives who are in a variety of different physical and nonphysical forms.

"The same is true within your own cultures, within your own civilization; your families have begun to gather together, to reunite. In the future you may find that you have long lost relatives camped at your front door, and they won't even know why or how they got there. They will just know that it is where they were compelled to be.

"This is because as your Earth begins to realign itself, it is bringing its original framework back together, a framework fragmented by humankind's bad gardening techniques. In her attempt to steer the course of nature back into a balanced flow, she will also be pulling you back into the origins of your more animal instincts. In this, you will begin to be drawn not only to nature, but also to those who possess your same lineage.

"Your immortal spirits are like threads of light woven into the tapestry of a divine source. Therefore, be it through an act of love or an act of hate, what each of you does on an energy level will affect all others. This is what makes up the probable flow of that which we call your collective consciousness.

Now, in addition to this connectedness, you also have commonalities through your genetic structures, your RNA, your DNA, and so on. This same kind of connectedness also extends through your family and into all hereditary groups. As you continue to raise your frequencies into the Christus energies, it is going to have not only an affect on humanity as a whole, but an even greater affect on those of your lineage.

"It is not unlike the 100th monkey theory documented by scientists. A certain species of monkeys, who were isolated on an island, were observed learning a mechanical skill, which they had never demonstrated before. Far away, on another isolated island, another group of the same species of monkey adopted the learned skill at about the same time, even though there was no physical interaction or communication between the two groups of monkeys.

"This is a simple example of how a collective consciousness works. All species are connected through their genetic structure, which is an energy framework that ties them all together. In a collective flow of energy, they literally have one mind. Within nature you see this kind of collective consciousness at work when you observe a flock of birds or a school of fish swerve and dance in the same direction at exactly the same moment. With one mind such a feat is effortless, for they share a collective thought, a collective consciousness. As people of heritage and culture you have the same bond, the same grid of frequencies that ties you together. Within your families, with those who share like genes and chromosomes, the connection is even stronger.

"So what does this mean? It means that your every thought, be it love or hate, will directly affect your family, your culture, and your humanity . . . no matter what. It means that when you feel ego-based anger or hatred toward someone else, you are also sending that thought to your own family, your nation, and your humanity who will then embrace that thought with you. That is how powerful you truly are. Remember? I told you that you were far more brilliant that you realized.

"I will tell you another secret. When you are in the flow of a passionate thought where you absolutely *know* that by so doing you are affecting the whole of the world, the energy of that thought is amplified a thousand-fold. In addition, if that thought was formed by a collective group, a collective consciousness and embraced by its collective passion, then the energy of it will be amplified a thousand-fold again.

"But you don't have to take my word for it. Just look at the predicament your planet is in. That is also the result of a collective consciousness. Not to mention your own human history, which has been a continuing saga of holy religious wars since the beginning of recorded time. In fact, in your 20th century more people were killed because of wars than in all of the previous centuries put together. You are currently living out the thoughts and emotions of your collective consciousness and that wellspring of ego-based intentions is what you now call Armageddon."

With these heavy and prophetic words, Shankara paused and once again threw several pieces of wood onto the fire. The hot embers made crunching sounds under the weight of the new logs as a flurry of tiny sparks scurried into the air. They disappeared into the night sky as he continued.

"For just a moment I want you to look around this gathering. What do you see? You see people . . . yes, and an animal or two. But what else do you find? Do you see the Chinese woman, and the Hindu man, the Gay couple and the Lakota professor? Look around and see if you can find the Russian pilot, the African journalist, the French scientist, and the American composer. Because you see . . . you are all here—because that is my game, and it was indeed my prayer, to wander into an alleyway and touch the world with the essence of my thought. In some way, and in some form, the entire globe is represented in this audience. Through your genetic structures, through your thoughts and emotions, I, right now, can affect the whole of humanity with one single thought, with one single prayer.

"And *you* thought that all of you had simply gotten lost in some alley by mere coincidence.

"Now, does that mean that I summoned all of you here on a special mission? No. It means that you have indeed summoned yourselves for the greatest, most powerful, and most worthy of missions. As for me, I simply sat under an oak tree one day and said, *Divine Spirit, bring me a vision of what you really look like. I want to see your face, your character, and every color of your rainbow.* Unfurling his arms toward the crowd he said, "And here you are.

"You think that, because you are only one person, you are so small, with only a small thought, and a very small prayer. When you embrace the wisdom that you are indeed the awakening Buddha, the awakening Christ, then your *knowing* will amplify your thoughts and prayers a thousand-fold and everyone that is of your family, your culture, and yes, even your nation will be uplifted by your vision."

Shankara then not only walked in my direction, he squatted down directly in front of me. His face and hair were like the silvers and grays of an ocean with his eyes flickering the sun's reflection on it. I felt washed by his close presence, bathed in the volume of his high energy.

"But what about you?" he began. "You are just a composer, and an unsuccessful one at that. What could you possibly do that would affect anyone, let alone the whole of humanity? After all you are sort of a mutt in your own right. You don't really even know what your heritage is, some jumbled concoction of something or other. Sort of a bastard, aren't you?"

He reached up and with the backs of his fingers stroked the side of my beard in a single motion. With great compassion, he said, "You are the only one here who speaks all of these different languages." Smiling at his own words, he added, "You see . . . music is the universal language. It is heard, felt, and understood in all dimensions alike. It can travel from spirit to spirit without any instrument and without any ears. That is why many of these people here have heard your music within their minds on the many journeys we have taken. I have sort of been using it to guide them through some doorways. Your symphonies have been heard in galaxies afar. In the silence of your studio you have been composer to the Gods, and you didn't even know it."

Rising back to his feet he turned and once again addressed the crowd. "That is the kind of wisdom all of you will be gathering in the days to come; you will learn to communicate through telepathy and heal your physical ailments with sounds and frequencies . . . and more, and more, and more.

"In the days to come you will begin to reclaim the wisdom that is already yours, learned expressions that are a part of humankind's accumulated wisdom. There is a realm, which is in a dimension of its own, that stores all learned knowledge of everything that the immortal spirits have gained throughout their journeys from the beginning unto this present day. To some, this realm is known as the Akashic Record, and it literally is the mind of God.

"It is available to anyone who would speak to the wind or whisper into a night sky for the truth of who they are. Those who have touched even a glimpse of this wonder will tell you that it is more vast than any universe. In times past some of your more advanced civilizations have reached to connect with this realm, some even creating temples and chambers to be used as passageways into this understanding. Today such places are now your ancient ruins, places where your archeologists continue to dig for the truth. A few of you here have been on great expeditions to find such a place."

Without warning, he stopped his monologue and again wandered over to stand in front of us. Directing his words to Michael, he said, "It is for you to understand that as you travel on your search, be it to Peru or somewhere else, that the Akashic Record is not just a room that you step into one afternoon. It is a moment granted to the pure of heart who are willing to leave behind everything that they possess as knowledge for yet higher wisdom. These new understandings will literally unravel all of the wisdom they were so sure that they had already mastered. Contemplate this on your quest.

"As far as this Room of Knowledge that you search for, is it indeed a place where an ancient civilization once sought this Akashic Record? Yes, it is true. Underneath the ruins there is a chamber well-hidden from the masses, but it does not require a secret doorway to enter, for the secret doorway is inside you.

"Most importantly though, I want you to realize that this room you seek is actually a library in itself of the wisdom that had already been attained at that time. You would do well to begin by just exploring this place, for it is there you will also find the images that have pulled and tugged at your memory for ever so long. And remember . . . opening the doorway requires nothing less than a leap of faith. . . . Understand?"

As he stood facing the people with the fire blazing at his feet, the golden flames lighting his form caused his image to appear larger than life. His shadow, some twenty feet behind him and projected several stories high, seemed more real than his physical form. Once again he spent a few seconds examining the many faces as if he were reading the lines of a story. Then smiling graciously, he continued.

"And so I have given you all that I know of the truth in this world, and in that we have traveled from the perils of your humanity to the true wonder of your spirit. For some of you this was far more than you ever wanted to know. For others of you it will be a place for you to begin. And yet for still others, who have tasted the wind, you know only to say to me . . . more, Shankara . . . more . . . more . . . and more.

"What more can I give you, when in truth . . . you already know everything. What more can I show you . . . when there is so much that you have already seen."

For a few seconds he stared into the fire. Reaching up, he touched his fingers to his mouth, allowing them to slide down over the contours of his beard and chin.

"But you are after all the children, the reaching hands of a most Divine light. So in light of that, yes, I will give you more."

32

The Sword of Compassion

As for myself, I actually felt quite satisfied, having already been given all the secrets of the universe. But, despite my copious concerns, I now had the distinct impression we were about to be handed even . . . more.

"If I were to give you," he began, "just one element, one profound tool you could carry like a sword, I would give you the sword of compassion. With such a saber you can slay all of your doubts and conquer all of your fears.

"An act of compassion encompasses all of those impossible solutions of *Walk away . . . Stand on higher ground . . . Love beyond measure.* Such a gesture will invoke these elements traversing from one to another with no particular sequence. Through an act of compassion you can *love beyond measure* by going into the pain of others to experience their fear and sadness. Then you will be challenged to stay centered within your being and *walk away* from their illusion. In other words, for a short time be in their world but not of it. Then, you can climb out of their self-made dungeon and return to your divine truth, where you will find yourself *standing on higher ground.*

The true power of a compassionate act lies in your ability to move out of the illusion after you have experienced it. You can only raise others' degradation to a higher place after you know how it feels. This does not mean that you carry their burdens for them, but that you embrace them for yourself.

"By mastering the illusion, you provide an example —a possibility—a pathway of how they can move out of the same drama if they choose. Your real gift is to bring light into their darkened scene. Show them that there are indeed steps out of the dungeon, but remember . . . you can never save them.

"To be in an act of compassion . . . is to *save* no one. If you pull a drowning man from the ocean, and through your rescue he does not gain the wisdom of that experience, he will simply fall back into the ocean the following day. On some level that was where he was choosing to be. Therefore, your act of saving another is really just an act of saving yourself from an identical illusion—one that you placed yourself into through your compassionate act. You can show them the means by which to move through their woe, but they must find their own passage. Only they have the ability to save themselves.

"Now, when you step into the dungeon of someone's life, there is always the strong possibility you will get caught in the overwhelming realism of the same drama. This is why an act of compassion is so great, because it is not simply your motion of pity for another. It is *you* mastering the same illusion that has them held captive. Your highest ability in this measure of love is to see their illusion for what it is—a very real and tangible illusion. To show them that they are simply caught within a moment in time—is your greatest act of love for them.

"This is a most powerful love. It's also a love of no conditions; a gesture given as though it is thrown to the wind. How well can you love another without anything attached to that love—without a list of conditions? Through the purity of unconditional love, your action is like a sword of truth that can cut through the most horrible of dramas. In this way you give of yourself so that you can graciously receive their woe and bring it to the light—not so you can bring it to your conditions—the conditions of what you are willing to do without stepping too far into the muddy water.

"In addition, compassion is not an element of your suffering to gain something for others. Some of you think that this act has to do with some burdensome deed you must do. Not at all. Compassion is your ability to see within *their* sad eyes the shining eyes of a Jesus, a Buddha, or a Shiva. It is to bless and honor them no matter how great the degradation appears.

"And what do you attain from this? Do you become a Christ or a Buddha because, as you do your act of compassion, God will mark it on your score card and say, 'Alright then, now you have only twenty-seven more similar gestures to perform and you will be granted ascension' . . . or whatever?

"Not likely. In the bigger scheme of things, the disease that is in another . . . is really, the disease of you. You are one entity, one light, dispersed in a multitude of physical forms. To be in an act of compassion is to reach and receive the mirror of you. It is to be in the prison of your own life where there are others who carry the reflection of the degradations you have yet to master. You must recognize these elements as a part of you because they are a part of the whole—the collective consciousness.

"Therefore, a compassionate act has not only to do with your unconditional love for another, it also has to do with your unconditional love for you. This is one of the greatest difficulties you have in this dimension. You think that you need to have a reason for the act of self-love, some excuse that will make you worthy. The love of self is without conditions. It is without an agenda. There is just you and the act itself. And who can be the only betrayer of such an act? Only *you* . . . by *you*. And if you haven't noticed—it is *you* who betrays *you* in this . . . all the time. You punish and deny yourself a complete connection with your divine source . . . all of the time."

With these words, he stopped briefly, as if waiting by the road for someone to catch up. Then he moved on.

"As you begin to embrace this process of compassion, you will also begin to understand that in every event it will also be an extraordinary act of courage. On your planet, and especially within your more competitive cultures, there is a great spoof that an act of courage is to armor yourself with a lot of muscle and ego. You then attack and defeat those whom you have deemed are the bad guys so that you can then proclaim yourself as one of the good guys—the winner of some dense drama. In such a display, you win nothing. You simply feed the fire of an existing tragedy, allowing the illusion of it to own you even more. In a realm of higher understanding, the macho heroes of your wars and injustices—and of most that are depicted on your movie screens—are really considered the buffoons of your time. This is also true of your overpaid gladiators, those whom you call your sports heroes. They would do well to begin mastering their own egos. Through *this* kind of quest they would soon come to an understanding of what courage really is.

"To jump into a raging ocean to help another who is drowning or to leap into a blazing inferno to keep someone from being burned is an act of both courage and compassion. This is because, for at least a few moments, one must be in the clutches of the event and share in the drowning, or the burning. If your act of courage has anything to do with competing for a prize or status, then it is simply the act of a buffoon floundering in an ego-based existence."

A few outbreaks of laughter sounded throughout the crowd. Probing the audience with his eyes, he waited until it was quiet.

"It is also important to remember that compassion only hangs about as *pity* when you feel sorry for someone else. Compassion becomes an honorable *virtue* when you enter the cage and free the tiger.

"And if forgiveness is your act of compassion for others, you would be better off to let your forgiveness be . . . that you do not judge them in the first place—that you simply recognize that they slid into the quicksand of the Gray World. In this way you allow your own humility to be the suit of clothes that you wear as you take this journey on the path of compassion.

"Through an act of compassion you can know all of humanity and travel into every nuance of this dimension.

"Through an act of compassion you can find the truth of

that which you so long to be.

"So, can you go there—stepping into the Gray World, stepping into the pain of others? For a brief moment can you journey into their woe and become them? Can you stand in the realization that you are not separate from them—that you are one being, one entity, one life force, one light? Can you step down into the dungeon of their fears and feel what they feel— become what they are? Can you then find your way back, focusing on that place of light inside you? Stone by stone, step by step, can you raise yourself back to the truth, no matter how deceptive and horrible it all looks? Can you do this . . . no matter what?"

Then raising his voice he asked an unexpected question, **"Do you want to try?"**

Like myself, I could feel many others trying to shift into the direction he had taken us.

"Right here, right now," he continued. **"Do you want to try your new sword of compassion? I am sure that amid this great woe of humanity we can find someone who will welcome your efforts. For you see it is really very simple, you don't even have to decide who it will be. So . . . shall we journey?"**

It was hard to know if there was an answer to this question. I couldn't help but wonder if there would ever be an answer to such a question. But as I watched some of the people around me adjust their coats and blankets, I got the unmistakable impression that they were preparing for more and that I was about to find out what "Shall we journey?" actually meant.

Shankara then carefully kicked the logs on the fire so that the embers would be separated and the flames die down. This caused the entire arena to become even darker and more mysterious. As his own silhouette started to change into a less defined image, his alluring words continued.

"So now settle yourselves deep into the comfortableness of you.

"Breathe into your body as though you could dissolve its shell.

"Listen for the music that calls from inside you and then courageously . . . close your eyes."

33

The White Stone Steps

You feel yourself moving through space, traveling a great distance, far from the life and the physical expression you have known, far from the footprints that you've left in the Gray World. You're on a path, one that you walk to the house of a great lord. Perhaps it is the temple of a Buddha or a Jesus—maybe the ashram of a Shiva—the garden of a Blessed Mary. It is a place where the entrance is always open for it has no doors, nor are there glass panes in the window spaces. You see it clearly now, this great structure of white stones, with greenery and soft flowers that trail along a grand archway.

With impeccable reverence you walk up white stone steps until you find yourself inside this holy palace. You stand in the center of a large room with an open beam ceiling whose portals reveal clouds and blue sky. White marble corridors, lined with white columns, span out in every direction. Long streams of light filter through the ceiling's openings, illuminating the green foliage that hangs about the rafters.

You look all about for the face of this blessed one, this one whose house you have entered, but there appears to be no one there. Searching from room to room, you find nothing but stillness and quiet. Only emptiness hangs in the hollows of this space. The long corridors resound as echo chambers waiting for any sound to come into their dormant passageways.

Then . . . in the distance . . . from where you know not,
there are faint cries, soft moans that ring of suffering from
somewhere beneath you. Like captive whispers they call from
somewhere in the house.

You enter one of the long corridors, following the feeble
voices. The calls draw you to a stairway at the end of the hall
where a series of dark gray steps descend around a curved
wall and into the shadows. You can tell by the dim amber
light that it is only the effort of a few frail candles that
illuminate the way, as rough stone steps walk themselves
into the darkened stairwell.

You go down, step by step, your body sinking lower,
the sound of each footfall taking you farther into the void.
As you descend into the coldness, the muffled cries
grow stronger, their lament reaching out, trying to find you.
You are frightened and sickened by the feeling.
Still you know you must go.

A dense wave of sadness comes up from the darkness below,
from the depths it moves through you,
settling into your heart.

At last you come to the bottom of the stairs, to a massive door
that is worn and scarred. The door is unlatched and slightly
ajar, revealing a crack that beckons you nearer.

Cautiously, you push on the door,
the desperate sounds growing louder.
You hesitate briefly amid the pitiful cries.
Then you take a deep breath and enter the dungeon.

Inside you see the forms of many beings.
Like shadows, they huddle along the walls and in the corners.
Their garments are dark, rough and soiled with draped cloths
pulled up around them,
covering their faces.

Their voices are muffled by the shrouds that mask their faces.
Only the stare of their eyes seems to penetrate the cloth.
You know that they see you, but still they hide themselves,
hiding the vileness that you can only imagine.
Slowly, you approach them, drawing nearer to their presence
that now fills your nostrils with the stench of disease.
You want to see them, but you're terrified of that moment
when they're actually revealed.

Their moans seem to surround you with desperate sounds,
tones that walk about with lives of their own.
Stepping closer, you surrender to the inevitable task
and pull the cloth away from one of the faces.

A vision of horror stabs into your being,
with a mound of disease that has consumed a face.
Desperately you reach into the depths of your mind
for any other image that might cancel this sight.
In a panic you lift the cloth from yet another face.
This one is scarred and scabbed all over.

You reveal another, more horrible than the last,
until you simply cannot bear to see anymore.

Then, all around, others stand and unmask their features.
They wear the sores of fear and hatred, of jealousy and greed.
Every tragic and degrading scar now stands to greet you,
for they are the helplessness of you, the wretchedness of you,
the victim . . . and the vileness.

They stand and approach you—they want you to help them.
They reach out to embrace you because you are so pure.
They cry out with their woe. They surround and touch you,
until you are sure you'll be mobbed and become them.

You turn and run,
desperate to escape.
You bolt for the open door
and slam it behind you.

Safe outside the door, you are alone in a space of total silence, a world away from the vile reflections.

Then . . . quite softly, a voice calls your name. You hear it over and over, this meager cry, and you're sure you recognize the cantor of this call.

You try desperately to put a face to the voice, but no image will come. You push at the door and listen through the opening for the call of your name, for some familiar trace.

Then, your mind begins to paint a portrait of a broad face with strong features that seem almost oversized for the small body they belong to. As your memory becomes clearer you remember the image of a man standing on a wooden crate, his silhouette shaped by a kerosene lamp that floods the rest of your vision. You know him well, his play and his jest, and the poetry he inscribes with a fine yellow chalk.

You push open the door and listen again. The voice says, "I am here in the darkness—somewhere. Do you see me?"

Without hesitation you move in the blackness, your eyes struggling to find a face in the shadows. You follow the voice as it calls and calls, to a dimly lit corner where you find him, hunkered down low, a cloth draped over his face.

You say to him, "Is it you?" For a second you wait, but there is no reaction. Slowly, you pull away the cloth from his face until you see the one you remember so well.

Looking up through sorrowful eyes, he speaks, "It is I . . . I am here, and I am trapped."

You look all about for the chains that bind him, but like the unlocked door, you can find nothing that holds him. Gazing into the wretchedness of the fear that has claimed him, you cannot help but see the glow of past joys and of laughter and humor that shines through his sores. The memory of playful antics still lingers in the sad image that now cradles his form.

In view of this cage that has no lock, you ask, *"But why are you still here in the disease of this body? Why do you not go? Are you not finished with this human adventure? You have been the wisest of us all, so why do you not fly and set yourself free?"*

Silence is the only response. Again, he covers his face with the ragged cloth, hiding the fear that has entrapped him. You want to take this fear and tear it from him.

You remember a great tiger once trapped in a cage, lying lifeless on his side, with sad and broken eyes. You remember the magic of how you once became him, moving into the essence of such a beautiful beast.

You are reminded of words in the wind, that you are all one being, a part of one light, and as such you can step down into the dungeon of his fears. You can feel what he feels, and well up in his tears. For a moment you can step into the spirit of his being.

So with great care you pull away the cloth and reveal his face—his deformed shell. Then with all of your love, with a compassion that you knew not was inside you, you reach out with your feelings into the sadness of his being. You probe him with your courage, searching with your love for the emotional chain that now holds him captive.

You look into his consciousness to see through his eyes for the one fear that holds him within the death of his body—the one fear that keeps him from going into the light. You embrace his woe until a barrage of words form around the burden you are feeling.

"What will happen when I let go of my body? Will there be only freedom as Shankara has told me? And is all that I believe in my mind really true? Is there indeed a Divine Spirit? Is there truly a white light? And when I pull from this body to awaken its wonder, will Shankara catch me in the palm of his grace?"

All at once you realize that his words are your words—his voice is your voice. You allow yourself to be pulled into the sadness of his being until the face that you now gaze at . . . is the face of your own. His eyes are your eyes. His tears are your tears, and the fear that has claimed him has now become you. His breath is your breath, his pain . . . your pain, and you feel yourself fall into the fear of his death.

You feel yourself losing, forgetting who you are. Defeated by depression and helpless in this woe, you hunker down in the dark sadness of it all. The drama closes in on whoever you were, as you pull the cloth shroud up to cover your face.

Then . . . in that very instant before you cloak your eyes, you see a thin stream of light stretched out across the floor. A beautiful beam that seems so out of place, a rare braid of light that only you have noticed. It trails out from a crack that was left in the doorway. You stare at this light-stream and ponder its journey and wonder how it ever could have found its way here.

That's when you remember from whence you came. That it was you who brought such a fine thread of light—who cared enough to enter this place.

You allow the ragged cloth to fall to the ground, and you step to the edge of the stream of light—tracing it with your footsteps—walking the line. You follow it to the crack in the door, pulling it open to find the gray steps and the candles that now burn brighter than ever. You breathe into a body that feels most familiar, and yet there is something quite different that you can't overlook. It's as though when you walk, you are not alone, and your coat is now of a slightly different color.

You begin your ascent from out of the dark, when something seems to pull at you from behind. You look back at the door that has swung itself closed leaving only a tiny crack for an opening. You push on its face widening the crack so this stream of light that once trailed the floor is now a large wash covering several stones. Like a portal it illuminates a shape on the floor just waiting for someone to stand in its glow.

Then you return to the stairs climbing up and around the curved stone walls, welcoming each candle along the way. From far up the stairwell, you hear the faint sounds of music. It's a melodic passage that pulls at your emotions. The music guides you past the place where you started to a white stone staircase that spirals into a tower.

And although you're not sure, it appears there's a light that burns at the top of this ancient spire. Not that of a lamp or a candle flame, but more like a glimpse of the setting sun. You breathe with each step, longing to see the mystery that beams tiny rays of light down through the tower. You anticipate the magic of what you will find, at the top of the tower, at the top of the world.

In the crown of the tower there's a round stone floor and a wooden ceiling. Evenly spread around the curved stone walls are arched openings making a lighthouse effect of rock-framed windows looking out in all directions.

You stand in the middle of the round stone floor. Watching the window openings of blue and white light, you rotate in a circle and are awed by the vastness of an infinite sky. You let yourself spin around and around until the room itself starts to turn on its own. You twirl and you turn without any boundaries, a circular flight from the center of your being.

In a state of euphoria, you sink down onto the white stone floor. The windows of white and blue sky continue to whirl around like a magical carousel of light. You feel mesmerized by the feeling of your body letting go. You allow it to happen. You surrender to the bliss.

Without your noticing, the windows have become still and you find yourself lying in the center of the floor. You gaze into the vastness of a white and blue sky, and wonder what it would be like to reach through a window. What would it feel like to touch the sky—or become the wind—or become the light?

You approach one of the windows and reach as far as you can, but the window is massive and still too high. Then you look down at the hand that reached for the sky, a hand that is now so tiny and delicate.

You marvel at the wonder of what you have found,
for the hand is attached to the child of you.
    You feel the little hand . . . and the magic of little arms,
and the innocence of a body that is, oh, so small.
And although you cannot reach the window, you notice as the
light comes in, it shines on the middle of the floor—a spot
so bright, it's as if the sun itself has sat upon the stones.

You go to this luminescent stone and sit in the beam of light.
You feel its warmth and the wholeness of being surrounded
by the spinning carousel of bright windows.
Steadily, the light grows brighter and more alive.
It shines in from all directions,
igniting small particles that hang like dust in the air—
sparkles in the rays of sunlight that stream in the openings.

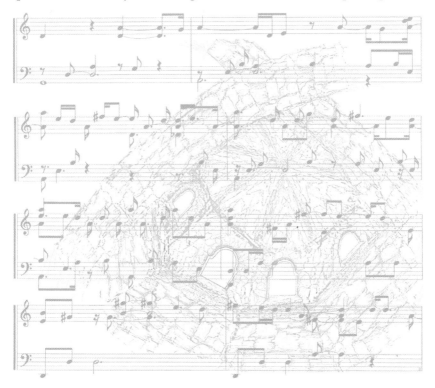

You reach out to touch the suspended white glitter.
Like magic it lands as light upon your hands.
So you reach to touch more of the sparkling dust
that illuminates inside the cups of your palms.

You breathe into your body and into your hands.
You breathe into the shimmer of light all around you.
Reaching into the light, you feel the sparkles blend into you.
They saturate your being in an ecstasy of bliss.

The light blends into the white stone room,
as though the windows have grown larger,
blocking out the shape of the floor and walls.
You bathe in the sparkles of white-blue light
surrendering all that you are to the euphoria of them.
There is only bliss inside you now . . . the tingling of tiny stars.
You lose yourself inside the flow of this feeling,
so you open for more . . . and more . . . and more.

You are the opening.
You are the space that was once the window.
You are the truth, the white light, and the sweet glow of bliss.
So you let go . . . and let go . . .
and let go. . . .

You are the long lost children of a Divine Source, the forgotten Gods in a dimension of time and space. You are the most adored of all that was ever created. You are the ongoing gift . . . of ongoing life.

To be in the knowledge of this . . . is your birthright. To be in the wisdom of this . . . is your divinity. And all that you reach for in the truth of this . . . can be found in a moment of bliss.

I will be with you always.

So much I love you.

Namasté

34

Exit, Stage Left

Even before I opened my eyes I could tell there was something unusual about this particular journey. It had actually come to a close. And although it was true that I'd experienced an incredible passage within this ascending sojourn, it was also quite unlike the others, for at its completion I had not fallen into any kind of unconscious state. I was still awake and alert. There was also a certain finality to it that filled me with a great curiosity as to what it all meant, including his very last phrase *Na-ma-stay*.

Opening my eyes, everything was exactly as I had remembered. The same group of people, the majority of whom still had their eyes closed, were gathered around the same fire, within the same canyon of brick walls that were no less luminous than when we began. However, the fire had obviously been stoked, its bright yellow flames now lighting up the arena.

Shankara was sitting quietly, sculpting the edges of his beard with the backs of his fingers—a motion I had come to recognize as a symbol of his contemplative patience. He appeared to be focused on Mohan, who was still perched on his wooden barrel, with legs folded and hands in his lap. His eyes were closed, and his head was tipped slightly forward as if he had fallen asleep or into an unconsciousness.

I watched as Shankara then rose and walked toward Mohan. He made his way through the meditative crowd with a presence and a stride that looked almost ceremonial in its manner. Mohan showed no sign of movement, holding his frozen pose—a lifeless posture. Shankara stopped directly in front of Mohan's perch and then performed a gesture that I found to be most bewildering.

Placing his hands together in a prayer-like manner, leaving an open space between his palms, he leaned forward and bowed down very low to Mohan. This long slow bow was the noblest I had ever seen. Delivered with such excellence and grace, it seemed to cry out that it was the most important of gestures or perhaps the final bow Mohan would ever receive.

That's when I knew . . . there would be no more jests, that the lights had come down, and the curtain had been drawn. The play had finally ended . . . and Mohan was gone.

Like an anxious child, I came to my feet with my tremulous heart pounding rapidly. Excitedly, I climbed through the crowd, in and around and sometimes over the people. I had to see for myself, up close, and for certain, if he had indeed passed on, right here among us. Was it possible that he in fact was the architect of his own departure? Was it as Mohan had said, *that it was only the chimes at the window who'd tell as he gently brushed by on his way to the wind?* Had he truly become the wind? Had he fulfilled his wish and stepped out of his body at the time of his choosing? And was it possible that I had somehow helped him in this passage, or perhaps others had—or all of us?

I stopped short of his small platform and slowly moved around him, peering into the peaceful expression on his face, wanting to see what was secret and silent behind his eyes. I trembled, not really knowing how to respond, whether to cheer or to weep, for both feelings were with me in abundance.

My mind searched for the jovial personality it knew so well, while my soul tried to drink in the very notion of what might have just occurred. Soon Emily, Michael, and Jessica joined me in my visual exploration. They were followed by the rest of the crowd, everyone gathered round looking for that same miracle—pondering the possibility of what was before us. A reverent hush seemed to engulf all who were witness, a silent *awe* that rippled out from the vision of what we were seeing.

From behind me, I felt two small delicate arms reach around my waist. Then Sharee's face pushed its way through the crook under my right arm. She peered in like a child hoping to see the spectacle, but not wanting to see it alone. Affectionately she pressed her head against the side of my body, holding me close, as though she had done it a thousand times before. She gazed at Mohan with tears in her eyes and an astounded smile that seemed to contradict the former. The innocence and vulnerability of her childlike gesture caused my own heart to stumble, the tears puddling up in my eyes, a lump swelling in my throat. Surrendering to this emotion, I allowed myself to hold her as we watched in awe and total wonder. I looked up at Shankara and found his own expression to be full of pride, an honorable smile that told all that could be said without words.

Awestruck, I asked, "Will he return?"

"To where?" Shankara said.

"To here. . . this place. . . to his body . . . his home."

Pausing for a second, he replied, **"He already has . . . returned to his home, that is. And never shall he wander from it again."**

There was nothing to do but stand there and drink in that instant. Nothing else mattered, nothing at all. It was Shankara who finally ended the silence as he turned to Father Mathews.

"Take him with you, and care for him well. Let there be no embalming or anything of the sort, and from here do not let his body touch the ground. Rest him in a place for three days and nights, and allow nothing to disturb his peaceful silence.

"After this span of time, return him to the fire, and cremate him in a blaze of glory. Then take his bones and the bowl of his ashes to the bowl of the vast and infinite ocean."

Then Shankara looked at me, **"Perhaps you will help . . . deliver him from this place."**

I stared at Shankara, not sure what I was to do. He smiled and nodded his head as though giving me permission to proceed. Strangely enough, it also felt that, whatever I was about to do, I was to do it alone and with great reverence.

Then Father Mathews gestured to me and said, "We can lay him in the back of the bus I brought from the church. I have it parked up on the main street."

That's when I knew that Shankara was asking me to carry Mohan's body to wherever it needed to go. I felt very honored to have been given the task.

So I squatted down slightly and pushed my chest against Mohan's back. Reaching around him with my arms, I placed my hands under his crossed legs, trying to pick him up and hold him in his current posture.

At first his body felt slightly rigid and molded into that form. Then it collapsed into itself, like a dried rose bud being touched for the first time. I juggled and balanced him as best I could until he finally folded into my arms and lap like the body of Christ in the statue of the *Pietà*. To my surprise, his human form smelled of sweet honey and subtle musk. And although it took all I had to carry him, I knew I had discovered a strength I never had.

So we walked, Father Mathews and I, making our way back out through the crowd, the people parting as we came as if for a procession. All eyes peered at the one in my arms, eyes of tears, eyes of laughter, and eyes of total awe. We moved in silence through the gathering, both of us unable to convey words, or perhaps not wanting to find any.

At the edge of the assembly, I turned to take one last look at the people, as if somehow I knew that there would never be another night like this. Throughout the crowd were faces and expressions so loving and profound that I couldn't help imagine what a glorious world it would be if these were the only gardeners of this humanity.

As I turned away to continue our journey to the main street, something pulled at my emotions. Turning my head, I found myself immediately drawn into a visual trance with Shankara, who seemed to stare right through me for a moment or two. Then he bowed his head and smiled slightly, making me stumble in my quest, a part of me not wanting to leave at all. I returned the gesture as best I could and then continued on.

Our journey to Father Mathews's vehicle was long and silent, neither of us desiring any great drama around what we were doing. Yet I was amazed as we left the alley and entered the main street that no bystanders bothered to react to the fact that I appeared to be carrying a dead man. Anxious to be away from the complacent onlookers, I was glad when we came to the bus and our walk down the public street was over.

I expected an old yellow school bus. Instead, Father Mathews was driving a tan late model VW bus, with more than a few dents and a little mold here and there. When he slid open the side panel door, it looked as if this particular vehicle had been used for everything from distributing food to the homeless to delivering children to the soccer field. So in a way it seemed appropriate that today it would become the hearse for a poet.

As I laid Mohan's body down through the side door of the bus, a small journal fell out of Mohan's coat and landed on the ground. After Mohan was safely arranged in the bus, the good Father picked up the book and handed it to me.

"No, it's not mine," I said. "It belongs to Mohan."

"No, Jared," he replied solemnly, "I believe it's Mohan's journal. Therefore, I think it now belongs to you."

He slid the journal into my coat pocket and reached for some worn and ragged-looking blankets from the back of the bus. He draped this makeshift shroud over and around Mohan's body. But as he pulled the ragged cloth up to cover Mohan's face, I impulsively grabbed the priest's arm, remembering the journey I had taken into a dungeon where I had once before pulled that mask away.

Father Mathews realized immediately what I was doing and why. He gave me a comforting smile. "Yes, you're absolutely right. Mohan is one of the few—or perhaps the only one we know—who was able to pull off the veil of his human adventure. We had best not cover his face again or . . . ." Then with a sheepish grin, he added, "Or he will undoubtedly haunt us for sure."

We both laughed, welcoming the comic relief. Besides, laughter around anything that had to do with Mohan seemed to be more than appropriate. After a short while, Father Mathews chuckled to himself. "What . . . what is it?" I asked.

"I was just thinking," he said, "of how Mohan would have preferred to be taken back to the church. But I just don't know how we would keep him from falling off the hood of the car."

I cracked up—not only at what this man, a priest, had said, but at the realization that his comment truly sounded like Mohan, as if he were here with us now, still turning and twisting the obvious into the sublime.

As our laughter subsided, I asked, "Do you want me to come with you?"

"No, this is sort of my department. And with Mohan I knew that this day was just around the corner. I will have plenty of help at the church."

So we said our goodbyes, and I soon found myself standing alone, late at night, on a nearly abandoned street. I didn't quite know what to do with myself, but I did wonder if Shankara or the others were where I had left them. With nowhere else to go, I walked back down the alley toward the arena.

The place was completely deserted, as if no one had been there at all and nothing of such magnitude had even occurred. Only a few orange embers of the fire kept a vigil. The sight of this vacant space brought to mind something Shankara had once said—there would come a day when all of us would doubt that any of this was true; we would doubt that he had ever been here at all. He said something about his being like the wind and that it would be our own ability to *know* that would give us tangible proof that any of what we had experienced was real. It seemed almost funny to me now to imagine waking up in a world where there no longer was, nor ever had been, someone named Shankara.

Sitting down close to the warm coals, I pulled Mohan's journal from my pocket. I held it near the fire to catch the last few minutes of light. The notebook itself was beautiful, made of a light-green parchment-like material with pages of a rag-type paper. Inside the front cover Mohan had written one line that he signed at the end.

My letters to the wind . . . . . Shankara

Mohan

As I turned the page, I knew that what I was about to read was very personal—something extraordinary that had occurred between Mohan and Shankara. I wondered if I was even capable of understanding this kind of connection. And yet I knew within my heart it was something I was hoping to experience. I was also well aware of my total intrusion into these very private thoughts, but my passion to know . . . to be able to have even a glimpse of their communication was more than my inquisitive spirit could overcome. There were only a few lines on each page, and yet there seemed to be more than enough words to fill up each piece.

I felt you smiling again.
The Earth moved all around me.
My bones rattled with your joy.
Won't you laugh through me some more?

Touch me,
and I'm a river,
and I cannot stop the rains.
My flood waters reach for you.
Drink me in and dance.

I caught you playing in the stars again.
You know . . .
no one really looks for you there anymore.
You'd better surround yourself with clouds
if you want to be noticed.

Each time you raise my cup,
I overflow into it.
My glory is your river.
Wash me.

I am well-seasoned wood.
Light your fire inside me.
Sprinkle my ashes over your bottomless ocean.

His words struck in me a desire to probe every possibility, to explore not only my relationship with myself, but my relationship with spirit—with a voice in the wind, which, up to now, I had been too frightened to call out to. If this is what it meant to indeed be a madman, then a madman I wanted to be. Hail to the Village Idiot who lives in the Land of Bliss.

Huddling down close to the fire, hoping to use the last few seconds of readable light, I turned to read his final words . . . the words to his friend, Shankara.

How can I hold you,
    when you touch me from inside?
How can I see you,
    when you look through my eyes?
How can I tell you,
    what no words understand?
How many roses,
    can I hold in one hand?

35

Fame and Fables

I had the sneaking suspicion that, despite being on my way to mastering the more refined virtues of honor, patience, humility, and compassion, I would nonetheless want to immediately behead anyone who awakened me from my tranquil slumber. Be it the phone, the doorbell, or perhaps hoof prints prancing on the roof, there seemed to be no escape. After all, where does one go? How does one hide? And how does one graciously tell the person now calling on the phone that the timing, is BLOODY INAPPROPRIATE! Grabbing the receiver, I barked a horrific woof, "WHAT!"

"Yes," came the calm and calculated voice of the man on the other end. "Would this be Jared Grayson?"

"Yeah! . . . WHAT!"

"My name is John McDowell. We connected several weeks ago . . . about possibly producing some of your music."

"What?"

"In fact, I believe we had an appointment, but I guess there was some miscommunication. At any rate, I would still like to meet with you . . . if you're interested?"

Completely stupefied, I carelessly allowed the receiver to slip out of my hands. I wrestled with the tangled phone cord like a line with a crazed fish I was trying to pull into my unstable vessel. For the next few seconds all I could catch was a slice or two of his voice as the receiver danced at the end of the coiled cord.

When I was finally able to reel him back in, I heard him say, "Are you still there? Grayson? Are you there?"

"Yes! I'm still I . . . I mean here . . . yes . . . me . . . I am . . . here." McDowell waited for just a second and then continued.

"I'm not really sure what happened with our last meeting. Maybe you're not really interested, but just in case it was something else, I thought I'd try again."

"No . . . I mean, yes . . . I . . . I'm interested. It was an emergency—that day I missed the appointment. I tried to call your office but there was no answer. I guess I figured that—"

"To tell you the truth, I probably wouldn't have called back, but I have a client who is putting together a movie project, and he's insisting that we use some of your work. A couple of months ago I played him one of the audio tapes. He thinks a couple of your compositions would be perfect for his film."

Having my ego stroked a bit helped me compose myself. Sounding slightly more coherent, I asked, "So which compositions? I mean which ones specifically?"

"They were a couple of pieces from a tape that had a lot of bold passages. I think one of them was titled *Opus for a New World*. Yes, I remember, because he really liked the music, but not the name. Anyway, we can talk about that when we meet. Would today be alright?"

"Yes, today would be good . . . very good."

"How about later this afternoon . . . around five at my office?"

"Yes, that would be fine."

"Good, I'll see you then."

"Yes, I'll be there (*click*) this time." Dead air filled the receiver.

In total shock, I just stood there in my boxer shorts and fallen down socks. Then I started to laugh, I mean really laugh. I thought of what Shankara had said just the night before—I needed to hold on to my hat because we were just getting started. This had to be what he meant. All I needed to do was get out of my own way and let go, then wonderful things would start happening.

I galloped about the house trying to prepare myself for the afternoon's event. Checking the phone machine, I found a message from Sam Stiltson at the hospital.

> Hi, Jared, Sam Stiltson here. That was some night last night. How are you doing? After we got home, Marshal and I weren't exactly sure if we'd just climbed onto a rocket ship or managed to get off one.
>
> Anyway, the reason I called is that I saw that woman again, Adrian Anderson, who visited your uncle—or I guess I mean Shankara—while he was still in the coma. This time I saw her at the pharmacy. I asked her if she was interested in what had happened to him. She said yes, though she acted somewhat skittish. So I asked if she had been in touch with you, which caused her to bolt immediately. I tried to pursue the matter, but she said it wasn't her place. Then out the door she went.
>
> I stopped at the pharmacy and got her current address: 499 West Olive Street. Phone number is 965-933-8044. Anyway, let us know what happens. See you later.

It did seem awfully strange that this woman would be so panic-stricken about talking with me. She obviously wasn't telling all that she knew. Which is why, after a series of unanswered phone calls, I decided to spend the early afternoon paying Adrian Anderson a little visit.

Her home was on the west side, an old Sixties rambler, with a brick veneer skirt and a very bad paint job. Overgrown shrubbery nearly covered the place, which made it easy for me to sneak up to the front door without being seen. I knocked a couple of times and then stepped to the side so that she would have to open the door to see who was there. And just in case my suspicions were right—that she had been avoiding my calls—I prepared to slide my foot inside the door when she opened it.

An attractive woman came to the door. She looked to be in her late fifties, with a light complexion and strawberry blonde hair pulled back tightly in a bun. When she first saw me, she smiled politely like I was one of her neighbors. Then, a split second later, she reacted and tried to shut the door.

Quickly I slid my right foot and hand into the opening. She saw this coming and cleverly kicked my foot out and slammed the door on my hand.

I yelped like a helpless pup whose paw had been stepped on. Grabbing one hand with the other, I doubled over from the pain and howled. "No, not my fingers, anything but my poor fingers." She came charging out to rescue me, chanting an apology.

"Oh, my God. Are you alright? I'm so sorry. I didn't see your hand there or I wouldn't have—oh God, should I call a doctor?"

Feeling my hand and fingers, I found no broken bones. I attempted to reassure her that there wasn't any serious damage, even though I knew that I wouldn't be playing a lot of Mozart or Chopin for a while.

"Come in and sit down," she said. "We'd better put some ice on that." Leaving me in the front room, she dashed around the corner to the adjoining kitchen. Through the space above the counter I could see her fishing ice out of her freezer, placing it into a plastic bag. Over her shoulder she called out, "Keep that hand in the air above your head or it will swell up like a melon." Returning, she laid the bag of ice on my hand and rattled off a stream of comments politely scolding the both of us.

"You really shouldn't have come. If you hadn't come none of this would've happened. It's none of my business anyway. The only reason I stopped by the hospital was to see how Ben was doing. I shouldn't even have done that, but after not having seen him for over ten years, well, I just wanted to know if he was okay. And I know, I shouldn't have said I was Clair Grayson, but they asked if I was his wife—which I sort of was—but then they asked my name as they were writing on some form, so I said I was—"

"Wait . . . wait a minute. What is this really all about? And why don't you want to talk to me?"

When she finally calmed down, I was invited into the kitchen where we sat at a large round table. For a few seconds she stared at her nervous hands. She then began to tell her story.

"I'm Adrian. I lived with Ben for many years. We got together after Clair died. Although we were never married, we lived in the same house for about six years. We had a good time together, and then it was time to move on. I have no regrets, and I really doubt that he does either. Our reason for separating had more to do with his wanting to live out in the mountains and my wanting to live in the city. This all happened after your parents passed."

"But what does this have to do with me?"

"You see, this all happened long before I met Ben, and I always thought it was wrong they didn't tell you. Children have a right to know where they come from. I didn't actually find out until years later. Ben made me swear to never say any—"

"What! What are you trying to say—I was adopted?"

"No, that's not it. And what you first need to understand is that when they started out they were really trying to do something good. Their intentions were very high, and Ben and Clint were the best of friends. He said they were closer than any two brothers he ever knew. That's why they did it. That's why they felt it would work out for everyone."

"What are you talking about? What did they do?"

She paused to pick up the bag to get some more ice. I caught her by the arm and slowly guided her back to the chair. For a few seconds there was silence.

"Early in their marriage, your father found out he couldn't have children. Your mother Rose—on the other hand—could. They considered adopting, but Clint wanted a child of his own lineage, his own bloodline—this was long before in vitro fertilization. That's when Clint came to Ben with his idea. He had read about a Native American tribe where if a man was not able to have children with his wife, his brother would be asked to impregnate her. So . . . that's what they did."

I sat there in a strange kind of shock as if I had been reading a story book only to find several pages missing.

Finally I said, "So Ben is my biological father?"

"Yes," she answered, "and don't be mistaken, I'm also saying they didn't use test tubes or turkey basters to accomplish this feat."

"What, you mean—"

"That's right, and that's also when all the trouble started. I guess they thought that they could handle it, that they were such good friends that having Ben and your mother share a few nights together was all for a worthy cause, that it would produce a baby and benefit everyone. Well, they were right. And for the most part, I believe it did benefit everyone—here you are, and no one would have ever experienced your life if they hadn't been so bold. But after you were born, things were never the same between those brothers. I think they tried at first. Ben told me that Clint and your mother would ship you off to the lake every summer to spend time with him. He said it was never enough time, though. I guess they all just slowly drifted apart.

"That's why I always felt so bad about it. I thought you had a right to know—especially after Rose and Clint had both passed on, and you and Ben were the only ones left. But he made me promise never to tell. I think after awhile there were just so many bad feelings and so much embarrassment, that Ben thought it best not to stir the whole thing up again."

I sat there stunned. A part of me felt very angry that I never knew who my father was. Yet there was also a part of me that grabbed onto the possibility that my real father might be alive.

"Jared," she said, "the most important thing is that what Ben and Clint and your mother did back then, they did out of their love and respect for each other and their desire to bring you into the world. The rest just didn't happen the way they had hoped. And me, I'm just a bystander in all of this who has told you the story the best I know how."

Adrian waited briefly watching for my reaction, then added, "Are you alright?"

As I drove back through town, I asked myself the same question, was I alright? Within the combustion of my emotions and this startling information, was I actually . . . okay? For the most part I felt fine, which I guess was why I was questioning my mental state in the first place. The fact that my parents were so dysfunctional for all those years would take some adjusting to. Yet my confusion and sadness around my past seemed overshadowed by this notion that my father was still alive. It was also quite possible he was connected to a spiritual being who I was relatively convinced was . . . was . . . well, I didn't know what he was, but whatever he was, it was extraordinary, and something I wanted to explore.

Adrian and I had spent a couple of hours talking and drinking coffee before I said my goodbyes and was on my way. I went straight to McDowell's office, my nervous haste causing me to arrive nearly twenty-five minutes early. Having no desire to sit and think about all of the news Adrian had just bestowed on me, I opted to cross the street to browse through a small bookstore called Bala East Books.

Inside, I was nearly overwhelmed by the aroma of incense. Sitar music filled the room as I wandered among the dark shelves looking blindly at the books with no idea what I was doing there. Occasionally, I pulled one from the shelf and fumbled through it—looking mostly at the pictures—finding it difficult to keep focused on foreign names and phrases. I continued this charade as if I were being watched. Then purely out of self-consciousness, I purchased a package of incense. The woman behind the counter looked East Indian and had a small red dot on her forehead.

As I received my change and started to walk away, she said, "Namasté." I stopped short, remembering that I'd heard Shankara say that same word the last time I saw him. I turned back toward her. "What does that mean . . . what you just said, Namasté?"

She replied, "It's a kind of salutation like hello or goodbye only its generally spoken from a place of spirit, as an honorable gesture. Translated it means, 'I bow to the divine in you.'" Then she giggled a little adding, "And I guess that means whether you are coming or going."

I smiled and said, "Thanks, that's nice." She smiled back and proceeded to help the next customer. I stepped out into the street.

It felt strange to be in such a familiar part of the city for such a different reason. I had parked only a couple of blocks from the entrance to the alley where the fireside gathering had been. In fact, the convenience store where I had been mistaken for Jesus was at the end of the street. In an odd sort of way it felt like a familiar neighborhood.

McDowell's office took up the first floor of a beautifully restored building with a Gothic facade. A couple of granite steps led up to a heavy wooden door with a thick pane of beveled glass. Inside, the foyer led up eight or nine steps to a carpeted landing that spread out into a spacious waiting room. Several burgundy velvet armchairs resided on either side of a small white marble table. Two antique floor lamps gave the room a warm tone and the ambiance of an old library or private sitting room. To one side there was a large desk where a woman was busy gathering up papers and assorted envelopes. She had her coat on and appeared to be preparing to leave.

"Oh," she said, having noticed that I was standing behind her. "You must be Jared Grayson. Mr. McDowell is expecting you. I'm leaving for the night, but I will let him know that you are here. Go ahead and have a seat."

I laid my satchel filled with music next to the marble table and oozed myself into the plush velvet chair. I felt like a gold ring being slid back into its jewelry case. That's when it all started to sink in; I was in the waiting room of my dreams. Fame and fortune were but moments away.

Beyond the secretary's desk was a large mahogany door. The name John McDowell was spelled out with inlaid gold letters. It gave me an incredible feeling of permanence, as though from here one never had to look back.

A few minutes later, the woman returned. "He will be with you shortly," she said. She picked up her purse from the desk and disappeared down the granite stairs.

I took up my leather satchel and held it in my lap as if it were my first born and I was about to introduce it to the world. Within the plush armchair of my success, there was no doubt that life had definitely taken a turn for the better and the magic was finally happening. Even the news about Ben being my father seemed to be changing inside me. The truth was in the here and now—he was my father and some facsimile of him was still alive. That was all that seemed to matter—though, where he was or how to find him was still a mystery.

I also thought of my recent interaction with Sharee. There at the fireside arena, as we gazed together at Mohan, I felt something extraordinary, a wholeness I'd never known before. It made me believe in possibilities again. It gave me hope that maybe that sweet connection was the start of something much, much more.

Just then the mahogany door opened and a voice said, "Grayson?"

Standing about five-foot-nine was a stout well-groomed man. He wore a white silk shirt and a finely-tailored gray suit which accentuated his blue-gray eyes. He was around my age with an evenly-tanned complexion and a gray mustache that was tweaked at the ends. His thick salt-and-pepper hair was short and spiked so the bulk of it stood on end. We shook hands in a businesslike manner and then entered his private office.

The first thing I saw was a large desk with a dark green marble top. A high-backed brown leather chair with strips of gold trim sat behind it; matching gold accessories were scattered on top of the desk. Several more of the burgundy velvet chairs did their best to hide the ebony grand piano glistening in the corner.

The wall behind his desk faced the street and was divided into six tall narrow windows with gold-trimmed Venetian blinds. The remaining walls were tastefully decorated with gold-framed awards, gold-framed pictures of McDowell with celebrities, and gold-framed posters that seemed to be the focus of the collage.

It was all too perfect to believe. Although a part of me wanted to just be there and say nothing at all, I readily welcomed the words that came next, "Well, Grayson, I consider you a very lucky man. I have a client who's crazy about your work. He's got a movie project going and thinks your music would be perfect. The best part is, the guy is extremely wealthy, which is what makes this my kind of project. Here," he said pointing to one of the velvet chariots, "have a seat. Hang up your coat on the rack if you like."

By this time I was feeling rather warm, so I opted to take him up on his suggestion. As I hung up my coat, something else fell from the coat rack. Reaching down to pick it up, I discovered it was a beautiful white silk scarf with an exquisitely embroidered M at each end.

For several seconds I couldn't turn around; I couldn't even move. I stood there staring at the white scarf in disbelief. This had to be a mistake, an odd coincidence. Yet there seemed to be no escaping the incriminating evidence.

My mind began to arrange the pieces of this puzzle: This building is on the same block. There must be steps from this office to that very place in the alley. But was it the same scarf, the same face—the eyes of a Jesus, the eyes of a Satan?

As I stood still facing the wall, I caught a glimpse of him reflected in the glass of one of his gold picture frames. There was no doubt. It was him. John McDowell was the one crouched down in the alley with the syringe. He was the chameleon. He was the madman who had suckled my fingers and then, a moment later, devoured them.

Here I was, in his office about to place my destiny into his hands. I could feel my dreams dissolving, my doubts and fears mounting up with a calvary of possibilities being forced to retreat.

And there was no changing the true reality of this, the *other* half of this duality. As he sat in his leather-bound chair, behind his fine marble desk, John McDowell was still the consummate example of my elusive success, the model of the dream that I had yet to achieve. He was the lord of musical accomplishment, the Robin Hood of undiscovered masterpieces. He was everything I had wanted to be. He was that . . . and more.

My brain scrambled to come up with some sort of plan, some way to prevent my demeanor from exposing my true feelings. Perhaps I could just play along and—

"Grayson . . . is everything alright?"

"Yes," I blurted out. "I was just noticing all of the photos and gold framed awards . . . very impressive."

"Well, this business has been good to me." Then changing the subject he added, "But today we're here to talk about you. Have a seat and let me tell you about this project. Bru Chandler is the man putting it together. I don't know if you have heard of him, he's new to the movie business. I think he made his real fortune in the timber industry, land use and development . . . that sort of thing.

"Anyway, this movie is an action adventure about a race of beings—aliens I guess you would call them—that secretly invade our government. The storyline is built around a couple of old war heroes who are called out of retirement to save the country from the invasion. I've read part of the screenplay, and it really has a wide range of possibilities, as far as music is concerned. There are action scenes where whole cities are destroyed as well as a few love scenes . . . and a lot of other stuff, but my point is, he's really trying to do a story about an alien invasion that is believable. I think he wants to send out the message that such a thing could really happen and we as a planet need to advance our military capabilities far beyond what they are.

"For example, with your music, he hears *Opus for a New World* as a triumphant ending for when the aliens are destroyed and the heroes gain back control. I think if they can actually do this kind of scene in a way people will take seriously, it could be very effective, especially with that piece of music.

"For now, Chandler would first like to have a meeting with you so that you can become familiar with the script. I will oversee the music end of it as well as be the music director when it comes time to put the sound tracks down. Your part is to bring in what you have already composed and fill in the holes where other things are needed. Chandler is totally sold on your music so there won't be any problem striking up a very choice deal." Lighting a cigarette from a gold case on his desk, he took in a long drag. As he exhaled a dense stream of smoke, he said, "So what do you think?"

I found myself remembering what Shankara had said about there being more advanced cultures that would be coming to interact with us as we moved out of our more barbarian ways. I thought about the likelihood of our common origins, that they were family, perhaps even the better part of us. I thought about—

"So Jared . . . you haven't answered me. I asked you, what do you think?"

I waited for just a few seconds before I answered.

"I think . . . no."

"What?"

"No . . . I think no."

"So what are you saying?"

"I'm saying no, the price is too high."

"I don't understand. What do you have to lose?"

"Everything . . . I think."

"I really don't follow what you're saying."

I hesitated before I answered. "I don't know that I do either, but I'm very sure that the answer is . . . no, I'm not interested in promoting that kind of a project."

"But Grayson, be real about this. You have never even had any of your music produced before. This is a sure thing. Chandler will put enough money into this project so that, even if the movie's a flop, it will still be played in every theater in the country. You could easily get a great soundtrack release from this. At this point in your career, how can you be so choosy? After all, everybody has to settle for less than their ideal the first time out."

"No." I replied. "Because this isn't *less* of anything. It's more . . . more violence, more vengeance, more killing, more hatred, more negative propaganda about alien life. That's all it is, just more of the same."

Then totally impassioned, I looked him straight in the eye. "When has there been enough? When will the feeding frenzy for promoting some kind of cheap rush through violence and vengeance stop? When does everyone quit selling out to profit by producing some kind of real or illusionary pain!"

Abruptly I caught myself; in my excitement I had nearly climbed over the top of his desk.

"I'm sorry," I said. "I didn't mean to raise my voice. I guess all I really have to say is . . . no. I thank you for the opportunity . . .

but no. I'm not interested."

I stretched out my hand. After a strong handshake, he commented in a bewildered tone, "Alright, if that's your choice."

It took only a few seconds to gather up my satchel and retrieve my coat, once again revealing the white silk scarf that hung like a banner on the coat rack. As I opened the door to take my leave, I turned back. When our eyes met I said, "Thank you for your interest . . . and your time." Then unexpectedly, he widened his eyes slightly as if he were zeroing in on a face he recognized. For an instant, I was sure he remembered. Then to my complete surprise he said, "Grayson . . . I do admire your passion about this." I stepped through the door and closed it behind me.

As I stood at the top of the stairs, an assortment of emotions battled with each other, each vying for dominance. A part of me wanted to scream at all of the unconscious people who were still feeding on the violence produced in movies and television. Another part felt betrayed by the spiritual path I was on, by Shankara and all of his prophetic words, the bliss I had yet to find. I also felt betrayed by my family who couldn't even tell me who my real father was. Then there was the dream I'd been chasing—to have my name on the same marquee as the John McDowells of the world. This was the greatest betrayal of all.

By the time I reached the door at the bottom of the steps, only one emotion remained. I felt alone. I wanted to squat down in the corner and pull my coat over my face.

I wondered where all of the people were—the rest of the conscious people. Didn't anyone else feel this way? Was all of humanity so seduced by the Gray World that all anyone could do was spin around in selfish indulgence and futility?

Exasperated, I pushed open the door and propelled myself out onto the sidewalk, back into the world I found to be so hollow.

I carried that feeling home with me, my own depression holding me captive into the early morning hours. Sleep seemed to be my only escape, for it was the one place I could go where my life wouldn't follow.

36

Color Me Home

I was soon to discover that hiding the phone before going to sleep was not really the answer to not being jolted into reality before I was ready to wake up. (*RING, RING*) I was also realizing that when you're only half awake it's even harder to remember where you hid the phone the night before. (*RING, RING*) Having stashed it in one of my drawers (as I was now remembering) wasn't such a bad idea, but then I had to remember just which drawer it was hidden in. (*RING, RING*) . . . (*RING, RING*) . . . (*RING, RING*).

"Yes! Yes," I garbled out. "What is it . . . for crying out loud?"

My sleepy ears were assaulted by the soulful and excited woman on the other end, who spit out her words uncontrollably.

"Jared! It's Emily! Quick! Turn on your TV. Quick, turn it on. That woman, she's on. Your friend Jessica, she's on right now. She's gonna *sing*, Jared. Hurry up, turn it on."

I stumbled into the next room, turned on the television, and began flipping through the channels. I put the phone receiver back up to my ear and frantically asked, "Which station, Emily . . . which channel?" It was then I discovered that the phone I was talking on had become a free spirit of its own, its cord detached and dangling in the air.

Finally, in my random search, I ran across Jessica's face on the screen. She looked drastically different from how I had seen her on TV the first time. In fact, she looked absolutely incredible.

I felt so happy and excited for her. And even though she always made me a little nervous, I couldn't help but feel proud of what she was doing.

Cathy Collins, the host of the show, sat beside her. I turned up the sound midsentence as Collins asked Jessica about leaving her television show on the religious channel.

" . . . Can you tell us what really happened, why you actually left the show?"

"Cathy, I know what kind of press comes out of this sort of thing and what kind of rumors get started. That may even be why I was invited on this show . . . because the producers thought I might bare my soul with some scandalous story. After all, why would a successful woman with her own television show, who preached as though she had it all together, just suddenly walk away?

"Well, I didn't have it together, not really. After I was involved in an accident that could have killed someone, I started to look at my responsibility around that, which in turn prompted me to look at my responsibility for everything in my life. I had always preached . . . give all your problems to Jesus. Well, one day I believe Jesus started giving all my problems back to me saying, 'You are no less than I am, so quit whining and handle it yourself.'"

"Really," Collins replied, chuckling slightly under her breath. "But what about all of your followers, the people who watched you . . . well, religiously?"

"They're beautiful people and incredibly sincere. But there was a kind of helplessness about it all with so many people looking up to me as some kind of a guide, a model of whom they should try to be. One day I took a close look in the mirror and I didn't like who I saw. She was someone who had been created to satisfy the image, to satisfy the cameras. In an attempt to become the perfect spiritual woman I became a plastic talking doll reeling out Bible scripture and phrases like 'Praise God' every time someone pulled the string. I had created somebody that wasn't anybody. My show was no less than a soap opera, programmed to be delivered the same way it had a thousand times before.

"Now, I am simply trying to take all of that and give it some value—fill in the empty spaces with the truth of who I really am."

Cathy Collins appeared to have no idea how to pursue this train of thought, especially within this type of interview. In fact, she reacted as if the interview had gone off track. In an attempt to change the subject, she asked Jessica another question.

"So you are going to sing for us today?"

"Yes, from some new material I have been putting together."

"Yes, and I hear that you have not only gotten a great response from it already, but there has been some interest in a movie project?"

"Actually, there is a small group of producers and directors who have gotten together to create a film that would bring out an awareness of who we really are as spiritual beings. The music I am now pursuing is of that nature. We have talked a little bit about doing a movie with orchestrated journeys. Something that would simulate tangible adventures into other dimensions of the spirit world."

Once again dodging the content of Jessica's response, Collins asked, "So did you write the song you're going to share with us?"

"No, the lyrics were written by my friend Mohan who recently passed on. In fact, how I came upon the lyrics in the first place is kind of an unusual story. I saw him out in front of St. Martin's Cathedral one afternoon. I had seen him in the distance, acting as though he was writing on some scraps of paper. As he got up and walked away, I noticed something had dropped out of his pocket. I picked it up and discovered the lyrics of this song."

"So Jessica, what you are saying is that these lyrics simply fell out of someone's pocket and into your hands?"

"Yes, sort of."

"That is so magical. So then I assume that you got together with him later and put the whole song together?"

"Yes . . . it was sort of that way."

As I sat there watching her, I knew exactly what she had done. She found those lyrics the day I left her to follow Mohan. Then later, she put them to music so that his words could live on. He probably never even knew that she had done it. What a wonderful way of honoring his work. I thought about how incredible his poems were and how fantastic it was that his profound thoughts were about to be heard by millions of people. Jessica was an amazing woman. She was just . . . wonderful. Resting back in my chair, I listened as the interview continued.

"So he wrote the lyrics and you wrote the music?"

"No," Jessica answered, "actually the music was written by another friend of mine, Jared Grayson."

"WHAT?" I yelped, the word lifting me out of my chair. "ARE YOU NUTS? ARE YOU COMPLETELY OUT OF YOUR MIND? Oh no . . . please tell me she didn't. Please tell me that this is not what she kept trying to talk to me about. Oh God, not on nationwide television. Oh God, tell me she didn't."

"So," Collins continued, "you were really just the glue that put it all together."

"Yes . . . I guess you might say that."

With full force, I whined, "Oh . . . my . . . God."

"So then, Jessica, what is this song about?"

"Well, I think if we could ask my friend Mohan right now what these lyrics were about, he would likely say something very unpredictable like—what would you have them be about? And then he might say, perhaps they are about a lost child who has been separated from a mother or a father, a sweet soul who knows that somewhere over that rainbow is a place called home.

"Or perhaps they're about a man or a woman who follows an ancient melody in search of the greatest of lovers, possibly someone known from before.

"Or maybe it's the prayer of someone like Jesus or Buddha who has bloomed within his being all the colors of the rainbow, so that he might walk into the bliss of his enlightenment.

"Or perhaps, it's about someone, anyone, who has longed for the truth. Someone who called out to the wind one day and then actually stopped and listened until the voice came back—a voice that said remember the grace of who you are and that it's time for you to come home to that truth."

Completely stupefied by Jessica's lengthy response, Collins finally asked, "So, Jessica, what is the name of this song?"

"It is titled . . . *Color Me Home.*"

"Very good." Then looking out into the crowd, Collins announced, "Ladies and gentlemen, would you please welcome to our stage . . . Jessica Williams."

As the people started to applaud, I once again began to whine, "Oh my God, here it comes. She's actually gonna to do this on television. Doesn't she know she can be sued for this? There's the intro. Oh no . . . here it comes."

You touch me from the stars,
and reach inside my lucid dreams.
You dance inside my breath . . .
in crystal shades, of blues and greens.

You color in my world,
and weave within my tapestry.
And all the shades of you . . . ignite the colors, in my mind.
Color me home.

Sail me home.
Hold on to this trembling heart.
And cast out your words . . . upon my waters.
Oh, don't let go.

Sail me home.
On lavender oceans.
Into your arms.
Color me home.

You're everywhere I go,
in every face that comes my way.
You're each familiar voice . . . I remember,
from somewhere far away.
And when the night is still.
You come for me inside myself.
And lead me to a place . . .
where the mountains meet the wind.
. . . Where starlight begins.

Sail me home.
Hold on to this trembling heart.
And cast out your words . . . upon my waters,
Oh, don't let go.

Sail me home.
On lavender oceans.
Into your arms.
Color me home.

I could not hold back the flood waters of thirty-eight years, not when what I had just been handed was as beautiful as this. In one fell swoop she had done what no one had been able to in a lifetime. I felt as if I had at last been born. My music was being ushered into the most beautiful of surroundings by the most beautiful of companions. It was wonderful. It was perfect, and it was far more than I could have ever imagined. I wept like grown men do in their private moments.

As the crowd applauded, Jessica smiled and bowed her head graciously. After being embraced by Collins, Jessica disappeared from the screen. I turned off the television hoping to preserve the triumphant emotions I was feeling for just a few more minutes.

I looked around at my humble home, the place where that music had been created. I noticed the piano, how dusty it was, and how it had aged over the years. There was the piano bench, which always seemed to have old sheets of music peeking out from under its lid trying to get out, trying to be heard. I glanced at the fireplace and remembered the many fires that had burned long into the night, and the mantelpiece where—

The clothes—Ben's plaid shirt and the rest of his clothes—they were gone. I had left them on the mantel.

Quickly, I rose to my feet. I searched all around the fireplace in vain. I ransacked what was left of my rational mind for an answer. Why Ben's clothes? Who could have wanted them?

Sitting down on the couch, I took a deep breath, trying to expel my panic. Then with a rush, it came to me—Shankara.

This realization was followed by an even more disturbing thought. Perhaps it was like the story Michael showed me, about the holy man who borrowed the body of the king for a short while. When he pulled his spirit away, the king died his natural death. Shankara is giving Ben back his clothes and quite possibly his fate . . . death—Oh my God.

All at once a thousand pieces began falling into place, including the fact that Shankara had said he would leave shortly after Mohan died, and Mohan was already gone.

That is what he meant by *Namasté*. It had nothing to do with hello; he was saying goodbye, which is why he tugged at my attention at the last gathering.

Ben always said he wanted to die at the cabin. He was up hiking in that area when he fell and hit his head. Perhaps in some unconscious way he had purposely gone there to die. Then I realized, that's where he is now . . . that's where my father is, the father I've never spoken to as my father. Shankara has put Ben back into his life so he could play out his destiny. He's gone back to the cabin . . . he's gone back to the lake.

As my jeep sped past the last of the city streets and onto the old highway, I could feel my life slipping past me. All of the events that had led up to this moment, were becoming blurred and distorted as if parts of them had never really happened.

I felt isolated by the dread of my speculation, the possibility that Shankara might step out of Ben's physical form leaving us forever, as well as leaving my uncle—my father—to play out the consequences. It was difficult to know what was real—what was possible. I guess there was a part of me that hoped there might be time, just after Shankara left Ben's body, when I could get medical help before Ben perished.

It was beyond my reasoning why I had been challenged by so many recent experiences, feeling that I had come so far in my understanding only to have it all pulled apart by this one incomprehensible situation. Here I was, standing in the middle of my life, having just found out the true identity of my father, yet quite possibly never having the opportunity to know him as such. And ever present on my mind was Shankara—who may have vanished like the wind.

With my rapid exodus from the city, I made record time. It was not long before I found myself turning up the old gravel road that would take me into the mountains. Swerving around a corner, I felt my back wheels slip, which startled me into the realization that I was driving dangerously. Yet it didn't seem to matter. All that I cared about was *that chance*, that one chance I had of finding Ben before it was too late.

Perhaps I was naive, wanting so much for there to be a storybook ending to this disjointed drama. Or perhaps the real truth was that all of these events were part of some divine order, despite my panicked perception. Yet, if I were to fail just to learn a lesson that some superior being had intended for me—to provide me with some tragic but profound wisdom—then this was one lesson that I was desperate to change.

I raced against time and against my fears, feelings that seemed to call out that whatever was to happen had already been set into motion. Be that as it may, I pushed forward, pressing down on the gas pedal each time the road straightened giving me the opportunity to accelerate.

At last I came to the end of the road where I found the two forestry buildings and the old general store. I slid on the loose gravel as I brought my jeep to a grinding halt. Climbing out, I charged to the front door of the rustic store. Unlike the last time I had been here, it was closed and uninviting. Finding the knob locked, I banged several times and shouted, "Hello, is there anybody here?"

A muffled voice finally answered, "We're closed for the day."

Calling through the roughly-planked door, I pleaded, "I just want to ask you a question. Have you seen a big man, very tall with white hair and a beard?"

For several seconds I waited, but there was no response. Quite possibly, by this time, I was simply on a futile chase, but I couldn't take the chance. Whatever the outcome . . . I had to know.

Just then, the door lock clicked and the door opened a crack. As the old hermit's face appeared, he yammered out what I wanted to hear.

"Yeah, I seen him. Hard to not notice that one . . . not that we get a lot of people around here anyway."

"So you saw him?"

"Yeah? . . . ain't that what I said? To tell you the truth, I thought the whole thing was pretty strange. He didn't even come into the place. I heard some kinda rig pull up and then take off again. Well, I figured it was just someone turning around. Then, I looked out the door and there he was, in the middle of the parking lot. He stood there and didn't move, and then real sudden-like he took off and headed up the trail toward the granite peaks. Pretty strange I thought . . . him with no backpack and no bedroll . . . and no rig to come back to. Even made me wonder if he was alright . . . in the head, you know. Or maybe he was a fugitive that was gonna hide in the mountains or something. He didn't even have a coat, and it gets cold up in these parts at night."

"What was he wearing . . . did you notice?"

"Just a plaid flannel shirt, sort of dark green and red, I suspect."

I leapt off the porch and headed towards my jeep. Shouting back to the old timer, I asked, "So about what time was that?"

"Around noon, I think," he said. "If you're going to catch up with him, you'd better hurry."

37

I Do Believe in Ghosts

To my surprise, the trail, although not well-traveled, seemed quite familiar from my last expedition here. Fortunately, I was able to *not* make the same mistakes as before, relinquishing myself of the need to switch back and retrace my steps. In addition, I had no threat of a storm surrounding me— no rain to cause the rocks and terrain to be slippery and hazardous.

Reaching the summit, I climbed over the last few boulders between the granite peaks. There I was greeted by a beautiful orange and lavender skyscape; the brilliant hues of color were dabbed about like brush strokes of a painting by Monet or Renoir. Captured by the majestic scene, I was momentarily oblivious to where I was standing. This was the same outcropping of rocks I had fallen from before. As I stepped to the edge of the cliff's face, I was mortified by how far the drop was—how dangerous a place this had been. Had I seen this ledge in the daylight the last time, I would never have attempted to climb down.

Picturing myself scaling over the rounded contour of this rock reminded me of the madman I had been on that stormy night. And yes, my lone pine tree was still standing there, some fifty feet tall. Its green branches were about ten feet from the edge, level with my waist. Touched by the wind, they waved slightly as if once again inviting me into their swaying arms. Via the tree was the route I had taken before, but from this perspective I was amazed that I had survived such a fall.

Off to the right, a path carved out by hikers traversed down the rocky side of the mountain. Frantically I started down the trail, running whenever possible. Along the way, thick brush and windblown trees scraped and scratched me until one branch snagged my denim shirt and spun me around. Losing my balance, I stumbled and rolled head over heals.

I landed in a thicket, captive in its woody arms and prickly stems. As I pulled myself slowly out of the bushes I heard my shirt tear. Cold air hit my bare skin, sending a chill down my spine. One pant leg and both of my shirt sleeves were torn. The back of my shirt was ripped; a long piece of cloth trailed down like a tail almost to my knees.

Shaking off the fall, I followed the last of the path to the edge of the lake. I crashed through the remaining overgrown brush until I came to the back of the cabin. Leaning against the log structure, I tried to catch my breath. Then in a frightened and nervous voice, I called out, "Ben . . . Uncle Ben. . . ."

Hearing the sound of my own voice made me feel even more distressed, as I could sense my body trembling from the uncertain terror of what I might find. I climbed onto the porch leading around to the back door where the dock connected and extended out to the lake. As I rounded the corner, it was as though the cabin itself had grabbed me by the shoulder, forcing me to stop and take in the gloomy sketch now before me.

He was there . . . at the end of the dock, a silhouette against the sparkling water, slumped down in a rocking chair. His dark image was perfectly still, the only movement—the mist slowly disappearing off the lake. His head lay against one shoulder, and his arms were unfurled, hanging limp on either side. In the late afternoon light, his white hair stood out starkly from the dark green and red flannel of his shirt. A few inches below his right hand was an old wooden pipe that had spilled the remains of its tobacco. The scene was more tragic than I had feared, more sorrowful than I could have imagined.

I knew he was gone, and yet the feeble voice inside me held on to the slightest hope, whispering with words only a ghost could hear. "Ben . . . are you there. . ? Can you hear me . . ? Ben."

Only the loons on the lake answered back, their eerie calls a most unwelcome sound. My chest felt tight, as though my torso had been snared and bound. I wanted to weep, but something held my emotions rigid and frozen, as if time itself refused to allow me quick passage through this heart-rending event.

Slowly I hobbled across the dock's wooden planks until I stood next to him and could see his face. His closed eyes gave him an empty expression as though he might have been resting there for a thousand years.

With just the slightest ray of hope, I rocked the chair and whispered, "Ben . . . Ben." The chair creaked back and forth, its voice silenced when the momentum was gone. I picked up the pipe and held it in my hands, the cold polished bowl was yet another reminder of the hours that had already passed.

Somehow I knew that this was how it was meant to be, that it had all played out exactly as I would have imagined. Nevertheless, I felt cheated, robbed of a lifetime, or robbed of even a few minutes of seeing him alive and well as my father. I didn't know what to do or how to react. Anger and grief boiled up inside me. It boiled to the surface, trying to find a way out until I could no longer contain it.

I turned and ran back across the dock and past the cabin, into the refuge of the woods. I did not know if I was running from something or running to something. I simply ran in torment with no direction at all.

As I galloped haphazardly past the trees and bushes, a single word kept coming to the surface, swirling in the eddy of my emotions. "Why?" I snarled. "Why here? Why now? And why him?"

I ran, my feet and words both stumbling without purpose, "Why me? . . . why now? . . . WHY NOW?"

I began scrambling up the side of the mountain, as though I could somehow find my way up the steep terrain and out of this scourge of emotion. With the last of my strength I stretched and pulled my way up onto a boulder, quite possibly the same platform of rock where I had awakened so many days ago, naked within the essence of a great tiger, wearing only my own fur and skin and some newly found scratches.

Filled with a sense of total defeat, I was too maddened to weep, even though traces of tears found a way to seep from the corners of my eyes. The tears rolled down the sides of my face, then seeped into the grain of my beard.

I sat slumped over in a puddle of confusion, with so many pieces to the puzzle now missing. Ben's life as my father was one missing piece, his body resting silently in an old rocking chair. He was exactly where I would have expected to find him, at the place he had chosen to die, with one last smoke of his pipe, looking out at the lake. This image of him appeared quite normal, part of the natural order of things destined to happen.

Yet that same lifeless form, that expressionless face, left me with a huge empty space, not only within my conscious reality but at the core of my spirit, a vacant cavern where the presence of Shankara had been. He was also a missing piece, the empty space made even more barren because it felt as if he had never been there at all. I could already detect my mind trying to erase his noble expressions, those familiar gestures so much a part of his personality. With him gone, I could feel his words fading, his messages and his stories becoming hazy and gray like morning mists that hang over silent waters a moment before the warmth of daybreak dissolves them away.

How readily the concrete experiences of my journeys began to feel like imagined fantasies, remnants of my close call with madness, from which my human mind now pedaled rapidly to escape. Madness seemed to be the middle ground between the belief that either *all of it was true* . . . or . . . *none of it was true*. Without the tangible proof of Shankara's presence and words, I was caught inside that middle madness, being pressed to go to one side or the other.

I could feel the rigidness of my past pulling me back toward the likelihood that *none of it was true*, as if it were part of some paperback novel I could put back on the shelf to choose another.

Yet, to do so also meant putting the part of the story called God, the Divine Spirit, back on the shelf, and that posed an altogether different problem for my poor brain to unscramble. If I believed that *all of it was true*, I had to look very closely at . . . what *did* I believe? Or perhaps what was more important, *what did I truly know?*

As I staggered about in search of some reasonable resolution, I could feel aspects of my body, mind, and spirit drifting away from each other, as if they were choosing up sides—*either all of it was true, or none of it was true.* Only the influx of my breath and my passion to stay conscious kept me from unraveling completely. Yet, within my more connected moments, I repeatedly found myself returning to the same questions. "What do I believe? And what do I know? What do I believe? What do I know?"

Feeling both feeble and deranged, I fumbled and pulled at the torn section hanging from the back of my shirt like a great tail. For an instant, I felt as if I were some powerfully perplexed lion who had sat down on his haunches to contemplate his problems.

"What do I believe?" I said out loud. "What do I truly believe? Do I believe in extraterrestrials? Do I believe in miracles? Or what about spirits? Do I believe in spirits? Shankara is now just a spirit, like a ghost he is . . . so do I believe in ghosts? Yes. I do believe in ghosts." Pulling nervously on my tail, I mumbled, "I do believe in ghosts, I do . . . I do—"

Then it happened. I snapped.

Jumping to my feet, I stretched out and leaped to the edge of the boulder. From the depths of me, I roared into the sky, "NOOOOOOOOOO!"

With a snarl and a growl I swiped with my paw at the clouds and roared again, "NO! . . . NOOOO!"

From that platform of massive stone, I shouted, "NO! . . . NO, I AM NOT A LUNATIC! . . . AND I HAVEN'T GONE STARK RAVING MAD! . . . I KNOW IT WAS REAL . . . ALL OF IT! . . . AND SHANKARA, I KNOW THAT YOU'RE HERE

SOMEWHERE! . . . AND I ALSO KNOW THAT I WENT ON
THOSE JOURNEYS! . . . AND I KNOW I HEARD YOUR
VOICE IN MY HEAD, and I know that you're here somewhere
now. I know it . . . I know it . . . I KNOW!" My final words
echoed throughout the valley. (*I know . . . I know . . . I know . . .*)

As the last of the echoes faded away, I collapsed back down
onto the boulder. Exhausted and distraught, I mumbled, "I know,
I know . . . I know you're here . . . and I know that all of this is—"

"Of course I am."

"What!"

**"Here—of course I'm here. With you gallivanting all over
the woods like some crazed carnivore, where else would I be?"**

"What? What did you say?"

"I said . . . of course I'm here."

"But where? I can't see you."

**"Seeing is not a necessary part of this kind of
communication. You can hear, can't you?"**

"Sort of, I guess. But why didn't you answer me before?"

"I did!"

"But why couldn't I hear you?"

"Because you didn't want to."

"What?. . . But why?"

**"Because you weren't really sure that you wanted to know
that, well . . . all of this was real."**

"But why now?"

**"I guess you could say that you finally found a reason that
gave you the passion to decide . . . to finally know."**

"But I don't understand."

"Yes, you do . . . or you wouldn't be able to hear me now."

"But what actually changed? Why is it different now?"

**"Well, as you so deduced yourself a moment ago: either all
of it had to be true or none of it. Therefore, having made the
choice that it was indeed all true caused your pituitary gland to
open up a bit more, awakening some of the dormant portions of
your brain to be able to explore this new understanding . . . the
understanding that you can actually hear through the**

frequencies of unlimited thought."

"What?" I said, once again finding myself in a cerebral fog. "What are you talking about?"

"Gather yourself together, and we will dialogue as you walk. Some active motion in your body and fresh oxygen will help keep this new frequency open."

I rose to my feet and began retracing my path back toward the lake. The voice of Shankara (of course) continued on with his explanation.

"When you stretch yourself into a pure act of knowing, because you have grown tired of the futility of beliefs and conjectures, your spirit awakens dormant cells in the brain to accommodate the parameters around this new knowledge. In a mechanical sense, it is really just an evolutionary motion. In your case, the achievement has been far more noticeable because it has given you a new ability, a new kind of perception. And even though this all seems very new to you now, it is really a type of telepathy that you employ outside of this human form all of the time. Do you understand?"

"No," I said, "but go on."

"Well, in truth . . . you do have some understanding of this, at least on some level, or you wouldn't be able to hear me now."

"Exactly!" I replied, playing along.

"You will also begin to realize that the sound of my voice is really just a frequency, one that I transmit with a certain texture or dialect so that you can tell it apart from your own thoughts . . . like a signature."

Facetiously, I remarked, "Somehow, I doubt that I'm going to have any difficulty telling your thoughts apart from mine."

Chuckling, Shankara filled my head with a sense of bliss and said, **"You're probably right."**

"I *know* . . . I am."

When we reached the cabin, I once again saw the haunting image of Ben in his old rocking chair. The scene held me captive. Silence soon infiltrated our dialogue as though I had been allowed that time to meld together these two different realities, that of the past, and that of the future. Within this space, I felt my grief again close in on me, but this time there was a reverence about it, which somehow made it all more acceptable.

Ben, as he had always done in the past, had placed his rocking chair at the very end of the dock. I made my way out to him and cautiously moved around in front of the chair to look at him more closely. Lowering myself on one knee, I gazed into his face, perhaps hoping to commit his final expression of memory on this solemn occasion.

My eyes followed the contours of his broad features and the turn of his beard. I saw *myself* in him for the first time, the resemblance that others had always noticed. It made me wonder, more than ever, what it would have been like to know him again, to have him in my life, a life moving so swiftly into such new understandings. My grief stirred the child in me, who remembered well this same scene, sitting at the end of this dock, in this rocking chair. Without even thinking, I spoke to Shankara.

"But why did it have to end this way? Why couldn't I have known him, just for a short time?" At first there was only the whisper of a soft breeze, and then I again heard Shankara's voice.

"Perhaps you should really be asking, why were you given this recent opportunity to interact with him at all, to at last know he was your father? Was this not a great gift—to have seen him just for a short time? And what of the gift that he has given unto you . . . to have surrendered the last of his precious days, to accommodate the spirit of I, for the greater exploration and expansion of you."

I stopped short within my own sadness. I had never considered that Ben might have somehow chosen to be a vessel for Shankara, as an offering to myself and others.

"How blessed you are to have only the sweetest of memories, the most noble of encounters to remember him by.

"Now . . . as you stand here observing what has happened, see the event, the truth for what it is, for so often such things may not be as they appear. In a higher understanding the events that occur in your dimension may carry with them a greater

truth, a more expanded purpose.

"**This, his participation, was indeed a glorious gift . . . that even sadness and pity can never tarnish.**"

I had no doubt that this was true, for I had only the fondest of memories of him. I wondered just how many people could say that about anyone that they knew, especially a member of their immediate family.

Turning around, I sat on the dock directly in front of Ben, my feet dangling over the edge. I swung my legs back and forth and remembered doing the same thing many times before as small boy. The memory made me feel like a child again, with Ben's enormous boots sitting on either side of me. I could remember hanging on as he tucked them under my arms. With a rush he would raise me into the air, above the edge of the dock and over the water. Then the rocking chair would roll again bringing me back to the dock, only to lift me a second later, again and again until I had laughed myself into tears. It was a great game we had played when I was small, just Ben and me, that old rocking chair, and his enormous leather boots.

Then suddenly, with the sound of a loud breath and a snort, those same boots lifted completely off the dock, the shock of which lifted me clear into the air. Briefly, I was nothing but arms and legs flailing in the breeze, and then (*SPLASH*) a jolt of cold, cold . . . cold, cold water.

I twisted and turned in the freezing water, gasping for air, searching for something solid. Then I was grabbed by the shirt collar and pulled up to the surface. With a blast of sunlight and a wash of fresh air, I heard an old familiar voice from above me.

"What the hell is this?" he said.

Chuckling, he added, "By God, you never know what you're gonna fish out of this lake. What are you doing in there, young fella? You damn near scared me to death. I thought I was having a bad dream or something."

Reaching down he grabbed underneath my arm and lifted me up, asking, "Who are you anyway? And how did you end up in my lake?"

"It's Jar . . . red," I garbled out with a mouth full of water. "It's Jared."

"Jared?" he questioned. "Young Jared?"

Together we pulled my wet carcass out of the icy water and onto the dock. I dripped like a wet dog, completely dousing the surface of the dock.

"Jared?" he asked. "Is that you, really?" Chuckling he added, "Well, now I know I'm dreaming."

"No . . . I don't think so," I said, coughing up my last mouthful of water. "This is the part that isn't a dream."

"What?" he said rather puzzled. Pushing the rocking chair out of my way, he added, "So what are you doing up here?"

I spent the next few seconds wiping water from my eyes, trying to fully bring myself into this new reality. As my vision cleared, I saw that he looked exactly the same, that is except for the very confused expression, an expression that I had never seen on Shankara.

As I gazed at this living being, it was as if the cold water had instantly washed away my grief, like someone had simply changed the channel. I remembered hearing one of Shankara's last comments, "*So often such things may not be as they appear.*"

Then realizing Ben was still staring at me, wanting an answer to his question, I said, "I guess I came looking for you."

"You did? Why? I mean, how did you know I was here?"

"It's a long story," I said, wondering if he truly had any idea of why he was here or how. Then I realized that this would be as good a place as any to start, so I just went ahead and asked him.

"So Ben, how about you? Why did you come all the way up here? Why now?"

"Well, I guess I came looking for me, too."

Somewhat surprised, I asked, "What do you mean?"

"Well, Jared, the truth is that I have been paying my share of visits to the doctors these days. They tell me that I've got some thin arteries in my head. They say it could be dangerous, like I might just check out one afternoon without warning. Well, that kind of news sorta makes a fella start looking at things, taking more notice of what's important, of what really matters. That's why I came back up to the lake. This place used to be real important to me. I think I've discovered that it still is."

Rubbing the back of his head, he continued, "And even though I haven't been here that long, I already managed to have a bad fall. I slipped and hit my head coming around the outer side of the granite peaks. It was hurting pretty good for a while. I'm not sure, but I guess I must have made my way here and then sat down in my chair to sleep it off. This always was a fine place to take a snooze."

Then, as though he might have been trying to change the subject, he laughed and added, "And it's still a great fishing hole. Look what I caught here today, and I didn't even have a fishing pole." Playfully he grabbed me by my soggy ragged shirt and tugged me around. "Too big to throw back."

This was the uncle I used to know. Then he noticed the many tears in my wet shirt and trousers. Smiling inquisitively, he asked, "So how have you been, young fella . . . and . . . whatever have you been doing with yourself?"

By his bewildered look, I wasn't sure whether he meant what had I been up to this morning or what had I been doing since I was nine. I did know, without a doubt, that he had no recall of the last several weeks and that it would take the rest of a lifetime to explain what had happened to the both of us.

I took a couple of minutes to give him a generic answer, having no clue what to say or where to begin. As far as all of the drama around my knowing that I was his son, it was enough right now just to know he was my father and that he was alive and smiling. There would be lazy afternoons and long summer nights to remember the rest of our story.

For now I was content simply to be the soggy wet pup that he had pulled from the lake, a surprise that seemed to fill him with an enormous amount of joy. And perhaps later he would tell me of all those missing years that had passed and of all those summer days that had been so good to him in his life.

Together we took the long way around the edge of the valley and up between the granite peaks. We said goodbye to the lake and promised to return soon. Then we climbed down the other side of the mountain to my jeep and drove back to the city, back into our lives as if it had all happened the way it was intended.

On the trip home, I tried to explain to Ben what had happened to him, how, after his fall, the forest service helicopter had taken him to the hospital where he had been in a coma for several days. I ended that explanation with—supposedly in a state of delirium he somehow made his way out of the hospital, back up the mountain, and down to his rocking chair, which was where I found him—with three or four weeks missing in between.

I realized that this was a difficult story to believe, but the more detailed version, which included Shankara stepping into Ben's physical body, was not really an improvement on the problem. In time, I would fill in all of the details, but for now Ben seemed quite content to be a medical mystery who had somehow wandered the city for some time with temporary amnesia, his only memory being some extraordinary dreams. In fact, I believe he must have returned from his adventures with a certain wisdom of his own. He seemed quite open to my amazing stories—willing to look at, and leap into, a myriad of different possibilities. I told Ben to write down the dreams and details he could remember. Perhaps these missing pieces would help us fill in some of the vacant spaces of what had happened to him in the last several weeks.

Later that evening, we stopped by Ben's house to pick up some of his things, and then I brought him home to stay with me for a few days. Even though he was feeling fine, and only lived about four miles away, we agreed that it would be best if he wasn't alone, at least until we could get him to the hospital for some tests.

The synchronicity, the magic, and the mystery of all that had happened that day made me take a long hard look at my life, at which part was real, and which part was illusion . . . and which part was the very . . . real . . . illusion.

I had watched elements of my world magically become part of a greater truth, bringing me a sense of fulfillment unlike I had ever known. Jessica's interaction with my music was this kind of a creation. She was a brilliant and courageous woman, who had somehow managed to reach into my life and pull the best of me out of its hardened shell, birthing me and my music into the world. She had the ability to touch people with her presence and transform a dream into something very real.

Yet someone else remained a mystery, a young woman who had moved me like no other. Sharee had been but a sweet stranger in my world—one who had given me back a part of my life—the ability to see all of the possibilities. She reminded me to be young and foolish again . . . and to want to take chances . . . to want to be in love again.

I decided that I was going to tell her all of this. No matter how old and foolish I was. No matter how crazy it appeared. My first order of business was to tell her how I was feeling, because now I truly did believe in taking chances.

I spent the midnight hours at my piano, dreaming the dream, playing with the possibilities. Before I was finished, I had fallen in love with some of those possibilities, reminiscing with an old piece of music—a love song I had written long ago. I immersed myself in the notes, the melody line becoming my fantasy. Like a restless ocean, the music pounded back and forth, the words falling passionately into place.

As the last notes were played through the haze of my longing, I pulled myself from the ivory keys, and found my bed. I fell into a deep sleep, leaving my piano to be calmed by the silence of the night, the last few phrases still lingering in the dark.

With lavender memories,
and blue horizons,
and all of the colors we'll bring to the dance.

Tonight we'll dance in the twilight,
till long after the morning
has chased all the stars from the sky.
And then we'll call on tomorrow
just to bring us the magic,
and then we'll gather it all of this life.

Here, we are . . . lost together.
Now and forever . . . into the night.

38

Balloons and Beyond

This was indeed a glorious morning for I woke of my own volition, ready to explore my life with not one phone call, one door bell, or one rat-a-tat-tat having spurred me into the arousal. Such a day as this would be devoted to chasing possibilities, especially beautiful ones named Sharee. Unlike my drowsy dawns of the past, this morning I was full of energy as if I were nineteen again and nonsensical enough to believe it.

I also found that Ben had most definitely made himself at home in my kitchen during the night. This I could tell by the empty milk glass on the counter and the cookie crumbs scattered about the room. I had to admit it was a welcome mess and not too different than messes I had left on many a night. Perhaps moonlight cookie raids were a hereditary trait—sort of a . . . like father, like son characteristic.

Strangely enough, with him there, it actually felt like the world was finally in right order, as if all along there had been empty chairs in my life waiting to be filled. I remembered Shankara saying that during this arduous time of our Earth's evolution, families would be quite magically gathering together again. He said, *you may find long lost relatives suddenly camped at your front door and they won't even know why, or how they got there.* How true I had found that to be.

This morning, though, I was anxious to fill in some of the other spaces in my life. All night I had thought about Sharee.

My capricious obsession reminded me of how I felt some twenty years ago when I was so very taken by my first love, Katherine. She had been my one and only until she ran off to Nepal with some guru by the name of Shankara something-or-other. How odd that I was having the same type of feelings for this woman Sharee at the same time that yet another Shankara had shown up in my life. Perhaps what the Shankaras of the world had once taken away . . . they were now giving back.

As I daydreamed, I was well aware of how foolish I was being. More than likely, I was way too old for her, but that didn't seem to matter. Even if she wouldn't have me, I knew I would hold on to the exuberance I was now feeling, and I could walk away ready to pursue another, ready to fall in love yet again. I guess that's why I was so giddy and excited about finding Sharee. The desire and the pursuit itself meant as much as the outcome.

I was also excited about calling Michael, at what was now seven o'clock in the A.M.. Today, it was my turn to have the devious pleasure of rousting someone else out of bed in the early morning hours. To my surprise and childish disappointment, I found Michael already up and on his way out the door.

"So Michael," I said, "where are you headed so early on a Sunday morning?"

"This isn't early," he exclaimed. "I'm usually up and out by this time every day."

"What a ghastly thought," I replied. "Anyway . . . Michael, I wanted to let you know that Ben is here with me now. I found him up at the old lake cabin. It appears that Shankara is no longer with him, you know, as him, or whatever. And from what I can tell, Ben doesn't really remember any of what happened in the last several weeks. He looks good though and seems quite well."

"Really," he replied, with a hint of disappointment in his voice. "So . . . Shankara has moved on . . . . Well, he did say he would be leaving the physical experience shortly after Mohan had found his way. I guess I'm not that surprised, but I am a little sad. It's like the end of an era. But as I think you have already discovered, Jared, Shankara is never really gone, not unless you want him to be, and maybe not even then."

I chuckled, "Yes, that's true. I'm beginning to find that out more and more."

Abruptly he added, "Listen Jared, I really am running out the door, I've got to rendezvous with someone this morning and—"

"You've got a date at eight o'clock in the morning?"

"Well . . . yeah, as a matter of fact I do, so we will have to talk later, maybe this evening."

"Alright. But real quick, could you tell me if you know where I could find Sharee? Have you discovered a way to contact her yet?"

"Yes, I have, I got her phone number at the last gathering. She is at 965-670-4476, but you won't find her there now. Yesterday she told me that she was going on a hot air balloon ride early this morning out at Marisa's Vineyard, you know, where the park is. So listen, Jared, I've really got to run."

"I understand, thanks for the info."

"I'll call you this evening."

I sat there in the middle of my empty kitchen staring at my cat Jethro, who was staring back at me wondering why I didn't get off my rump and let him out. It was not until that very instant that I realized just how giddy and foolish I was about to be. I—was going to Marisa's Vineyard, to the magical land of balloons and fantasy rides. If I hurried, maybe I could get there in time to talk with Sharee before she went up. I had to do it. I had to tell her, and I had to do it right now before I lost my nerve or came out of this sweet madness.

After listening at the door of my spare room, I decided that—due to the sheer volume of snoring—I would just leave Ben a note and not wake him. From the assortment of socks and boots scattered about my living room and the trail of cookie crumbs from the kitchen to the proverbial room-of-snoring, I felt quite confident that he had no intention of going anywhere. So, grabbing my keys, I headed out the door on what I hoped would be a grand adventure.

Marisa's Vineyard was on the outskirts of town, but not that long a drive from where I was. I also knew, from having watched the balloons take off and land there before, that getting one up and into the air could be a long process. I had high hopes that there would be time to speak to Sharee before her departure.

As I rounded the final corner and drove out onto the field of wild grasses, I found myself entering a scene almost surreal in its tranquility. A brilliant blue sky held suspended an assortment of puffy orbs, sculptured balloons of varying sizes and colors. Their bright designs of yellows, greens, oranges, and lavenders spiraled and turned in flowing patterns. Like planets they hung in the air, perhaps a dozen in all, those very close as large as mountains, and those far away as tiny as moons.

In the center of the field, about fifty yards away, were two balloons completely inflated but still on the ground. I jumped out of my jeep and started across the pasture.

I ran toward the balloons, trying to appear happy but calm, and not at all panicked. Several people were gathered around each of the balloons' baskets, and I could tell that the passengers had already been loaded for their journey, anxiously awaiting their ascent.

As I got closer, I slowed my gallop. I recognized Sharee in one of the baskets, smiling and waving as if quite surprised to see me. The massive spiral of the balloon's yellow, orange, and lavender color soon blocked out the sun, leaving me in the shade of its eclipse.

The basket of this particular balloon was about seven feet off the ground with one man holding on to a long taut rope and another hanging on to the bottom of the basket. I got the impression that their launch had been delayed momentarily as the men on the ground conversed with the one running the controls inside. I ran up and likewise held on to the bottom edge of the basket.

"Sharee!" I exclaimed, desperate to catch my breath. "There is something I have to tell you." She was smiling down at me, hovering from above like an angel, the long silk fringe of her white shawl dangling over the edge of the basket.

"What is it?" she said, already chuckling at the spontaneity with which I was pursuing her. Her expression looked playful, and she seemed eager to hear my response, her eyes sparkling with bright anticipation. I got lost in them for a second, and then I just blurted out what I had to say. In front of God and everyone, I spewed out the words that my poor heart could no longer contain.

"I'm totally taken with you!"

"What?" she said with both laughter and embarrassment in her voice.

"Yes, completely smitten."

Playing along with my blissful insanity, she laughed out loud, as did the crew holding on to the balloon and the three or four other people in the basket.

"It's true!" I chortled.

"But Jared—"

"I know this is a surprise, and you may think I'm nuts, but I had to tell you."

Then the man piloting the controls said, "I think we are ready to lift off."

"No wait!" I spouted. "Sharee! Just a date . . . one chance."

Giggling, she said, "No, Jared, I can't."

"But why?" I said, looking more foolish than ever. "I'm not so old . . . I just look that way."

Still laughing, she turned away as if she were addressing someone else inside the balloon. Then she returned giggling to say, "No, Jared, I can't."

Directing his comment to me, the pilot said, "We're gonna take off now . . . you're gonna have to let go of the basket."

"Sharee!" I insisted, "is there another man? That's okay. I'll just . . . run him off."

At this she really laughed. "No, Jared, I truly can't."

"But why?"

"Because," she started to say, "because I was the one who took the key and got into your house."

"What . . . well . . . that's okay. I'll give you your own key, and you can come and go as you please."

"No, Jared, you don't understand. I'm the one who took the letter and the sheet music from your desk, the letter from Katherine Mason."

"Yes . . . she was my first love. I know, but I don't mind. You can have *all* of my old Dear-John letters if you want."

"No, no," she said giggling. "You're not listening. I was also the one who got into your mailbox. I was trying to get back a letter I'd written . . . with something I have to tell you."

Then the pilot called out to the crew, "Alright, let her go!"

"Sharee! Then tell me now!" I cried out, trying to hold on to the basket.

"No, Jared, this is not the time or the place."

"But I'm crazy about you."

"I know. I'm crazy about you, too."

As the balloon began to lift into the air, I hung on to the bottom of the basket, causing it to tip and jostle.

Abruptly, the pilot shouted, "Let go of the basket, you love-sick lunatic."

"No!" I shouted, "Sharee! Not until you tell me!"

"Jared! No! I can't!"

Unable to hold on, I let go and watched as the balloon continued to rise.

Then, with a rush of adrenaline that surprised even me, I ran up and grabbed one of the long ropes hanging down from the side of the basket.

"But why!" I shouted like the true madman I had become.

"Jared!" she called down laughing, "I can't, Jared . . . let go, you crazy nut."

As the rope rapidly slipped through my hands, I cinched down on it time and again, occasionally lifting off the ground. In this fashion, I danced along the grassy pasture, sometimes in the air, sometimes not. Without a doubt I was making a total fool of myself, yet I wouldn't have traded the feeling for anything.

"Jared!" she cried out. "You're crazy . . . let go!"

"Just tell me!"

"No!" she said. "Not now!"

I suddenly realized that the last of the long rope was slipping through my hands. Playing the court jester right up to the end, I grabbed tight to the last of the rope. As it slowly lifted me off the ground, I looked up, only to find that Sharee's face had disappeared behind the edge of the basket. Dramatically, I called out one final plea, "But what is it . . . just tell me what . . . WHAT IS IT?"

For an instant, my feet left the ground, and I was suspended in time and space, my whole reality silent and poised for the final outcome.

Then I saw Sharee's bright face appear over the edge of the basket, her eyes wild with excitement, her smiling expression about ready to explode. Then she said it. She just blurted it out.

"Katherine Mason was my mother . . . *I'm your daughter!*"

I let go of the rope.

Like a feather I floated back to Earth. In fact, I don't even remember touching down. I do remember staggering blissfully about. And I remember that sprinkling of laughter and those small words that came falling from above. "I love you, Dad."

Surrendering to the moment brought me to rest on my rump, in shock, in amazement, and in total joy. That was why I had been so attracted to her—why she felt so familiar. She was a part of me. . . a wonderful part.

Once again I looked toward the sky as the rainbow balloon drifted into the clouds. Sharee was still giggling and waving, as was Michael Talon, whose face now appeared next to hers. Such a fool I was—the greatest of fools—and so glad to be such. Without a doubt I had finally filled the essence of my true identity. I most certainly *was* the Village Idiot and quite contentedly so.

I waved to the tiny colored ball in the sky as the faint voices and laughter slowly faded into the blue. Then, to my complete surprise, this blissful scene was disrupted by the rumble of a car crossing the rough pasture. It was headed in my direction, headed directly for me. As the car came closer, I could see that it was a gold Rolls Royce, very much like the one that had sent Mohan catapulting into the air. As the car came even closer, I could tell without a doubt that the driver bouncing around inside was Jessica.

About sixty feet away from me, the bucking Rolls Royce came to a rocking stop with a small billow of dust trailing after. In a flurry, Jessica threw open the door, got out, and slammed it. With the gusto of a wild boar, she stomped toward me bellowing out in full voice. "There's something I have to tell you!"

At about twenty feet away, she shouted, "I've been waiting, and I can't wait any longer."

At about ten feet away, she exclaimed, "And you may think that I'm nuts, but I just have to say it. . . ."

At point blank range, she grabbed me by the shirt and simply said, "Ah . . . hell." And then she kissed me.

Well, I was so damn surprised that I didn't know what to do. So . . . I kissed her back.

We laughed for a long time after that. Then we lay down in the tall grass and wild flowers and waved our arms and legs at the tiny balloons so far above, pretending they could see us and were waving back. Where this relationship would lead, I had no idea. But as I watched some of these new possibilities unfolding I found myself quite comfortably out of control. This too was a reality I was responsible for—even though I was oblivious as to how I had created such bliss. Perhaps in the days to come I would discover my secret. Perhaps it wasn't a secret at all.

39

On the Morrow

It has now been long past a year since that last night Shankara walked among us . . . there in the firelight arena . . . our schoolroom at the end of an alley. I have honored that event, and the experiences that followed, as my wake-up call, a kind of semi-anonymous alarm that finally went off in my head, igniting my memory and causing me to begin to put some of the pieces together. As a result of this epiphany, I periodically find myself calling out to the wind, even though there is not always an answer. But sometimes, when the moon is just right, or when the trees stand still in spite of the wind, I discover that I'm caught up in a profound conversation. At first, I seem to be talking to myself again. But then I realize that the voice, the other half of my dialogue, has an old familiar dialect. A jovial irony weaves in and out of thoughts and wisdom that reach far beyond my own daily babble.

Of course, there's always the blissful feeling—that euphoric sensation that accompanies that moment—when I catch myself midsentence and start to laugh saying, "Oh, hello Shankara, when did you arrive in this conversation?" He always allows me that brief time, where, instead of my asking for a word with him, I just start up a conversation with myself, and he stealthily steps in. I suppose its easier for me that way, at least for now. Besides, I know it's a part of the game, a part of the juggling of—*Is it real, or isn't it?*—*Do I know that I heard a voice, or do I just hope so?*

I guess it all depends on where you stand when you talk to the wind, whether you are on a mountain top gazing into the stars, or stuck in traffic trying to pulverize some other driver with negative thoughts.

Sometimes, when I hear music in my head, I know Shankara's sitting on my shoulder. He gracefully confiscates one of my own compositions to announce his presence or to accompany me on yet another of his soul-searching journeys. Of course, one can't be sure which was created first, my music or his journey. At any rate, I have discovered that, at times, the two have found a kind of marriage. So when I hear one of those compositions from out of nowhere, I know he's around—being the voice from beyond—trying to send me a message about something or other.

Because of that voice, I see the human experience quite differently now, allowing so many other possibilities to exist in this reality. I'm far more conscious of the world around me and of our planet struggling to bring back a natural order, the divine balance humanity has nearly destroyed. We have no choice now but to become better gardeners of our wondrous Earth and to evolve our state of consciousness into a unified cause that revolves around that balance. I think that's why this crazy idea—that we are the awakening Christ—isn't so farfetched to me now. After all, that is surely what it will take to save us yet another dance in this our earthly sojourn.

I now understand that to walk in the footsteps of a Christ or a Buddha is not really about being holier-than-thou. It's about being responsible for all of my decisions. Not just the conscious ones but also those unconscious choices that manifest into so-called accidents, the ones that are much more difficult to own up to. But as Shankara once said, either all of it is true or none of it is. This chemistry of thought and emotion creating physical matter and tangible events must apply to the entire fabric of the universe, or it doesn't make sense. When I look at the world around me, and the intricate balance of our evolution, the environment, and humankind's many cultures, I know beyond any doubt that this is indeed how the universe works and how our history was created. Looking at our world now in the throes of such deterioration and demise makes me realize with crystal clarity what can be created on a planet overrun with self-serving egos. It had to have taken a great deal of powerful manifesting to sculpt humankind's current predicament.

I suppose that's why this idea of us as individuals being responsible for our every thought is so important. When I contemplate everyone's collective thoughts as a whole, and how positive and powerful those collective thoughts or prayers could be, well, the possibilities seem endless. I guess that's also why Shankara's prediction of a handful of Christs or Buddhas waking up here and there in all of the different cultures of the world seems like a very logical way of raising humankind into a higher state of consciousness. In fact, at times I have this incredible urge to just shout it out from the nearest mountain top, "AND ISN'T IT ABOUT TIME!?" Our weather patterns and our planet's terrain have become totally erratic and unstable. We have numerous nations playing out ancient and senseless holy wars, trying to annihilate each other through ethnic cleansing or nuclear and chemical warfare. Our children murder each other in their schools as though they are playing video games or mimicking Hollywood's movies. I mean, how many more signs do we need? How much more Armageddon do we have to experience before we as spiritual beings make spiritual evolution our priority? Isn't everybody tired of the competitive dog-eat-dog existence, where whole lifetimes are spent trying to outdo somebody else or get back at somebody, scraping after the rush of gaining some material goods or a few minutes of fame? "WHAT ABOUT SOME OTHER POSSIBILITIES, PEOPLE!"

I guess that's why I feel that the greatest gift I received from my time with Shankara was my experience of his guided journeys. These adventures brought very real sensations of bliss and ecstasy into my whole being, possibilities that I had never known before . . . at least not in this lifetime. These sojourns proved to me that there is something beyond this constant recycling of our human survival. Those experiences of harboring the spirit of an animal, or walking up a white stone stairwell into a carrousel of light, convinced me beyond any shadow of doubt that I'm not just a physical body. I am pure spirit, and my light and my life force extend into everything around me, including every person, no matter their gender, race . . . or extraterrestrial status. Now I walk with a totally different perception, one that has far more to do with what I feel than what I've been told.

I watch the people who come across my path, and I witness some of them in their unconscious behavior—their totally selfish approach toward the planet and humanity. It is then that I quickly realize a very simple truth—they just don't know. They're not bad people and, for the most part, not particularly malicious. But the fact still remains—they just don't know. They have never felt what it's like to soar effortlessly over a glistening river or to have their bodies filled with the sensations of a sparkling bliss that makes even laughter seem mundane. If they ever experienced such things, they would undoubtedly begin stepping out of the illusions of the Gray World and no longer be absorbed by depression or worship the deception of that altered state called the ego. Surely they would then realize that there truly is a Divine Source of which we are all an intricate part.

I suppose that's why I now have so much compassion for the ones who don't know and why Shankara's solution to the problem seems so simple and logical. More often than not, I find that I *walk away* from the negative probabilities of the human drama. Once I experienced a taste of bliss in my consciousness, the illusion of the recycling dramas seemed rather obvious and quite redundant. More and more, my body is becoming like a barometer that can easily detect both the ego's lower frequencies of deception and fear and nonhuman frequencies from electricity and pollution. When I see in the newspapers that nations are still warring with each other or striving for nuclear advantages, their rationales are foreign to me. I feel like an innocent child who has to be told time and again why it is that one group of people wants to murder another; I always ask the same question . . . "And what was that worthwhile reason again?"

Within my own consciousness—now feeling almost naive when confronted by these notions of competition and violence—I find myself quite naturally, *standing on higher ground* . . . effortlessly. Of course, on a day-to-day basis, I, like everyone else, am bombarded by people's unconscious behavior and all of the mayhem in the world. So when I feel myself being pulled into those illusions, or surrounded by some kind of deception that is clouding my perception, the first thing I try to do is—not judge it. I try to stand in a higher place, not a place of judgment, but a place of higher understanding for whatever it is in the human experience I am witnessing. Then I do just that, I witness it and do my best not to be caught up in it.

Every time I sidestep away from these recycling dramas, I'm immediately drawn back to the Earth. I long to sink my feet into some soft warm sand or stand on a high peak and stretch out my wings as far as I'm able. As I do, the truth comes back to me instantly, and I have to laugh, pondering the question myself— whatever was I doing down there mucking about in the Gray World? The truth makes a lot more sense, and is infinitely more fun, no matter where you're standing. And sometimes, when I'm standing on that peak, I take the opportunity to speak to the wind, laughing at myself for not having called up a breeze sooner. I say, "So Shankara . . . where the hell have you been?" and he says, *"Right here with you . . . where the hell have you been?"*

With Shankara, it's easy to know *love beyond measure*, because that is all he ever does. In fact, I think that's all he knows how to do. Bliss—with a sense of humor. What more could you ask for?

Sometimes, when I'm in a situation trying to decide what it would be to *love beyond measure*, I just think about how Shankara would handle *me* in the same situation, and then the answer becomes clear. I have also found that this kind of loving or compassionate act is very addictive. I want more of the feeling . . . and more and more. Each time I step beyond the measure of love that I experienced the time before, I feel myself becoming lighter, as if I were climbing stone steps to the top of a mountain, each effort raising me up to where I can see better and further than I ever had before.

So much of the time it all seems so elementary. But, does this mean that I have all of this figured out—this journey to enlightenment, this profound motion of stepping into the shoes of a living Christ or a Buddha? No—not at all. On a daily basis, I still find myself face down in the mud, my pants having fallen around my ankles, wondering what just happened and what kind of joke that Supreme Being is playing on me now. But the big difference is, now I can laugh about it. Now I get the joke—it's just a part of an illusion that we are playing out for real, and we will probably get another stab at it later. And if I don't totally get the joke, then at least I pretend to, because basically it's a lot more fun, and I know that just around the corner, if I pay attention, the higher understanding of it will undoubtedly end up in my lap.

One evening, not so long ago, I saw Mohan step from this human experience and into his next adventure. In that very second, I knew he had gotten the joke, that he had solved the puzzle. For him, there came that moment in time when there was no longer any doubt. He simply knew the truth of who he was, and then there was just bliss . . . and forward motion. I know this to be true, not because I have mastered the wisdom myself, but because Mohan told me so in the words of his memoirs. I found his message on one of the last pages in the small green book that Father Mathews had given me that evening when I laid Mohan into his poor man's hearse. Since then I have given these words music and a melody.

Before I ever read these verses, I thought Mohan had accepted his death and gone on to something better because he was leaving a cruel world and the decay of his cancer. But in the last of his days, as he walked on this Earth, the words of his sonnet reflected something quite different.

Be this Heaven?
Or somewhere beyond the skies?
Be this tomorrow?
Or somewhere beyond time?
So much like a vision . . . yet so real . . . I dream
through the day.
Are these but Earthly shadows now seen . . .
in a different way?

Through broken skies,
Through awakening eyes . . . I see.
Clearer somehow,
Beyond all the doubt . . . I finally see.
That, heaven is. . . .
Heaven is here.

Within the valley,
there'll be no shadows.
Only delusions
born out of sadness.
Beyond the mirrors . . . beyond those shades of gray.
There's brighter memory where music
and children play.

Through broken skies,
through lavender eyes . . . I see.
Clearer somehow.
Beyond all the doubt . . . I finally see.
That heaven is. . . .
Heaven is here.
Heaven is. . . .
Heaven is here.

For Mohan, this life had become nothing less than a joyous platform from which he took flight. One day, I hoped to be able to truly understand these profound phrases and such an awakened perception, to be able to see through clearer eyes, and know such simplicity. One of the things I loved most about Shankara's having been with us was that, time and again, I watched him come upon others like Mohan and so easily find within them the absolute beauty of who they truly were. He would first uncover their hiding place and then send them off in that same direction so that they could find it for themselves.

Shankara had an extraordinary passion for innocence; he could find a piece of it even in the shrewdest of characters. Like a penny waiting to be found, or a clear marble that had fallen deep into the camouflage of a rippling creek, there was a treasure in each person, which he could always bring to the surface. He looked for what was most precious in every man and woman, no matter how well they had disguised it under their artificial demeanor. Then he would pick up their virtue like the forgotten penny and say to them in the sweetest of confidences, "*Could it be that you have lost this pence? I have found it to be so shiny that surely it would be missed by someone. I felt that perhaps it might be yours.*" And then he would hand it to them, their own innocence reflected back to them in the glimmer of his clear blue eyes and his wry smile. I often saw him in this act, bringing out the most endearing qualities in what were frequently the most unlikely of dispositions.

Now and again I have thought about Shankara's description of how one might address beings of a dark nature such as Lucifer or Hitler. He said to recognize their degradation, and then with one finger, reach inside them and pull a thread of color from their spirit, from the truth of who they really are. Then take the thread and repeat the motion until you have dressed their being in a tapestry of color, the colors of their forgotten identity. Through such an act it was as if Shankara saw these dark spirits as no different than anyone else, just members of the family, no greater and no lesser, on a unique adventure, exploring their vision, for no other reason than to do it.

I myself had never truly known what it was to be a family before. Nor did I ever imagine just how large and diversified a family could be. But now, as I sat contemplating, looking out at the people around me, I knew that I was beginning to see the reuniting of *Oh-ma-ta-quiasin* (all my relations).

It was on this day that Ben and I invited what had now grown to be our own family to come to the lake cabin and spend the afternoon having a summer's banquet. As it turned out, Ben owned much of the property in the area, including the lake; and with some serious money and a little ingenuity, we were able to have a road constructed coming in from the other end of the valley. It took over six months to build, and although it was no freeway, it did give us a way in and out of the place, as well as a rough and tumble ride along the way.

Ben had not only stepped happily into the role of playing my father, but he also became my best friend. For him and for me, it was as if we had started up again right where we left off . . . here at the lake cabin. On the day I told Ben that I knew he was my father, there were a few tears and a little sadness. Yet I believe that because we found such joy in having been given a second chance, it was easy to dismiss what we could only imagine had been lost. Looking back, Ben once said to me that he had never really understood that the *truth* was all that really mattered and that anything else was just a downhill slide, even the slightest alteration of the truth could change the course of people's lives forever.

In the last year, since Shankara's visit, we had all experienced a great shift in our lives. As for myself, it was as if my bad luck had finally changed. I knew, of course, it was I who had changed. By taking responsibility for even a handful of my past failures and frustrations, I saw the universe magically turn about, surrounding me with a myriad of possibilities.

The song *Color Me Home*—that unrehearsed collaboration between Mohan and myself—became a big hit for Jessica. For the most part, the public thought it was a love ballad, but those of us who knew Mohan realized it was much, much more. The song became the title cut from a CD Jessica released, which contained several of my other compositions. The creating and producing of this music was a part of the romance Jessica and I were enjoying. So far our relationship had stayed just that—a romance—perhaps neither of us wanting to lose the magic of a new love affair.

Jessica was an independant woman. She stepped boldly into her blooming career, always sending out a message of encouragement for people to find their own way and take responsibility for their lives. In fact it was because of Jessica that I decided not to go back to teaching. Instead I chose to gather up a satchel full of my compositions and produce a CD of my own. At this time in my life, I truly did have something to say and, without a doubt, I had nothing to lose. I realized, of course, that starting a career as a songwriter/performer at the age of forty was a little preposterous—but not doing it at all seemed even more unimaginable. For Jessica and me, the pursuit of such music had become a blissful journey, full of magic, adventure, and unexpected changes.

Today, we were also witness to the changes in many others, some twenty or more who had come to celebrate with us. Most of them had been part of a group who, like ourselves, had gathered one evening in an arena of old brick buildings . . . to listen to some stories . . . to listen to the wind.

Father Mathews arrived with Father O'Brien, the Irish priest whom I had originally met at the hospital. He was the one who had first suggested that Ben have an exorcism, an event that we both now acknowledged was a worthwhile experience, regardless of the unpredictable outcome.

The priests came with many stories of how their church had been changing in ways both good and bad, with people searching desperately to find the real truth about their lives. With all of the confusion brewing in and around their religion, both priests had finally decided that the *real* truth was where the bliss was— and that's where they wanted to be. Father Mathews said that he had already spent part of a lifetime giving sermons about fear, guilt, hell, and damnation, so in the future, he wanted to preach about creating bliss.

My neighbor Marshal and his partner Sam had arrived, and as usual, were bearing boxes of food for our celebration. Sam had become Ben's primary physician and often said that as happy as Ben was now, he probably would outlive us all. Marshal, on the other hand, had become a familiar fixture in my kitchen. I often came home to find Jessica and him bounding around in the pots and pans, whipping up some kind of a sauté this or a soufflé that. Both Marshal and Sam had become very good friends of ours. They always brought a lot of joy into our household; they were a true example of how love transcends gender and the crippling beliefs of what is socially acceptable.

Emily and her six-foot-six giant-of-a-husband had also joined us. They had been through some changes as well and had apparently learned a great deal about all of that animal energy and where it could lead. In fact, the doctor had told them to prepare for twins as they were now about to have a litter of their own. Emily was only seven months along, and she was already the size of a prize-winning pumpkin. As I expected though, it didn't slow her down in the least—she was carrying on in her own ecstatic world, where I was sure there was never a quiet moment. I remembered her telling me the story of how, in the hospital, Shankara had said that the reason he talked to her and not to any of the others was because *She allowed the possibility to be, and because she believed that life was present even in the most silent of situations.* It was difficult to imagine Emily being in anything that resembled a silent situation.

My daughter Sharee had no trouble finding herself a home. She not only set up house with me, she also took up residency with Ben at the lake cabin. I guess you might say that she created for herself a home wherever she went. Everybody so loved having her around, including her dear old dad. She told me that after the death of Katherine, her mother, she left Nepal with the sole purpose of finding me.

As a child, she was raised near a monastery where one of her teachers was a holy man by the name of Ramya Shankara Ananda.

It was Sharee who had taken dictation for the letter from Shankara that had been sent to Michael, the letter I read at his house. She had no idea when she came looking for me that the letter and I would end up in the same scenario. She also said that I was the one who led her to find her old teacher Shankara—to discover whose human body he had stepped into.

Apparently, on the morning I got the call to go and identify Uncle Ben, she was outside my house waiting in a taxi—trying to muster up the courage to see me for the first time. When I came bolting out of my house, headed for the hospital, she followed.

Later, after I left the hospital, she went in to see who I had been visiting. That's when she found him. Shankara—who had first stepped into Ben's body during an encounter with Michael in the mountains—made his second appearance with Sharee that very day. She discovered her teacher had walked into the physical expression of the grandfather she didn't even know she had. That's why she was rifling through my mailbox—trying to intercept the letter she had written telling me I had a daughter. She had decided not to give me the news just yet, for she knew that with Shankara on the scene, change was in the wind and something extraordinary was in the making.

For the past several months, Sharee had been gallivanting around the world with my destined-to-be son-in-law Michael Talon. Their widespread tour had landed them in a variety of places, including Portugal and South Africa, as well as Nepal where Sharee had been raised. They had taken the trip to visit some of the sacred sites and to begin a kind of networking for the worldwide distribution of Michael's book, *The Blissmaker*. We had not seen them in several months, and part of our celebration today was to welcome them home. We were all anxious to hear about their adventures.

After devouring our picnic banquet, we sat around with our

half-filled glasses of wine and listened to the stories of our worldly travelers.

"So, Michael," I called out across the table, "what all did you discover on your expedition?"

He reached into his bag and pulled out three or four small books. He stood up with the books in his arms as though he were about to give some great declaration. "Today," he began, "Sharee and I have returned to be reunited with all of the people we know and love as our family. Well," he said, holding the books out in front of him, "let me introduce you to some of the other members of your family." He then allowed the books to tumble down onto the table.

Everyone sat staring at the books not knowing what to think. Then Emily, who was closest to the deposit of literature, grabbed one of the books and read the cover, *"The Life of Raha Muumba.* That means Blissmaker . . . The Life of the Blissmaker."

"That's right," Michael replied. Then he picked up another book and said, "This one is called *Words of the Wonnestifter.* In German, Wonnestifter means one who bequeaths joy. This one over here is titled *El Creador de Goso,* which translates from Spanish to creator of joy." Taking a copy of his own book, *The Blissmaker,* out of his bag, Michael added it to the assortment of books on the table.

"But Michael!" I said. "What does it all mean?"

"Well," he began with a cocky smile, "I think it means that our friend Shankara has been popping up everywhere . . . kind of like the wind, if you know what I mean. For the most part, these books are unique in that they are each about different cultures, written in different languages, with stories of people's various adventures. There is a common thread, though; all of them refer to a spiritual being prompting them to be on that quest. Most of their journeys were about finding the truth, or some kind of wisdom, and almost all of them described their guide in some way that translates into 'The Blissmaker.'"

At this the table came to life with an assortment of astounded comments. Then Michael interrupted by saying, "But there was one particular story I found in Nepal that I thought might interest you all. I have had it translated from Sanskrit into English."

Pulling the smallest of the books from the table he continued. "This apparently was a story that a spiritual guide told to someone who was ill and frightened of dying. Strangely enough, the piece is titled, *The Search for Ultimate Bliss*."

Suddenly Ben erupted, coughing and spitting wine all over the checkerboard tablecloth.

"Ben!" I called out, "Are you alright?"

Clearing his throat, he finally responded by saying, "What . . . what did you say it was called?"

"It translates into something about ultimate bliss . . . *The Search for Ultimate Bliss*."

Rising from the table in a flurry, Ben began a very brisk and determined march to the cabin.

Jessica called out to him saying, "Ben, is everything okay?"

Without turning his head, he waved and said, "Yes, I will be right back."

We all just sat there wondering what had caused him to react so unexpectedly. From the cabin came the sound of a few rattling drawers, followed by another march of footsteps that soon ushered Ben back to the table. He carried with him two or three pieces of folded paper, which he carefully opened up as he walked along.

"So Jared," he said, half laughing with excitement, "do you remember the day that I fished you out of the lake . . . the day I told you that I fell . . . the day I had that strange dream?"

"Yes, I remember."

"Do you also remember that I said it was like a story and you told me to write it down?"

Stepping up to Michael, he gave him the handwritten pages. Anxiously I asked, "Michael, what is it . . . what does it say."

Smiling, Michael looked up and said, "It says . . . *The Story of Ultimate Bliss*."

All around the table amused comments and laughter arose until Michael handed the pages back to Ben and said, "Read your version of the story, Ben. We want to hear it in your words."

Ben smiled shyly and then sat down and stared into the pieces of paper. We all waited in silence for a few seconds until he looked up and said, "Well, I'm not really sure how it all happened, that is, when I was actually told this story. I just remember walking along the west ridge trying to find another trail down to the lake. I was feeling pretty poorly at the time, not physically, but just sad about my condition with the doctors saying that my time here could be short, that I could check out at anytime. I was brooding over this, which was probably why I fell—because I wasn't paying attention to what I was doing.

"I remember just lying under the trees and it being more night than day. Someone was telling me a story, almost like a bedtime story. I don't remember seeing anyone, just hearing a voice. As I have tried to remember and reconstruct the story, I have occasionally heard that same voice in my head, helping me to write it down just as I heard it the first time. I realize now that the voice was, and is, Shankara. I also believe that this story is about Shankara himself. He tells about one of his lifetimes here and his experience as a young boy with one of his teachers. It's really a story within a story; a teacher gives the young Shankara a kind of parable to ponder."

"So Ben," Sharee asked excitedly, "tell us . . . read the story."

Slowly he laid the pages down on the table and cleared the hoarseness from his throat. He closed his eyes and took a deep breath. With a slight nervousness in his voice, he began to read.

40

The Story of Ultimate Bliss

There was once a young boy who was stretching hard to become a young man—

Abruptly, Ben stopped and glanced at everyone around the table. We all could sense his uneasiness, his feelings of vulnerability. Receiving smiles of encouragement, he looked back down at the wrinkled pages and continued.

The young boy lived with his family on a hillside overlooking the outer portion of a poor and ancient city. In this place all of the buildings were made from stones carved out of the Himalayan mountains. Their home was very close to a monastery where a small group of monks lived.

At the edge of this monastery was a courtyard where a fine garden flourished during the growing season. This area also harbored several trees and a couple of stone benches where the monks would come and sit or sometimes meditate. The young boy often wondered about the monks, about their meditating and their lofty thoughts. He tried to imagine what they contemplated, pondering whether or not these holy men really had all of the answers, for even though he was only ten years old, he had some pretty profound thoughts himself.

Day after day he watched the monks in their courtyard. Often he would see one very old man with a gray beard and gray hair braided into a long tail. Because he was the oldest, the boy figured he must be the wisest of them all. So one day, as he saw this old man wander out to the bench, the boy decided to go and pester him a bit—ask him some questions.

As he entered the courtyard, he found the old monk scratching abstractly in the ground with a long stick for no apparent reason. Within a very short time the boy's ten-year-old curiosity got the best of him, so he called out, "What are you doing?"

The old monk did not look up; he just kept scratching on the ground. Then to the boy's surprise he finally replied, "I am gardening."

Well, thought the boy, that wasn't a very enlightened answer. It was very cold out. There were no leaves on the trees, and all the plants had died back for the winter. Obviously, it was not a very good time to be gardening—the monk's answer only heightened the boy's curiosity.

Stepping a little closer, he asked, "What is it that you're gardening?"

The old man still did not look up, but he did answer, "I am gardening my life."

Well, now the boy felt he was getting somewhere—talking about life—something quite profound. And although he did not understand how the man was gardening his life by scratching in the dirt, he thought it was a great opening for him to ask some philosophical questions of his own. So he jumped right in as an obnoxious ten-year-old would and asked, "Well then, what is the purpose of life?"

At last the old man looked up from his scribbling and peered at the young boy from beneath his eyelids.

"Why do you ask this?"

"Well," the boy stuttered, "I don't actually know."

The monk then lifted his head and looked directly at the boy saying, "Come . . . and sit down. I want to tell you a story."

He sat with the old man, who returned to scribbling in the dirt. Then the monk began to tell him his story.

I once knew a young man who was a fine gardener, who throughout his early life had worked on his land, which like himself had been healthy and abundant. But there came a day when he found himself at a place in his life where he was very disturbed and ever so frightened. You see, this gardener had been born into a family that for many generations had experienced a hereditary disease. Many of the people of this lineage had perished as young adults, for that is when this particular disease would become active. As a child he lost his papa and an uncle in this way.

The young gardener knew that this disease was now upon him for he had seen two dark spots under his arm—signs of this disease and of what was to happen. As he had seen with other members of his family, he knew that once the spots began to appear it would be only a year or so before his life would end.

This desperate gardener decided to visit a holy man who lived in a far away temple—for he had heard that this one was very wise. If anyone could help him with his problem it would be this holy one.

After waiting many days outside the temple, the gardener was at last allowed to see this holy man. He told him of his plight and of the short time he had to find an answer to his problem. He showed him the two dark spots under his arm and pleaded for his wisdom, some way to change his fate.

For a very long time the holy one was silent. Then at last he said to the gardener, "There is something you can do, but you must have great integrity in this and make no mistakes or it will cost you your soul. All human beings incarnate into the human experience for the purpose of discovering the one event that is the pinnacle of that lifetime.

"I can only help you, my young friend, if you find this one element—your highest purpose. You must go out into the world and find the one experience and then come back and tell me what it is. If you can do this, I can tell you how to cure your disease. But if you fail to discover the right one, that which is your highest purpose, it will surely cost you your soul and you will die a horrible death.

"You will know when you have succeeded because the sensation of it will bring you the most joy you could ever know in this lifetime. It will be your ultimate purpose. It will be your ultimate bliss.

"Only the highest bliss will guide you to your true purpose; anything less will be a disaster. Bring me the answer to this riddle, and we can change your fate."

The young gardener was very excited, for at least now there was a possibility for him. Courageously, he went out into the world and into his life to discover and experience his ultimate bliss.

He started with what had brought him the most joy in his past, and then he expanded on that joy. With a fervor he sought after his bliss, always trying to outdo the joy of the experience that had come before. Many times, he would have blissful encounters, greater than anything he had ever known, but he could not be sure that it was the most blissful moment he could know.

Through this quest he became very focused, very refined, never allowing himself to become distracted by anything that did not help him find his bliss and discover his true purpose. He searched and searched, always making sure that each experience was more blissful than the one before, always climbing the ladder to what would be the highest bliss. Time and again he would come to the pinnacle of his joy, and yet from that blissful space he felt that he could imagine even more. Therefore he knew that a greater bliss must exist, and he would continue on his quest.

Then this old man, who was telling the story, just stopped as though the story was finished. The boy could only hold his curiosity for an instant. "So what happened! Did he ever find his ultimate bliss? Did he ever find his purpose in life . . . that one thing?"

The old monk said, "No, he never found it. He could never be sure that it was his ultimate bliss. He always felt that there could have been something grander, that there could have been something more."

"But what about the disease?" he spouted. "Did he ever cure the disease?"

"No," he said to the boy, "he never did."

The boy just sat there for a time, pondering. Was that the answer to his question? Was the purpose of life to find your ultimate bliss? For the most part this made good sense to the boy, but he couldn't help but wonder why a story about bliss had such a sad ending.

The boy, not knowing how to respond to the story, eventually got up from the bench and began to leave. As he walked away, he contemplated the old man's earlier words about gardening his life. Feeling the need to at least say goodbye, the boy raised his hand and waved to the monk.

The old monk, who had returned to his scratching in the dirt, likewise raised his hand to wave, which caused the boy to stop abruptly as though he had been snagged by a branch. For a time the boy just stared back at him, at his smiling face, at the wave of his hand—but mostly at the two dark spots on the underside of the monk's arm.

Then his eyes met the eyes of the old man, eyes that seemed to nod inside the boy. He felt the monk surround him with his smile and bless him with his wisdom. It was then that he realized that the monk was really the young gardener in the story who had indeed lived to be an old man. He understood that long ago some holy man had tricked the monk into looking for the ultimate experience of his bliss, spending nigh seventy years of his life searching for that one thing. He had focused on his bliss until he now sat in his old age. The disease was still with him, but it simply had not moved. It sat with him like an old friend, reminding him always to be in search of his ultimate bliss.

Slowly Ben put the pages down, and for a few seconds no one broke that sweet silence. Surprisingly, it was Father O'Brien who offered a comment.

"You know,'" he said, "that story reminds me of something that happened to our friend, Father Angelo."

The name sounded familiar, but offhand I couldn't place it. I looked over toward Father Mathews, who sensed my question.

"You remember, Jared, he was the priest at Saint Martin's Cathedral who attempted the exorcism on Shankara."

"Yes," I said, "now I remember. That last time I saw him he had become ill."

"That's true. In fact, since then his health has deteriorated rapidly. He has gotten to the point where he can't take care of himself, so they've moved him out to the Sacred Heart Convent.

The nuns there care for him daily, but he just sits and stares, even when I last visited him."

Interrupting, Father O'Brien exclaimed, "But that's what I'm talking about. Something happened to him just two nights ago. I haven't had a chance to tell you yet, Father Matt. He is much better now. The nuns say it was nothing short of a miracle. Sister Anne, who is in charge out there, told me what happened just last night.

"It was late in the evening, and they were in one of the smaller chapels having quiet time. They were all gathered in a circle, with some of them knitting and others writing letters. Father Angelo was there, sitting in a chair, even quieter than usual. In fact, Sister Anne became concerned that he might have passed away right there in front of them. So she knelt down at his side and tried to wake him.

"Quite suddenly, Father Angelo took them completely by surprise by rearing up and taking in an enormous breath of air as though he had literally come back from the dead. Well, apparently it scared all of the sisters half to death. Then miraculously, Father Angelo opened his eyes, raised up one knee to support his arm under his chin and then with great confidence said, **'Good morning. . . . How have you all been doing?' "**

Instantly, I looked at Michael and Jessica, and then at Sharee as a chain reaction of astonished faces began ricocheting off of each other until the entire table exploded with laughter. With chairs rocking and hands slapping the table, it was not long before plastic glasses and utensils were zinging into the air and a roar of giggles and laughter was rumbling across the lake. This outburst of laughter was unlike anything I had ever heard. In fact, I'm sure it wasn't really laughter at all. It had to be bliss.

Pure and unlimited . . . unbridled . . . bliss.

"Are you sure?"

"What—yes . . . yes, I'm really quite sure."

To the reader:

"The truth is within you,
and it is now time for you to step forth to remember,
to claim your divinity,
to return to the wisdom and the knowledge,
to complete the task that you started long ago.

"You are remembered by those who reach to walk through you
with their love.
You are loved by wingéd birds that long to fly with you,
and great beasts that stand and stretch to roar through you,
by voices in the wind that call out unto you,
who brush by you, and stir you, and reach to love through you.

"You are surrounded by sweet familiar voices that have come
now to tell you,
that no matter how great the illusion appears,
in your todays, and your tomorrows,
you are not alone.

"Within the wind, is the sovereign message,
that you are so loved.
For you are the lost children,
the forgotten Gods.
You are the blooming Buddha,
the awakening Christ.
The time is now,
for you to remember.
The time is now,
for you to come home.

So much I love you.
Namasté"

The musical pieces, journeys, and songs that you have just experienced are part of a collection created by author/ composer Royce Richardson. Full versions of the narrated journeys and songs are available on the CDs listed below. These can be purchased at www.Blissmaker.com or from this publisher. Short clips of many of these works can be heard at our website.

This appendix also provides the page numbers in this novel where these items appear. Included is a listing of the stories and poems of *The Blissmaker*, some of which will be published as children's books in the days to come. Publication dates and much more information can be found by going to www.Blissmaker.com.

The CD below, which is included in the deluxe edition of this book, presents the journeys of *The Blissmaker* with fully orchestrated musical scores and voice narration. These can be played to enhance the reader's experience of the novel, or as part of one's meditation practice.

The Forgotten Garden
  (The Blissmaker, p. 38)
Grrrr . . . *(The Blissmaker, p. 105)*
Ancient River   *(The Blissmaker, p. 155)*
Burning the Shadows
  (The Blissmaker, p. 233)
The White Stone Steps
  (The Blissmaker, p. 375)

The CD depicted below contains songs presented in *The Blissmaker* as well as other pieces written and sung by Royce Richardson.

Winds Along the Canyon
(The Blissmaker, p. 117)
Dreamwalker *(The Blissmaker, p. 3)*
Save Us A Dance *(The Blissmaker, pp. 63,279)*
Alright by Me
Be This Heaven *(The Blissmaker, p.451)*
Sail You Home *(The Blissmaker, p.65)*
I Remember
My Lady of the Moon *(The Blissmaker, p.94)*
Don't Feed the Bears *(The Blissmaker, p.120)*
Color Me Home *(Blissmaker, p.416)*
Lost Together *(The Blissmaker, p.434)*
and many more.

Coming soon —

The Blissmaker Audio Book

A narration of the story that includes the music and words of the songs and journeys.

A compilation of Royce Richardson's instrumentals, some of which are mentioned in this book, will be made available on CD in the future.

Index of Topics and Teachings